Beautiful Illusions

ANNIE JOCOBY

Vinci Books

By Annie Jocoby

Illusions

Beautiful Illusions
Deeper Illusions
End of Illusions

Vinci Books

vinci-books.com

Published by Vinci Books Ltd in 2025

1

Copyright © Annie Jocoby 2013

The author has asserted their moral right to be identified as the author of this work in accordance with the Copyright, Designs and Patents Act 1988. This work is a work of fiction. Names, characters, places and incidents are the product of the author's imagination or are used fictitiously. Any resemblance to actual persons, living or dead, places and incidents is entirely coincidental.
All rights reserved. No part of this publication may be copied, reproduced, distributed, stored in any retrieval system, or transmitted in any form or by any means, including photocopying, recording, or other electronic or mechanical methods, nor used as a source for any form of machine learning including AI datasets, without the prior written permission of the publisher.
The publisher and the author have made every effort to obtain permissions for any third party material used in this book and to comply with copyright law. Any queries in this respect should be brought to the attention of the publisher and any omissions will be corrected in future editions.
A CIP catalogue record for this book is available from the British Library.
Paperback ISBN: 9781036707262

The EU GPSR authorised representative is Logos Europe, 9 rue Nicolas Poussion, 17000 La Rochelle, France
contact@logoseurope.eu

Chapter One

IRIS

I woke up in a strange hotel room. Cotton mouth, a strange, sweet taste on my tongue, a feeling that every muscle was bloated and filled with liquid. My head was pounding, my hands shaking. My hair hurt, and the light streaming through the window was just.too.bright. I attempted to run one hand through my hair, but the hand was caught in a massive tangle. I pulled on my hair and then gave up. The tangle wasn't going to come out. I felt nauseated, and the sensation that came over me was that I was about to hurl. I swallowed hard several times until the feeling passed. I had no idea where the bathroom was, and the last thing I wanted to do was throw up in the bed. Where was I? And who was this guy in this bed? A head of dark hair, but the body was covered in a sheet. He was breathing heavily, evidently knocked cold.

I surreptitiously snuck out of bed, hoping my clothes were around somewhere. On tip-toe, I prowled around the room. It was a very nice room. A suite, in fact. I didn't have time to look around. I had to get out of there. I got on my hands and knees, looking under the bed. Nothing was there. I crawled around the room, becoming frantic at the prospect of being unable to find my clothes. I finally got up and tip-toed out of the room and into the next room.

Through bleary eyes, my head pounding like a Stewart Copeland drum solo, I finally saw my clothes in a pile. My precious red Mary Jane Jimmy Choos, which I spent way too much on, were next to the white sofa. My skirt and shirt were next to them.

I breathed a sigh of relief.

I looked at my hand, which was shaking. I didn't know if I was shaking because of the situation or the effects of the hangover.

Probably both.

I got dressed and then realized I had no idea where my purse was. Panic started anew in my throat. By now, I was beginning to understand that this particular suite was gorgeous. Modern art on the walls and the furniture was modern as well. Distinctively modern. Soft white leather, chrome feet. Marble coffee table in front. Enormous flat-screen TV. There were orchids on a glass table by the window.

This guy certainly had taste.

Just then, I heard my ringtone. Radiohead's *Creep*. It was across the room, and I shot over to my purse. My ringtone was so fucking loud! I immediately silenced it. But the phone helped me find my purse, so there was that.

Then I crept out the door, shutting it gently behind me.

In the cab on the way home, I tried to piece it all together.

Where was I? I was doing shots in a bar. Happy Hour. I met a guy last night. Obviously. I couldn't remember much about him. I couldn't pick him out of a lineup at this point.

You're too old for this shit. It had been a good five years since I was in college, and college was the last time I had this kind of slutty one-night stand. I didn't remember why I started drinking so much. My thoughts were hazy, and I felt exhausted like every cell in my body was filled with alcohol.

Let me see...I was going to meet a guy off the internet. That didn't pan out. Of course. The dude didn't show. And I...went up to a guy and started chatting with him. Which was totally like me. When I'm drinking, anyhow. Otherwise, I'm painfully shy and insecure about myself.

I only remembered a few details. Most things were a blur.

I examined my phone, holding my breath. *Please, please, please let there be no dialed calls late last night.* Shaking, I looked through my log of dialed calls. Drunk-dialing would be just like me. There should be an invention where the phone can tell if you've had a few too many and prevent you from calling anybody.

Nothing was on the dialed calls log.

I sighed in relief.

Then I just sighed.

I'm too old for this shit.

I looked again at the call log to see who'd called me this morning. It was my best friend, Debbie. I called a cab, then called her on my drive home.

"Yeah," I said. "What's up?"

"Hey there, girlfriend, how you doing?"

"Great, great." Or, I would be doing great if I didn't have the overwhelming feeling I was about to hurl. The motion of the cab was literally making me gag.

This was going to be a long cab ride home.

"Oh, I did something really stupid," I said.

"What's that?"

"I met somebody and went home with him. I just got done taking the walk of shame, and I'm in the cab right now."

"Awesome," she said. "You need to get laid. How long has it been?"

"Since the early stone age," I said. "At least. One thing, though."

"What's that?"

"I don't remember any of it. I have no idea who was in the bed next to me this morning." *Oh, God, this is so embarrassing.*

"So, what're you doing now?"

"I gotta pit bull rescue to do. I really don't feel like it. I just want to go home and go to bed. And puke. I need to seriously puke. But that dog needs me, so I gotta go."

"That's too bad. I was calling to see if you wanted to have lunch somewhere."

"Maybe tomorrow. Sunday brunch, maybe."

"Sure, let's meet for brunch."

We decided to meet at a restaurant that was central to both of us. It was a place that served a hearty brunch buffet. Right at that moment, though, any kind of food sounded unappetizing, to say the very least.

I went home, made myself throw up, changed, and then went to the abandoned house where a pit bull was left in the basement after the owners were foreclosed. It was scary how many of these calls we got. I went to the house, permit to enter in hand, opened the door and went downstairs. There was a 9-month-old puppy down there, whining and barking. When she saw me, her entire little body squirmed with delight. I kneeled down, and she licked me on the face profusely. I had a bag of food, a jug of water and a bowl, and I fed her and gave her the water. She wolfed down the food, looked to me for more, and gulped the water.

"There, there, my little one," I said. "That's all you can have for now, but you'll get more in the shelter, I promise." She licked me some more as I unchained her, leashed her, put her in my car, and took her to a shelter. I had a large carrier in the car, and I could hear her whining.

I prayed she'd find a forever home quickly.

Pit bulls really are the sweetest dogs.

After my rescue mission, I headed home and passed out on the couch.

Oh, I'm never drinking again.

Chapter Two

On Monday morning, I arrived at my law office, where my assistant greeted me. Melinda had hair that was variously blue or green in the front, and when I called her, I was subjected to a Ramones song. I didn't generally dig the Ramones. The Sex Pistols, maybe, but not the Ramones. Still, she was fun, cool and efficient. Everybody loved her, including me.

I noticed a guy sitting on the couch in my peripheral vision. I was surprised to find out I had somebody coming in.

I looked quizzically at Melinda.

She motioned me to come a little closer. I bent my head down, then she said in a low voice, "this guy's here to see you."

I looked at the man, and my heart quickened. He was the most beautiful man I had ever seen. In.my.life. Thick dark hair. Eyes greener than I'd ever seen. He looked at me, an impish smile on his chiseled face, and when he smiled, I noticed his teeth were perfect like he spent his entire younger years in braces. He was wearing an expensive-looking tailor-made grey suit with a silk shirt underneath. Italian shoes.

I wondered why he'd be in my office. He definitely didn't look the type who'd be slumming with a bargain-basement divorce lawyer like myself or filing for personal bankruptcy. Those were my two major areas of practice. I also did some criminal law, and he certainly didn't look like the kind of guy who'd need a criminal attorney. Well, maybe a white-collar criminal attorney, but those are the bigwigs in the high rises. I was as far from a bigwig as you could possibly imagine.

At the same time, he looked so familiar....

No. It couldn't be.

Beautiful man stood up and smiled broadly.

Tentatively, I said, "Hello. Can I help you?"

His smile disappeared. He ran one of his hands through his thick mane of dark hair, his head slightly cocked down, his mesmerizing eyes looking at me questioningly.

I drew a breath.

His face turned red. "Uh, I'm here to see you."

"Oh, ok, sure. My office is right there," I said, pointing to the door.

What the hell?

He followed me in. Files were piled on the desk, on the floor, and on top of the computer.

"Sorry about that," I said, frantically taking the piles on the desk and throwing them to the floor behind me. I was suddenly nervous and had no real idea why. This guy was magnetic, so he made me nervous, but it was more than that. I couldn't quite place him, but my subconscious mind knew exactly who he was.

My subconscious just refused to communicate with me at the moment.

"Have a seat."

He sat down on the red tweed chair. My office was small, about 10 x 10, which was all I could afford. Although I was an attorney, I definitely wasn't highly paid. I spent most of my time worrying about people who didn't pay their bills and chasing after them. Plus, my student loans from 7 years of schooling were choking the life out of me.

He still had a quizzical look in those beautiful green eyes.

Then he began. "You don't remember me, do you?"

I bit my lip and raised my eyebrows in an expression that said, "No, sorry."

He looked down. "I'm really embarrassed. I didn't know you were that drunk the other night."

At this point, I could feel my heart in my throat. No. It couldn't be. Never in a million years would I end up with somebody who looked like him. Never.

I must've been on some kind of candid camera show. There was a Canadian show called *Just for Laughs*, where actors played pranks on unsuspecting people and filmed their reactions. This was probably what this was, although I wasn't aware that there was an American version.

I took a deep breath, not wanting to jump to conclusions, and said, "I'm so sorry. I don't know what you mean."

"Harry's Bar. You and I doing shots together. Any of this ringing a bell?"

It was my turn to be embarrassed. Actually, it should've been my turn to be embarrassed when I first saw him. It was now becoming clear, but I didn't think I'd ever catch the eye of a guy like this.

And I didn't think I'd ever see my hotel mystery man again.

"Um, did any of those shots happen to be te-killya?" I asked.

He smiled. "A few."

I felt tears coming to my eyes. I had no idea why. I lowered my head, putting it in my hands, and then peeked through my hands at him.

He was smiling again, and I was completely captivated. God, this guy could completely light up a pitch-black room. Just the same, ending up with him was a lucky shot on my part that no doubt included beer goggles for him. I was halfway decent looking and could lose a few pounds, but this guy belonged with a Giselle Bundchen clone.

"Gosh, I'm so embarrassed. I didn't act a fool, did I?" Of course I did. I usually did act a fool after tequila.

"Not at all. You came up to me, and before I knew it, we were chatting like old friends. We talked for hours about everything from liberal politics to Oscar Wilde. I was quite impressed with your knowledge of *The Importance of Being Earnest.*" He paused. "I think we even talked about the Kardashians."

The Importance of Being Earnest. I read that play after seeing the movie. But I wondered why I'd be talking about that. Still, it was impressive for me to find somebody who even knew who Oscar Wilde was. I couldn't count how many times I'd met a guy who thought Tennessee Williams was a country singer.

He was looking embarrassed again. "I think I owe you an apology."

I raised an eyebrow and cocked my head slightly. "For what?"

"If I would've known you were that, uh..."

"Smashed?" I said helpfully.

"Yeah. Well, I wouldn't have..."

"Taken me to a hotel room and torn my clothes off?" This was like a mad libs game.

"Yeah."

Oh, the irony. I ended up with a jaw-droppingly beautiful man who was literate, and I didn't even have a good memory of it. I hoped I enjoyed it at the time.

Didn't matter. If I didn't remember it, it didn't really happen. In my mind, at least.

Then it struck me. Why was he here? And how did he find me? The only thing I could think of was I left something in the hotel room, and he was enough of a gentleman to return it to me. But I couldn't imagine what I left there.

I realized something else. This guy was intimidatingly beautiful, yet I felt completely comfortable with him. Mesmerized, captivated, excited – but also completely comfortable.

Like he said, I felt I'd known him all my life.

He was still smiling at me impishly, his head slightly downward, his mouth half-cocked.

"So, I was wondering..." he began, his hand running through his thick mane again. "I was wondering if you'd be interested in having drinks with me sometime."

He wasn't looking me in the eye. Almost like he was shy. This guy, shy? He no doubt had women dripping all over him. Which almost made me turn him down. He had to be a womanizer. Anyhow, he was stratospheres out of my league. Light years. He was the Starship Enterprise, and I was Earth.

Or so went my brain. My heart, however, was noticing how comfortable I felt in his presence. Heart overruling brain, I simply said, "Sure."

He smiled. "Friday night at Harry's? We can meet for Happy Hour and go from there."

"Want to return to the scene of the crime, eh?" I asked with a smile.

"Something like that."

At that, we made a date to meet at Harry's at 5:30 on Friday.

After he left, Melinda said, "Oh, sweet Jesus, that guy is beautiful. Where did you find him?" She was mock-fanning herself as she talked.

I smiled. "You wouldn't want to know." *Your boss is a ho.* "Now, shoo, get back to work."

Friday couldn't get here fast enough.

Chapter Three

Friday was finally here. I couldn't quite believe this beautiful guy wanted to see me again, and it occurred to me, much to my acute embarrassment, that I didn't remember his name. I didn't know how to ask him about that.

I was in rare form, sleeping with a guy I'd just met and getting that schnockered in the first place. It had been at least since college since I'd done something like that, and have no memory of it the next day.

Maybe he slipped me a roofie? God, I hoped not. I wouldn't want to think a guy like that would be a rapist. Lord knew he wouldn't have to resort to that to bed a woman.

No, I got that wasted all on my own. That was what happened when I started tequila shots. The old shirt that said "One tequila, two tequila, three tequila, floor" summed up my reaction to that particular liquor. But somehow, I not only acted coherently but charmingly as well. Astounding.

That afternoon, I left the office early for a hair appointment and a Brazilian. Yowch! They should use Brazilians as a torture method for enemy combatants. That would get them talking in no time.

Not that I was planning on sleeping with the guy again that night. My sober self was much more old-fashioned than that.

Meeting him out, I was wearing my only pair of nice shoes, the red glitter Mary Jane Jimmy Choos from the night I met him. Those were my lucky shoes. They sure were lucky the other night, anyhow. They were high-heeled, but that was good because I needed the height. I stood 5'2", and this guy was at least 6'1".

I pulled on a slimming black dress with a halter neck, which was always my most flattering neckline. I felt self-conscious about my 30 extra pounds, then tried to banish the thought. A bit of foundation to cover up my freckles, some mascara for my light eyelashes, some lip gloss, and I was ready to go.

I got to the bar and looked around. Harry's was a classy upscale cigar bar where they served 30 different kinds of martinis, along with a limited menu mainly consisting of olives, hummus and different gourmet pizzas. It attracted an older crowd of sophisticates attracted to the expensive martinis and even more expensive cigars. The place was smallish, but it wasn't a hole in the wall, as it was two levels and had a patio. The interior walls were cherry wood, as was the enormous bar, which ran the length of the main room. The floor was covered in white tile. The artwork in this bar favored Toulouse Lautrec – brightly colored, with dancing girls and advertisements that looked like they were from the turn of the century. The crowd ranged from mid-20s to mid-60s, but most of the people in here were in their early thirties, by the looks of it.

Beautiful man was already there. I looked at him and

lost my breath momentarily. Dressed down in a blue short-sleeved shirt that brought out the marine flecks in his otherwise green eyes, with grey casual pants and black shoes, he looked like a Ralph Lauren model come to life. The short sleeves displayed his lean and muscular arms, and he looked like he didn't have an ounce of fat.

He stood up when he saw me, a broad smile on his face.

Now I was shaking. Not sure why I was having this reaction now. In my office, I felt much more comfortable. Maybe because it was my home turf. But here, in the bar, I felt intimidated.

I'd have to resist the urge to drink tonight. Alcohol was always my crutch in awkward social situations. Or any social situations. I was quite shy. Or insecure, at least.

He met me halfway and gave me a big hug. His body was warm and incredibly hard. He must've lived at the gym. I could hear his heart pounding as my head lay against his chest.

We sat down, and he ordered a Dewar's and water for him, a Grey Goose dirty martini for me.

So much for my vow not to drink tonight.

Well, I'll only have a few.

The drinks came shortly, and I knew I had to get the name issue out of the way.

"So," I began.

"Sorry, before you say anything, I just wanted to tell you that you look beautiful."

I momentarily forgot my words. I pondered anew the possibility that I was on some kind of candid camera and that my humiliation would soon be on YouTube. I then just managed to say, "Thank you."

"Now, you were saying," he said, looking at me with a soft expression.

I took a deep breath. "This is the most embarrassing thing I've ever had to admit. But I, well, you know, I had a lot to drink the other night and-"

"Ryan. My name is Ryan." He was still smiling, and his eyes told me he thought it was humorous that I forgot his name.

I could feel my face flushing. "How did you know what I was going to ask?"

He shrugged. "I figured that if you didn't remember me at all when I came into your office, it stands to reason you didn't remember my name, either."

"About that. I hope you don't think I make a habit of going home with men from a bar."

"Damn. I was hoping to get you hammered again and get you to pick up a girl and do a three-way," he said with a smile.

I laughed at that. "Sorry to burst your bubble," I said.

"Well, I understand you're embarrassed. But don't be. It was, uh, fun."

Fun. I wished I could've remembered.

"Anyhow, I could say the same," he said. "I hope you don't think I'm some kind of manwhore."

"No, no, I don't think that at all." I paused, tucking my hair behind my ear and sipping my drink. It was salty and slightly sour. As I picked one of the olives from the little red toothpick to put in my mouth, I saw Ryan watching me interestedly. "I also wanted to apologize for just, you know, leaving in the morning."

"Yeah, I was disappointed. I wanted to take you for breakfast."

"I was totally embarrassed for being there. It was shitty of me to do that, though."

"Well, I was glad you gave me one of your business

cards at the bar. Otherwise, I would have to do some serious research to find you." He took a sip of his scotch rocks. "And I would've tried to find you. Make no mistake about that."

Wow. I must've been really charming the other night. Or really "fun."

He was smiling. "I know we're doing this backward, but we need to get to know each other."

I couldn't remember what I told him, so I didn't know if he knew the basics about me. This was so awkward, not knowing if what I told him would be something he'd already heard.

"So, what do you know about me?" I asked him.

"That you're an attorney who aspires to do something else. Maybe become a writer or an animal rights activist. You want to eradicate all big money from politics and liberate every factory farm animal on the face of the earth. That you have gorgeous red hair."

Ryan crunched on some ice thoughtfully, then shook his now-empty glass and looked around for the waitress. She was there in a flash to take our next order. Then he continued. "And you think *The Importance of Being Earnest* was the funniest story you've ever read."

"Wow. I really was spouting off, wasn't I?" I knew that I tended not to have a filter when I was drinking, but I still couldn't believe I told this guy my life story in one sitting. And, of course, I was a hypocrite because, while I was a deep animal lover, I ate chicken and fish.

"No, not spouting off. You just came off as....passionate. You think about the world even though you know you can do little about it. That's refreshing. You're like a realistic idealist." He picked up a bar napkin, laid it down, and started doodling on it. The guy was quite an artist. Not looking up, he proceeded. "And the fact you said an Oscar Wilde play is one of your favorites really drew me in. Because he's one of my favorite playwrights too."

I blinked, not quite grasping what was going on. It all seemed surreal. As surreal as the drawing on the napkin was turning out. After it was done, he handed it to me with a smile. "For you," he said.

The drawing was a like a miniature Dali painting, with little melting hearts into fingertips and a single eye hovering above. It was charming, and I couldn't believe he put it together so quickly.

"Impressive," I began. "So, let me guess. You're a graphic artist?"

He shook his head. "Bank CEO."

"Ah. Should've known."

"Why is that?"

"You looked like a CEO the other day. All suited up."

He stirred his drink, squeezing his lime into it. His eyes didn't meet mine.

I instinctively knew something was wrong, so I asked him.

"Nothing's wrong. I just like you, that's all."

"I like you too," I said. But why did he seem to not want to talk to me about himself?

Then he asked, out of the blue, "Do you mountain bike?

"I've never been, to be honest."

"Would you like to try? I know some great trails here in town."

"Well, I don't have a bike for that. I have a road bike and used to like to do that, but I haven't lately. As you can probably tell."

He ignored that last comment. "I have a bike you can

borrow if you like. But only if you want to go." He had the puppy-dog expression again.

I took a deep breath, not knowing what I was getting into. "Ok, sure. When would you like to go?"

"Uh, what are you doing tomorrow morning?"

"No special plans, actually."

"Pick you up at 8?"

"Sure."

I was starting to feel the dirty martinis working on me. I looked at this martini, my second, and made a mental note to stop. I wouldn't get liquored up again - the guy might think I had a drinking problem. Plus, I didn't want to sleep with him that night. My experience was that a relationship that started with sex ended up being a relationship all about sex, and I wanted to get to know him before hitting the sack with him again. As I said, I was an old-fashioned girl at heart.

At least, I was when I was sober.

Our conversation continued from there for the rest of the evening. It continued when we left the bar to go to dinner at a steakhouse. Natural, flowing, easy, never an awkward moment of silence. It was as if we were childhood friends who grew up together and knew every intimate detail about one another. We were finishing each other's sentences by the end of the evening.

But, as we talked, I casually looked around the restaurant. As I did, I noticed quite a few people staring at Ryan. Not just women but men, too. Even the ones you'd never suspect.

I immediately felt self-conscious. I was somewhat cute, but this guy was magnetic, and everybody in the bar knew it. All the dirty martinis in the world wouldn't erase the self-doubt creeping into my brain with every lustful glance I saw from the patrons at the bar.

With a sinking heart, I knew I'd have to cut it short before I became too involved with a guy who was stratospheres out of my league.

My hand shaking, I began, "Ryan, this has been an amazing evening. But I don't think-"

I never finished my sentence because he was over on my side of the table in a flash. He put his hand in my hair and gave me a soft kiss. Electricity shot through my body, and I realized I was no longer breathing. My heart stopped for a brief second, and I was trembling more than ever. He looked into my eyes with his penetrating green eyes with long, dark lashes.

"Iris. I can tell you feel I'm better than you, but I don't want you to think that. I like you. I really like you. I want to spend more time with you."

I wasn't hearing him. His kiss had stunned me, had made the rest of the world stop. I could hear my heartbeat and breathing but could hear little else. I continued just to stare at him. He was still kneeling before me, his eyes pleading a little. I could also see desire in his eyes.

"I...." There were no other words. I blinked rapidly, coming out of my brief catatonia.

He was finally standing up, his hand out. I stood up too, and he grabbed my hand and smiled.

I still couldn't speak.

"I paid the bill. Let's get my car, and I'll drive you to yours."

I dazedly followed. He opened the door, and the night air brought me to my senses. It was still over 90 degrees, even though it was 11:30. He held my hand as we walked down the street. My hand was trembling a little. My legs felt like spaghetti.

He was talking. "Now, with mountain biking, you must feel in control. You have to make the bike and the trails your bitch. That's the secret. Don't worry. You'll get the hang of it. We'll begin you on the slightest grade of trail, although you'll soon get bored with that and want to graduate to a bigger trail. But I don't want to rush you."

I must've had a look of horror when he said that because he hurriedly added, "But only if you feel comfortable."

God, I feel dumb. Why couldn't I talk?

We were soon at his car, and I felt even more intimidated. The guy had a brand-new Porsche Taycan, an electric car that retailed for over $100,000. More than I made in two years in my dinky one-woman law firm.

He opened the car door. Before I entered the door, he leaned me up against the car and put his hands on my shoulders. Then he put one hand in my hair as he leaned to kiss me again.

I stopped breathing again. I heard his heartbeat, which was surprisingly loud. The kiss was longer and deeper than the one in the restaurant. The jolt of electricity I felt during the first kiss was stronger now, coursing completely through my body. My heart was beating fast and hard. His kiss remained soft, his lips feathering on mine, his tongue lightly gliding just inside my mouth.

He was an amazing kisser.

After what seemed like an eternity, he broke away. I looked up, and he was looking at me, smiling, his hand still in my hair. His other hand was gently around my waist. I was still shaking. Smiling, he gestured for me to get into the car. I stumbled into the front seat, my legs giving way beneath me. I was vaguely aware of him fastening my seatbelt, then getting into the driver's seat next to me. Once he got into the driver's seat, he leaned over and kissed me again, feathery, light. Then we were off.

We drove silently to my car, a beat-up 15-year-old RAV4 named Priscilla because she was purple. I still didn't have words, and he was probably tired of trying to fill the silence. But, at every stop light, he would gently take his hand off the steering wheel and place it in my hair, gently running his hands through my mane and sometimes stroking my cheek.

We finally arrived at the battered car, but I somehow didn't feel embarrassed about it. And it wasn't until I arrived home that night, after driving home with the radio on, feeling that every love song was written especially for me, that I came down to earth. He'd kissed me again before I got into my car. His kisses were tender and sweet. He was very respectful, keeping his hands around my waist and in my hair. That kiss at my car lasted a while.

I wanted it to last forever.

However, getting home brought me back down. Madison, my kitty cat, gave me her usual greeting when I came in the door which was pawing the cork disk on the floor while mewing. I looked around the apartment. It wasn't a bad apartment, just quite small. I'd painted the walls a dark shade of green in the living room (there wasn't a dining room), and the bedroom was painted a dark shade of rose. Above the fireplace was an enormous Andy Warhol print of Jacqueline Kennedy. I wasn't really a fan of either Warhol or Jackie Kennedy, but, for some reason, that particular picture drew me in, and I had to have it.

I plopped on the couch and thought about the night. Was I dreaming it all?

Then I drifted off to sleep. I dreamed about a beautiful dark-haired man who swept me off my feet.

Chapter Four

Ryan arrived at my apartment at 8 AM, just like he said. I'd come down a little since the previous evening, but I couldn't bring myself to clean up the apartment. I was too wired.

And, oh, God, I didn't have biking shorts! I couldn't possibly bike without biking shorts!

He was knocking at the door. At this point, I had to find my keys, as they went missing sometime during the night, and my cell phone, which went missing somewhere else. I tore around the apartment, lifting up magazines and newspapers, throwing everything out of drawers, tossing the couch cushions repeatedly. I kept looking in the same places about 20 times as if they would magically appear in these places when they clearly weren't there before.

"Just a second!" I called. *Shit, where are these goddamned things?* I opened up the refrigerator, and there were my keys. *Go figure.* This gave me an idea – I climbed up on the counter to look on top of the fridge, and my cell phone was there. *Bizarre.* I got the idea to look on top of the fridge because it occurred to me that I might've put the cell phone up there because years ago, I put a pair of glasses on top of the fridge. Of course, I was drunk at the time. But, last night, I was drunker than I had ever been. Not literally, just high from the evening.

I opened the door breathlessly. "Gosh, I am so sorry. I overslept. Um, I can't go."

He looked perplexed. "How come?"

"I wasn't thinking last night. I don't have a pair of biking shorts."

"Ah, well, you aren't getting out of this so easily, my friend." He smiled impishly.

"What do you mean?"

"I picked up a pair of biking shorts for you."

"This morning? Already?"

"Yeah. Dick's is open early."

I was surprised to find this out. Somehow, I was suspicious that he got the shorts yesterday afternoon. *Presumptuous.* Or, God forbid, he bought them for somebody else. *Whatever.*

"Huh. What's the real story?"

"You caught me. Actually, I have a friend who knows the owner of Dick's. I called in a favor and asked him if he'd let me shop early this morning before the store opened."

I was impressed.

"Just a sec. Let me bring them up and make sure that they fit." And he was gone.

In about a minute, he was back, shorts in one hand, his other hand behind his back.

"Here, try these on."

"Ok, but you can't come in." *He can't possibly be ready for cyclone alley, as my mother would say.*

The next order of business was putting on the shorts.

They fit perfectly. I threw on a t-shirt, then realized Ryan's bike probably had clip pedals. Luckily, I had an old pair of clip shoes and threw them on. However, I couldn't find my helmet.

On my way out the door, I grabbed a Slim Fast shake, shook it, and downed it. *That's all you'll have until lunchtime.*

I opened the door. Ryan was chatting with my across-the-hall neighbor. Funny, she never even said hello to me. Ever. She was giggling animatedly, flipping her hair, batting her eyelashes. *Give me a fucking break.* I looked at her, and she looked back. Daggers from her. *Bitch.*

Ryan immediately turned his attention to me. "Well, Sheila, it was good to meet you."

"You too," she said, giggling and hair flipping. Eyelash batting.

Turning to me, Ryan asked, "How did the shorts work?" He had a pair of clip shoes in one hand and a helmet in the other.

"Great, great. Wow, you think of everything."

"You already have the shoes. But do you need this helmet, at least?"

I nodded. "I can't find mine anywhere." He handed me the helmet, and I adjusted it to fit my head. "Actually, let me see those shoes. Those look nicer than mine." And, indeed, they were. I put them on. They fit better than mine as well. "You get all these things at Dick's this morning?"

"Yeah. After I went home last night, I realized I didn't ask you if you had the right gear, so I decided to pick this stuff up. I'm glad I did."

"Everything actually fits perfectly," I said, thinking about the irony of him bringing me shoes that fit perfectly. Cinderella popped into my head for a brief moment.

"Then let's get going."

Once in the car, Ryan grabbed my hand and kissed it, then kissed me.

We drove along in silence for a few minutes. I was back to my silent mode. This was all so bizarre to me. I'd experienced this kind of crazy ardor before, usually from some weaselly loser who won't stop calling me. Never from somebody like Ryan.

We got to the trails, and I immediately felt the whole scenario was not for me. For one thing, I was terrified of going down the steep hills. We started out on some flat trails, and this was fine. I could roll along and keep up. However, when it came to the steep downhill trails with all the rocks and branches, I couldn't go down them because I was too fearful. The few times I tried, I wiped out and landed painfully on rocks. Ryan was always very good about this, coming to my aid, and he was ready with some bandages and Neosporin, but I ended up with a great deal of road rash for my efforts.

And biking up these steep hills? Forget about it, although Ryan was an expert. I watched his sinewy legs peddling up those hills, and I momentarily forgot my misery. Only momentarily, though.

Finally, we arrived at one of the streams he was talking about earlier. He had lunch ready, with turkey sandwiches and granola bars. We got our water bottles out of the cages on the side of our bikes and sat down beneath a tree.

"So, how're you doing, beautiful?" he asked with a gentle smile. I saw him looking at the road rash sympathetically.

"I don't know if this is for me." I felt defeated.

He smiled. "Relax. We can try again if you like. If you don't, it's no biggie. Really. Honestly."

I shook my head skeptically, remembering that we'd also talked about how he loved to ski last night. He skied black diamonds. I had to Google this, not knowing what black diamonds were, then discovered they were the most difficult courses. "I don't ski, either," I said miserably. *This guy will get so bored with me.*

"Sweetheart, it's ok. I like you. I don't care if you're not into adventure sports. I'm impressed you're trying this. Most girls wouldn't." He tousled my hair and lay down on the ground beside me. He patted the ground, and I lay down as well. He kissed me slowly, lightly, and the familiar jolt of electricity coursed through my body. I didn't recall ever feeling this way about anybody. At least not this amount of electricity. I could tell he was feeling just as much electricity because I could sense it from him.

We lay there for a little while, kissing passionately yet innocently. I wanted him to strip off my clothes right then and there and explore my body eagerly with his tongue.

Looking into my eyes, Ryan said, "We should probably get going before it starts getting dark. The trail exits onto the street, which might be better than taking the trail all the way back. I think you've had enough mountain biking for the day."

Truer words were never spoken. So, we followed the trail for a little bit, then were soon out on the street. We biked the 10 miles back to the car, me struggling to keep up but not wanting him to know. I wanted him to think I was better than I really was.

"What would you like to do now?" Ryan asked when we got to his electric Escalade, which apparently was his other vehicle and was made just for him, as it had yet to come to market, and put his bikes away.

"I'm starved," I said. I just had that little Slim-Fast shake for breakfast, then the turkey sandwich and granola bar for lunch, so I was pretty hungry after all this exercise.

"I hope you don't mind, but I'd like to cook for you this evening."

My eyes grew huge. Cook? He can cook? *Riggghhhht. Next thing you know, he'll tell me he does his own dishes.* I wasn't used to men who cooked. My old boyfriend lived on Doritos and frozen pizza, which was typical.

"That sounds fantastic," I said, smiling. "But I need to shower and change."

"Of course." He took me home, kissing me goodbye. "Pick you up at 5?"

I nodded. Then went inside, showered and fed the cat. Right at five, he was back, dressed in jeans and a polo. He looked adorable.

We went to his house in Hallbrook. Hallbrook was the neighborhood where Joe Montana lived while playing for Kansas City. It was now the home of CEOs, hedge fund managers, venture capitalists, large-firm law partners, heart surgeons, and probably more than a few drug kingpins. It was the ultimate in gated communities.

We arrived at his gorgeous and enormous Tudor revival home. The home had a brick and wood façade, with three of the signature wood triangles on the outside of the home. The driveway was a circle drive. The front of the house was surrounded by flowers and perfectly manicured bushes. A vaguely Japanese fountain was in the middle of a little courtyard, surrounded by marble benches. The front door was adorned with a stained-glass bird and looked like it cost more than my car brand new.

My legs felt like spaghetti as we walked up to the house.

I felt more comfortable walking in, as he had two very

friendly mutts who ran to greet him. "Maximus" and "Brutus" were two rescue mutts, he explained, who were about to be put down before he saved him. One was a pit bull mix. Because I rescued pit bulls, I felt a special affinity for this dog. Instinctively, upon meeting the dogs, I lay down on the floor so that they could come up to me and lick my face, which they did, being dogs. I rolled around with them for a while, and Ryan did the same, lying on the floor with me and the dogs.

"Looks like you really love dogs."

"Definitely. I want one so bad, but I can't have them in my little apartment. So, I rescue them instead."

His house was beautiful inside, spotless and elegant, with just enough masculinity. The kitchen was large, with an 8-foot island in the middle. The kitchen counters were entirely made of Italian marble in a dark blue color. His kitchen cabinets were made of real cherry wood, with more stained glass on the cabinet doors. The kitchen tile was mosaic patterned, with rust, blue, yellow and greens blended in. *My entire apartment could fit in this kitchen*, I observed.

This was the first room I hung out in, but he gave me a tour of the rest of the house. The living room was about 1,000 square feet, with cherry wood hard floors and throw rugs with various patterns on the floor. The ceilings were vaulted, with a skylight at the top. The furniture was modern, with leather sofas, coffee tables and end tables that were glass-topped and marble-bottomed, and tall lamps with crystal bells and brass stems. An enormous fireplace was on one of the walls, with a 10-foot by 10-foot mural done in the style of Thomas Hart Benton above it. Upon closer observation, I realized it was a Thomas Hart Benton original. *Oh, shit.*

He saw me looking at the mural. "I got that from my parents. Tom was a friend of my father's."

Benton grew up and made his art in the Kansas City area. Ryan's father was probably prominent in Kansas City business, so that makes some sense. "Yes, my father also knew a local artist," I said stupidly. "Her name was Marjorie Holman. She did two portraits of my sister and me." *As if Marjorie Holman could match up to Thomas Hart Benton.*

The rest of the living room appeared as if an interior decorator had designed it. And, of course, there was nothing out of place.

"Here, make yourself at home," he said, gesturing to an empty stool next to the kitchen island. I observed the pots and pans above my head. They were copper-bottomed and looked very professional. I wanted to know if this guy could really cook.

He opened up a bottle of wine. "I hope you like this."

I sipped the wine. It was smooth, full-bodied and fruity. It was very good. "I like this. Where did you get this?"

He looked a bit embarrassed. "I, I, I, um…" It was his turn to stutter. He turned bright red. "Listen, Iris, I don't want you to feel intimidated here. I guess I should've warned you about the Benton."

Yes, but what does the Benton have to do with this wine?

I looked at him, puzzled.

"I really like you. I mean, I realllllllyy dig you. I don't want to scare you away."

I looked at my wine, taking another sip. Very tasty. I looked up at him expectantly. He was acting very strange. He'd been so confident before.

He took a deep breath. "I actually, uh, I actually own a winery in Italy." The "own a winery in Italy" was mumbled softly as he looked down at the floor, so I had to ask him to repeat it. Which he did.

I nodded my head. *Well, that makes sense. What's so wrong with that?* I looked at him, furrowing my brow, wondering why he was so embarrassed. "My dream man!" I joked.

He looked relieved. The color returned to his face. Nothing would surprise me anymore about this guy. He told me last night he went to Harvard for his undergrad and Oxford for his MBA. He also told me that his father was a CEO for a major utility company in town. Plus, he owned a Benton mural. Owning a winery went perfectly with this guy.

He smiled. "You surprise me sometimes."

I smiled back. "I do? How?"

"Well, last night, you seemed so nervous around me. I get the feeling that you might not be used to... things. But the Benton and the winery didn't seem to phase you."

"Maybe I'm getting more comfortable around you somehow."

He smiled. "That's great." Then he kissed me tenderly while longingly stroking my face.

"I'm gonna steal that painting, just so you know. Benton is one of my favorite artists.

"Mine too. It's only fitting to have his art in my house since he's such a large part of this area."

I nodded, then suddenly realized how badly I needed to use the restroom. "I need to use the little girl's room," I said with sudden urgency.

"Around the hall to your right."

After returning from the restroom, I felt a little more queasy. Thomas Hart Benton was one thing. de Kooning was another, and he had an original de Kooning in the hallway leading to the bathroom.

Good lord, this guy has millions hanging on his wall.

He looked a little sheepish. "I guess you saw the de Kooning, too, huh?"

I smiled, nodding slowly. "Pour me some more of that Italian wine." *Lord knows I need some now.*

Whatever he was cooking smelled divine. It was clam sauce with a little butter, wine and garlic. He brought out a freshly baked loaf of bread, baked, evidently, by hand. He also brought out some Caesar dressing in a container. Also, freshly made. He chopped some romaine lettuce and then shredded some Parmesan Cheese. The entire meal was simple and freshly prepared.

As we sat down to eat, he raised his wine glass. "Cheers! Bon appetit!"

I smiled. On my first bite, I was amazed. More than amazed. "Oh my God, this is delicious! I feel like I'm eating in the best Italian restaurant!"

He smiled, too, blushing profusely. "Try the bread."

The bread was infused with rosemary and something else. It, too, was divine. "This bread is amazing! What herbs did you use?"

"Rosemary and lavender."

Lavender. Who would've thought?

Even the butter was delicious. It was herb butter, and Ryan explained that he'd melted the butter with garlic and herbs, then let it set up.

Then the dessert. Ginger pear flan. "I found the recipe in one of my cookbooks."

After dinner, he finished giving me a tour of the rest of the magnificent house. There were six bedrooms, including one that had been converted into an enormous office. I smiled upon entering the office, seeing he was human, after all – he had papers everywhere piled up, randomly, on his desk, and magazines were strewn all over a table. Some of the magazines were related to his work as a CEO of a large bank - *Inc.* and the *Wall Street Journal*, for instance. But some of the magazines were more relatable to me – he also had subscriptions to *People* magazine and *Entertainment Weekly*. These were two of my favorite magazines. He also appeared to have subscriptions to *GQ* and *Maxim*. And I had to smile upon seeing several copies of *Star Magazine*.

He looked embarrassed. "Guilty pleasure," he said.

"I love that magazine too!" I said, smiling. "You always gotta know the latest Harry Styles stories."

We'll get along after all.

I also noticed a life-size stuffed Donald Duck in the corner. I looked at Ryan, thinking he would explain the enormous bird. He didn't say anything about it, though.

While seeing the office made me relax, seeing the rest of the house intimidated me once more. The house had everything – a wine cellar, a game room, a home theatre, a fully-stocked wet bar, and fireplaces in every bedroom. The master suite was magnificent, and the master bathroom was....there were no words. Sunken marble tub, which could comfortably seat several people. Brass fixtures, marble counters. Even the toilet looked expensive. The seat was heated and featured a bidet.

I was in awe, to say the least. *This home must be worth at least a million dollars.* Plus, the home backed up onto a golf course.

I drew an enormous breath, trying to banish the thought that I'd never fit in here. Ever.

There was one room with a closed door. Ryan didn't open the door to this room. I thought it was odd, as he happily showed me every other room.

I let it go.

After the tour, we went back downstairs and lay by the fireplace in the living room. He played with my hair and stroked my cheek. We drank the wine from his winery, finishing one bottle and opening another. Music played in the background, an Ipod mix of Frank Sinatra, The Silver Sun Pickups, Gotye, Muse, Johnny Mathis, The Police, Green Day, and Adele, with a little Def Leppard and REO Speedwagon mixed in for good measure. Very eclectic tastes, much like myself.

He was staring at me, not really saying anything, just gently playing with my hair, lying next to me on the rug. He kissed my forehead lightly.

"Do you want to spend the night in the guest bedroom? I've been drinking so don't want to drive."

I looked at him quizzically. I was anticipating a full-on seduction, but he'd barely touched me.

"Sure."

He led me up to one of the guest bedrooms. It was some guest bedroom. Like the kitchen, my entire apartment could fit into this bedroom, and a fireplace was in the corner. An enormous sleigh bed was in another corner of the room, and the carpeting was a muted blue. The nightstand was cherry wood, like most of the house, and the room had an enormous walk-in closet. Above the bed was a magnificent piece of artwork, another original, although the artist wasn't familiar. He saw me looking at the piece of art. "I got that at a local art gallery," he explained, "on a First Friday."

"First Friday" referred to the first Friday of every month, when the art district's galleries stayed open late to the public, and thousands of people jam the streets, walking from one gallery to another. I sometimes went to these affairs, not necessarily to buy art - I couldn't afford any of it

- but to be amongst the crowds of people and to take in the festive atmosphere. Plus, I generally liked to admire art.

He tucked me into bed, kissing me on my forehead. "Get some sleep."

"I had fun this evening. Thanks for everything."

At that, he turned out the light, leaving me in the dark. Sleeping beneath an unknown artist.

Chapter Five

I woke up at 6 AM. I couldn't sleep. I woke up earlier, at 3 in the morning, wondering where the hell I was. Literally. This often happened to me even when I was in my own bed. I'd wake up and panic a little, thinking I was in some dark alley or dungeon, until my conscious mind caught up and realized I was in my own bed. That happened last night, only it was worse because it took me several minutes to understand I was safe.

Or was I?

I was feeling nosy. I crept to the room Ryan didn't show me. I figured he kept his secret child porn stash or S&M gear there. *He doesn't want me to know that he's a freak.* I had to find out before I got in any further with this guy. Alternative sexual practices were not my thing, never had been, and never would be. I didn't care how nice, hot and rich he was. If I found whips and chains in there, I would be outta there. No questions asked.

I opened the door. What was in there stunned me. It was not an S&M room at all. Far from it. It was a baby's room. The walls were pink, and the room was done in Hello Kitty. There was a crib by the window with a little mobile above it with tiny giraffes, elephants, hippos and zebras. Stuffed animals were everywhere, and a rocking chair was in the corner. I opened the closet door, and cute little dresses and shirts were hanging up there with care, and tiny shoes were lined up on a shelf. On the dresser was a picture – of Ryan, a stunningly beautiful blonde woman, and a beautiful little girl.

Huh. He never told me he had a child. Well, that wasn't a big deal. I loved children, although I didn't want one of my own. *He'll tell me eventually about his kid. But why did he keep this room secret?* I answered my own question – he probably just forgot to open the door. That was all. He wouldn't want to hide that he had a child – there wasn't a reason for that.

I tiptoed out of that room and prepared to come down the stairs.

From down below, I could hear Ryan talking on his cell phone, so I decided not to bother him just yet, as I wanted his full attention.

But what I heard stopped me in my tracks.

"Listen, Alexis, I'm tired of your petty bullshit. I bought you that goddamned Porsche you demanded. I don't know what else you want except maybe your airplane." Ryan was talking in a loud whisper, not necessarily shouting, but definitely not trying to be quiet. He was pacing the floor, and it appeared that he was talking to himself like a schizophrenic. Of course, he had in a Bluetooth, but still, it looked odd – like the homeless people you see in the library talking to somebody who wasn't there.

There was a long pause. Ryan's pacing was frenetic, and he was pulling on his hair. Not running his fingers through it but pulling it with both hands. Then - "Yes, I know I have my own airplane, but you don't understand, I earned that."

Geezus, his own plane? Really? I was intrigued, utterly intimidated, and scared to death at seeing him this way, all at the same time.

A shorter pause as I saw Ryan pick up a stress ball, and squeeze it, no longer pulling on his hair. Then – "Oh, yes, I did. Yes, I did. Trust me, after what that bastard did to me, I earned that and more. Besides, you forget that I work for a living."

What bastard? Who did what to him? Oh, how I wanted to retreat back into the bedroom and not listen to this, but I stayed, my feet rooted to the ground.

Another long pause, about five minutes. Now he was again pacing the floor, having thrown the stress ball against the wall. He looked like his hand was going through the wall next. Then - "What kind of fuckery is that? How dare you bring that up? We're divorced, I gave you all I'm going to give you, and blackmail will get you exactly nowhere."

Oh, lord – blackmail? My mind was racing now. Ting, ting, ting, just like a computer, my thoughts started racing about what was up with all this. I felt like crying – just when I was starting to let down my guard....

Maximus and Brutus were getting into the act, coming up to him to comfort him. He was sitting on the couch, and they tried to lick his face. He hastily pushed them both away and started towards the door to put them out. Then he picked up the stress ball again and paced some more. Then - "Go right ahead. Go to the press. It isn't my ass that's on the line. It's his."

Jesus – the press. Must be something bad. The computer started whirring again. Ting, ting, ting.

A long pause, then - "Goddamn it, I'm not going to keep

buying your goddamned silence. This has to end, Alexis, one way or another. So, go ahead with your little plan. You've got no proof anyhow. Remember, our divorce decree has a gag order, so you can't use those depositions against me."

A silence of about one minute as Ryan was now at the Benton painting, putting his left hand on it protectively, as he said, "Goddamn it, I told you that you can never have the Benton, so why do you keep asking me about that? How many times-"

More pacing, then "I know that the de Kooning is much more valuable, but you can't have that one either, and that's that."

Still pacing, and pulling on his hair, then "No, the Cezanne is off-limits too, but, Holy Christ, you know that. That's been in my family for years, and you know why I have it now. You know why, so quit asking me about it."

Cezanne? What the-

More pacing, and he opened the door to go outside. I immediately ran back into the room and opened the window to hear. Now he was pacing around outside.

"You'll get nothing more. You'll never be satisfied. I could buy you a fucking Greek Island, and you'll come back for more."

He made his way back into the house, and I rushed to where I was before, up above. Then - "I won't give in to blackmail."

Then - "Little shit."

I tiptoed back into the guest bedroom, afraid of him knowing I heard any of that, much less all. *Why do you have to be so nosy?* I also was afraid of going downstairs. He couldn't be in a good mood after all that. I lay back in the bed, half expecting him to storm in here, ripping the covers off me and kicking my ass out. Or, worse, ask me why I was still there. Well, maybe that wasn't worse. Equally bad.

Tentatively, I opened the door and looked down at Ryan in the living room again. He was pacing the floor, muttering to himself. I could make out various words. "She can't do this." And "She won't do this." Then he was on the phone again. "Sheldon, it's me..... She's threatening to go to the press again...Tell me again about the terms of the gag order... That's what I thought. She can use what she knows. She just can't use the legal proceedings against me. But she can use what she found out through me during our marriage...I know, I know, she wouldn't have agreed to our divorce terms otherwise, but, goddamn it, I wish we had a more airtight gag order on her...I know. I didn't think she'd be so vindictive, either...God, you think you know somebody....Well, the good news is that she has no proof of anything without those depositions. I'll just deny it all...Yes, I know it's his ass, not mine...I don't know why I care how much trouble he gets into... He just scares me still. Plus, if this gets out, it'll be humiliating for me...No, it's not that... Yes, well, thanks, Sheldon, for answering the phone on an early Sunday morning...Good to talk to you too...Yes, I didn't forget about racquetball. On my schedule...Bye."

Sheldon. Sounds like a lawyer's name.

After he got off the phone, he dragged himself to his couch, slumped his shoulders, and put his head in his hands. I quietly went back into my room and shut the door, then cracked it open a little to hear if he was coming to see me.

To my surprise, he got on the phone with somebody else. "Nick," he said. "I really need to see you." At this point, Ryan was sitting on the couch, the dogs sitting next to him. He was petting them calmly while he spoke.

Pause. "Well, I'm kinda spiraling right now." At that, he

pulled on Maximus' ear. The dog yanked his head away. "I'll tell you later. I just, uh, really need you to see you right now...Tonight would be great. Maybe we could get a drink?"

My heart plummeted to my shoes. Nick? Who was Nick? Nick – girl, boy? Nicolette, Nicole, Nikki? *Oh, lord, I knew it! Dude's got a girlfriend.* I bit my nails, not worried about the manicure. *Don't jump to conclusions. It might be his brother. Or sister.*

After careful consideration, I decided to play it off like I'd never heard that conversation. Any of the conversations. Although warning bells were going off in my head, I didn't want to confront the matter. I was nuts about this guy, so sweeping danger signs under the rug seemed the thing to do.

Suddenly, he was calling for me. "Iris?" I could hear him coming up the stairs. My breathing started coming rapidly, more and more so as he approached the door. I ran back into the bed, pulled the cover over my head, and thought better of it. That would be a dead giveaway I heard all of that.

Instead, I pretended to sleep.

He quietly opened the door. Then he sighed and closed the door behind him. He went back down the stairs. My breath caught. *I hope that worked. God, I hoped that worked. I hope he really thought I slept through all of that.* Then I thought – *how long should I wait to come down the stairs?*

I decided to wait a half hour more. It was now 7:30. He didn't have to be anywhere, so hopefully, I wasn't bothering him too much.

The second I opened the door, he spun around where he was downstairs. He smiled wanly. "Hey, beautiful," he said without his usual enthusiasm. Encouraged, I made my way downstairs, and he was already coming up the stairs, so we met halfway.

Putting his arm around me, he said, "I hope you slept well."

"Yes, yes, I did. Thank you very much for letting me stay."

"Well, I couldn't let you drive after all that wine."

"Excellent wine. You have very good taste."

"Well, that was a particularly good year because it was so dry that year." He smiled. "Global warming is actually a good thing for vintners."

"Oh?"

"Yeah. The drier it is, the better the crop."

"Huh?"

"Well, when there's too much moisture, the leaves tend to get moldy, and the grapes don't grow as well. The sugar also gets more concentrated in dry weather."

"Learn something new every day!"

Surreptitiously, I looked at his face for any sign of the emotional turmoil he was apparently going through. He looked a little wan, a little less engaged, a little more distracted. But he was hiding it well. I felt mixed emotions about that. *If he could hide his emotions about this, what else would he be good at hiding in the future?*

I waited for him to say anything about the conversations this morning. He had to know that there was at least a chance I heard something, although I hoped it was not in his mind that I heard as much as I did.

"Um, let me fix you some breakfast." Well, "fix" wasn't quite the term, as he had cheese strata already in the oven, which was now coming out and cooling.

"Did you prepare that last night?" I knew stratas were usually an overnight thing because the bread has to soak up the egg and cheese, but I didn't recall him making anything last night.

"Yeah. After you went to bed, I got this ready. I wanted to make something nice for you for breakfast. And, for the record, I'm impressed you know about cheese stratas."

"Well, I'm not a total food philistine," I said with mock indignation.

"Never thought you were." He was distracted - he apparently thought I was being serious when I acted offended.

He sliced the cheese strata and garnished it with some berries and cream. "Bloody Mary or Virgin Mary?" he asked.

"Bloody, please."

He smiled at that. "My kind of woman. Now, shoo, go meet me on the terrace."

I went out the sliding glass door that opened into his backyard. The "backyard" was more of a palatial terrace. The back patio was paved in lightly colored stone, overlooking an in-ground Olympic-sized swimming pool. A 10-person hot tub gurgled just above the pool. The hot tub was also built in-ground. I walked to his dining table, which also sat 10 and was situated under a canopy. Beyond the pool and hot tub, I could see roses, daisies, geraniums, mandevillas, and a gazebo. There was also a fully-stocked wet bar outside, underneath a little Tiki hut, right by the pool.

Ryan appeared, bearing a tray with his plate and mine and two Bloody Marys. I felt weird sitting at such a large table.

"Love, would you rather sit by the pool?"

I looked towards the pool, noticing a smaller table with an umbrella attached. "Sure, but let me help you with the food and everything."

"No, I got it. Just meet me there."

I went down the steps to the table by the pool, Ryan behind me.

Sitting down to eat, I bit into my strata. "Oh, I'm in heaven! Where did you learn to cook?"

"Here and there. I picked up a little all my life."

I felt glad he didn't tell me the clichéd "My nanny taught me to cook." Or something like that.

I took a deep breath, wondering if he'd say anything about the unfolding drama. To my surprise, he did.

"My ex-wife called this morning."

I tried for the right expression. Not exactly surprised, but not like I knew something, either. *I hope I get this right.* "Oh?"

"Yeah," he said but then said nothing more.

The breakfast was soon finished. We barely said a word to one another over the delicious strata and the spicy and wonderful Bloody Mary. Not sure how to play this - if I stay, am I intruding? If I go, does he think I'm no longer interested? - I opted for eating and running. "Hey, thanks for everything. You're an amazing cook. I hate to eat and run."

"Yes, yes," he said, sounding miserable. "Um, let me show you out." I looked at him quizzically, suddenly remembering I didn't have my car there. I wondered if that occurred to him as well. In a split second, it did. "Oh, shit. Hold on a second." He went into the other room with his iPhone. He came back in a few minutes. "I'm terribly sorry. I just called my driver. He'll be here in about five minutes."

Jeeves is driving me home? NOT a good sign. I sighed inwardly. *I knew this was too good to be true.*

Daniel, his driver, was there in five minutes, driving a Cadillac Escalade, just as Ryan had promised. Patting my head a little before I got into the car, he said, "Thanks, Iris. I had a very nice time."

That's it? Not even a fake promise to call? Not even a half-hearted "I'll see you later?" I nodded my head. *Bastard.* I immediately banished that thought. *Not a bastard. A nice guy who's dealing with a nasty problem I can't even begin to fathom. Well, maybe he is a bastard, if this Nick person is his girlfriend. Estranged girlfriend? Sister? Woman he wants as a girlfriend?*

Smiling, I waved.

But he already had his back turned and was walking into the house.

Chapter Six

Sitting in the back of the Escalade, I willed Daniel not to be a chatty driver. I couldn't deal with that right now. I bit my lip, willing myself not to cry. *Daniel will no doubt report if I cry, so keep calm.* Then I thought, *ha, Daniel won't report anything. Ryan won't ask because he won't care. Daniel has probably seen it all, anyhow.*

Thankfully, Daniel was stoic, not even trying to make small talk.

Once inside my apartment, I let loose a torrent of tears. I had no idea why I was crying. I barely knew the guy. Except I actually had known him my entire life. That is, I'd known the idea of him all my life – the seemingly perfect guy. Dare I say – Prince Charming? So, I was upset because I assumed I wouldn't see him anymore.

That week sucked. Dragging myself to work, trying not to snap at clients, barking at opposing counsel, writing ever nastier letters to them.

"Your client better get her ass off that couch and stop sponging off my client," read one letter.

"Tell your client to get off the crack and bong hits and take care of the kid, or we'll get a modification agreement faster than you can read this," read another.

I was on an "ass" kick in that because I was loving that word. I wanted to use it in some fashion in every letter I wrote. I refrained when writing my motions to the judge, however. But even those motions were more aggressive than usual, although not quite as blunt as the letters to opposing counsel.

And one client, in particular, sent me into Defcon 1. He showed up to plead for a DWI, and when he arrived at the courthouse, the smell of alcohol on his breath nearly knocked me over. It was fresh alcohol, too, because it actually smelled like vodka, as opposed to smelling slightly sweet, which was what vodka smelled like on a person's breath after some time.

"What the fuck?" I asked him. The alcohol was strong on his breath, and his eyes were bloodshot. He looked like a mess.

"What?" he asked.

"Oh, no, you didn't. I know you didn't booze it up before seeing the judge about your DWI charge."

"I'm going to jail," he slurred. "I wanted to have one last hurrah with my friends."

"What did I say that made you think you were going to jail today? I said you're gonna get probation." I was apoplectic. "Well, probably not now. That judge will take one look at you and one smell of you and throw you in the clink for sure. And that would serve you goddamned right." I shook my head. "You aren't paying me enough for this bullshit. You couldn't pay me enough for this bullshit."

Then I looked around. The guy was there by himself. "Where's your ride?" I demanded.

"I couldn't find a ride."

"Then where's your bus pass?"

He looked at the floor and said nothing.

I was stunned. "Oh.my.God. You drove drunk to the courthouse to answer your drunk-driving charge?"

He hung his head and continued to say nothing.

"Well, fuck this noise. I'm withdrawing from your case."

"What? You can't do that!"

"Oh, can't I? Where's the rest of the money you promised me?"

"I'll send it to you when I get paid."

"Bullshit. I'm withdrawing."

When the judge called my client's name about an hour and a half into the docket, I stood before him.

"I request a move to withdraw your honor."

"Why is that, counselor?"

"Rule one violation, your honor." Every attorney knew the rule number one for clients – always pay your attorney. The bastard paid me $250, owed me another $1,000, then drove drunk to the courthouse. *You can't make this shit up. Nobody would ever believe me if I told them.*

"Motion granted." Turning to my client, he said, "Now, young man, your new court date is August 20th. You must have new counsel by then. Do you understand?"

My client nodded mutely.

"Oh, and another thing. If you show up in my courtroom drunk again, I'll have your case transferred to the state for prosecution. That'll mean you won't face probation or possible jail time, but prison time. The big house. Do you understand?"

My client nodded.

"I didn't hear your reply."

"Yes, your honor."

Turning to me, the judge asked, *sotto voce*, "Counselor, did your client drive here?"

"He did, your honor."

The judge motioned to the bailiff. "Take this man and put him in custody. He apparently drove drunk to get here." The bailiff grabbed my client by the arm and led him away. He didn't protest.

The judge shook his head. "Now I've seen everything."

That client wasn't the only one to piss me off that week. He was just the worst. I found myself wanting to strangle at least 6 people for various reasons.

"You were cooking meth while your kid was in the house. Take this offer or leave it," I said to a criminal client who was, amazingly, being offered probation yet didn't want the offer. "Or should I say, take this offer, or I'm gonna withdraw because you aren't listening to me, your counsel."

"Oh, good lord, you want sole custody of your child because your ex-husband was late taking her to band practice? Seriously?" I asked another, rolling my eyes.

By the week's end, I realized I was cracking up. I could usually handle idiot clients, but that week, I just couldn't. It was because of what happened with Ryan. *What is wrong with you, Iris? You.barely.knew.the.guy.*

The weekend was finally approaching. I dreaded it and looked forward to it at the same time. While I no longer had to refrain from chewing out various clients with their excuses and whining, which was good, I also had nothing to look forward to that weekend but my DVR.

Which was bad.

My fault. My friends were calling all that week, wanting to see how I was, wanting to get together. I didn't answer any of the phone calls.

I'll call them when I'm feeling better.

Chapter Seven

I dragged myself home. *Friday night, let's see what's on Netflix.* I wanted to see a limited series called *The Queen's Gambit*. It was a story about a chess prodigy who learned the game in an orphanage and then went on to beat the best in the world, all during a time when women really didn't play chess. I'd heard great things about it, and there were only 6 episodes, so I could probably watch the entire series that evening. The other option was watching *Downton Abbey* for the thousandth time - I'd seen every episode of the period British drama four times - but the chess thing appealed more. I'd had enough of rich people and wanted to see a story about a girl who came from nothing and made good.

Feeling slightly cheered at the prospect of watching the series, I opened up a bottle of wine and sucked it down from the bottle, not even bothering to pour a glass. The series was as good as I heard, as I got sucked into Beth Harmon's story right away and finished it around one in the morning.

In the middle of the night, I was snoozing on the couch

after drinking an entire Two Buck Chuck straight from the bottle. I was dreaming about there being somebody at the door. Knock, knock, knock. I tossed a little, putting the pillow over my ears. Knock, knock, knock, knock, knock, knock, knock, knock.

Go away.

Gradually, I started to realize the knocking was not in my dreams. I stumbled to the door, looking out the peephole.

Huh. Looks like Ryan out there.

Nah, I'm seeing things. I went to lie back down on the couch.

Then a voice. "Iris? Are you there?" Knock, knock, knock, knock, knock, knock.

I got back up off the couch and opened the door. Ryan was in the hall, looking stinking drunk but still beautiful. He was dressed formally in a silk dress shirt, dress slacks, and expensive Ferragamo wing-tipped shoes. He was wearing a Rolex watch, one I'd never seen before. He wasn't wearing a jacket or tie, but I surmised those items were a part of his ensemble earlier in the evening.

I'd have slammed the door in his face if I was self-respecting. *Coming here, in the middle of the night, after not calling all week and showing up drunk to boot.*

Then I remembered I was drunk, too, so I let him in.

"I'm so sorry, Iris, for dropping in like this. I was over at Bristol's for a fundraiser. I'm so sorry," he repeated.

Bristol's Restaurant was a tony seafood restaurant just up the street. Of course, "tony" was a relative term, this being Kansas City. This town was not exactly known for its seafood.

I was vaguely aware the apartment was a mess. My depression was such that I didn't want to do anything but lay around on the couch and watch Amazon Prime and Netflix shows all week. Thank God I didn't really eat that much, though.

The main problem was the wine bottles. I'd been making a point to recycle them, but unfortunately, curbside recycling had not yet hit my neck of the woods. At this point, there was an entire garbage bag filled with empty wine bottles which had accumulated just that week, all of them Two Buck Chuck - thank God for Trader Joe's!

He looked sheepish, standing in front of the door, which was still open. "I wanted to call."

Yeah, you should've called, so I could've tidied up a bit. Oh, well, nothing can be done about that now.

It occurred to me I should probably have him at least sleep off his apparent drunk.

"Hey, it's okay you didn't call," I lied. "You can stay here tonight or until your drunk wears off. Let me get you a pillow and blanket."

"Iris....." He started, looking pained. "I hope you don't think I'm only coming here because I got too drunk to drive."

Something struck me. "What time is it?"

"It's around 2 AM."

2 AM? This is a goddamned booty call. "What time does Bristol close?"

"I don't really know. The fundraiser was over around 9."

I narrowed my eyes. "Yet here you are at 2 AM."

"Well, some of us went out afterward to Harry's."

Harry's. In Westport. A good thirty-minute drive. "Yet here you are."

"I took a cab here."

I raised an eyebrow. "Daniel busy?"

"He didn't answer his phone."

"Oh." I looked at him. *You could've come right over when the fundraiser was over instead of waking my ass up. Then again, I was at the height of drunkenness at 9 PM, so it may be good you're here at 2. I feel at least slightly coherent.*

As if reading my mind, Ryan said, "I'm so sorry. I should've come right over when I was across the street."

I merely grunted at that one. "Let me get you a pillow and a blanket, and I'll drive you to your car in the morning."

"No need. My car is over at Bristol's."

"Good, I guess you can just walk on over there when you sober up," I said with gritted teeth. My head started to hurt because my jaw clenched as I spoke to this guy.

"You're angry. I don't blame you."

"Listen, I'm used to being treated like shit, so not sure why I ever thought you'd be any different." I *was* used to this kind of treatment. Booty calls, no calls, text-message break ups, dropping off the face of the earth, ghosting, any number of coward's way out. Carrie Bradshaw stated once that there was a right way to break up with somebody, and it didn't involve "an e-mail, a doorman or a missing person's report." That line always stuck with me because that seemed to be the *modus operandi* of the modern male.

However, I melted a little as I looked at him. His beautiful face was contorted, and he appeared to be about to break down in tears. I made fun of tearful guys on *The Bachelor*, but in real life, men's tears got me every time.

"Come on in, make yourself at home," I said, my anger gone. I smiled wryly. "What's mine is yours." This had no meaning whatsoever, considering Madison was my only property. Well, that and my furniture and computers. And my ancient car, Priscilla, of course.

He came in and sat down on the couch. Madison leaped

on his lap, purring loudly. I was stunned. *She never goes to anybody but me.* Madison was a sweet kitty but usually very shy. Yet she went to him like he was offering her Beluga Caviar. That was a good sign – they say animals are the best judge of character.

If he's good enough for Madison, he's good enough for me.

"I'd offer you a drink, but...." *Let's see what I have.* "Actually, let's see how this is." I grabbed my vanilla soy milk and mixed in some butterscotch Schnapps. I tasted it. *Not bad at all.*

He smiled as I offered him my new concoction. "I probably need another drink like I need a hole in my head, but if you're offering, I'm taking."

He took a sip. "Say, that's pretty good."

"Well, it isn't vintage wine from my own winery, but I guess it'll do." I was feeling more comfortable around Ryan. I didn't care that he saw my trash bags overfull with wine bottles.

I noticed everything wasn't right with him, though. He was staring at the plastic cup holding the vanilla soy milk-butterscotch Schnapp's concoction and I saw him shaking a little.

"There's something wrong, isn't there?"

He looked at me. "No, nothing. I just feel bad for hurting you."

I narrowed my eyes. I knew better, but I didn't push.

He smiled, although it wasn't really sincere. "This drink's pretty good. Did you invent this?"

"Not really. It's called throwing together whatever I happen to have on hand."

"You're a regular MacGyver."

I had to laugh at that one. "MacGyver" was a word I

often used for people who were resourceful and able to create things out of everyday household items.

"Yes, a drink MacGyver. You'd be amazed at the things you can put together if you really make an effort."

He smiled again, wanly, then sipped the last of his MacGyver cocktail. I sat beside him, obsessing about the garbage bag of wine bottles.

I took his cup. "Would you like another?" I asked, moving towards the kitchen.

"Actually, it's pretty late."

"Sure, you're right. I'd give you my bed...."

"No, I can't put you out like that."

"Really, it isn't a problem."

He looked up at me. "I hope it's not too forward to ask if we could sleep together in your bed? I mean, I promise I won't try anything. I know we started out as a one-night stand, but I really want us to be about something other than sex."

"Not a problem," I said, excited about sharing a bed with this hunk of a man.

"Thanks for accommodating me on such short notice."

"Don't be silly. I'm thrilled to have you."

We lay on the bed, fully clothed, on top of the covers. Ryan lay behind me, one arm wrapped tightly around my waist, his free hand gently stroking my hair. "Mmmm, this feels nice," he said. "Really nice." He reached his face around and kissed me gently on the mouth with little feathery kisses. I immediately felt his erection after the kiss, through his pants, even though his pants were somewhat loose, as they were suit trousers. He self-consciously turned his body slightly so that his lower half was no longer pressed against me. "Sorry about that," he said.

I lay there quietly, afraid to speak. I hoped he thought

I'd just magically fallen asleep. I didn't want him to feel embarrassed.

He just lay there next to me, his lower half facing the ceiling, his torso still pressed up against me, his fingers still stroking my hair, his other arm still wrapped tightly around me. "Beautiful hair," he purred. "I've always loved redheads." His lower half remained facing the ceiling. I could feel his breathing, could feel his heart pounding. When he kissed me, his breath tasted of Dewar's. He smelled of a very faint cologne.

My breath was catching, and I was trembling. His hands never explored my body. I could tell he was trying very hard to be a gentleman, but I wanted his hands to explore my breasts and everything else. I wanted his kisses on my thighs, back, and neck. But we both were trying to behave. *With any luck, there'll be plenty of time for that.*

Still, it was nice to know I turned him on. The evidence was certainly there. I fell asleep with Ryan wrapped around me, except for his lower body.

I'd never felt so safe.

Chapter Eight

The next morning, I woke up fairly early. Ryan's entire body was now wrapped around me. He was still sleeping soundly. I attempted to extricate myself, as I had to use the bathroom, but, when I tried, Ryan held on tighter. He was mumbling. "Stop, stop, daddy. Daddy, please." I didn't quite know what to do. *What was he dreaming?*

This guy was becoming ever more complicated. But I knew I was at least starting to fall for him, and not because of his beauty and apparent wealth. I was falling for him more for his kindness.

He woke with a start, looking at me, not quite seeing me. Then he plopped back down on the bed, pulling the covers around him, facing the wall. I seized the opportunity to use the bathroom at that point. I then tiptoed into the kitchen.

After about an hour, Ryan appeared, still fully clothed.

"Hey," I greeted him, Ajax coating the kitchen sink, and me scrubbing it diligently. My dishes were now in the dishwasher, which was humming quietly.

"Hey." He looked beautiful, more than ever, because he now had a look of vulnerability. "I'm sorry about last night."

I looked at him. *Sorry about what? I hope he wasn't apologizing for his erection. Probably not, he was probably apologizing for coming over so late.* "Um, don't worry about it." That covered anything that he'd be apologizing for.

"No, no. I was pretty shitty, coming over here in the middle of the night."

I smiled. "Better late than never."

"I should've called you."

"Please don't mention it." I looked in my fridge and found some turkey bacon. I also had some eggs and a tube of biscuits. *That should do it. It's not a cheese strata and berries with cream, but it will do in a pinch.*

I cut the turkey bacon in half, then started to fry it. "I hope you like turkey bacon."

He smiled. "Actually, I love it. I like it better than regular bacon."

"Me too." I was half expecting him to make some excuse to dash out the door, realizing he made a huge mistake in coming here, so I was relieved he wanted to stay for breakfast.

"Can I help?"

"No, I got it." After the bacon was done, I poured the eggs into the same pan, adding a little bit of olive oil and minced garlic to the pan. I had already put my Pillsbury biscuits in the oven, and they were almost done. I dug into my freezer and opened up a can of orange juice concentrate, and squeezed it into a container, adding water to mix it up.

Everything finished, I produced two plates - I had to interrupt the dishwasher cycle to get them- and piled some bacon, eggs, and biscuits on each plate. I set the plates down on the counter and then got two TV trays out for us to eat on.

"Sorry," I said, feeling embarrassed again, "I don't have room for a dining room table, so I have to eat on these TV trays."

He smiled, sincerely - the first sincere smile I'd seen in awhile, to be honest. "Not a problem."

"So, what are you up to today?" Ryan asked.

Besides laundry? "No real plans."

He seemed suddenly shy. "Would you like to hang out?" he asked, not looking me in the eye. *He seems afraid of rejection.*

"Sure, what did you have in mind?"

"Well, I chose the last activity. Your turn." His face was instantly brightened.

"Um, well, let's see....How about we pack up a picnic basket with some roasted chicken, some bread, some wine and take it out to the park by the art gallery? I think there is a Shakespeare play there tonight. Let me look in the paper...." I brought out the paper, turning to the art section. "Yes, see, *Twelfth Night* is playing."

"I love that play!"

And we were off. I drove him to his car, just up the street, and he followed me back to my apartment complex so I could drive with him in his car to the park. We stopped by the Hen House to pick up a roasted chicken, and I packed the chicken into a picnic basket that I had picked up at a thrift store a few years back. We also picked up some roasted new potatoes and roasted green beans. A bottle of Two Buck Chuck completed the meal, along with a small loaf of bread. I had also packed an Indian blanket, but we had to stop by his house to pick up two small lawn chairs for the evening performance. Also, Ryan wanted to check on Maximus and Brutus and change his clothes, of course. He was still wearing his dress pants, silk shirt and Ferragamo shoes from the night before.

"Daniel checks on them when I'm away, but I want to see them for at least a little bit before we go," Ryan said, referring to the dogs.

"Why don't we bring them along?" I remembered that dogs were welcome in that park.

"Sounds great." So, when we stopped by his house, Maximus and Brutus were harnessed. They leaped about, excited to be going. He also got two lawn chairs.

"We better take the Rivian." We went into the garage, and Ryan packed the dogs, in their carriers, into the Rivian, along with the two chairs, and the picnic basket filled with goodies. I loved this car - it was an all-electric SUV, sporty and sleek and super expensive. I tried not to think of that.

Driving to the park, Ryan held my hand the whole way. Every other stoplight, he kissed me softly. I watched his groin, remembering last night's erection. *I hope that isn't a problem now.* However, it became evident that it was. There wasn't much hiding it, the guy seemed enormous. I privately worried about that but felt excited at the same time.

He blushed. "I better stop that for awhile."

I blushed, too.

We got to the park and tossed around a frisbee and a ball for the dogs. "How old are they?" I asked.

"Maximus is 2 and Brutus is around 8 months."

"No wonder they're so frisky."

"Frisky is not the word. Spastic, hyper – those are good words."

And indeed they were.

We lay the blanket out on the lawn, and then got out the

paper plates, and plastic cups. He poured some wine for us both, and I broke apart the chicken. "Is a leg ok?" I asked.

"A leg would be great."

I piled a chicken leg, about four new potatoes and a spoonful of green beans on the plate.

Ryan produced two pillows after our lunch, and he lay down on one of the pillows. At his urging, I laid my head on his stomach. I felt his eight pack beneath me without an ounce of fat. His body was sinewy, muscular and lean. He stroked my hair contentedly. "I never thought I could feel this way," he purred.

"What way?"

"Happy, fulfilled."

I played a little dumb. "But you were married."

"Yeah," he said, simply. "But I never felt like this with her."

"Then why did you get married?" *A logical question.*

"Shhhh."

I kept quiet. The mystery will remain for now.

After a few minutes, Ryan admitted "I was so sick last week when I thought I might never see you again."

"Why did you think you would never see me again?"

He took a deep breath. "I don't know. I'm going through some stuff and I thought maybe it wasn't so good to get involved."

"But you changed your mind, right?" My heart sunk when he said those words.

"Yes. But I have to deal with issues with my ex-wife. You probably heard me talking to her when you spent the night."

"I didn't hear anything," I lied.

"Oh, well, I guess that's a good thing. But I wanted to talk about her because she might become an issue."

"Why would she be an issue?"

"Because she won't go away."

"What does she want?" I didn't like the prospect of an ex-wife coming between us but what choice did I have?

"She wants stuff, even though the divorce is all settled and has been for awhile." *No mention of the blackmail and the threats to go to the press with...something.*

In due time.

I lay there, silently. It was so difficult trying to determine how much to pry. I needed to make sure he knew I cared but I didn't want to push.

I was walking a delicate line and I knew it.

"What kind of stuff is she still wanting?"

"A new Ferrari, an airplane, that sort of stuff." *It sounds like he's joking, although I know he's not.*

"How long were you married?"

"Two years."

At this point, I was dying to find out everything. Why did they break up after only two years? Why did he marry her, when he apparently didn't love her (he said he never felt about her the way he felt about me. Considering he'd known me for less than two weeks, that wasn't saying a lot for their marriage)? And, especially, what information was she using to blackmail him?

In due time.

He volunteered some information then. "I married her because she was pregnant."

I thought about the baby room. *Here's where he'll tell me about his child.* However, what he said stunned me.

"So you have a child, right?"

His face darkened. He said, softly, "No. At least not a child who's alive."

I blinked, feeling the tears coming to my eyes.

"I'm so sorry. What happened?" I thought about the baby room some more and how it was so perfect. Nothing was disturbed in that room. I immediately felt so sad, knowing he must have loved his child very much. The evidence for this love was in the pristine condition of that room. I now figured he didn't want to show me because he wasn't ready to talk about her.

"Mia was born healthy. She died at the age of 6 months. SIDS." That was all he said. And I could tell from his tone and his body language that this was all that he was going to say.

"Oh, I'm so sorry…" What was there to say?

"Yeah, it was a tough break. Alexis was never the same after that, and our marriage, which wasn't all that strong to begin with, just went downhill. I found her in bed with Paul, my former driver, one day when I came home early from work to surprise her with a trip to Italy. I had it all planned out – the blindfold, the limousine taking us to my private jet, the whole nine. I wanted to cheer her up. It was like a kick in the gut, to say the least." *I like how he slipped in there that he had his own jet. He must be getting more comfortable talking to me about his wealth.*

"Geez." Again, what do you say to that?

"Yeah. I kicked her out. During the divorce, I found out how dirty she can fight."

"Oh?" *Come on, tell me everything that's going on.*

But he left it at that.

"Yeah. Hey, listen, it must be getting late. The show starts at 7, and we should head over to get a good seat."

"Sure." I felt disappointed, but I also felt that he'd slowly reveal what was going on with the blackmail thing. I found myself genuinely caring about what was going on, as opposed to wanting to know for nosiness, which, I admit, motivated me before to want to find out.

We made our way out to the outdoor theater. It was dusk now, and the cicadas were buzzing in the trees. Those bugs were so loud but I'd never actually seen one. There were apparently millions of them, however, judging by how loud the sound was.

We ended up not even using the lawn chairs, preferring to simply spread my Indian blanket on the lawn. We poured our wine into some plastic wine cups and drank the wine while the dogs, tired out from chasing around various balls and frisbees earlier, lay beside us. The park was packed, as this was a free show. It was something I tried to make every year.

As the night wore on, I tried hard to keep up with the action. *Twelfth Night* was a play I'd learned in college, but Shakespeare had always been exceedingly difficult for me to follow. However, the experience of being there – under the stars, with thousands of other people, on a warm summer night, with the most beautiful, sweetest man I'd ever met, was intoxicating.

Ryan was laying behind me on the blanket, and I was leaning against him. The dogs were beside us, snoozing and snoring. I started to notice he wasn't watching the play at all, but, rather, was staring at me. I felt a little strange and thrilled at the same time.

"You're not watching the show," I teased him, when I turned around for the millionth time to see him staring at me, instead of the play.

"You're right, I need to watch the show. I actually do like this play. I thought it was hilarious when I studied it at my high school."

I laughed. Who was I to control him and make him

watch the show? If he was that into me that he couldn't take his eyes off me, then....*Oh, stop it, you're sounding so full of yourself.*

"Would you like some more wine?" I asked.

"Nah, I'm ok."

"Ok, then."

The play ended. "We better pack all this stuff up," I said, already beginning the process of getting everything together.

He looked strange, wide-eyed.

"Is there anything wrong?" I asked. His demeanor had changed 180 degrees from just a few minutes before. I felt a bit alarmed.

He wasn't hearing me, but was staring off into the distance. He shook his head. "She's following me now?" He looked down, his expression now looking perplexed.

Who was following him? It couldn't be Alexis, he probably would be upset. He just seems mystified.

But there was unmistakably a woman coming toward us. I started to feel nauseated. The woman was the typical supermodel type that I'd been noticing all over town since I started hanging out with Ryan.

The woman was kind of bizarre, to be honest. Here we were, in an outdoor setting, and she was dressed in high heels. She was also dressed in slim black pants and a colorful top. She was wearing full makeup, although she really didn't need to. I could tell that she was the kind of woman whom commanded attention. I noticed more than one man's head turning as she walked. She was tall, slim, blond and stunningly beautiful, and carried an Hermés Birken bag.

Her bag was no doubt worth more than my car.

Ryan stood in his spot, as if he couldn't move. He wasn't looking at the woman, but it was if he was trying not to.

The woman was now about three feet away. "Hello, Ryan." I looked closer at her face. She looked so familiar... Then it struck me. She was the woman in the picture with Ryan!

"Alexis," Ryan said calmly. *So this is the infamous Alexis. Why doesn't Ryan look upset to see her?*

She turned her attention to me. "And who is this?" She looked amused. I could tell that there was no way that she would have imagined that I was his date.

Ryan put his arm around my shoulders. "This is Iris. Iris, this is my ex-wife, Alexis."

I held out my hand to shake hers. She ignored it. She raised one eyebrow, looking at Ryan. "Your date?" Her expression was one of amusement mixed with disgust.

"Yes, my date." He turned to me. "Would you excuse me for a second?" I nodded. He looked at Alexis. "Let's go over here and talk for a second."

I stayed, rooted, holding the dogs' leashes and wondering what to do. My instinct was no longer that I should run. At the same time, like the fateful morning I heard him yelling at Alexis over the phone, I wasn't looking forward to being around him after this.

I watched Ryan and Alexis because they were within viewing distance. I tried to make out what they were saying. I heard Alexis yell "I'm sorry, but you're not exactly taking my calls." Ryan was talking in a low voice, so I couldn't make out what he was saying. Alexis apparently wasn't above making a scene. "You know what I want. I want you. But if I can't have you, I want the Cezanne." *Again with the Cezanne. How come I haven't seen this painting?*

I sat back down on the ground. The blanket was

wrapped up and in my arms, and I didn't feel like laying down the blanket, so I just sat on the grass. People were everywhere, talking, wrapping up their stuff, walking towards the exit. Kids were blowing bubbles. Babies were crying. Dogs were running about on their leash. It was a festive atmosphere and was a great evening up until now.

I felt sick to my stomach.

I heard Alexis say "Well, maybe I should tell your new little girlfriend about this, what do you say about that?" At that, he looked back at me, worried. I instinctively looked away. I heard her say the word "Nick" and the word "Benjamin." I narrowed my eyes. *Isn't his father's name Benjamin? Who is Nick?* It seemed Alexis would tell me things Ryan was afraid to because it seemed there was no reasoning with this woman. She had ammunition and she was going to use it.

Now he was trying to placate her. I couldn't make out anything he was saying but he was putting his hands on her shoulder in a conciliatory gesture. He definitely didn't appear to be angry with her.

Then I saw her start to cry and he put his arms around her. "I miss you, I love you," I heard her say more than once. *How is he going to get out of this? Is he going to get out of this?* I could imagine his dilemma. If he broke away from her and left her where she stood, she'd raise hell and rat him out to me. But he can't really stay there with her, either. *Maybe I should make this easier for him. But how?* This relationship was getting trickier and trickier to navigate. Remembering I made the exact wrong move last time by bolting, I decided just to stay put for now.

I also unmistakably heard the word "Mia," uttered by Alexis. *She's grieving her child, and so is he. They went through something unimaginable together. I could never begin to fathom what they are both going through.* Now she was really sobbing. They'd been talking for about 20 minutes and the park was increasingly emptying.

It wouldn't be long until we were kicked out.

I sighed. We were certainly off to a rocky start, although the highs with this guy had certainly been worth it. I was impressed, however, with how he was handling this situation. Here was a woman on a roller coaster of emotions, going from yelling to crying, and he wasn't losing his cool at all. It was quite a bit different from the first time, when I heard him yelling on the phone with her.

I caught him looking back at me, his face clearly saying "Help!" I stayed rooted where I was, though. I figured he'd come to me when he is ready. It wasn't my place to interrupt.

Now he was finally coming towards me, Alexis in tow. *Was she there all alone?* "Iris, I need to take Alexis home. I hope you don't mind if she comes with us in the car."

I didn't protest. I simply nodded.

He looked grateful. "Thank you so much for understanding." Glancing over at Alexis, Ryan said "Alexis apparently took an Uber here."

Yeah, of course she came here by Uber. She knew you'd have to drive her home. I looked at Alexis. She looked devious.

The three of us made our way to the Rivian, the dogs being hauled by me on leashes. Ryan made no attempt to hold my hand, of course. He barely even walked with me. Alexis was walking very close to him, trying to cling on to his arm, but I could tell he wasn't having it. I could just imagine what was going through his mind at this point. My heart went out to him.

To my surprise, my heart went out to her as well.

We made our way towards my apartment, to my dismay, in silence. *I'm being dropped off first? Not a good sign. Not a good sign at all.* Alexis was in the front seat and I was in the back with the dogs.

Ryan dropped me off. He opened the door, and I got out. Alexis was in the front seat, glaring at us both. He kissed me on the forehead. "I'm so sorry for this," he whispered. "I'll see you later."

At that, he got back into driver's side, backed up the Rivian, and drove off.

Chapter Nine

Awkward parting was starting to become a pattern. As it turned out, the last awkward parting was my fault. This time, I knew I did nothing wrong. I sighed. I was surprisingly not that upset. After all, the last time I left him, I assumed I would never see him again. I wasn't going to jump to that conclusion this time. I was on a roller coaster but preferred to stay on it for now and see it through.

I hope he feels the same way.

I half expected him to appear at my apartment again that night, after talking Alexis down off the ledge.

However, that didn't happen.

He did, however, appear at my apartment the next day. "I was hoping you'd be home," he said, as I let him in the door. "I'm so sorry for the drama. I'm also sorry that I keep dropping in on you."

That's ok. The apartment's clean this time. I had actually just gotten finished with my laundry – I couldn't sleep the previous night because of what happened at the park, so I decided to be constructive and get my laundry done. All five loads of it. I ended up washing all the clothes which were thrown on the closet floor, and they were now hung up or put into drawers, depending on the type of clothes they were. I also was able to sort out my dry-clean only clothes from the pile, and these were stuffed into a garbage bag. This garbage bag was by the door, so that I hopefully wouldn't forget to take them to the cleaner's the next time I was out and about.

"Actually, that isn't a problem," I said, referring to him dropping in on me again.

He looked relieved and surprised. "I can't believe you're not infuriated after what happened last night."

"I could tell Alexis was very emotional. I could also tell you were in a bind."

He looked at me, then kissed me passionately. "You're an amazing woman."

I smiled. "Thanks, you're an amazing guy."

We went out onto my balcony, and sat down, my feet up on the wooden rail. I had prepared some iced tea. I was drinking way too much lately and had to take a break.

I looked at him expectantly. He wasn't saying anything, just staring straight ahead.

"How do I say this to you...." He started to open his mouth to say something, thought better of it, then resumed to staring straight ahead.

I started to feel worried. I naturally figured that whatever he was trying to say, it wouldn't be good news for me. I immediately felt selfish for thinking this thought. He was going through something terrible, it was probably even worse than it looked, and I was only thinking of myself.

But that wasn't really true. My heart went out to him as well. I was not yet in love with him, although I knew I would get there if I let my guard down. However, at this point, with all the drama and the secrets, it was impossible to trust him completely.

Staring at his glass of iced tea- it was an actual glass this time, I'm proud to say - Ryan began with "I've known Alexis for a long time. Since middle school. We dated off and on in college. She was at Yale when I was at Harvard." That surprised me. Alexis didn't really look like the academic type.

"Go on."

"She and I..." He took a deep breath. "Well, let's just say that I've not always been as, as, as....clean as I am now."

I furrowed my brow. The message was somewhat cryptic and could mean any number of things. He was shaking. The ice was rattling in his glass. He also was playing with his thick hair, his dominant left hand running through his mane, again and again. He was not making eye contact at all.

He took an enormous breath and went on. "Well, you know, there's a lot of money in prep schools, and a lot of bored kids. Most of us were less supervised than we should have been. I was no exception."

Another deep breath. He went on, not looking at me. Then, he did look at me. "Um, Iris, I feel that I could have something really special with you. That's why I'm here. I need to come clean with a few things about my past. If I didn't see a future with you, I wouldn't be here right now. It would just be so much easier just to pretend that last night didn't happen, and it would be so much easier for me to walk away from you, as opposed to having to tell you these things."

Things? There's more than one issue?

"Alexis and I...we were very much into...Oh, Christ, I

need to just come out and say it. It's a part of my past, it isn't me now, it isn't a big deal." Huge breath. His visibly shaking hand once again smoothed his thick dark hair.

Huge breath. "We were heroin addicts. There, I said it."

I nodded. "When?"

"From age 17 until age 25. I kicked it with methadone. She still struggles."

So he was a heroin addict until just 8 years ago. And he was an addict for 8 years.

He looked at me, trying to gauge my reaction. Surprisingly, I had very little reaction. I guess because I felt that I had seen it all in my lifetime, and this really wasn't a big deal.

"You haven't done this since you were 25?"

He looked pained. "I, I, I, I...." Now he was shaking again. "I hhhadd a relapse, uh, last week."

I looked at him, not saying a word. He went on. Another huge breath. "I went to see her last week. She called me last Sunday, as you remember, before you woke up. Well, she called back, the next day, and told me she had taken pills and was waiting to die. So I went straight over to her house." He shook his head and continued. "I don't know why I allow her to still manipulate me like that. Anyhow, she was actually fine."

I raised my eyebrow. This was getting interesting.

"I was pissed. But she had some high-grade stuff, laying out on her coffee table. She threatened me. She told me that she was going to go ahead with taking all the pills she had in her house if I left her that day. And she threatened to do this if I didn't shoot up with her."

"So you-"

"I'm not proud of it." He sighed. "The good news is, I

seem to be well past the addiction. I had no desire to continue after that."

I chose to believe him about this.

He went on. "Trust me, after all Alexis and I have been through, it has been tough on both of us to stay clean. She's done it, just barely. She white-knuckles it so she relapses all the time. I've completely kicked it, and I know now, more than ever, that I've no desire to go back to the way I was."

I made a face. "You still love this woman?"

He looked perplexed. "No, why?"

"I guess I just don't know why you would sacrifice your sobriety for her games."

"I don't really know, either. I guess I always believe her when she says she's on the edge. I wouldn't want that on my conscience – that I could've helped her and didn't."

"Yeah, but Ryan, there's helping her, and then there's intentionally self-destructing because she's manipulating you."

He looked ashamed.

I didn't say anything more. The guy no doubt had beat himself up enough about it. *I just hope the drugs really are in the past.*

And there's more, I know there is. But the confession of his addiction seemed to take a lot out of him, and I could tell there would be no more heart-wrenching admissions coming from him today.

We sat in silence for awhile, drinking our iced tea. I didn't tell him I had Googled his father that morning. I couldn't remember his father's name, but when Alexis said the name "Benjamin" last night, it struck a chord. So, I Googled his father, using the search terms "CEO", plus the name of the utility company, plus the years Ryan told me his dad was active, and I found out that his name was

Benjamin Whitney. I felt a little amused that, up until then, I didn't know Ryan's last name. I figured it probably was also Whitney, although I couldn't be positive.

As casually as possible, I said "Well, what's past is past. I do, however, want you to be honest with me about this. If you ever feel like relapsing, please tell me. I'll help you, I promise. I won't judge you."

He looked grateful "You probably think I'm a basket case. Therapy, drugs, a crazy ex-wife."

And there's more still, I know it. For one thing, there's somebody named Nick. But what else?

"Hey, we all have our cross to bear."

I knew that I was, once again, taking a risk by taking it all too lightly, but I wanted to move on to more serious concerns. Like what he was hiding from me. The drug thing was kind of bad, but, if I was to believe what he is telling me, it was in the past. So it wasn't that big of a deal. But I sensed there was another, larger, bombshell on the horizon. I just didn't know how to get it out of him just yet.

He smiled the wan, distracted smile I saw that one Sunday after the screaming match with Alexis. Now I knew Alexis was not only a gold-digger but also crazy.

Yet, somehow, I was going to try to hold onto Ryan the best I could.

How to bring up the father? I have a feeling the father had something to do with what Ryan is hiding from me. Casually, I said "I hope you don't mind, but I was fascinated about what you told me the other night about your dad."

His face instantly changed. Panic, fear, anger all flashed through his eyes. I wondered why he didn't have a hard time talking about him the other night. Come to think of it, he really didn't say much about him, except that he was a retired CEO of Flash Utility, being active from 1975 to 2003, then left it at that.

"What was fascinating about it?" His voice had a hard edge to it now. He sounded demanding, sarcastic.

"Well, you didn't tell me much. I'm trying to find out more about you."

"You don't need to know about my father to find out more about me."

I suddenly felt that I was wrong to Google the man. But the morning when he was talking in his sleep, begging his father to stop something, made me want to find out more about Benjamin Whitney.

"Well, I Googled him…"

That was a mistake. I suddenly saw rage in Ryan's eyes. Then he looked away.

I went on "You know, it occurred to me, after looking up your dad, that I didn't know your last name."

"You still don't know my last name." His voice was very hard-edged.

I was getting somewhere. But at what price? "It isn't Whitney?"

"No. It's Gallagher."

Time to drop it. But it was too late. Ryan was standing up and backing out of the apartment. "Thanks for the iced tea," he said, opening the front door. "I'll call you," he mumbled.

And he was gone.

Chapter Ten

After Ryan left, I was back on the couch. I didn't feel as miserable as I did the last time. I was more confused. *OK, so he and Alexis were drug addicts together. Big whoop. Rich kids doing drugs in a tony private school? That's almost a cliché. That's definitely not what he's really worried about. Even if Alexis "went to the press" about that, who cares? Ryan is an unknown, except that he's the son of a prominent businessman. Yeah, it's kinda bad that he did drugs with her the other day, but if he says he doesn't want to do it anymore, I choose to believe him.*

I couldn't concentrate. I gravitated towards the computer, mindlessly flipping through Yahoo! stories about the world's fattest dachshund, and what Taylor Swift was up to that week. Some relationship advice was also on the Yahoo! front page, so I flipped to that. I even flipped to my Tinder account. *Hmmm. Two different guys are hitting me up.* I put that on the backburner, for the time being.

I drummed my fingers. Sighing, I got on the Google home page, typing in the words "Benjamin Whitney." The usual came up – his biography, his causes, the news about his retirement, the news about how Flash had lost money in 1999, but Benjamin still got a $30 million salary that year. There were stories about how he possibly was forced into retirement because he just didn't have the business acumen anymore. *Yeah, so what? CEOs are forced into retirement all the time.*

Taking a deep breath, and doing something I hadn't yet done - probably because I just now learned his last name - I Googled "Ryan Gallagher." I came upon notices that Ryan Gallagher is on Facebook. Not the same guy. There was another story about a Ryan Gallagher, with an accompanying picture. Definitely not the same guy. There was a Ryan Gallagher who was an artist, but I glossed over that, thinking it probably wasn't him. *Nothing bad so far.*

Then I Googled "Ryan Whitney," deciding to go ahead and do a search only on the Google news page. This bore fruit. Apparently his drug abuse had made news at the time, as he had spent time in a Mexican jail trying to smuggle some drugs into the country. He was 22. *A drug dealer, too?* I read the story carefully. It turned out that it was small-time, just some pot, and he was only in the Mexican jail for three days. Since he's the son of Benjamin Whitney, this passed as news. I found another article about him entering rehab. Again, this was only news because of his father. His picture accompanied both articles. He looked quite a bit different – thinner than he is now, his hair was longer, his shoulders were hunched, and he did not look happy. *Would you look happy to have your picture taken as you're led into a Mexican jail or going into rehab?*

Ordinarily, this stuff might alarm me, but he already told me about the drug abuse, so I wasn't all that surprised that he was in the news for it. And it wasn't like it was national news. These articles were from the *Kansas City Star*, so the story was pretty contained.

The one thing that did interest me and set off little alarm bells, is that Ryan's last name *is* actually Whitney. *Why would he tell me his name was Gallagher?*

This gave me an idea. Getting on Wikipedia, I typed in the name "Benjamin Whitney." Under "spouse," it became clear. Benjamin Whitney's spouse's name was Margaret Gallagher. *Well, that mystery is solved. Ryan is using his mother's maiden name.* Margaret "Maggie" Gallagher was an opera singer born in Ireland.

Why was Ryan using his mother's maiden name?

I skimmed the article, as I was mainly interested in Benjamin's personal life, so I skipped ahead to that section. Then something in that paragraph made me completely lose my breath. The section read "In 1986, Whitney was accused of inappropriate contact with a minor child. Charges were never filed, but the child's education was paid for, leading some to believe the child's parents were bought off." *What? Where was that story on Google?* Then I remembered that anybody could add content to Wikipedia. Still, I'd imagine that Ryan, and Benjamin for that matter, were aware of this entry.

Why wouldn't Benjamin sue for libel?

Because truth is an absolute defense to libel.

I flipped back to Google news, typing in "Benjamin Whitney" and "inappropriate contact" "sexual abuse" and "minor." *Nothing.* Why would that be on the Wiki page and not in the news?

Because the story was buried. Completely buried.

It was all becoming clear. *No, no, no, stop thinking the worst. Maybe Benjamin doesn't know about the Wiki entry and somebody has it in for him. It's possible. Anything is possible.*

Somebody was at the door. It was Ryan. I shut down my computer, and deleted my search history. *You can't be too careful.*

I opened the door. He looked kind of drunk again. "Hey," he said.

"Hey. Come on in."

"Sorry about earlier."

"Not a problem. Come in, sit down." *RuPaul's Drag Race* was playing on the television. *If the messy apartment, the wrecked car and the general brokeness of my situation doesn't scare him off, trashy television probably won't either.* Nevertheless, I clicked it off.

I had invested in some better wine glasses since the last time he was here. I also had signed up for a wine-tasting class so I could provide some better wine than Two Buck Chuck. However, at this time, it was Two Buck Chuck or nothing. I poured a couple of glasses of wine, then joined him on the couch.

He looked at me. "I need to tell you something."

My breath caught. *Is he going to tell me something about his father?*

I waited, expectantly.

What came out of his mouth was not what I was expecting. "I'm in love with you," he said. He continued to stare at me. "I know that sounds crazy, we've only just met."

Yes, crazy, but he told me he was possibly falling in love with me after the first date or so. Take this with a large grain of salt.

He continued. "God, I just can't stop thinking about you. Since the moment I met you, I haven't been able to stop thinking about you. I even dream about you."

I felt flattered and overwhelmed. Well, he certainly was laying it on thick. I wanted to tear down my walls and really believe what he was saying, but it was unbelievable. He hardly knew me, and he could, literally, and I do mean literally, have any woman he wanted. Any woman. And I hadn't forgotten that there was somebody named Nick in the picture. Until he was ready to tell me about who she is, I refused to trust him. Not to mention his complicated relationship with Alexis. There were just too many issues around this guy.

He continued. "All I could think about just now, after I left your apartment, was how I hoped that you still want to keep seeing me. I hope you believe that I don't have a need to go back to the horse. I mean, I'm an addict, I will always be, I guess, or so they told me in rehab. But I realized this week that I don't want it anymore and probably never will again. I hope you believe that."

"Of course I believe that." And I did. There really wasn't a reason not to. *Well, except for his relapse...*But I immediately put that out of my head.

"I just can't believe that crazy Alexis, my drug abuse past and the fact that I regularly see a therapist isn't scaring you away."

"Come on, we all have our issues." *Some have more issues than others, but still...*

"I'm being serious here. I'm in love with you," he repeated. "I can see myself spending the rest of my life with you."

I furrowed my brow. What was he saying? Why me? What about Nick?

"I know, I know," he continued. "I hardly know you. You hardly know me. I know it sounds nuts, but I see you. I see your kind and generous heart. I see your sense of humor. I don't really know myself why I feel so strongly. I just know I do. I also think that you don't judge me. I mean, how you handled the Alexis situation…I fell in love with you right then."

The Alexis situation. What did he mean?

He continued on. "I mean, you didn't come over and demand that I pay attention to you when I was talking to her at the park. You somehow understood that Alexis had to sit in the front seat last night and that I had to drop you off first. You somehow understood the whole situation. I couldn't believe how good you were about everything. Most women would have pitched a holy hell bitch about that situation, rightly so. Not you. You understood."

Well, I'm glad I have you fooled because I didn't really understand. I just didn't know how else to react.

"Then when I just now told you about my drug problem, you didn't bat an eyelash about it." He hesitated. "Actually, after I calmed down the Alexis situation last night, I had some time to think, and that was when I realized I wanted to marry you. I just couldn't imagine another woman who would be so calm about what was going down."

Whoa, whoa, whoa. Marry me? I could feel my breath heaving, my heart beating.

"Well, it wasn't just the Alexis situation," he continued. "That was what capped it off. It's…I don't know, I just feel comfortable around you. Like I've known you all my life."

I took a deep breath. "How much have you been drinking?" A rude question, I knew, after all he had just told me, but I figured that most of this was alcohol talking.

Then again *in vino veritas* – "in wine, there's truth."

"I had a couple of beers at Houlihan's," he said, referring to the bar and grill down the street. "And a couple of Dewar's and water."

I nodded. *How long was he gone from the apartment – about*

three hours? He probably drank a lot in those few hours and he's loaded now and babbling at the mouth. Still, he didn't look *that* drunk. His eyes were not bleary, his speech was fine, and he didn't stumble. However, I remembered my Uncle Jack. That man could literally drink all night long and never slur a word. So Ryan might be drunk and just not showing it.

He looked at me, his face wounded. "I know you think I don't know what I am saying, but I do. I think I loved you the first time I saw you." Then he started humming a tune, then singing a familiar Randy Newman song, *Marie.* His voice was melodic and nice, unlike mine. *Is there anything this man can't do?*

He smiled. "My mother used to sing that to me when I was a little boy. But she used the name Ryan instead of Marie, of course." He looked wistful.

"That's very sweet."

"Yeah." He looked up at me, and for some reason, I thought of him as a little boy. "She wasn't in my life much. My father and she divorced when I was ten. I lost contact with her altogether until just recently."

I nodded. I wondered if he was going to tell me about her opera career.

He did hint a little. "She was a very good singer. I always loved that song."

"Did you have a mother figure growing up?"

"Not really. Benjamin never remarried. He was too focused on his career, I guess. Although my best friend's mother was a female role model for me. She was a very kind person, like my mother."

He didn't elaborate further.

My heart was pounding and my head was swimming. It was so much to take in all at once. He loves me, or is in love with me, he has a crazy, yet strikingly beautiful, ex-wife, he is a heroin addict. *All of these issues in such a beautiful package.*

"Your mother, what was her name?" I played dumb.

"Maggie."

"She's Irish?" I pretended to guess by hearing the name.

"Yes."

I waited for him to say more about her, but he didn't.

"So…" He began. "What do you think about what I just told you?"

I knew that question was coming. "Well, I'm flattered." *Poor choice of words.* "Let me start again. I…" I took a deep breath. "It's really soon." I finally said.

He looked hurt. "You're right."

Way to go. But what should I say?

We drank our wine in silence for a few minutes. I was feeling really uncomfortable. My emotions couldn't keep up with everything going on between myself and Ryan. I was still stuck on why he would like me, at all, in the first place, and now he was talking about marriage. I guess I was having a hard time believing any of it was real.

I was looking at him, thinking he was going to leave at any moment. Why stick around, when you just poured your heart out, and the girl isn't responding? The thing of it was, there was a part of me, buried deep within that brick wall, that wanted to confess that I loved him too.

But I couldn't admit that to myself, so I really couldn't admit it to him.

He stood up. *Well, that's it, you chased him off once more.* He put out his hand for me to grab, which I did. Standing, he hugged me tight, putting his hand on my hair. I could smell his aftershave, and his breath that smelled vaguely of Scotch and beer. Once again, my breath caught, and then started coming back more slowly than before.

Then we were kissing, slowly, tenderly at first. It was difficult to kiss him standing up, as he was so much taller than myself, so we ended up kissing back on the couch. He kissed my neck, my shoulders, his sensuous lips running lightly, from one shoulder to the other, then on my cheeks, then kissing me on the lips again. I ran my hands along his back, feeling his rock hard muscles. He was laying on top of me, so I could feel his erection through his pants again, but, this time, he did not attempt to move so that his erection was no longer in contact with my body. I was breathing, faster and faster. I could hear my heart, or maybe it was his. It might have been both of our hearts, beating together, faster and faster.

Somehow, I got his shirt off. I gasped a little at the sight of him. Every muscle rippled in his chest and abs and his arms were large and lean. He resembled a swimmer - long, lean, cut and hairless. *This isn't happening. This perfect specimen is not in my living room.* But it was happening. I was aware that I was breathing very hard. Now my shirt was off. He was kissing my stomach and my braless breasts, working his way up to my neck again. He gently touched my breasts while he kissed my lips hungrily. His erection was growing ever harder by the second, but he was patient. I, however, was not. I unbuckled his belt and unzipped his pants. I was stunned at the size of his erection, now making a huge tent of his boxer-briefs. I sighed. *This might hurt, especially because you haven't had sex since....well, let's just say it's been a long time. Except the first time with Ryan, but you don't remember it, so that doesn't count.*

He was just down to his socks and boxer-briefs at this point, his massive erection still pitching a tent. I took off my own jeans, as he seemed hesitant to do this. *Oh, God, what about protection?* We were being careless, but I was on the pill.

We never discussed this before, but he whispered in my ear "Are you using anything?"

I nodded.

Both of us got completely naked, but Ryan did not enter me for a long time. He was too busy exploring every inch of my body with his tongue. I gasped when his tongue reached my sweet spot. He was so gentle, using long strokes of his tongue, flicking it in and out of my genitals. Then, when I was just about to climax, he switched to slowly licking the inside of my thighs. *How did he know I love that?* I thought as I came to a powerful climax. For an hour, he kissed me - kissing my mouth, kissing my breasts, my legs, my lady parts, then my mouth again. I could feel his bare erection just outside the opening, while he lay on top of me, kissing me all over.

I was being driven crazy. I wanted him to enter me. He was so close. I could literally feel him, as I have felt him for the past hour. Then, he finally entered me slowly. I gasped. He was huge, so he had to go very slow. This didn't seem to be a problem for him, though. He slowly, slowly ground in and out, kissing my lips while he thrust. It hurt a little, because it had been so long for mé with anyone, let alone with somebody as large as him. However, we had so much foreplay that I was ready to receive him. My breathing was so heavy I felt I would pass out, but, instead, I came to a powerful climax, more powerful than anything that I had ever experienced before.

He was whispering in my ear "You're so beautiful, so sexy. I love you." Then he was gently nibbling on my ear while he thrust slowly in and out, his hands exploring my breasts once again.

After about an hour of his slow, rhythmic thrusting, he began to go faster and faster until he came inside me. I could feel his legs shaking on top of me. My own legs were shaking as well. I felt lightheaded. He lay on top of me, clutching his arms around my neck, breathing rapidly. I could still hear his heart pounding. Or maybe it was mine? My arms were shaking, badly. I needed a drink of water, but he was still on top of me.

Then he was kissing my lips again, passionately. I moved onto my side, and we lay, side by side, on the narrow couch. He was behind me, stroking my hair, kissing my neck, and my back. I turned my head because he gently put his hands on my cheeks so that my head would turn, and he kissed me passionately, his body still behind me. In what seemed like no time at all, he was hard again. He entered me from behind, slowly thrusting. He whispered "I want to make this last a long time," so he slowed his thrusting down still further. Slowly, slowly he slipped his amazingly hard cock in and out. Because of all the lovemaking from earlier, I received him much better than before, so there was no pain at all this time when he entered me. He wrapped his arm around my neck from behind as he thrust.

As I said before, it was painful at first the first time we made love, simply because of his size. Now, his size was perfect, because I was opened up to him completely and I was wetter than I'd ever been in my life. He whispered "I want to make love to you all night." These words turned me on further, and I climaxed for what seemed to be the hundredth time that night.

This time he thrust, slowly, for an over an hour, kissing me passionately on the mouth through most of it. When he came for the second time, I was shaking even worse than before, and I really needed a drink of water.

He was stroking my hair, and staring at me. I asked "hey, are you thirsty?"

"Dying, actually."

We were in an uncomfortable position right now, both of us sideways on my small couch. Ryan fell off the couch, onto the floor. "Oh, shit, I'm sorry," I exclaimed, but he was laughing. I noticed, for the first time, that he still had his socks on.

"I guess I got carried away," he said, gesturing to his socks. Which made both of us laugh.

I got up to make both of us a drink of lemonade. When I came in, Ryan had laid a blanket on the floor, just in front of my fireplace. He patted it lightly, and I laid down next to him.

While both of us drank our lemonade, Ryan was the first to talk. "That was nice," he said.

I took a deep breath. "Very nice." I felt tongue-tied, as did he, apparently.

He continued to stroke my body, leisurely with his hands. He became hard again, and he laid on his back. I climbed on top of him, kissing his torso lightly until I came to his erection. I gently licked the top of his penis with my tongue. His size was going to be challenging for this, as well, but I managed to get my mouth around him, sucking him while my tongue simultaneously caressed his shaft. He moaned and breathed harder. He started to thrust a little in my mouth, but I put my hands on his thighs to stop him. I wanted to be in complete control of this. I slowly sucked and licked, grabbing his balls lightly with my hands. My tongue gently explored his balls, then gently explored his sphincter. He groaned. "No girl has ever done that," he managed. "Please don't stop." I didn't stop, putting my tongue inside his sphincter, then slipped one of my fingers in there. I returned to sucking his massive erection while my fingers explored inside his sphincter. This was too much for him, and he climaxed inside my mouth. There wasn't much of an explosion, however, as he had come inside me twice in the past few hours, which meant that it also didn't taste bad.

I could feel his breathing rapidly. I laid down beside him. He lay quietly, breathing hard for about five minutes. Then he said "I've never had a woman do that to me. That was amazing!"

I admitted to myself that it wasn't my first time doing that. I had some fairly kinky boyfriends in my past, and this was just one thing they liked to have done to them.

"Well, I have some tricks up my sleeve." I laughed. I was feeling giddy, like on a sugar high. My limbs were still shaking, worse than ever now.

He laughed, too, then kissed me passionately again. *This guy is the Energizer Bunny* I thought, as I felt him growing once more. Again, he was inside of me, thrusting harder this time. I could take it now. I would not have been able to take the aggressive thrusting earlier, but I was so swollen inside I could take anything. This time, it was more animalistic sex, less tender kissing and stroking and looking into each other's eyes. He rocked his body so I was on top of him, and I rode him hard for a long time. It was going to take some time for him to come this time, because it would be his fourth time that night.

And, indeed it did. Even with the animalistic nature of this particular encounter, he stayed hard inside me for well over an hour. I stayed lubricated that whole time - I was so turned on by everything. Him, his feelings for me, his vulnerability, his hotness – everything became like a mental salad for me and I had never been so turned on in my life.

This actually did go on all night. We made love a total of seven times that night, and, when the morning came, we were both exhausted and spent. We finally fell asleep around seven the next morning, his arms wrapped around me from behind, both of us still lying on the blanket on the floor.

It was Sunday, and, when we woke up at 2 in the afternoon, I realized that he would have to leave soon. As much as I wanted to lay there forever, making love, he did have a job to go to the next day. But he still wasn't finished with me. Immediately upon waking, he had an erection, then entered me without foreplay. Somehow this was ok, even though I should have been so sore that making love again would have been impossible. He lasted around 45 minutes this time, one of our shorter love-making sessions.

After we made love that afternoon, both of us were starving. I didn't feel like cooking and there was nothing really that I could have cooked right then anyhow, as I hadn't been to the store in awhile. So we got into his Porsche and searched for a restaurant. We ended up at Sullivan's Steakhouse, which was a trendy, yet comfortable, restaurant with a large patio and a hip, suburban business-type crowd. I settled in with my extra dirty martini. He tried a Tanqueray and tonic.

I didn't even notice the gawking this time. Well, I noticed it, but it didn't bother me as much as it did before. Ryan was still focused on me completely.

He smiled shyly. "You were amazing last night."

"And this morning and this afternoon," I laughed. He smiled discreetly.

"I really wasn't prepared for that when I came over."

"Yeah, it took me by surprise, too."

He suddenly looked pensive. "I said some things yesterday when I came over..."

Here we go. He's going to walk them back and tell me to disregard them. I actually hoped that he *would* walk them back and disregard them. But, no – he continued. "You didn't really respond to what I said."

He's going to pin me down yet. "Well, I…I guess I'm just cautious. I've been hurt. A lot. I have a hard time believing things." *And there is some mysterious person named Nick in your life. Please tell me about that.* I continued. "I've heard men tell me that before, and I've also heard empty marriage promises before. It's difficult when you're in the dating world to know if somebody is being sincere or if they are really just a tool. And you are just so magnetic, handsome and intelligent. You can have anybody you want. Anybody you want."

"I understand that," he said. "Really, I do. I just want you to know that I'm different than the guys you've known in the past. I'm really crazy about you."

I just shook my head. "What are the words to that song about the word that isn't said enough yet also too much?"

"Those three words are said too much, yet not enough," he sang from Snow Patrol's hit song *Chasing Cars*.

"Right. You have a great voice, by the way."

"Thanks," he said without enthusiasm.

"Anyhow, I have a hard time believing things. Blame your sleazy brethren for using the love word to get women into bed." I was trying to make a joke, but it was falling flat.

"I said something else to you."

Oh, now he wants me to elaborate on how I feel about his wanting to marry me. This might be slightly trickier.

"Yes, well, let's see. I guess I would have to say that if we go out for a long time, like a year, and you really get to know me and I get to know you, we can talk seriously about…that other thing." There, that should cover it.

Again, other men had ruined that talk for me as well. I had heard the empty marriage promises, early on in the relationship, too many times. I was wise to that game too.

He looked me square in the eye. "This isn't a game, Iris. I know it's soon, but I knew that I wanted to marry you from the moment I met you. You felt it too. I noticed you from across the bar and I was going to talk to you and then you came up to me. And I knew. You'll find out soon enough that I'm serious about this."

Let's just drop this, shall we? "Where is our order? The waitress is taking forever." She really wasn't, but I was desperate to change the subject.

He sighed, resigned that he wouldn't get more out of me on this subject.

Changing the subject quickly, I said "So, Maximus and Brutus. How'd you pick them out?" I was impressed that he had not one, but two rescue dogs, including a pit bull mix.

"Actually, this is going to sound crazy, but I got them when everything was falling apart. I was grieving over Mia and Alexis was just starting her ultimate crazy shit. I didn't know about her and Paul at the time, but she was distant and pushing me away. So, I went to the shelter to try to comfort myself and I found those two mutts there. They were brought into the shelter together and I just fell in love with both of them."

"What were they named before you got them?"

"I didn't change their names. They were going by those names for several weeks so I didn't think it was fair to them."

"So they were true strays, or did somebody bring them in?"

"True strays, from what I understand. Brutus, the pit bull mix, would've been put down immediately in a lot of cities around here." This was true. Some of the suburbs had active pit bull bans because of several maulings. He continued "That's so unfair to indict an entire breed because of what shitty owners do to some dogs to make them mean."

I nodded vigorously. "I know, it's totally the owners. I happen to love pit bulls, but, at the same time, I feel for them when I see them around town. For some reason, I always imagine the worst, that they are a part of a dog fighting ring, even if they are just out and about with their owners. That's why I had to become active in a pit bull rescue group. They are the sweetest dogs, but have such a bad reputation, which is tragic and undeserved."

"I feel the same way. And your compassion for those animals is one of the many reasons why I'm in love with you."

We chatted a little bit more throughout the meal. I deftly avoided the serious subject of us and our future, but I really wanted to find out a bit more about his background. However, I noticed earlier how his father was a sore subject, so I had a difficult time figuring out how to approach it.

I finally opted not to approach it at all.

After dinner was over, we went back to my apartment. I figured that he would leave that night, because, after all, he did have to work in the morning. I also had to work in the morning, but my schedule was cleared for that day, so I really only had to get caught up on paperwork. A lot of paperwork. He surprised me, however, when he followed me into my apartment. "Do you mind if I spend the night with you again?" he asked me before coming up.

"No, no, of course not."

"I mean, of course, I have to be at work in the morning, so we're going to have to get some sleep tonight. I just really don't want to leave just yet."

"Yes, of course."

But that night was the same as the previous night, as we

made love for hours, in my bed that time. Finally, at 3 AM, I announced that we had to get some sleep, because he wasn't going to be very productive at work when he had to go in at 8 that morning. He agreed, attempted to sleep, then made love to me again.

"You're going to be exhausted in the morning."

"Exhausted and happy."

I was amazed at his libido. And the thought crossed my mind that maybe he was one of those addictive personalities and I was just another of his addictions.

Banish the thought.

He did manage to get up and leave my apartment at 6 AM, so that he could go home and change for work and get there by 8. I was sad to see him leave, of course, but I knew I would be seeing him soon.

Chapter Eleven

Weeks went by, and Ryan and I managed to spend every evening together. It was somewhat difficult because both of us had animals. It was decided that, since he had two dogs, and I had one cat, that we would spend most of our time at his place, instead of mine. I took Madison over with me when I visited. This was a much better arrangement than both of us hanging out in my apartment, not just because of the animal situation, but also because his place was a palatial mansion, and mine was, of course, a tiny hovel.

However, one day, I arrived home, after being away for a few days, to a most unpleasant surprise. There was a note on my door asking me to go to the office. The property management people wanted to see me.

I felt like I was a bad kid going to the principal's office as I approached the clubhouse.

"You wanted to see me?" I asked after I arrived in the property manager's office.

"Yes, Ms. Snowe. Sit down."

I took my seat across from the glaring woman. I never

could stand her, and, now that she was a good nine months pregnant, she was bitchier than ever, probably because of the hormones.

"We have become aware that you have a cat in your apartment."

I turned red. I never declared Madison, preferring not to deal with the hassle of paying a pet deposit and the extra rent for a pet. I couldn't deny her existence, although I didn't really know how they found out about her.

"Yes, yes, I do."

"I'm very sorry, Ms. Snowe, but you are in violation of your lease. You will have to vacate the premises within 30 days."

30 days? Unfuckingbelievable. Granted, it was my fault for trying to pull a fast one, but still….

"Wait, wait, wait. I'm sorry about the cat. I'd be happy to pay back rent for her and a deposit." I calculated it in my head. It would be tough to swing the extra money, but I'd manage.

"I'm terribly sorry, but we have already found a new renter for that unit."

I was dumbfounded. They were kicking me out? I wasn't aware that the units were in such high demand.

I was shaking my head. "Isn't there anything I can do?"

"I'm sorry Ms. Snowe."

I sighed. My mind went blank. *Well, this is a fine how do you do. Now you have a forcible eviction on your record and a cat. Plus, your credit is generally shitty because of the Yellow Page ad default* – I had taken out a full page ad in the Yellow Pages that I was unable to pay.

Who's going to rent to you now?

I imagined myself homeless.

I could always move in with my mother. My nephew

had recently moved out of that house, so there was an extra bedroom.

I went back up my apartment. It was an off night from Ryan, because he had a fund-raiser to attend, as he frequently does. I'd found out over the course of the last few weeks that he sat on the board of several charities, so doing fund-raisers was one of his job descriptions. I was pleased to learn that one of the charities was close to my heart, the Humane Society. But the fund-raiser tonight was for the Rose Brooks House, a battered woman's shelter. It was being held downtown in one of the large hotels.

My phone rang. It was Ryan. "Hello, beautiful," he said. This was his standard greeting for me.

"Hey. I thought you were at a fundraiser?"

"I am. They're getting ready to start the silent auction, so I had a minute, and just wanted to call and say hello."

"That's sweet." I wasn't in the mood to be talkative.

"So, what're you doing?"

Contemplating living on the streets with my cat. "Nothing, just watching a little television." My viewing habits were classed up a bit, as I was getting ready to watch *Mad Men* on AMC+.

"I wish you were here." We'd actually discussed my going as his date. He wanted me to, I didn't. I wasn't ready for that just yet.

"Yeah, me too." This wasn't a lie. Those things could be boring but they could sometimes be fun. And the food was generally passable, if not great. At any rate, the food was better than what I had in my fridge. I was spending so much time at Ryan's house that my fridge was more threadbare than ever.

"Well, honey, the auction is going to start, so I'll talk to you later."

"Later."

I ended up getting Hardee's that evening, picking up a newspaper at the gas station. *I better look at the rooms for rent or anything I can find. Hopefully somebody who won't do a credit check.*

I went to bed around 10 PM and the door was knocking at 11.

"Hey," I greeted Ryan.

"I was in the neighborhood?" He looked sheepish.

Yeah, right. Your fundraiser was downtown, a good thirty minutes away. If you were in the neighborhood, it was because you drove to it. I found that humorous.

"Ah, you're here for your booty call," I said, walking back towards the bedroom.

"Well, yes, but I missed you tonight." He grabbed me and spun me around and kissed me passionately, his tongue hungrily exploring my mouth. He tasted of red wine and dark chocolate.

We parted, as I started walking back to the bedroom. I expected him to follow me.

I turned around and saw him looking at the newspaper folded on the coffee table. I had circled several ads for rooms for rent in red.

"What's this?" he asked.

Oh, geez, this is embarrassing. I still got embarrassed when I was caught up doing stupid things.

"Madison is here illegally," I explained. "Illegally" was not quite the right word, but it was all I could come up with just then. "I mean illicitly," I corrected myself when I thought of the right word.

"And?"

"And I have to move out. In thirty days."

He looked happy about this.

"Exactly why are you smiling?"

"Sit down."

I sat down and he sat down next to me on the couch.

"You could move in with me."

Oh, hell no. Hell to the no.

"That's very sweet of you to offer, but I can handle this on my own," I lied.

He looked crushed. "Won't you at least consider it?"

I shook my head. "Impossible. It's too soon."

"I don't think so. We get along. Things are going really well."

"No. The answer is no. Now come to bed, if you want."

But of course, moving in with him was exactly what I did. I put in applications for leases all over town, but, just as I thought, my forcible eviction and lousy credit put the kibosh on all of them. I knew Ryan was secretly rooting against all the apartment complexes. I wouldn't have been surprised if he paid them all off, one by one, to deny me.

Of course, it wouldn't take something that nefarious to get me denied at these places. My history did that all on its own.

Finally, I called uncle. But first, he had to meet my family.

At his house, when I finally confessed that I was going to take him up on his offer, I put the stipulation of meeting my family. There was no way I would move in with him, making such a serious step, without them first meeting him. Ryan readily agreed.

I figured this was a good time to see if there was some reciprocity in this.

"So, you're finally going to meet the fam."

"Yes, and I'm excited!"

"What about you?"

"What about me?"

"Well, is your family ok with some strange woman living in your house?"

His mood darkened. "I don't know."

This was a reaction I expected, yet didn't expect. I knew there was something going on with the dad, and I had a pretty good suspicion about what. However, my suspicion was so horrible that it couldn't be imagined. Yet, the proof was there – at least one night a week, Ryan talked in his sleep, begging his father to stop something. I wished Ryan would open up, but apparently he wasn't ready for that just yet.

I didn't push.

What I didn't expect was that he'd react this way about his mother. He loved his mother and was apparently close with her again, after being estranged for many years. After his father's divorce, he wasn't allowed to see her anymore, and his father told him that this was Maggie's choice. It wasn't until he was an adult, and sought her out, that he learned the truth. It took some work and some family therapy, but they got past their differences and worked at re-establishing a relationship. Now they were close. Christ, he took her maiden name as his own, although he never did admit to me that this is what he did.

"So you don't want me to meet-"

"Iris, just drop it, please." His voice was hard-edged, as it always was when the subject of his father came up. And he used my first name, which was never a good sign with him.

I was perplexed. *What about my meeting Maggie?*

But the conversation about his parents ended there.

Chapter Twelve

The night was upon us for him to finally meet the family. He had been warned about what to expect, so there was nothing that would make him run for the hills. And the night went just as I thought it would.

Ryan brought my mother a bouquet of wildflowers and a limited edition Barbie Doll for her collection. He presented my sister with a box of Christopher Elbow chocolates, which was a boutique chocolatier in Kansas City. For my father, he had picked up a signed copy of *Atlas Shrugged*, one of my father's favorite books. I knew that the book set him back, and the doll did too, but money was no object, as usual.

We met at a Japanese Steakhouse. I wasn't quite ready for Ryan to see my parent's townhouse. My apartment was the Taj Mahal compared to their place. They had an untrained dog, so their carpet constantly smelled like pee, and my parents were sloppier than I could ever hope to be. I figured Ryan would be better off with a small dose for this first night.

The dose he got was bad enough. I loved my family, but they were a little quirky. My nephew also showed up, and he was loud. His speaking voice was loud to begin with, and he had a quick temper and tended to cause scenes in restaurants, dropping the F-bomb as many times in a sentence as possible.

My father showed up in his usual Japanese gear – a Japanese headband, a Japanese robe and a white t-shirt on underneath. Ryan was amused by this get-up and thought it was cute. My mother wore a colorful shirt that I had bought her for her birthday one year. My nephew wore his usual jeans and plaid shirt, topped by an enormous straw hat. My sister was, as usual, dressed to the nines, wearing high heels and a lacy blouse.

The night wore on, as my family sat around the long table, watching the chef prepare our food. It occurred to me that this was not the best set up for Ryan to get to know my family, as we sat in a long row. It was difficult for him to talk to anybody except the people sitting next to him, one of whom was myself. Still, I could see him talking to my father animatedly.

Since Ryan had given my father the Ayn Rand book, my father took that as a sign that Ryan was interested in Ayn Rand, and he started talking about Randian philosophy. I could catch snippets of their conversation. To my surprise, Ryan knew a lot about Ayn Rand, and was prepared to debate my father about her ideas.

I heard him tell my father "I'm quite sure she was a very intelligent woman, but I don't agree with social Darwinism or objectivism."

"Yes, but we can't let the social safety net get too out of hand." I rolled my eyes at my RINO father. The Republican party wouldn't want to have anything to do with him – the guy was pro-choice, pro-gun control, pro gay rights, and pro legalizedn marijuana. He was also passionate about green technology. Yet he called himself a Republican. Go figure.

I heard Ryan expound a little more about her philosophy, which showed that he had a deeper understanding of her work than I gave him credit for.

Meanwhile, I was talking with my mother. "So, what do you think?"

"Well, he's certainly easy on the eyes. He seems like a real gentleman, too."

"That he is," I said, truthfully.

"Do you love him?"

Again with that word. "Yes." And I realized, perhaps for the first time, that I really did love him.

Ryan made his way to sit beside my mother. It was a bit more difficult to find topics of conversation with her, as her interests ranged from trashy television to tabloids. Nevertheless, Ryan found common ground, talking to her about The Rachael Ray Show and other cooking shows, and about various episodes of *Flip That House*. I was amazed again at how well-rounded he was.

With my sister, he talked politics, and, again, their views were virtually identical, so there was not a disagreement there. My nephew joined in with this conversation too.

All in all, Ryan was a hit with everybody. He just had a way of making people feel at ease, and he really went out of his way to engage in conversation with each and every one of them about things that interested them. I was amazed at how deftly he handled everybody.

If anything, my sister said he was "too good to be true."

Which I suppose that he was. The other shoe was going to drop soon, I told her. I really believed it when I said that to her.

But I wasn't quite prepared for how it would drop.

Or how quickly.

Chapter Thirteen

It was about a month after I officially moved in with Ryan when it happened. We were doing exceedingly well together. I curbed my messier habits, and I took a cooking and wine class so I could do my part in the kitchen. Ryan was an excellent cook, and I managed to get out of him that he spent two summers taking cooking courses in Italy when he was at Oxford.

As he explained "I was living in Europe anyhow, I might as well have taken advantage of it." Indeed. He was an expert Italian cook, but could also cook all kinds of other cuisine – Greek, French, Spanish, even Moroccan and Turkish food. "I became fascinated with the Mediterranean way of preparing food while I lived in Italy," he explained. So, he took cooking classes here in the states that would help him prepare Mediterranean food in general.

As for me, I wasn't a bad cook necessarily. I could follow a recipe for the most part, but was not yet well-versed in how to throw together gourmet meals without a book in front of me. So, like everything else, Ryan was well ahead of me in the cooking arena. I wanted to do my part, as much as I could, to help with the cooking, so I enrolled in a cooking course.

I actually told Ryan how far I had come from my horrible cook days, just a few years earlier. "I'm a passable cook now, but, just a few years ago, I'd take frozen chicken, put it in a pan, put the stove on high, then be shocked, shocked when the chicken came out raw on the inside. I knew when the food was done because the smoke alarm would be going off."

He found that amusing.

"Beautiful, you're an excellent cook. I love your Osso Bucco." That was something special I prepared for him one night, using a recipe. To my credit, it did turn out nice.

Anyhow, it was my night to cook. Up until that night, everything was going well. He taught me how to mountain bike without fear, and I was getting better at it. He was also trying to teach me how to ski, and that was harder, but I was trying. We went to independent movies at least once a week. We spent time with friends, his and mine, having somebody over at least every other week for dinner. We went to the casinos together about every other week. And we made love every night before we went to bed and every morning before both of us went to work. We also pursued separate interests, as I continued with my pit bull rescues, and he pursued tennis and photography.

In short, we were getting into a nice routine of contentment.

Not that all was perfect and rosy. We had our arguments, usually over petty things.

"Goddamn it, Ryan, would you stop flipping the channel? I mean, I don't mind it if you want to see what's on while our show is on commercial, but I really hate it when you flip around and don't return to the program we were watching."

That had happened three times now. We'd be watching a show, I'd be getting into it, then, when the commercial comes – boom! Ryan was off to find something else. It was driving me crazy.

Instead of arguing back on this particular evening, Ryan clicked off the channel and went to bed without a word. He was in a shitty mood, which I saw him in more often than I would've liked.

He, on the other hand, would get on me about minor things as well. "Why are you always forgetting everything I tell you? Why don't you make a list?"

"I do make a list."

"Oh, yeah, well, where is it?"

I had to admit I couldn't find it.

"I bought you that iPhone so that you could keep track of things. Why aren't you using it?"

Because I couldn't find it, either. When I admitted as much – "I don't know where it is right now. I think it might be at the office," Ryan threw up his hands in frustration.

"You're driving me crazy! The way that you forget everything all the time, I constantly feel that this is *Fifty First Dates.*" *Fifty First Dates* was a movie we had rented one night from Amazon, because Ryan said the main character reminded him of me. I instantly got the reference – the main character was a woman who had a short-term memory problem, and literally couldn't remember from one day to the next. I chuckled at the time that this was how Ryan saw me, but he was evidently irritated about my forgetfulness, and wasn't joking in using that reference.

Plus, Alexis was still in the picture. Ryan was surprisingly patient with her when she called, not like that one morning when I heard him yelling in the phone. She even showed up on a fairly regular basis and he'd invite her in to watch television with us. She was usually drunk when she showed up and would talk throughout the show.

Sometimes she'd show up on a Saturday evening, when Ryan and I would be going out to see a show or go to dinner. Such as one Saturday evening when we were heading down to the Glenwood Fine Art theater, a theater that showed independent movies and revivals, to see a revival of *Citizen Kane*.

"So, what are you guys up to tonight?"

"Going to the Glenwood to see *Citizen Kane*," Ryan said.

"Isn't that an old movie?"

I looked at her, dumbfounded. *She's a Yale-Educated lawyer, and she doesn't know about Citizen Kane?*

She clarified. "I mean, of course it's an old movie. I just didn't hear that it had been remade."

"Actually, we're going to see the original. There's been no remake," Ryan said.

"Oh." She stood there, kinda looking around. "You know, I love old movies, especially on a big screen."

So I said "Would you like to go with us?" *Please say no.*

"I'd love to."

This happened more frequently than I would like, and I was puzzled as to why Ryan was being so nice to her. But, far be it for me to tell her to get lost. If Ryan wanted her to get lost, he'd tell her.

Which he never did.

He did apologize for her intrusion, though, explaining "You know what they say. Keep your friends close and your enemies closer."

I sighed. I knew Alexis was blackmailing him. With what, I hadn't exactly ascertained. But he didn't know that I knew that, so I kept quiet and accepted her role in our lives. Besides, she was really pretty harmless, if annoying. And, of course, whenever we were out together, there was always the assumption that the two stunningly beautiful people were together and I was the adopted sister to one of them. I accepted that too.

I had the patience of Job.

However, on this night, Alexis came over and was definitely different. She came over, unannounced, as usual, but she wasn't her usual spacey, but sweet, self. She was belligerent.

"Shit," Ryan said, looking out the door. He locked it with the deadbolt. "Hide!"

I made a face. Hide? Why would I hide from Alexis? In spite of myself, I was starting to consider her to be a friend.

I ran up the stairs to the guest bedroom with the artwork from the unknown, where I spent the first night in this house.

Alexis was pounding on the door. "I know you're in there, you little shit!"

Ryan looked panicked. I was up above, looking down at him. He looked shaken.

"Let me in there right now! I mean right now!"

He ran up the stairs as I retreated back into the bedroom. "Stay in here!"

"What's going on?"

"She's really high. I knew it the second I looked out the door at her. Her pupils are dilated beyond belief and she looks a mess."

"High on?"

"I'd say cocaine." *Cocaine. What are we, back in the '80s?* "She's also probably manic. She tends do more cocaine when she's manic, which, of course, just makes it that much worse."

Oh, she's bipolar? That explains a lot. "Why didn't you tell me she has bi-polar disorder?"

"I don't know, it probably didn't come up."

Alexis was pounding, louder and louder. "You open up or I'll kick your precious stained-glass bird in, I swear I will!" At that, she started kicking the door, on the wood part, just below the bird. The door was enormous and solid, but the bird wasn't. Alexis would shatter that bird, there wasn't a doubt.

"Stay here! Don't move," Ryan said as he ran back down the stairs.

He ran to the door, unlocking the deadbolt.

"Where is she?" Alexis demanded.

"Where is who?"

"Who do you think? What do you see in that toad, anyhow?"

"She's not here." Ryan didn't address the "toad" comment, but I guessed that was just as well.

"Well, then, I'll wait. What do you have to eat?"

"Why do you want to talk to her?"

"Nunya."

"It is my business, Alexis. Why do you want to talk to her?"

"I saw Nick today. I ran into him at the liquor store." *Him? Nick is a him? What the hell?*

"Oh, shit. Alexis, you wouldn't..."

"Oh, wouldn't I? Listen, I don't have anything against your little rando of a girlfriend. She seems pretty nice, actually. I'm only looking out for her."

"Alexis, please." Then he lowered his voice, but I could still hear what he said. "I haven't told her about that."

Told me about what? Oh, lord, what now? What next?

"Why are you lowering your voice?" Alexis was no dummy, even when she was high. She immediately figured I was somewhere in the house because Ryan lowered his voice. "She's here somewhere, isn't she?"

"I told you, she isn't here."

"Bullshit." Now she was coming up the stairs. I hid in the closet. She was immediately in the room. She opened the closet door. "Oh, in the closet, huh?" Ryan was right behind her. She looked back at him. "How appropriate. Now you're both in the closet." Alexis laughed wickedly at her own joke.

What does that mean? And who the hell is Nick?

She rubbed her chin, looking at me. "Nah, I can't do it." Then she turned to Ryan. "You know what I want. I want that Cezanne. I know where all the bodies are buried. Every last body. I'll burn you to the ground. To the fucking ground." *I hope she's using "buried bodies" as a figure of speech.*

I didn't speak.

"I'm going now," Alexis said, stumbling down the stairs.

Ryan was on the phone with Daniel. He knew she couldn't drive, although she apparently drove over here. Daniel was over in less than five minutes.

"Oh, hell no. I'll drive myself," Alexis said upon seeing Daniel. However, Ryan had already gone through her purse and taken her keys. "Where are my keys? Give me those fucking things."

"Here, Alexis, drink this glass of water before you go."

"I don't want water." But she drank it anyway. Ryan nodded to Daniel, who was standing in the doorway. Within 10 minutes, Alexis was passed out on the couch. Ryan and Daniel picked her up and put her into her Range Rover.

"Thanks, man," Ryan told Daniel.

"Of course. We have to stop meeting this way."

"Don't forget to bring her back to her car when she sobers up."

He nodded. "I know the drill by now."

"You're a lifesaver, buddy."

Daniel nodded and drove off, with Alexis passed out in the passenger's seat. I wondered what kind of drug Ryan gave her to make her pass out like that, when she was so wired before. Must've been something pretty potent.

I looked back at Ryan, who looked shocked and shaken. He was literally shaking, too.

Now you're both in the closet. What the fuck?

I was scared to ask. "What was that about?"

"Excuse me." He took his phone into the other room. "Yes, Dr. Halder? Thanks for answering the phone so late. No, no, I'm ok. Do you have an afternoon open sometime this week? As soon as possible? I need about three hours of your time, if possible." He stood, silently, on the phone for about five minutes. "Wednesday. Anything sooner?" Then "Yes, yes, I understand. Thanks for clearing your schedule for me on Wednesday."

He came out. "What are you doing on Wednesday at 1?"

"Well, let's see," I said, looking at my iPhone. Ryan bought that for me as a gift the first week I moved in. "You need to be better organized," he explained when he bought it. I couldn't argue with that. "I have a couple of new intakes. I could always reschedule them." I was a little bit upset about getting into the rescheduling business again. I was trying to be more responsible. I couldn't lose my practice now, because then I'd be a total loser. Ryan wouldn't want an unemployed loser living with him.

"I normally wouldn't ask you to do that, but this is important."

"You want me to go to your therapist with you." That was a statement, not a question, because I knew the answer.

"Yes. Please."

"Ok."

Then I was on the phone with Melinda. She wasn't happy. "You're rescheduling again? You were getting so much better."

"Yeah, I know, but this is an emergency."

"Ok," she grumbled.

"Thanks."

I turned to Ryan. "Done."

He took a deep breath. "Ok, now you have to promise me something."

"What's that?"

"You won't ask me a single question about what Alexis said, or what you heard Alexis saying, until we can sit in Dr. Halder's office together."

Shit, that was in three more days!. My curiosity, and, I admit, panic, was killing me.

"Deal," I said, faking a smile.

He let out a deep breath. "God, I love you." Then he was back on the phone. "Yes, Dr. Halder. It's Ryan again." Pause. "Yes, I hope it's ok if I bring my fiancée in as well on Wednesday." Pause. "Thanks for accommodating us."

I looked at him. *Fiancée?*

I suddenly felt terrified for some odd reason.

Chapter Fourteen

The three days that I had to wait to see Ryan's therapist was sheer hell. Over and over again I heard Alexis' words "Now you're both in the closet," and I couldn't stop obsessing about who Nick was. Now I knew that Nick was a man, and...*No, no, stop that. It isn't that.* I was sorry that I ever agreed to Ryan's condition that I not talk to him about what Alexis had said before Wednesday.

It wasn't exactly fun being around Ryan, either. There was an elephant in the room that neither of us could address just yet. My mind was going 1,000 miles an hour, considering all the possibilities. While Alexis chose not to reveal Ryan's secret to me that night, she did plenty of damage without coming right out and telling me what was going on. Perhaps that was her objective.

She played her hand perfectly.

I realized that one of her main goals was to get Ryan back any way she possibly could. Yes, she wanted material possessions, but it had always been clear to me that for her, he was the ultimate prize. Perhaps she was just putting something out there that wasn't true at all in an attempt to put doubt in my brain about Ryan. With me out of the picture, she could worm her way back into his good graces, perhaps.

These were all the thoughts going through my mind as I tried to concentrate on work. Such concentration was impossible.

It was very discouraging. I was dealing with the reality of my burnout, at the same time that I was anticipating a major bombshell from the therapist.

I wasn't having a good day.

I came home and Ryan was waiting for me. A huge bouquet of roses was on the table. There was also candle light and I could smell dinner waiting for me. He opened a bottle of his wine.

"Love, I know you're stressed out. I'm so very sorry about all of this. I'm sorry to make you wait to find out what's going on. I wish that there was something I could do. I know dinner and roses won't take away your anxiety but I just wanted to make the gesture."

I had to admit, he was sweet. I hoped that what was revealed wouldn't be a deal-breaker, although I was very nervous about it.

Dinner was delicious, as usual. He made one of my favorite meals – potato gnocchi with sage butter, goat cheese and walnuts. It was savory and produced an orgasm in my mouth. He served it with a simple Caesar Salad with homemade croutons and homemade dressing. Dessert was Zabaglione with fresh raspberries. We went through a bottle of some of the finest wine from his winery.

After that meal, I was feeling better.

He led me up to the master bathroom. This was a magnificent bathroom with a sunken tub. We took off our clothes and climbed into the tub. He had run the bath to just the right temperature, and made sure that there were lots of bubbles. He lined up some of my favorite songs on the iTunes collection and they were piping through the speakers in the bathroom. We drank wine and relaxed in the enormous tub.

He gently massaged my shoulders with massage oil while he sat behind me in the tub. He shampooed my hair, giving me a gentle scalp massage. I leaned forward a bit and he started to rub my back with the oil. His hands massaged my back, then my shoulders, then my neck.

"Ooh, you are so tense," he said, his hands gripping my shoulders, trying to work out the knots. Yes, I was tense, but the tension was gradually starting to get better with every grip of his strong hands. We relaxed in the bathtub for a couple of hours, as I raised my feet out of the bath from time to time to keep from pruning too much. The water never got cold, as the tub had a built-in heating unit, similar to a hot tub.

After the bath, I lay down on our bed, while Ryan massaged my back with the oil, and the back of my legs. He massaged my calves and my feet, spending a good deal of time on each body part. I felt like I was having a professional massage. That was how good it felt. Then I lay on my back and he massaged my thighs and my arms. I was starting to completely relax when he started kissing me passionately. He made love to me, tenderly, slowly, like we were on the first night. I didn't want it to end. We ended up making love for a long time, tenderly, passionately, slowly. We were comfortable together, more comfortable than that first night, and we were starting to find out what each other enjoyed.

After we had made love for a long time on the bed, and

in front of the fireplace in the bedroom, laying a rug down in front of the fireplace, I fell asleep in his arms. I hoped this wouldn't be the last night for us. We'd made love that night like it could be our last night together, and the thought absolutely terrified me.

I whispered to him "I love you."

Unfortunately, he was already asleep.

He didn't get to hear the words he was so desperate to hear from me since that first date.

Chapter Fifteen

D-Day had finally arrived. I met Ryan at Dr. Halder's office, getting there slightly early and waiting in the waiting room for Ryan to arrive. He arrived shortly after me. We sat in the waiting room in silence, me flipping through a *People* magazine. He just stared into space. I could hear his breathing. I could even hear his heart pounding.

"Are you nervous?" I asked.

"Deathly," he said.

"Me too."

"Iris, I just have to get this out. I hope you can handle what is going to be said in here. I pray you can. If you leave me, I don't know what I'll do."

I patted his hand lightly. "Don't worry, I'm not going anywhere."

"I hope you're right about that."

"Oh, I'm quite sure."

Dr. Halder called us in. "Iris, Ryan?"

Ryan greeted him with "Hello, Dr. Halder. This is my, uh…"

"Fiancée?" Dr. Halder asked, looking at me.

Ryan looked at me. My expression was skeptical. *Why is he going to lie about that?*

"Actually, she is not my fiancée yet." He looked at me. "Yet," he repeated.

Whatever.

"Come on in, sit down."

There was a love seat in the enormous office. The office was overlooking a bluff and had a very nice view of the city. The windows were huge, and the ceilings were high, about 14 feet tall. I had to admit this was a very relaxing office, with a little waterfall in the middle of the room. Ryan and I took our place on the love seat.

"Now, Ryan, first for the preliminaries. We discussed what you want to do on the phone. I need you to sign your waivers of confidentiality." Ryan nodded, taking the papers in hand, reading them carefully. Meanwhile, I sat there, literally shaking. I made eye contact with Dr. Halder. He smiled.

"Nice day out there," he said.

"Yes."

"The trees are finally turning."

"Yes, this is my favorite time of the year." And it was. I'd always loved autumn in the Midwest. I loved Halloween and the way the air was so crisp during the month of October. I loved that the Christmas season was right around the corner, which was my second favorite time of year. I loved that it got dark so early.

Ryan and I had made a date for the following weekend to drive out to the country to see the changing leaves. *I hope we make it that far.*

Dr. Halder continued to make some small talk while

Ryan carefully read the confidentiality waivers. "Have you seen any good movies?"

We chatted about movies and about Chiefs football for several minutes. The Chiefs were finally a world-class team and the city was obsessed with them, as it should be. Not to mention the obsession with Taylor Swift, who was dating the star tight end for the Chiefs, Travis Kelce. I personally hoped they would get married and have beautiful, and extremely tall, babies.

Ryan was finally done with the confidentiality waivers. He inhaled and exhaled mightily. He nodded at Dr. Halder.

Dr. Halder began, addressing me. "Ms. Snowe, can I call you Iris?" I nodded. He began again. "Iris, do you know why you're here today?"

I looked at Ryan. He wasn't looking at me. He appeared to be studying the paperweight on Dr. Halder's desk, memorizing the design. "Not really. I mean, I have my suspicions."

"What are these suspicions?"

"Well, Ryan's ex-wife said something the other night, and I guess I need to find out what she meant."

"What did she say?"

"She said Ryan was in the closet."

Dr. Halder nodded, looking meaningful at Ryan. Ryan nodded his head.

"Iris, I need to ask you this. Do you believe in bisexuality?"

I gulped. This was heading just where I thought it would, and I didn't like it one bit. "Sure. I mean, Angelina Jolie is a bisexual, Fergie from the Black Eyed Peas has admitted to it, Megan Fox, Anna Paquin, Lindsay Lohan, Zoe Saldanas..." They were all women.

Dr. Halder nodded. "Those are all women," he said,

stating the brutally obvious. "Now, I know that this is going to sound odd, but do you believe in male bisexuality?"

I looked at Ryan, feeling uncomfortable. "Actually, I've always heard that there are no bisexual men. There are straight men, and there are men on the way to gay town." I scratched my chin. "Then again, I think I read that Marlon Brando admitted to being into men and Green's Day's Billy Joe Armstrong has too. So, I guess maybe guys can be into guys and not be gay."

Dr. Halder nodded again.

I took a huge breath and waited for Dr. Halder to continue.

"You see, the female bisexual is accepted in today's society. Britney Spears kisses Madonna on national television, and there's some controversy, but it's really not a big deal. As you noted, there are no shortage of female stars who openly admit to having had affairs with women."

I nodded. "Yes, that's true."

"What do you suppose would happen if, say, Brad Pitt came out and admitted to having had a love affair with a man, like Angelina Jolie had come out and admitted to having had an affair with a woman?"

"I don't know. I suppose his career would be over."

"Precisely. There's a double standard about this. The female bisexual is hot. Men have fantasies about two women together. Women brag about having same-sex affairs in college. It's cool to be a female bisexual. The male bisexual is not so accepted."

True.

Dr. Halder continued. "Do you know about the Kinsey study?"

I did know something about that. "Kinsey stated that

sexuality is fluid and that nobody is entirely homosexual or heterosexual."

"Right. Sexuality is on a continuum."

I nodded. "I don't really know what that means."

At that, Dr. Halder produced a little line chart with a moveable slide. He put the slide in the very middle of the line. "Here is an illustration of one's sexuality. On the left side is complete homosexuality. You are attracted to your same sex and only your same sex. On the right side is complete heterosexuality. You're attracted to the opposite sex and only the opposite sex. And right here, in the middle of this line, is a true bisexual. That person is attracted to men and women equally."

I nodded.

"Now, where would you place yourself?"

I moved the little slide far to the right.

"I see you moved the slide far to the right, as far as it can go."

I nodded.

"That means you have no attraction to the same sex."

I thought about it for a second. I remembered at least two occasions when I met women to whom I was extremely attracted. I even had fantasies about one of them. I also had a massive girl crush on my college roommate. And I often fantasized about women when I masturbate, especially voluptuous women that I encountered on the street.

"Let me change my answer." At that, I slid the little slide slightly more to the left. Then slid it a bit more after that.

"I see you moved the slide further to the left."

I looked at Ryan. He was still studying the paperweight.

"Yes, I have attractions to certain women."

"Have you ever been with a woman?"

"No." *Why is this suddenly about me?*

"Why is that?"

"I don't know. I guess I'm afraid to be."

"Afraid?"

"Yes. You know, it's taboo and everything."

"Ok." He looked at Ryan. "Ryan, would you like to add anything here?"

He drummed his fingers lightly on the side of the love seat we were on. He took the slide in his hands and moved the slide further to the left, much further than where I had moved the slide.

He looked me in the eye. "This is where I am at on the continuum."

The slide was just right of center.

"Oh," was all I managed to say.

Dr. Halder motioned Ryan to go on.

Ryan took a deep breath. He looked at Dr. Halder. "I can't tell her about this. Can you help me?"

Dr. Halder took the bait. "Ryan called me very distressed this week, concerned that you had found out about a man by the name of Nick."

"Nick, yes."

"Has Ryan told you anything about Nick?"

"No. I suppose that's why I'm here today, in this office, to find out about that."

"Yes. Ryan said he wanted a safe place to discuss with you his relationship with Nick, so that you can get your questions answered by a trained professional."

"Who's Nick?"

Dr. Halder looked at Ryan.

Ryan nodded.

"Nick has been in Ryan's life since Ryan was very young," Dr. Halder began. He again looked at Ryan.

Ryan looked at me, took a deep breath. "I can take this

from here." Taking another deep breath, he began. "Nick and I grew up together. We went to grade school, middle school and high school together and were roommates at Harvard." He continued, exhaling mightily. He played with his own hair, smoothing it back. He fidgeted with his collar. His hands went back to his hair, finger combing it.

He continued. "We were friends. Just friends. But he saved my life."

I looked at him, perplexed. *What was he talking about?* He continued. "Well, you know, I was really into drugs during my Harvard days. I was high all the time. The only reason why I got through school was because I paid somebody to take notes in class, and I'd use speed to cram for the exams. Nick wasn't into drugs at all. He was constantly trying to get me off them."

"Go on."

"The drugs weren't the only problem. I was also severely depressed in college. There were things in my childhood that were weighing me down, that I was trying to forget. So I took the drugs to try to numb the pain."

I nodded, silently encouraging him. He was having an easier time talking. "I was having a particularly rough semester. I was in an off period from Alexis and I was dating another girl. Things weren't going well with her and I was constantly having nightmares. Constantly. Every night. I mean, I always did well in school, but the pressure was always there. And my father…" He broke off there. His breathing was coming harder now.

Your father what?

But he didn't elaborate on that.

"Anyhow, the pressure was getting to me, so I bought a gun. I loaded it and put it to my chin. I was about to pull the trigger when Nick started knocking on the locked door."

His eyes were watering as he looked away in the distance. "I screamed at him to go away and leave me alone. He persisted. Of course, he had a key, but I had barricaded the door with a bookcase." More finger-combing, then his hands were on his pants leg, then he had his keys in his hands and he was flipping them around. Over and over. Dr. Halder tossed Ryan a little squeeze ball, and Ryan gripped it, squeezing it again and again. He wasn't looking at me at all.

He continued. "Nick came through our sliding glass door. We were on the sixth floor and we had a balcony. So did our next door neighbor, so Nick went to the next door neighbor, got on their balcony and leaped onto our balcony to come through the door. He risked his life doing so, as there were several feet between our balcony and their balcony. Once through the door, he tackled me before I could get the shot off."

I was feeling overwhelmed again. Nevertheless, I motioned for him to go on with his story.

"I hated him right then. I wanted to die and he didn't let me. But, later on that night, we were having a beer in our room, and I was feeling very thankful by then about what he did for me. And we, uh…" He looked at Dr. Halder desperately. Then started squeezing the ball again, his knuckles turning white. His hands came to his face, as he rubbed his cheeks and eyes. More finger combing.

"We kissed that night. And we got intimate."

My eyes were wide. "How intimate?"

"Just oral."

Just oral? I was going to have to wrap my head around this.

"Ok, then that happened that night. I can deal."

"Actually, it didn't end there. I mean, we were buddies

still, we were always buddies. But we started having oral sex on a regular basis." *Ok, so it was an on-going affair. Still manageable.*

"Where's Nick now?"

"He lives in Mission Hills." This was another ritzy Kansas City suburb, as ritzy as Hallbrook. "He has a wife and two children."

Ok, so Nick lives in town. "Do you still see him?"

"Yes."

"Do you still...." I made a meaningful face.

"Yes. Or, at least we did, up until I met you."

"Oh." There was nothing more to say.

I began again after finding my words. "How do you feel about him?"

He looked at Dr. Halder. "I love him." Ryan continued on. "Nick has been there for me through the absolute worst times in my life. Through the drugs, through the almost suicide, through the divorce, through losing Mia. He has always been there, rock solid for me. I love him very much as a friend, but I love him as more than a friend as well. He's been the only consistent person in my life. Ever."

"Where do we go from here?" I asked.

Ryan looked at Dr. Halder. "Go ahead and tell her what I told you the last time I was here."

Dr. Halder addressed me. "Ryan is very much in love with you. He sees a future with you. He also loves Nick."

"You guys don't..." I made a circle with my thumb and forefinger, and jabbed my other forefinger in and out of the circle.

"No. We've never done that."

"Good." *As far as I know, it's difficult to catch diseases from doing oral.*

This encounter was an education for me. I had my prejudices, as do most people, about men being intimate with other men. I didn't think there were male bisexuals. I guess I didn't think about men being the same as women in that regard. That, just as women can love people from both sexes, so can men.

"So, what're you thinking?" he asked anxiously.

"I'd like to meet this Nick."

"What else are you thinking?"

I was thinking that I was confused, more confused than I'd ever been. *How can he love me and a man as well?* But I just shook my head and said "nothing. I just need to process all this a little bit more, that's all."

Later on, after we'd arrived home, I realized I needed some time with all of this. It was too much to digest all at once. I had an inkling it was coming. Hell, I had a very large heads-up this was coming, with Alexis' cruel comment about both of us being in the closet. But, hearing the words was something different altogether.

Bisexual.

The man I love is bisexual.

Chapter Sixteen

Ryan met me at our home, arriving a few minutes after me. He didn't know what to say to me and I didn't know what to say to him. A large part of me resented him, felt he sucked me into his life without giving me pertinent details, such as his love affair with a man. I mean, if it was an isolated incident, or was on-going affair, but happened years and years ago, that would be one thing. But it was on-going recently. That was just a little too much to handle.

I had to get away to think about this. *See what happens? You move in with this guy, now this. You have nowhere to go.*

"How do I put this?" I began. Ryan was looking at me expectantly. I continued "I think I need some time to process this. If you don't mind, I'd like to stay with my mother for a few days."

Ryan nodded, but looked very hurt. "I figured you were not really ok with this."

"I don't know that yet. I might be ok with this. I might not be. I need some time to decompress and maybe do some research on this topic."

"Listen, Iris, I meant what I said. You're the most important thing to me."

I sighed. I'd gotten myself into quite a dilemma. I relied upon Ryan to save me, because I had no place to go when I was evicted because of Madison. Now, if I moved out, I really would have no place to go. Why would I do this? What was wrong with me? I left myself with no options. I should've known better.

I went upstairs and packed a light bag and put Madison in her carrier. She yowled and cried, because she, like all cats, hated the carrier. "Shhh, Maddy, don't cry," I said, stupidly. Madison wasn't going to understand my words. She was a cat. Nonetheless, I tried to calm her down as best as I could.

I turned around and Ryan was standing in the doorway, looking very upset. "You can leave her here, you know."

I shook my head. "She's my responsibility, but thank you. I've relied on you too much."

"I want you to rely on me, don't you understand?" He looked angry now. "I know why you're leaving right now. I pray you come back. I know why you need some time. Any woman would. What I don't know is why you're constantly keeping me at arm's length."

I was suddenly angry, irrationally so. Or maybe I was consciously trying to put a barrier between us because I was afraid that he would soon break my heart, and I wanted to break his first.

"I think you're full of shit. I really don't know how I could think any differently. You still don't really know me. And I certainly don't know you. Today proved that."

Then Ryan let loose with lightning quick rage. He took a crystal egg that was sitting on the dresser and threw it down below. It smashed into a million tiny pieces. "Goddamn it, why do you doubt me? I try to get you to understand how I feel about you, and you just shit on me! Fine, leave, never come back for all I fucking care. Leave! Just leave! I don't want you here!"

I was scared now, but, for some odd reason, not as scared as I should've been. *Been here, done this. He's turning out like all the rest after all.* I simply raised an eyebrow, picked up the yowling cat and my bag and walked out the door.

As I was getting into my ancient car, I looked up and there was something else that came crashing through the window up above. It was a vase. Maybe I was in shock, but I found it all somewhat humorous that he was destroying his own stuff, simply because I really didn't have anything in the house to destroy. I mean, I had clothes there...*woops, here come the clothes through the window now.* I sighed, picking them up off the pavement and throwing them in the back of the car. I waited, figuring he would throw all my clothes out, which he did. I spent the better part of an hour picking up the clothes off the pavement and packing them up in the car.

Then, with the cat yowling at fever pitch, and all my worldly possessions in the back of the car, I drove off.

Chapter Seventeen

RYAN

I didn't know how it happened, but the woman I loved was gone. Of course she was. Who wouldn't be? Who would really understand a man who's in love with his best friend? But she could never understand that I felt for her more strongly than I'd ever felt about anybody.

Not really sure why.

It just felt right.

And now she was gone.

I made my way to my bathroom. My head was in the toilet as I was vomiting out my guts. Something felt like it was torn out of me. Now there was literally nothing left, as I sat beside the bowl, my two dogs lying beside me.

Then I called Nick.

"Hey," I said to him. "Iris, is…"

"Iris is what?" he asked.

"She's…" I couldn't bring myself to say the words. There was a part of me that was in denial that any of this was true. In my alternate reality, Alexis never made her way over here and made a cruel comment. Iris was still here, in the dark, but here with me. She was still in love with me. Of course, in reality, I didn't really know if she actually was in love with me, or ever was. She never told me how she felt about me. She was inscrutable, elusive, and I never quite knew where I stood.

Well, at least that *was* true.

I knew where I stood now, unfortunately, with her. Nowhere.

"Out with it." Nick had no patience for this.

"Nothing." If I didn't say the words, they weren't true.

He sighed. "Do I have to ask Alexis about this?"

Hearing the word Alexis snapped me out of my pity party. "Don't talk to that bitch again," I said.

"Whoa. I thought you guys were getting along."

"*Were* is the operative word here."

"Okay. So you guys are on the outs again. I swear to God, over the past 20 years, you guys have hated each other for as many days as you've loved each other. It's just about even."

I didn't say anything.

"So what's the problem now?" he asked.

"That's what I'm trying to find out. She came over the other night crazier than I've seen her in awhile. She'd been doing lines of coke and was beyond pissed. She said she ran into you."

"Yeah, she did, at the liquor store."

"What happened to set her off?"

Nick didn't say anything.

"Well?" I asked.

"We slept together," he said.

Oh for the love of God.

He went on. "She's still in love with you, though. Of

course. She thinks you guys will get back together at any time."

I didn't say anything. I wasn't that upset about them sleeping together. That kind of thing had been going on and off for years. There was a period of time when the three of us were all together, before it all became too much, and jealousy got the better of us. But I still look back on those three months in college, when Alexis, Nick and I all shared a house in the Hamptons one summer, as some of the best times of my life. Before it blew up one morning when Nick brought home Rielle. Three was company, but four would be a crowd, and Alexis wanted no part of it anymore. Which made me wonder if she was into Nick at that time more than she was into me.

At any rate, after the summer was over, Alexis went back to Yale, Nick and I stayed at Harvard, and we didn't get into the threeways anymore. I always suspected, though, that Nick and Alexis were hooking up behind my back. And Rielle's, because she became a permanent part of Nick's life from the moment he met her at a clam bake on the beach.

Now he and Alexis were back to hooking up again. But why would that set her off against me?

So, I asked "Ok, so you guys slept together. Why did that piss her off?"

"Because she asked me about you and Iris. She apparently was under the delusion that Iris is just one of your fly by nights. You know, like you used to have before you met her," he said. "And I set her straight."

"Don't remind me of my pre-Iris love life." Before I met Iris, I was a manwhore with one stunning Victoria's Secret type after another. None of them made me happy. Not that there was anything wrong with them, but I was always looking for something more than a beautiful face and rocking body.

I wanted my best friend.

I found that with Iris.

I felt comfortable with her, safe with her, from the moment I met her. She just had that nature that put me at ease, and I knew immediately that I wanted to tell her everything. But she was so unsure of herself, which only made me like her more.

It made me want to protect her.

She has no idea how pretty she is. I'd always been a sucker for redheads, it was the Irish in me, but it was more than that. It was the way her eyes lit up when she looked at the doves at the bird feeder in the backyard. She could watch those doves for hours, a hot cup of Earl Grey tea in her hand, sipping it mildly while she watched the birds, entranced. She bought a book about birds after we got that feeder so she could know the different birds that she would meet every day, and always got excited when she saw a different one.

It was the way she wouldn't kill any bugs in the house. She gently puts the bugs on a piece of toilet paper and sets them free outside.

It was her hysterical laughter at the silliest things, and usually her laughter was in response to something I said.

It was the silly songs she sang off-key to the dogs every day, making up her own lyrics to familiar tunes.

It was the smattering of freckles that crossed the bridge of her nose, spilling onto both of her perfectly round cheeks.

It was the way she looked at me and how she could read me. I never had to say anything to her. She just knows. Like she has telepathy.

Most of all, I loved her because she wanted nothing from me. She just wanted me. That was what I loved the most about her. Everybody has always wanted something from me. Not her. She simply wanted me.

"You still there?" Nick asked.

"Yeah." I still couldn't bring myself to tell Nick that Iris was gone. The one woman in my life who got me, who really got me, was gone. And it was Nick's fault. And Alexis'.

No. It was my fault.

"What did you tell Alexis about Iris?" I asked Nick.

"That you're in love with her."

"Well, that explains everything. But I can't imagine why she would think differently – after all, Iris was living with me. Of course she's my girl."

"You wanna tell me what's going on?" Nick asked.

"She knows," I said. "Iris."

"Oh."

"And she's gone." Saying the words made them real, and I felt like somebody had taken a sharp knife and flayed my flesh from my body, inch by inch.

"Oh. I'm sorry, buddy."

I was silent. I couldn't talk.

"Hey, let's get a beer, huh?"

"Nah, I don't feel like a beer." I felt sick again.

I could hear him audibly breathing on the phone. "Well, you take care, buddy. Call me if you need me. Anytime." He paused. "I love you, buddy."

I said nothing for a long time.

"Me too," I finally said.

Then we hung up.

Chapter Eighteen

IRIS

I arrived at my mother's house, Madison in tow. I really didn't have any plans at that time for what I was going to do. I'd sold everything before moving in with Ryan – well, by "everything," I mean an old-school (non-flat screen) television, a couch and love seat, a bed, a dresser, a nightstand and a coffee table. It didn't fit in with Ryan's elegant décor, so I put an ad out on Craig's list and was fortunate enough to get some bites. Which was why I only had clothes over there.

I let the cat out of her carrier and she scurried to hide underneath a bed. Poor Madison. I knew how cats hated to travel and how they hated carriers. They weren't like dogs, who liked carriers, because dogs lived in caves long ago. Cats didn't really have that evolutionary gene with regards to carriers, so they hated them. Madison was no exception.

My mother was sitting at the dining-room table, looking over some offers for prizes that she hoped to win from some fly-by-night outfit or another. She was forever trying to win a big jackpot from some shady organization. I felt badly for her, being so gullible. She reasoned that somebody has to win, but I was always explaining to her that, for the prizes that she was shooting for, nobody won them. They were frauds.

But she kept trying.

"What're you doing here?" She was actually very happy to see me.

My boyfriend, the wonderful, perfect guy? Yeah, he's bisexual. "I wanted to come and visit for awhile."

"Uh, oh. Did you and nutso have a fight?" "Nutso" was her term for all my boyfriends.

"No, no fight." I lied. "I just missed you guys, that's all."

I went up the stairs with my bag in hand, and lay down on the rickety bed. This room was maybe 50 square feet and that was pushing it. There was just enough room for a wire shelf, a desk with a computer, and a double bed. The room was threadbare, tiny, but nice. The carpet could've used some work, though.

I came back down the stairs. "What's for dinner?"

"Well, you know, Michael and me don't usually eat that much."

"So that means...you at least have a frozen pizza in there, don't you?"

"Well, no. Maybe I can get Michael to pick up some fried chicken from KFC." At this, she phoned my dad, who was visiting a friend, asking him to pick up a bucket of chicken with all the trimmings on his way home.

That night, after my mother and I watched some reality TV together, I lay in the upstairs bed, trying to figure out what to do. *OK, so you're kicked out. You didn't qualify for an apartment because of your record. So, now what?*

I was surprised that my mind went there, first, before thinking about the Ryan situation. I just figured it was a moot point now and Ryan would soon be with some other unsuspecting female. I really didn't figure we'd get back together.

Why wasn't I more upset about this? Then, I figured that, once you get your heart broken once, I mean truly broken, the heart won't break again. And I suffered the massive heartbreak of my life about 8 years before. This was going to be cake.

Except it wasn't.

About three days into my visit, I couldn't get out of bed. I'd never felt so depressed in my life. By then I had to admit to my mother that Ryan and I had broken up. That was when it hit me like a flood. All the memories of us making love, hanging out, cooking together, laughing together, skiing and mountain biking, cooking for friends – all of this was now gone.

More than this, the idea of him was gone. The idea of being happy, of being with somebody I loved, who loved me, somebody who would never leave me – that was gone. And I couldn't bring myself to meet anybody else on my Tinder account, even though everybody always told me that the best way to get over somebody was to meet somebody else.

At this point, my life was in upheaval. My on-going struggle with the fact that I hated my job had never resolved itself, and it didn't look likely to. I wasn't the kind of person who liked to look for a job, so, when I fell into having my own practice, I thought it was where I should be. I didn't anticipate how it all would make me so miserable – the paperwork, the chasing down money, the constant phone calls and e-mails and whining. 20% of my clients made 80% of my work, and this was enough. Plus, I wasn't good about bookkeeping, so the IRS was like a wolf at the door, constantly.

I also saw little hope on the romantic front. Ryan was nuts about me – why, I would never know, but he was. Everything about him was perfect – his beauty, his kindness, his sexual prowess, his thoughtfulness, his sense of humor, his intelligence, his manners…I could go on and on. That he was rich was a bonus, but it was far from the only thing, and it wasn't even in the top 10, to be honest. So, now I was supposed to be happy with an ordinary schlub?

Oh, Ryan, you ruined me for the ordinary.

Of course, I knew that I would, soon enough, be ready to date the schlub down the block. I just would have to give him a chance and realize that nobody would ever compare to Ryan.

One good thing was, my sister and I were bonding again. We would hang out in her room, talking politics or watching silly movies.

We were watching *Up In Smoke* for about the hundredth time. My sister had pot – she always had pot, even though her work drug-tests her. She was sharing with me. Pot was something that I'd smoke if somebody else bought it and it was offered to me. But I had never bought it myself.

After about a half hour of toking, we were both extremely high. The pot was high-grade stuff, a "one hit wonder." Watching the movie I said "I love this part!" Cheech was sitting on Chong's lap in the driver's seat, because they had to switch places really quickly, because Chong didn't have a license. I started laughing so hard that tears ran down my cheeks. My sister was laughing too, right along with me.

Then we started talking a bit about what was going on.

"So, what happened to Ryan?"

"He had issues."

"Worse issues than any of your other boyfriends?"

"No. Just different."

"What do you mean?"

"I don't want to go into it." And I didn't. I couldn't bring myself to tell her, or anybody else, that Ryan had oral sex with another guy. How do you tell people that? I knew that most people figured that men who liked men must be gay and living in denial. Why can't anybody believe there are people in the world who love members of both sexes?

I actually did do some research on the matter. Wikipedia confirmed that, in the Kinsey study, some 37% of men had a sexual encounter with another man. I'd never seen that number before, and it was somewhat shocking. I also read an article about a bisexual man who was happily married. The man played with other men while he was married, and it was all copacetic with the wife. Perhaps I jumped the gun. Maybe I could've been happy, could've accepted it, if I would have given Ryan a chance.

If I only would've stayed.

But I ran. I ran before I gave him a chance to run me out.

Of course, as it turned out, it was really him running me out more than me running out.

Chapter Nineteen

For the next few weeks, I threw myself whole-heartedly into the pit bull rescue group. They were happy to have me working more again, as I was slacking off some after I met Ryan, I was ashamed to admit. I did five rescues in one week. One was abandoned, two were in dog-fighting rings, and two others were strays staying at temporary homes. All of the dogs were friendly, even the ones in dog-fighting rings. Doing this work always made me feel important, and gave my life meaning, so it was good therapy for me. It was also a great way to take my mind off Ryan.

I also tried to date. I dreaded the prospect, but I couldn't pine away for Ryan forever. I had to get back on the horse, so to speak. I just hoped I wouldn't start crying in the middle of it.

Date #1. An accountant. Dweeby but cute. Was going ok until….

"So, what do you like to do?" I asked him.
"I like to go to NASCAR races."
"What else?"

"That's all, really."

Date #2. Another lawyer. Was going fine until…

"Could you give me a pair of your underwear?"

"Uh, uh…"

"I need you to wear the underwear for about a month straight, then give it to me."

Yeah, sure, buddy, I'll be getting right on that one.

Not.

Date #3. A professor. We hit it off until….

"You know, you would've been considered to be a very beautiful woman 100 years ago."

"Why only 100 years ago?"

"They liked bigger women back then."

"I wasn't aware that 25 extra pounds is considered to be bigger, but, ok."

Then, one day, in late October, I got a phone call.

Not from Ryan, but from Alexis.

Chapter Twenty

"Hello? This is Alexis."

"Hey," I said without enthusiasm. She caused this, after all. Or, then again, perhaps I should be grateful for her, because, without her, I would've never suspected what was going on.

"I wanted to apologize for that night."

"Not a problem." I was long since passed that.

She was silent for a long time.

"Is there anything else? I have things to do."

"Yes. I was wondering if you could meet me for lunch."

Lunch? With Alexis? Oh, hell no.

"No offense, Alexis, but I…"

"Listen, I'm not asking on my behalf. I'm asking for Ryan."

My heart stopped for a second. Then I could feel myself hyperventilating. "What do you mean?"

"He asked me to call you."

Why would he ask her to call me? He doesn't even like her.

"I don't understand."

"Meet me at Sullivan's at noon tomorrow. I'll be there. I hope you'll be too." And she hung up.

Well, that was weird. Of course, I wouldn't meet her. The last time I saw her, she was absolutely crazy.

Still, Ryan told me she suffered from bi-polar disorder. That particular disease was something I understood. I grew up with that. I lived with that. Not myself, of course, but my sister and people around me. My heart went out to her. That was a tough break, having to live with a disease like that. It was so hard to treat, and even harder to diagnose.

I didn't really hate Alexis.

I understood her.

In spite of myself, I walked into Sullivan's the next day at noon. It was a Saturday, so there was a large lunch crowd of people who ordinarily wouldn't have the time for long, leisurely lunches. I saw her there, sitting in the back. She stood up and waved as I walked through the door, like she was waiting for me to arrive.

I made my way back to where she was. Alexis wasn't wearing much makeup for once, but she was more beautiful than ever. She was dressed down, wearing a simple sweater, jeans and boots, and a Louis Vuitton purse. Her blonde hair was pulled up in a ponytail.

She still would turn every head in the place.

I felt inferior to her, as usual. I, too, was wearing a sweater, but it was a sweater I'd picked up from a thrift store. The weather was getting crisp, as it was in late October, and the cold weather would soon be upon us. As it was, the temperature was in the 40s outside. My pants were a little tight, as I was eating my way through my stress over the lack of direction in my life.

At the same time, I felt a little proud to be joining her. It was like the most popular cheerleader in school inviting me out to lunch in high school. I didn't belong there, talking to her or talking to Ryan, for that matter, and somehow, there I was.

I found myself feeling nervous for some reason.

She was smiling. She had already ordered me a drink. A dirty Keitel One martini. "Ryan told me how much you love these drinks, so I took the liberty to order you one. I hope you don't mind."

"Not at all." I sat down, then downed the drink. I was going to need this drink.

Her blue eyes got wide. "Look at you! You go, girl!" She gestured to the waitress. The waitress was right there. "She needs another drink."

Like the first date with Ryan, I started to relax. The place was filled with people, talking, laughing. There were large parties getting boisterous, celebrating this event or that. It felt like a festive atmosphere. Plus, there wasn't any pressure, really. It was a woman I was meeting, not a potential mate, so I felt a bit more relaxed. I found myself getting in a good mood, in spite of myself.

I had another drink. I was now feeling a lot more relaxed. "So, girl, what's up?" I slurred.

She was smiling still. "I wanted to apologize about that last night we saw each other."

"You said that over the phone. What's really up?"

"Well, as I said, Ryan asked me to call you and talk to you in person."

"I don't understand. You guys aren't getting along." I didn't tell her that I knew about the blackmail. Somehow, I wasn't quite that drunk to accuse her like that. I also knew that if I brought that up, our conversation wouldn't go as well.

"Iris. Ryan and I have known each other since we were kids. I met him when we were both 13."

I didn't know that. He told me they dated on and off and did drugs together. I didn't know they went back that far. Then I suddenly remembered that Ryan once told me he met Alexis in middle school.

She went on. "We might not always get along, but we always get each other."

"So you guys have been talking?"

She looked embarrassed. "Well, yes. My meds...Ryan told you about my illness, right?"

I nodded.

"Anyhow. My meds were not quite right, so I spent a couple of months manic. I was off my rocker, unfortunately. And I was doing way too many lines. Which, of course, made it that much worse."

I looked at her silently.

She continued. "It all came to a head. I was wired and out of my mind. I humiliated Ryan and probably scared you to death. And I'm sorry."

She seemed completely sincere. "Apology accepted," I said, putting my hand on hers briefly, and touching her forearm.

Alexis continued. "I also said some things about you. That was really not called for."

"Oh, you didn't say that much about me."

"I called you a toad. You aren't a toad."

I felt a bit embarrassed. "Thanks for saying that."

We both got another drink. She continued. "Apologizing to you isn't the only reason why I'm here."

I nodded. Of course, there was something else.

Go on.

"As I said, Ryan asked me to call you and meet you. I owe him this much."

"I don't understand."

She sighed. "I've treated him really shitty. He doesn't deserve that. He's never been anything but kind to me." She shook her head. "He doesn't deserve the way I've treated him," she repeated. "So, when he asked me to do this, I agreed."

"But what does he want you to tell me?"

"He wanted me to explain things to you. He doesn't have the words to tell you everything."

Everything? There's more?

Of course there's more. There's something going on with the dad. Is Alexis going to finally tell me about that?

"What more is there to say? He has a male lover. It doesn't get much worse than that."

"I want you to understand why Nick is so important to him."

"I know about that. Nick saved him."

"Yes. But you don't know the whole story."

"Why don't you tell me?"

"I knew his father," she began, after hesitating for what seemed like a lifetime. "I met Ryan soon after his father divorced his mother. His father was…" She trailed off, visibly shaking. She gestured for the waitress, who was there in a few seconds. She ordered another drink for us both.

Was what?

She began again. "His father was very sick. Very sick. Ryan….well, his mother protected him when he was younger. Then, when they got divorced, there was nobody to protect him. Ryan was on his own, because his sister went with the mother when Benjamin and Maggie got divorced."

He has a sister?

She continued on. "His father did terrible things to him. When his father was with his mother, he physically abused him. He used to beat him with a belt for the tiniest things. If Ryan didn't wake up right at 7 AM, there would be hell to pay. If Ryan did not come to dinner at precisely 6 PM, there would hell to pay. Benjamin sometimes would just yell at him, but, sometimes, he did much worse." She shook her head, angrily. "Benjamin was a sick, twisted, sadistic son of a bitch."

I braced myself. There was more.

"His mother didn't agree with what Benjamin was doing, of course. His mother was a very kind woman. She was in over her head, though. She didn't quite know how to protect Ryan and Sarah. Sarah was four years older and was terrified of Benjamin. Maggie was terrified of Benjamin as well. Everybody was afraid of him."

I started to feel nauseated.

She continued. "Maggie and Benjamin divorced when Ryan was 10. I'm sure he told you about that."

"Yes, he did."

"Well, Ryan found this out later, when he was an adult, but Benjamin threatened Maggie when she left the family. Benjamin told her that he would have Sarah kidnapped and killed if Maggie had contact with Ryan. Benjamin said he would make it look like the person who kidnapped and killed her had it out for him because of his wealth. Maggie believed him, so she completely cut off contact with Ryan."

Now I was shocked. I expected Benjamin would be a bastard, but was not prepared for how much of a bastard he really was. I mean, who does that?

"Meanwhile, Benjamin told Ryan that Maggie didn't love him, and that she left because of him. Ryan was only

10. He didn't know better. He believed what Benjamin told him about his own mother."

The waitress was back with our drinks.

"This next part is something that Ryan repressed for years. It has just now been coming up in therapy."

I found myself still questioning her sincerity. Why would Ryan tell her all of this? What if she was lying about everything?

She continued. "Benjamin...well, Benjamin was lonely after Maggie left." She shook her head. "Ah, fuck it. Benjamin was a sick pervert. He used to ask Ryan to invite young girls over to the house, and Ryan would do that. He would invite some girls he knew in school. Then, Benjamin would molest them, would rape them. He got away with it because he was rich. The kids would tell, the mothers would get a new car, or whatever, and that was that."

I wanted to wretch. Now I was also visibly shaking. I felt hot tears welling up.

Alexis shook her head, tears in her eyes. "Benjamin continued to physically abuse Ryan. Scalded him with hot water, burned him with lit cigars, beat him, verbally abused him. Always told him he was a worthless piece of shit, always told him how much he hated him. What Benjamin did to Ryan was bad enough. However, Benjamin did even worse things."

Worse? How could it be worse?

She went on. "Benjamin would have sex parties at his house. I know you've never seen his house."

I shook my head. "No, I've never seen his house."

"Benjamin's house makes Ryan's house look like a fucking guest house. Benjamin's house is one of those 30 bedroom jobs, which sits on 10 acres of land. A very private place to live. So, when he had his guests over for these sex parties, there were never any neighbors to complain. Also, there were never any neighbors to hear Ryan scream."

I involuntarily put my hand to my mouth, then halfway covered my eyes in distress. Just the thought of my beautiful Ryan going through that made me want to find the man who made him suffer and make him suffer worse than anything he put Ryan through.

Burning that man at the stake would be too merciful.

She went on. "Ryan started growing into his looks about the age of 13. That was when I met him. He was going through puberty, becoming a man. He was always a cute kid from the pictures I saw, but he really started becoming a handsome young man when he hit 13."

I drew a breath. Somehow, I knew that what was to be revealed next would be even more horrible than what she told me before.

"Ryan was forced to attend these parties. His father promised Ryan that he would leave him alone if Ryan would entertain his guests. He saw that Ryan was becoming handsome, and he wanted to entertain his lady clients, so to speak."

Now I wanted to seriously hurl. I thought about excusing myself to go to the bathroom to decompress, but wanted to hear the rest of the story. Yet I really didn't want to hear it, because I was becoming more and more depressed by the second.

She went on. "Mind you, these were the upper crust of society. Doctors, bankers, lawyers, businessmen, CEOs. These were the kinds of people who would attend these parties. These were not the low-lifes on the street. These were the most respected people in the city. Plus, these people came from all over the country to attend these parties. They would come from Chicago, New York, Los

Angeles, Dallas, DC, Seattle, Pittsburgh – from everywhere around the country. They would fly in to attend these parties. And Ryan was made the guest of honor."

She rolled her eyes. "It makes sense, if you think about it. The men at these parties were middle-aged, paunchy, losing their hair. The women were the same way. Everybody was horny. Granted, the goal of these parties was for everybody to hook up with somebody, and all of Benjamin's bedrooms would be full of people during these parties. They would be doing threesomes with one another, while somebody else watched. Some of the rooms were reserved for bondage and discipline practices, and Benjamin would outfit these rooms with whips, chains, body bags, nipple clamps, leather suits, handcuffs, sex swings, you name it. Those were the hard-core rooms. Other rooms were more romantic, with fireplaces, wine and sunken tubs, where couples could just swap for the night. There were four-ways, and straight men blowing other straight men while their wives watched. Sometimes the wives would get gang-banged by four or more men while their husbands would watch."

I was just staring, shocked. *Is this how the upper class lives?* She continued – "And here Benjamin had this beautiful young man living with him. It was like a prize for everybody. Benjamin would force Ryan to attend these parties, and he would force Ryan to do things with the people at these parties against Ryan's will. And it didn't matter who was doing the requesting – men, women, married, single, gay, straight. Whoever was asking to have a turn with Ryan, his father obliged. And Ryan was too scared to say no."

I started to feel I was living in a dream. This story could not have happened. My Ryan could not have suffered like this.

She went on. "There was one lady in particular who attended these parties. She pretended not to be interested in Ryan. She was the only one, mind you. Everybody was into Ryan – every man and every woman there wanted to be with him. But she held back. She went to Ryan one night and asked him if he would like to come home with her. Of course, Ryan said yes. He would've done anything to get out of there." She shook her head "He was only 14 at this time. He'd been attending these parties, on a regular basis, for over a year, at the time she came to him to ask him to come home with her."

I stared at my hand, still gripping the latest martini. It was shaking uncontrollably. I put my thumb to my mouth and bit the nail hard.

She looked at me. "You can imagine what happened. Benjamin willingly let Ryan go and stay with her, for as long as Ryan liked." She looked devastated. "Ryan thought he was out of the hell hole. That he had finally found somebody who would take care of him, and not let bad things happen to him." She shook her head. "This woman was 34, 20 years older than Ryan. And, of course, she sexually abused him, every night. She probably thought she'd died and gone to heaven, having this beautiful young man living with her, having sex with her every night."

I was perplexed. "Why would Ryan have sex with her?"

"Well, as he told me, it was better than having to go back to his father's house and be forced to attend the sex parties. So he obliged her. He just didn't want to return to Benjamin's house."

"I don't understand. Why'd Benjamin let Ryan go to this woman's house?"

"This woman had a major account with Benjamin's company. A major account. If she pulled her account, it would've meant a loss of millions to Benjamin's company. So he just let her have Ryan to keep her happy."

Now I was feeling like I was going to throw up.

"That was where I came in. I was friends with Ryan before he moved in with Rochelle, the lady who took him in. I was also friends with Nick. Ryan didn't tell me what was going on, but I strongly suspected it. So I begged Nick to let Ryan come and stay with him and his family. My own family was in turmoil – my mother and father were divorcing at the time, and my sister was 15 and pregnant. If my family wasn't so messed up at that time, I would've taken him in. So Nick sneaked Ryan out of the house one weekend when Rochelle was gone – I think she was playing golf somewhere – and Ryan went to live with Nick and his family."

She smiled. "I wish I could've seen the look on Rochelle's face when she got home and Ryan was nowhere to be found. That would have been priceless!"

She continued. "Rochelle ended up pulling her account, she was so angry that Ryan had left. And Benjamin was also very angry with Ryan, but he didn't know where Ryan had gone to live. He hired a private investigator to follow Ryan home from school, and he soon found out where he was. However, Nick had told his mother and father what was going on at Ryan's home, and they helped Ryan get a restraining order against his dad."

She smiled. "Nick's father is an attorney and a good one at that. He wanted Ryan to go to the authorities, but Ryan was afraid to do that. Anyhow, Benjamin was also afraid that Ryan would rat him out, now that Ryan had support from others. See, Benjamin controlled Ryan, because he isolated him from others. He didn't allow Ryan to get support outside the home. Benjamin made a mistake allowing Ryan to go with Rochelle, because he lost control over him."

Benjamin wasn't so smart after all, I thought.

Alexis continued. "Anyhow, Ryan stood up to Benjamin, and threatened to turn him in. Benjamin wept, stating he was sorry for all that he did. Ryan ended up not talking to the authorities about his dad. His father reinforced his silence by giving Ryan the de Kooning and the Cezanne."

"I've never seen the Cezanne."

"Ryan lent it to an art museum in Paris."

Mystery solved.

"So, it had kind of a good ending. Nick's father helped Ryan get into Harvard, and Ryan stayed at Nick's house throughout his high school years. Ryan literally became like a second son to Nick's father, and Nick literally became like a brother to him." She sighed. "So, of course, they were best friends at Harvard, and they lived together all four years there. Ryan was doing drugs the whole time at Harvard, and Nick is, and was, as clean as a whistle. Nick wanted no part of Ryan's drug habit."

She now looked ashamed. "I, of course, did want a part of the drug habit. I feel so shameful about it now, but we were like Sid and Nancy back in the day." She smiled after seeing my face. "Well, an Ivy League School Sid and Nancy, but you get the idea."

I nodded my head, understanding her gist. There were Sids and Nancys everywhere, apparently, not just on skid row.

"So, you see, Nick means a lot to Ryan," she said. "An awful lot."

"But I don't understand why they can't just be friends."

"Well, the other is something that cements their bond. It brings them closer together. I know, I didn't really understand it so much, either. I did come between them a few times, though, if you know what I mean."

"Ryan and Nick are into that?"

"Sure. I mean, I was Ryan's girlfriend, and Nick definitely likes women, too, so he really didn't mind my joining in the fun." She smiled, apparently at the memory. "Good times."

"What's Nick like?"

"He's light, where Ryan is dark. Sandy blonde hair, green eyes. He's Irish, too, like Ryan - his last name is O'Hara."

"Is he as handsome as Ryan?"

"Well, nobody is as handsome as Ryan. Ryan could stop traffic on a busy highway. But Nick holds his own. He's very handsome in his own right."

"He seems like a nice guy, too."

"He's a very nice guy. But he doesn't take shit from nobody. He does not suffer fools gladly. I think Ryan was able to break away from Benjamin mainly because Nick let Benjamin have it. Ryan was afraid to tell the authorities, but Nick wasn't. If Ryan would've given the word, Benjamin would be in prison right now, instead of living off his family's billions for the rest of his life."

"So Ryan stopped Nick from going to the authorities?"

"Oh, yes. Nick wanted Benjamin to fry for what he did. But Benjamin was still dad to Ryan, the only biological father Ryan ever had. Of course, Nick's father became Ryan's surrogate father, so at least Ryan had some kind of benevolent father figure."

I was shocked, too shocked to say anything but "Wow."

"Yeah. Anyhow, as I was saying, Ryan is the nicest guy I've ever known. He really is as thoughtful as he seems.

After all he has gone through in his life, he should be hardened and mean. But he really isn't."

She shook her head, tears glistening in her eyes. "I blew it with him. Of course, I know he told you about Paul, but Paul wasn't the first. I was cheating on him from the start, really. I don't know why I was doing that, except that I was suffering from bi-polar disorder, and didn't know about that disease – I hadn't been diagnosed at that time. I didn't know that one of the signs of bi-polar was that you could become very sexually promiscuous."

She looked at me. I tried not to look judgmental. "Of course, that probably sounds like an excuse, but I couldn't help myself. I mean, as you probably know, Ryan's libido is pretty healthy. He gave me all the sex I wanted or needed. But I just needed even more. It was a high for me."

She sighed, heavily. "Anyhow, I blew it. I tried to make amends. Believe me, I tried. But Ryan just couldn't trust me anymore, so it was over. We had a tough time after we broke up for good and got divorced. I hated him and treated him terribly. We had vicious words for one another. I was irrational, and I blamed him for the breakup. I justified my affairs. I told myself that Ryan drove me to these affairs, somehow. But, of course, he didn't. None of it was his fault."

I looked at her, remembering the threatening conversation that she had on the phone with Ryan not six months ago, that morning when I stayed over at his house. What changed? How had they become friends again?

As if Alexis read my mind, she said "Ryan and I have managed to get past the animosity. He helped me get stabilized on the right medication. He went to my doctor's appointments with me, and stayed with me for the first week that I got the new medication, to make sure I was taking it the way I should. It's helped. Ryan would've been there for me, all along. I just had to stop fighting him and ask for his help. Which I finally did."

I smiled. This was sweet. She was sweet. I kind of saw that in her all along, but now I understood that she really was a good person. She was just sick.

She looked at me. "This is where you come in." *Okay...* "Listen, I blew things with Ryan, completely. He doesn't want anything to do with me, except be friends with me. I know that now, and I've accepted it. But you...." She looked a little rattled, shaking her head rapidly. "He's crazy about you. I mean, crazy about you."

Still? Even after he kicked me out?

"I don't understand. Why does he like me so much?"

"He doesn't like you. He's in love with you. He told me he felt like he had been struck by lightning at the moment he met you."

I blushed. "Why?"

She shook her head. "No offense, but I'm trying to figure that out myself. But all I know is that Ryan is completely in love with you. He told me he fell in love at first sight. So I guess it does happen, after all."

"I don't exactly treat him well."

"No, you really don't," Alexis said, honestly. "I understand why. Here's this guy, this drop-dead gorgeous guy, and he's crazy about you, and he has been from the first. I can understand why you don't trust it."

She went on. "But please, listen to me. I'd give anything to be in your shoes. To have him love me again. But that isn't going to happen. I really just want him to be happy now. I shit on him, repeatedly, and I can't take that back. But what I can do is to get you back together with him. That'll be my way of making amends for all I've done."

My heart went out to her. She really did seem sincere. I sighed. "So, I should go to his house and try to talk to him?"

"Number one, that's your house too." I looked at her, perplexed. "I know, I know, it seemed like he threw you out, but he was hoping that would be temporary."

"He hasn't even tried to call me. I've been at my mom's house for almost a month now." I was incredulous.

"About that..." She went on. "Well, to be sure, Ryan didn't call because he didn't want to pressure you. But also..."

But also, what? What now?

"Ryan is in Los Angeles right now. He's at a facility there in Beverly Hills."

"What kind of facility?"

"A mental health facility."

What? What the fuck...did my leaving devastate him that much?

Again, Alexis read my mind. "It wasn't all because you left. I mean, that contributed to it. But, mainly, it was because Ryan had repressed a lot of what happened, and it started coming back to him. I just found out some of the details, myself, when I visited him at his house before he made the trip to LA."

I sighed with relief. I would've been devastated to have been the cause of that much pain for Ryan. That I wasn't the one who drove him into a mental health facility relieved me greatly.

Alexis continued. "I knew about the father, but I didn't know the details about the sex parties and all the details about Rochelle. Ryan, himself, didn't remember about all that until a few weeks ago. Once he started remembering, the floodgates opened, and he had to check himself into a facility. It isn't a hospital, though. It's a beautiful, manicured facility that more resembles a resort than anything else. Ryan e-mailed me pictures of this place."

"How did he start remembering about Rochelle?"

"Well, of all things – he saw her. At a fundraiser. She shook his hand, and she wears a certain type of perfume. She had always worn the same type of perfume. When he smelled it, it all came flooding back to him. He started processing everything in his journal that night. He said that he wrote in his journal all night, then called into work the next day, and wrote in a fever throughout the day. He never calls into work, so, for him to do that – he must have been thrown for a loop."

"Do you think I should go to LA to see him?"

She looked at me "Duh! Listen, Ryan's in that place right now thinking you want nothing to do with him. He thinks you can't handle his relationship with Nick."

I just stared at her.

She continued. "You can handle his relationship with Nick, can't you?"

"Yes," I answered truthfully. Hey, bisexuality happens. I wouldn't be the only woman in the world who's dealing with this. Even John Irving had written a book about the topic. "Yes," I repeated. "I can deal with his relationship with Nick."

"Then what are you waiting for?"

"What do you want me to do? I mean, he's in the hospital right now, right?"

"Here." She produced a confirmation number for a plane ticket, one way, to Los Angeles. "You can use this confirmation ticket to leave at any time. I left it open for you, because I know you don't necessarily have a ton of flexibility and can leave at any time."

Now I was dumbfounded. "Did you buy this ticket for me?"

"Yes, but don't worry about it. As I said, I owe Ryan a lot, and I've put him through so much. It's the least I can do for him. Oh, and it's one way, because I would imagine that Ryan will be flying you home on his private plane. That's how he got out there."

I blinked. Private plane. Holy mother of God. I wondered how much he really got from his father to buy his silence.

"I'll pay you back."

"For the last time, don't worry about it." She was looking kinda pissed now. "Why're you so insecure about things that people try to do for you?"

I don't know, maybe because nobody has ever done these kinds of things for me?

"Ok, then, I won't pay you back."

"Thank you." She looked at me meaningfully. "Now, listen to me. If you hear nothing else, if you take nothing else away from this conversation, know this. Ryan's in love with you. He doesn't fall in love easily. I think I'm the only other woman he has ever loved. Now, don't question it anymore. Just go with it. He isn't going to hurt you, he isn't going to lead you on, and he will never, ever cheat on you. You have a good guy there. Stop blowing it with your insecurities."

Point taken.

We talked for a few more hours, just two gal pals out on the town. She learned more about me, about my family and my background, and I learned more about her. I learned that she was neurotic, but sweet, and her heart was in the right place.

I also learned, once more, a valuable lesson. That you

always need to look closer at people's lives. You can't just assume that just because they have beauty and wealth that they aren't touched by tragedy, heartbreak, cheating, and everything else that plagues us mere mortals. They put their pants on one leg at a time, just like the rest of us. The old saw was true, and here was proof.

Ryan was proof of this as well.

Both of them were beautiful illusions.

Chapter Twenty-One

The plane touched down on a Monday afternoon, over a week after my lunch with Alexis. Unfortunately, that week after we had lunch was hellish. I had two trials, one of which went, one of which settled, and I won the one that went. Sort of. If anybody can actually "win" a custody trial. You simply have to settle for not losing badly.

The trial that went was scheduled for Friday, so, of course, I couldn't leave. But the following week opened up for me, after some careful maneuvering of some new client intake. So, I packed my bags, asked my mother to care for Maddy, and left on a Monday morning for Los Angeles. I hadn't yet talked to Ryan, as he apparently wasn't allowed to use his cell phone at his hospital, and I wanted to surprise him anyway. Alexis had given me his patient number, so I'd be able to get in when I arrived there.

I arrived in Los Angeles, amazed at what I saw. It was early November, and back home, the trees were losing their leaves, and the temperatures hovered in the 40s and 50s all week. However, here in LA, all the trees had their leaves and the temperature was hovering in the 70s. Not exactly beach weather, but not exactly Kansas City weather, either. I had packed several sweaters, and I still needed them, because so many buildings were blasting their AC, but I definitely didn't need them outdoors. Except for in the evening, when the crisp air more mimicked what I was used to in the Midwest.

I also got a thrill out of seeing palm trees and bougainvilleas, neither of which grow in Kansas City, because they need year-round warmth and would die in the frost and freezing temperatures. The purple ice plant, with its multitude of brilliant purple flowers, were also in bloom, as these flowers tend to bloom when the weather cools off a bit, as it was here in Southern California. Everywhere, there seemed to be new life growing, whereas back home, the life was going dormant already, and would not re-emerge until the following spring.

It was a little disconcerting, actually. I wanted to see bare trees. That was what I was used to, and that was what was comforting to me. This place seemed like Candy Land.

I arrived at my hotel, also paid for by Alexis, who wouldn't hear of being paid back for this, either. It was a five-star hotel downtown, and my suite reminded me of a penthouse. It was at least 1,000 square feet, with two flat screen televisions, a sunken tub in the middle of one of the rooms, and two bathrooms done in marble and brass. Each of the bathrooms had their own enormous tub. There was also an enormous dining room table with a crystal chandelier overhead. There was artwork on the walls done in style of Tamara Lempicka, who was actually one of my favorite artists from the 20s. I'd flown here first-class, and Alexis was paying for my rental car, so, all in all, my little trip was setting Alexis back a pretty penny. Probably in the range of

$15,000, considering this room was easily $1,000 a night, probably more, and I was booked to stay for a week.

I was nervous to be seeing Ryan. It had been over a month since that fateful day. How would he be around me? How would I be around him? How was he going to be, in general? I knew he was depressed; at least that was what Alexis told me. Was I going to be welcomed here? Was he going to think I was intruding? Alexis told me that Ryan wanted me out there to see him, and that was why she was doing what she was doing – for him. But the reality might be different.

I had to calm my thoughts before going to the Enterprise Rental Car place to pick up my Volvo that Alexis booked for me. It was tricked out with everything that I could ever need or want.

I arrived at the place at 5 PM, just when visiting hours were beginning. The place was a huge and looked like a five-star resort, with manicured grounds, reflecting pools, spa services, and horse stables. I wasn't wrong in thinking this was probably the place where celebrities go when they were feeling "exhausted" or "dehydrated." I always admired Catherine Zeta Jones' decision to dispense with the bullshit excuses. She wasn't exhausted or dehydrated, she was battling bi-polar disorder, and she came right on out and told the world that. Gutsy.

The grounds were beautiful and perfectly manicured and there was a little stream on the grounds with benches and picnic tables surrounding the water. I looked around, hoping we could rendezvous out here a little to talk, and I'd brought a blanket to lay on, just in case.

I was hoping for the best, expecting the worst.

I hope there is the expected return on your investment, Alexis.

I went to the front desk. "I'm here to see client number 23897," I said.

She looked at her list. "Ms. Snowe?"

"Yes." This was a good sign - he put me on the visitation list already.

"Could I please see some ID?" I handed her my Kansas Driver's License. "Do you have a second form of ID?" I nodded, handing her a debit card. "Thank you." She buzzed me in. "Room 324."

I hoped I wasn't interrupting. I felt so nervous I could puke as I made my way to room 324.

It was a private room with plush carpeting, a leather love seat, a flat screen television and a queen-sized bed. In all, it was a cozy room, and the door was open. But Ryan wasn't there. I sighed, and sat down on the love seat to wait for him.

He arrived after about a half hour. I stood up as he walked into the room. He looked a bit tired, dressed down in jeans and a button-down blue shirt which brought out the blue in his otherwise green eyes. I let out a large breath, waiting for his reaction to my being there.

Without a word, he closed the door behind him, then walked towards me and took me in his arms for what seemed like forever.

Chapter Twenty-Two

Ryan was happy to see me. Extremely happy to see me.

It was such a relief.

"You came. You came. You came." Ryan just repeated this phrase over and over again. He had tears in his eyes.

I found myself crying as well.

"Of course. I had to, after talking to Alexis."

"I was so afraid you couldn't come. Alexis said she gave you the tickets and the accommodations and everything, but she wasn't sure if you could make it. She thought you might be too busy with work."

"That was the story last week. I cleared my schedule this week."

"Would you like to take a walk outside?"

"I thought you'd never ask." I was in a hurry to get out of this rather depressing atmosphere.

"I see you have a blanket in your hand."

"I do."

"And a picnic basket. Let me take that for you."

"Thanks, it was getting a little heavy." I'd packed

imported cheese and sparkling grape juice (I figured correctly alcohol wouldn't be permitted on the grounds), some dry roasted almonds, some whole-grain crackers, and some fruit. It would be a light supper, as I wasn't starving. I hoped he wasn't, either, but I had packed some cheese and hard salami sandwiches as well, just in case he wanted something more substantive.

"You think of everything."

"I try."

We walked, in the dark, although the grounds were brightly lit, until we got to an area just on the banks of the babbling brook. The area was surrounded by trees and flowers and it was very peaceful. There was a little bridge going across the brook. This would be an excellent place to meditate. We laid our blanket down and lay down while I unpacked our goodies.

"You always know the perfect thing to pack in these lunches." Ryan was smiling, the color coming back into his cheeks. He looked quite a bit less tired than when he first came in the room.

I fed him a grape, and poured out the juice in the little plastic champagne cups that came with the basket. As we ate our small dinner, Ryan was talking.

"I missed you. God, I missed you," Ryan said.

"I missed you too."

"I'm so sorry for throwing your clothes at you."

"Actually, that's ok. It wasn't the first time." I wasn't joking about that, either.

"It'll be the last."

I nodded.

We sat in silence for a few minutes. I found myself wishing the sparkling grape juice was wine.

He looked at me. The overhead light had illuminated

his eyes, making the little hazel parts around his pupil stand out. I could also make out specks of bright blue, which danced around in the bright green of the rest of his iris.

Those eyes, so beautiful, now seemed haunted to me.

It broke my heart.

"Alexis told me you guys had a talk."

"Yes."

"I asked her to call you. There was so much I needed to say to you but I just don't have the words."

"I understand. Thank you for sending her to me."

"I hope you aren't offended it wasn't me who told you all of that."

"Not at all." *How to address the elephant in the room?*

"What are you thinking?" Ryan asked.

"The truth? I'm thinking you're very brave. So very brave to have lived through all of that. And I now understand why Nick means so much to you. I really do."

He nodded. "I'm getting intensive counseling here. I needed to come here because it was a safe place for me to be after the memories started coming back." He looked into the distance. "I'd completely forgotten all about Rochelle until I saw her. I really didn't recognize her, even then. She recognized me, though." He smiled, wryly. "'Hello, Ryan.' Just like that. 'Hello, Ryan.'" He shook his head. "I didn't recognize her. She had to jolt my memory. She seemed offended about that, too, to tell you the truth."

He went on. "She asked me if I remembered staying with her for the better part of a year when I was 14." He looked at me. "I didn't remember it at all. She looked like she wanted to slap me." He chuckled a little, took a sip of the juice, then bit into a sandwich. He continued. "In my nightly journal, I started writing, free-associating. I described how she looked, how she sounded, what she said to me. I was writing and writing and writing. Then it suddenly hit me who she was. It was the perfume. It was so familiar to me and I suddenly linked the perfume up with her. I threw up in a trash can immediately."

I stayed silent, rubbing his back. It was his turn to tell me his story, as much of his story as he wanted to tell me.

He sighed. "Once I remembered who she was, I started remembering the parties." He shook his head angrily. "I started to remember why I got into drugs in the first place. Why I wanted to die that one time in college. Why I always thought about wanting to die. I couldn't live with what happened to me. I'd blocked it out for so long, but it came out in other ways. Self-destructive ways. The drugs, the suicide attempts...." *Attempts? Plural?* He went on "Well, actually, there was only one actual attempt. When I was 21, a year before the Nick incident."

He took a deep breath. "I tried to hang myself from a tree branch, but it broke, thank God."

I stifled a gasp, then grabbed his hand, putting my other hand on top of it. I clutched him, then drew his head into my chest, stroking his hair.

He continued. "I broke my ankle and was on crutches for two weeks. The other attempt wasn't really an attempt. It was more like I was going to go ahead and do it, and do it right, but Nick burst in at just the right moment. I was so angry with him for interrupting me, you wouldn't believe it."

He looked away. "I thought about it this time, you know. About killing myself. But Alexis called and she started on her crazy shit. She heard there was something wrong with me because of the way I sounded on the phone. She knows me too well. We've known one another for 20 years. She came over and convinced me not to do it. She urged me to get help. I told her I'd get help if she got help for her issues. So she did. She saw a different psychiatrist than the one she was seeing, and got a new prescription and got stable. I helped her, as I'm sure she told you."

I nodded.

"She agreed to help me. Once I was out here, she called and asked if there was anything she could do for me. I told her I wanted her to contact you, tell you everything, and see if you didn't mind coming out here and visiting me." He smiled. "And here you are!"

I smiled back. This would be such an awesome vacation, considering I was staying at a place I could never afford and driving a rental car I also couldn't afford. Yet, treating this trip like a vacation was the very last thing on my mind.

"What can I do?"

"Just be here for me. I'm having trouble coping right now and I really need you."

How could I turn down a plea like that? "Of course I'll be there for you. That's not even a question."

I had to be strong. But I wondered how long I would have to be out here in LA. I had a job to go to even if things were slow right now.

"How long will you be staying here?" I asked him.

"Three more weeks. I'm checked in here for a total of 30 days."

I tried to make a joke of it. "You see any celebrities in this place?"

"Well, yeah, but I can't tell you who they are. This is the place where they come when they are-"

"Dehydrated and exhausted," we said in unison. We both laughed at that.

Ryan said "Celebrities are people, too. They have issues, probably more than the average person. And this is a good place to work on things. It's very calm and peaceful and they have a world-class stable of doctors here. That's why I came here, specifically."

"You ever been here before?"

"No. This is my first time inpatient." He looked at me. "This isn't going to be easy for me. Those memories I repressed were awful, worse than what my father did to me. I know that sounds odd, but I could get more closure on what my father did because I was able to confront him. But most of those people at those parties are anonymous people. I can't confront them, so that's why I'm having problems."

"That makes sense."

"So what's going on back home?" Ryan asked.

"I'm here for this week, at least. Next week - let me check my iPhone." I pulled out my iPhone. "It looks like I can be here next week, too." *I'll just have to do some more rearranging. But he needs me, that's most important.*

"I owe you," Ryan said. "I know you have a life and it can't just stop for me. But it means the world to me that you can take the time out to be here."

I smiled tightly. I hadn't planned on being here two weeks, and it was a hassle even getting the one week off. Things would blow up back home, no doubt. I patted his hand reassuredly. He'd not yet known me well enough to know when I was covering up anxiety. I had all sorts of "tells" for that sort of thing, one of which was patting the person's hand.

It was getting to be 8 PM, and visiting hours were winding up. I packed up the food, what was left of it. "I think I'll just go to my car from here, if you don't mind," I said.

"I don't think you can do that. I think you have to go through the main door."

He was right, of course. If I would be able to just get to my car from there, anybody could do that. That wouldn't be that big of a deal for people like Ryan, who was there voluntarily. It wouldn't be so great for some of the other patients there. So we made our way back into the main building, holding hands.

"I wish I could stay," I said.

"I wish you could, too."

He ended up walking me to my car. He kissed my forehead. "Thanks again for coming. I'll see you tomorrow?" He looked hopeful.

"Of course."

I came back the following evening. This time, he was waiting for me by the front door, where the receptionist sits. I could see the receptionist eyeing him. He had his hands in his pockets casually. As usual, his beauty took my breath away. It occurred to me that the way that he looked was most of the reason why I felt insecure around him, even more than his wealth. I just never saw myself with somebody who looked like him. Yes, my past boyfriend were cute or even handsome, but they were never stratospheres out of my league like this guy.

And, somehow, his pain was making him even more beautiful. He always had a vulnerability I never could quite place. I never knew what the source was. Now I knew, and I also knew his vulnerability ran deep, deeper than I could possibly fathom.

And it was precisely this moment that I knew I was in love with him, too.

He smiled broadly as I approached. "Hello, beautiful!"

I always smiled when he called me "beautiful." Here he was, indescribably beautiful, and he thought I was, too. Of course, I wasn't quite the mess I was when I met him for the very first time. I was cutting my carbs lately, and the weight was starting to come off. I also started taking better care of my skin, making sure I was drinking lots of water and I'd even started moisturizing some. I'd also tried to get bi-weekly gel manicures, which were amazing, because they lasted the entire two weeks, just as promised. So, I was less of a toad than I used to be, so I guessed that was something.

But beautiful? That was stretching it just a bit.

I smiled back. "Hey!"

"Would you like to go out on the town tonight?"

"What do you mean?"

"I'm here voluntarily, so I asked if could leave tonight. They said I could. But I do have to be back by 10 PM."

"Let's go."

We made our way to where I was parked. "Do you want to drive?" I asked.

"Sure."

We found a beautiful Italian restaurant in Beverly Hills. The waiter brought us bread and water and I ordered a glass of Pinot Grigio and Ryan ordered a Scotch Rocks, which was his familiar standard.

"So," I began. "How was your day?"

"Pretty good. I've been doing intensive journaling and talking with one particular therapist about my memories. I've also done group therapy that's focused for people like me. People who've had sexual trauma."

I was afraid to ask, but I knew he wanted me to. I knew he needed me to know as much as possible because I was going to be his "person." I was finally starting to get that.

"Have you remembered anything new?"

"Just more details. I'm starting to remember some faces but the names still aren't clear to me."

I wish he could remember names. I wish I could put a hit out on each and every one of them, and that they would each die a slow, painful, death. Or go through what they put Ryan through.

"Rochelle. She still lives in town?"

"Apparently so. My therapy has been focused mainly on her. But I've also tried to place some names and faces of some of the other people who would attend the parties and would do things to me."

"What are you remembering about Rochelle?"

His face still looked relaxed, so I felt encouraged to ask him more. I figured I could tell when he was being pushed too far.

"Alexis told you the gist of it. Rochelle took me in and we had sex a lot. I was confused. I thought this was the way to please people and I knew I didn't want to go back to Benjamin. So I pretty much did what she wanted when she wanted it." He paused. "And sometimes she threatened me a little."

"What do you mean?"

"Sometimes she would handcuff me to the bed and would threaten not to bring me food or water if I didn't have sex with her. I challenged her one time about this, and she actually didn't bring me food or water for two days. Nor did she unchain me to let me go to the bathroom." He looked ashamed. "That was the worst part of it, even worse than being denied food and water."

I was holding my breath. I let it out. I wanted to kill this woman, slowly. I wanted to handcuff her to her bed and not bring her food and water for two days, and make her literally shit and piss her pants. Make her think she was going to die of dehydration.

Ryan seemed unruffled talking about this, though. He didn't seem as enraged as I felt at that moment. I imagined he had gotten his emotions out so he was able to somehow accept it. But I looked at my hand, which was clutching my wine glass so hard that I was surprised it didn't break. My hand was also shaking uncontrollably.

Ryan noticed this. "This is making you uncomfortable."

"No, enraged."

He put his hand on mine. "Do you mind if I keep talking about this or do you want to change the subject?"

"Go ahead. You need to talk and I promised to be there for you every step of the way."

He took a deeper breath. "What I'm trying to figure out through all this intensive therapy and journaling is why I liked the abuse."

I tried to make my face as impassive as possible. I didn't want him to see the curiosity and horror I felt when he said that last part.

He continued. "My therapist told me I was experiencing a classic case of Stockholm Syndrome."

I nodded. I had a passing familiarity with Stockholm Syndrome.

"I've come to realize that I depended upon her, and, at first, she protected me. Or so I thought. She took me away from that house, and that was really all that I wanted at first. Actually, that was all that I ever wanted, period, from her. Then, when I realized she wasn't my protector at all, but that I was essentially held captive by her - simply because the alternative was unthinkable, going back to Benjamin – I started to sympathize with her and didn't really see that what she was doing was wrong. It was my defense mechanism. I had no choice but to stay with her and I'd have done anything to please her. So I did. At least, that's what I'm getting out of therapy, as far as why I liked the sex and the abuse."

I waited for him to go on. I was trying to absorb this, all

I could, trying to understand him so I knew the best way to help him.

"I'm trying to work through this the best I can."

What a crazy bitch.

The waiter came around for our order. I had already told Ryan what I wanted to order, so Ryan ordered for me, like he usually did.

"The lady will have the chicken parmesan, and I'll take your Spaghetti Carbonara. The lady will also have a Caesar salad and I'll have your house salad."

"Very good."

After the waiter left, Ryan looked at me. "So how are you liking your accommodations?"

"Oh my God! I'm loving it! I could never afford this room in a million years for even one night, and I can't believe I get to stay there for 14 days and nights! It's also a lot of fun driving the Volvo. It sure beats my usual jalopy. Alexis must have spent a pretty penny for all of this!"

Just then it occurred to me that Alexis didn't pay for all of it, or any of it, for that matter. I narrowed my eyes. "Wait a second. She didn't pay for all of this. You did."

He looked embarrassed. "I didn't want you to feel obligated to me. But I also wanted to make sure I made it worth your while to come out here. Alexis made the arrangements but I paid for it. Sorry for the ruse."

I felt a little speechless. I felt obligated to him now, but, at the same time, I had to rearrange my life to come out here, so I guessed we were even.

I put my hand on his. "Thank you very much for the room and the car."

"Thank you very much for coming out here to be with me."

He took a deep breath. Several of them, in fact. He

appeared to be shaking a little as well. "I have another confession to make to you."

I nodded, covering his hand with my hand again.

"I actually ended up at the Beverly Hills place because I had a major relapse with the drugs." He looked ashamed. "When the memories started coming back so quickly and so strongly, I went back to my crutch from before. Before I knew it, I was right back into it." He sighed. "I was somehow able to catch myself before it got too far, because I knew that after a week of getting high that I had to get back into rehab." He looked at me with pleading eyes. "I hope you can handle all of this."

I looked into his eyes sincerely, my hand covering his. "Ryan, you're very brave. You couldn't help what happened to you in the past, when you were a little boy and an adolescent. You can help what happens to you today and I think you're amazing for helping yourself. A lot of people would just keep going on with the drugs after having a relapse and would OD or just keep going down the addiction road. You aren't doing that, and, for that, you're my hero."

He smiled, then stared at me for a little while, with compassion and love in his expression. I blushed and looked away, as I always did when he gazed at me intently. His eyes were too intense for me to look into for any period of time. He blinked a few times.

The waiter was back, pouring some more water. I ordered another glass of wine, and Ryan got another Scotch.

"I wish I could go back to the room with you," he said.

I smiled. "And have your way with me?"

"It's been way too long. Way too long. Way.too.long."

I smiled. "Yes, it has. It certainly has." But I got a little serious. "But you're raw right now. I don't want to confuse things. Maybe being physical isn't want you need right now."

"Maybe not. You're right about that. I'm getting confused about sex, because I'm realizing how much it was used as a weapon against me for so long. That's one of the things I'm trying to work through while I'm here. But I'd like to sleep with you. Just sleep and hold you like before."

"That would be nice."

"I know you have a beautiful room and all, but if you could spend the night with me, it would mean a lot."

I nodded. "Is that okay to do?"

"I already checked to make sure. You can stay with me tonight. I can have one overnight guest a week."

I smiled. The food arrived.

"This chicken parmesan is divine. Here, taste some." I put some of my chicken parmesan on his plate, and he put some of his spaghetti carbonara on mine. I tried the carbonara. "Delicious! We'll have to remember this place for later."

He nodded. "Yeah, this is an excellent place. Cute, too. I'm really digging the décor."

As was I. We clinked glasses.

That night, I spent the night with him in his room. He clung to me tightly the entire night, more tightly than ever before. It was a little uncomfortable for me, physically, as I felt like I was being smothered. One of his arms was wrapped around my neck, and another around my waist. His face was buried in my hair. But he didn't talk in his sleep that night and he slept soundly.

I wished that I could say the same.

I woke up the next day, feeling almost like I'd be taking the walk of shame. I'd have to walk past the other patients to leave the building.

Ryan wanted to have breakfast with me before I left, though. Then he said "My counselor would like to meet with you. I explained you were the person who would be with me most of the time when I'm in recovery. So she wants to tell you a few things."

"Sure. What time?"

"Right after breakfast would be good."

"Of course."

We made our way down to the cafeteria. The food there was excellent, not at all like the kind of food you might associate with a mental health/rehab facility. I ordered eggs benedict, suddenly feeling famished. Ryan got blueberry pancakes with eggs and turkey bacon. Both of us also ordered orange juice.

After breakfast, we made our way up to his counselor's office. The counselor was a woman in her 50s, with wild, curly black hair and glasses. She was attractive in a stereotypically librarian sort of way. She was dressed in black dress pants, a lavender silk top, and had on Christian Louboutin shoes.

"Dr. Silver, this is my girlfriend, Iris." *Back to being just a girlfriend, huh?*

She reached out her perfectly manicured hand, and I shook it. "It's good to meet you. Please sit down." She articulated every word.

I sat down in the large leather chair. Ryan sat in another leather chair. I wished there was a love seat that both of us could sit on.

She addressed me. "I understand that you're living with Ryan?"

"Yes." It went without saying that I'd be moving back in with him when I got back into Kansas City.

"We like to have these meetings with the support system to give you some understanding of what to expect."

I nodded.

"The first thing you need to know is that Ryan won't be taking any kind of prescription medication. That was his choice and it was determined that he doesn't need any kind of prescription medications. So you won't have to worry about making sure he's med compliant."

That's a relief.

She went on. "Ryan has experienced trauma, as I'm sure he told you. He's going through post-traumatic stress. He wanted me to make sure you'd be able to handle the issues which might crop up."

I silently waited for her to continue.

"There might be nightmares, avoidance behaviors, emotional outbursts. He might be hyper-vigilant about certain things. There's a chance he might experience anger and severe depression. We're going to monitor this, and I've contacted his therapist back home. She's giving him a referral to a psychiatrist who might be able to prescribe some medication if he experiences periods of profound depression. Right now, Ryan doesn't want to take medication - he feels he's strong enough to handle this on his own, but he's open to it in the future if it becomes necessary. Also, Ryan might experience persistent flashbacks. Additional memories may flood him at any time. Any further contact with Rochelle should be strictly prohibited until he's stronger and more able to deal with what happened to him."

Ryan looked at me. "I hope you can handle all of this."

"Of course. I won't let you down again."

He looked relieved.

Of course, I had practice handling people who were

having problems. My sister had suffered from bi-polar disorder for most of her life, so angry outbursts and suicidal depression had been things I'd experienced since as long as I could remember. Plus, I made friends who had mental disabilities, because I went through support groups with my sister and made friends through this group. One of the women whom I befriended, in particular, would go from 0 to 60 in the blink of an eye. She'd be nice as pie one moment, and the very next moment she would be screaming at the top of her lungs, right out in the driveway, in front of the neighbors. It was literally as if a flip was switched and she was off to the races.

So, yes, I had experience dealing with emotional upheaval. Not that I was relishing the role again, but Ryan was special enough to me by now that I knew I had to come through for him. He couldn't help what had happened to him and he needed me right now. Again, I wondered why he chose me, but, the fact of that matter was, he *did* choose me, so I was going to act like someone who was going to be his permanent person.

I was brought back from my reverie. Ryan was looking at me. "Is that ok?"

Oh, God, I was spacing out. What were they talking about?

I nodded. "Yes." To what I was saying yes to, I didn't know.

"Good. Then you don't mind moving back in right away."

Phew. That was something I would've said "yes" to anyhow. "Of course not."

He smiled and squeezed my hand.

I looked at the counselor. "Now, about the drug situation."

The counselor looked at me, then at Ryan, then back at

me. "Ryan and I are having an issue with that. Ryan, why don't you tell Iris what the issue is here."

Ryan nodded. "The counselor here doesn't like that I'm friends with Alexis because Alexis always has relapses with her drug issues."

The counselor looked at me. "Iris, what do you think about that?"

"Well, I like Alexis, a lot. She's really a nice girl when she's sober and not manic."

To this, Dr. Silver said "That's not the point. The point is, she's a bad influence. Ryan needs to make sure he changes his playground and his playmates, and Alexis was always Ryan's main playmate when it comes to drugs."

I said "I don't understand. Ryan told me he relapsed because of the memories flooding back after seeing Rochelle, and that Alexis actually intervened and made sure he got help here."

I thought about it. I was really warming up to Alexis. She'd become a friend and made the arrangements for me to come out here, even if Ryan was actually the one who paid for everything. I would be sad if Ryan had to cut her off, and it seemed Ryan was good for her, too. Ryan made sure she also got help. *But, once again, this is not about me. This is about him, and if Dr. Silver says Alexis should be cut off, then Alexis should be cut off.*

"If Dr. Silver thinks Alexis should be *persona non grata* than I guess that's how it's going to have to be."

Ryan looked defeated. Alexis had been in his life since they were 13. He'd known her for 20 years. Plus, Alexis might just start her crazy shit all over again, threatening him and coming over, pounding on the door, higher than a kite. I started to think there was wisdom in keeping her around myself, on our terms as opposed to her terms. If he cut her off, she'd be coming around on her terms, not ours, and that was not a pretty sight.

So, I looked at Dr. Silver. "Is there any way Alexis can remain Ryan's friend? I mean, she's been around Ryan for 20 years, and she'll just come over, anyway, even if Ryan doesn't want her to."

Dr. Silver stated emphatically "I understand she comes over unannounced. I suggested that Ryan obtain a restraining order against her." She looked meaningfully at Ryan "Of course, it's completely your free will and choice. But you know my position on it."

"I do," Ryan said. "And I'll make up my own mind. I wanted Iris' input, but it seems she's not really sure what to do, either."

Guilty as charged. Being definitive was never my strong suit.

Dr. Silver looked at both of us disapprovingly. Her look to me said "I can already tell you're not going to be what he needs if you can't even back me up on this."

I suddenly felt three inches tall.

Dr. Silver stood up and looked at her watch. "I think we're done here. Do you have any questions, Ms. Snowe?"

"No. Not right now."

"That's fine. We'll probably have another meeting before Ryan leaves."

"I'm only going to be in town through next week. I think Ryan is here for another week after that."

To this, Ryan said "Actually, I'm going to be leaving with you. I'm getting what I need here, so I'd like to leave a week early. Besides, you don't have transportation home, and I'd love to fly you on my plane."

Oh, yes, the private plane. That should be fun. "Are you sure? I don't want you to cut anything short."

Dr. Silver was now boring holes in both us. If looks could kill....

Dr. Silver turned to Ryan. "Could I have a word with Ms. Snowe in private, please?"

Ryan nodded and left the room. I suddenly felt like a bad child who was about to be scolded, or a bad employee who was about to be fired. I shuddered, remembering my firing when I was 22 years old and fresh out of college.

The feeling now was just like that feeling.

There was no beating around the bush. "Ms. Snowe, I hope you're taking this whole thing seriously. This isn't a time to play house and give him what he wants. You need to be the adult here and make sure he only does things which are in his best interest. Not yours, his. You need to stop thinking of yourself and think about him."

I was stunned. I wasn't aware that I was only thinking of myself. "I, I, I...." I couldn't find the words. I was instantly ashamed. "I, I am s-s-s-s-orry, I did-did-didn't think that I w-w-w-as only thinking of m-m-myself," I said. *God, this woman is intimidating.*

I couldn't wait to get out of there.

She raised an eyebrow. "You have to tell Ryan either that you will stay an extra week, or that you will leave without him, but he has to stay the entire 30 days. That last week is very important for his recovery."

I nodded assent.

"And you have to discourage him from seeing Alexis. She is going to pose problems for his recovery and may even trigger a relapse. From what Ryan tells me, Alexis is unstable on the best of days, and she often relapses herself."

I nodded again. *That's true. But she doesn't understand Alexis just comes over whenever she feels like it. She also probably doesn't understand that Alexis is prone to blackmailing Ryan when things aren't going right.*

We sat staring at each other for a few minutes. Then she spoke. "I hope that I have made myself clear."

I nodded. "Crystal."

Then she nodded, picked up some paperwork and started writing. I wasn't sure if she was writing something for me, or if she just abruptly, and rudely, started on other paperwork as a way to have me leave.

I soon found out it was the latter situation.

She looked up from her paperwork. "You can leave whenever you feel like it."

"Oh, oh, okay. Bye." I left and she never glanced back up from her paperwork.

Whatta bitch.

I walked out, a bit dazed. Ryan was waiting for me in the hall. "Is she always like this?" I asked.

"Pretty much."

"That woman has some etiquette learning to do."

He smiled. "What did she say to you?"

I was honest. "She said I need to look after your best interests in making decisions. That you might need some help with that. And she reiterated that Alexis shouldn't be a part of your life."

I sighed. It looked like I was going to have to clear another week on my schedule here so I could leave with Ryan. I reached into my bag, and looked at my iPhone. The week after next was filled with hearings – pre-trial hearings, bankruptcy meetings, even a sentencing hearing. *Melinda is going to be pissed, and I'm going to be broke as a joke if I'm going to pay people to cover all that.*

I blinked and sighed.

"Iris, it's ok if you leave when you were going to. Dr.

Silver is right, I need to stay the whole 30 days, but you can still fly home on my plane."

"No, that's ok. I'll stay here another week with you." I flashed a fake smile, knowing the logistics of that was going to be next to impossible.

Somehow, Ryan understood my dilemma. "I'd love for you to stay here, if it's at all possible. So, I just sent your assistant $20,000 through Venmo so that you can pay people to cover for you. I hope that isn't too presumptuous. Even if you don't want to do that, and you want to go on home and attend to your responsibilities, you can keep that money. It's my gift to you for being here."

"Does my assistant know what this money is for?"

"It's in your account, of course, but I e-mailed your assistant about it, explaining what the money is for. Does she have access to your account?"

"Yes, yes, of course." *Good thing I trust her.* "Let me call her and see if she can round people up to cover my hearings." *$20,000 will go a long way.* Then, it occurred to me this whole trip was setting him back some $50,000, or more, now, with the extra weeks of staying at the hotel and renting the car. *Guess he really does have money to burn.*

I bit my tongue, wanting to protest all the money he was spending, but then I remembered Alexis' reaction when I tried to protest her spending money on me. This was just how the rich were, I guessed. Money was literally no object.

I brought it up anyhow. "Ryan, I feel uncomfortable –"

He stopped me. "Shhh, love. You're doing more for me than any money can repay. It's the least I can do for you."

I said nothing more about it.

I called Melinda right there. She picked up. "What's going on? I got an e-mail from your boyfriend saying that he sent 20 Gs to your account so that you can hire people to cover your hearings for you the week after next," she said.

"I'm going to owe you big for this, but please call Lance, John, Terry, Amy and Rex to see if they have openings in their schedules to cover everything. These are simple hearings, they aren't complicated matters, just pre-trial stuff, a sentencing hearing and two bankruptcy meetings. See what they charge for doing this, and let me know." None of this would be a problem except, possibly, the sentencing hearing. It was a minor thing, too, a federal drug possession, but that client tended to be pissy and no doubt would be unhappy that another lawyer would be there when he was sentenced. I tallied up the possible bar complaints in my head. *You have to get it together. After you get back into KC, you have to hunker down.*

But something was telling me that would be easier said than done.

Melinda called back in a half hour. "John is open all week and can cover everything for $5,000." I nodded to Ryan, making the thumbs up sign to him. He smiled back.

"Good. Give him the files and make sure he meets with the clients beforehand, or at least talks to them on the phone, so they don't freak out."

"Okay."

"Thanks. There'll be a nice Christmas bonus for you. You've been a life-saver."

"Don't mention it."

Turning to Ryan, I said "Good news. Melinda found somebody to cover everything for $5,000. So – "

"So, you can keep the rest of the money for yourself." There was no brooking dissent here, as I could tell from his expression. He smiled. "Besides, I heard you say you were going to give Melinda a nice Christmas bonus, so that money will come in handy for that."

I started to protest anyway. "It's my pleasure coming out here and being with you. That money is too much. I-"

"Please let me do this for you." He looked at me. "In all seriousness, I know that this is a huge sacrifice for you. I know that coming out here is screwing up your practice. So I'm happy to be able to do something for you to make things easier."

I could only look at him. There was still a very large part of me that would never be able to get used to his generosity, simply because it was something I had never before experienced. I was never a spoiled child – my parents never had the money to spoil me. And my previous boyfriends, even if they had money, were pretty tight with it. Now, here was this guy who was willing to spend thousands of dollars on me without even thinking about it. It was disconcerting and felt wrong. At the same time, it was something he felt he had to do, so I tried not to protest too much.

He continued. "Besides, I wanted to show you some of my appreciation for sticking with me during this time. It may not be easy for you all the time, and I hope you can handle it all." He smiled. "But I think you'll be able to."

I thought of mean Dr. Silver and all she said. I had to get out of my own head and not think of my needs for once. This, too, would be difficult, because it had been my experience that, if I wasn't looking after my own needs, nobody else was, either, and I always ended up coming last.

This was all going to be a severe adjustment for me.

At this time, I knew it was time for me to leave for the day, so Ryan could get on with his intensive therapy and whatever else he had going on that day. "I have to leave now, I guess. Thanks for the breakfast and everything."

Ryan looked interminably sad. "I wish you could stay."

"Me too. But, I know you have work to do."

He nodded. "But you'll be back later on, right?"

"Of course." Duh. What kind of person would I be if I didn't spend time with him when he was sacrificing so much for me to be here, at least monetarily-wise?

I ended up back at the hotel room, and decided to watch some television and enjoy the sunken tub while I was there. It wouldn't hurt to do a little relaxing, and I found out how tired I was when I fell asleep in front of the television. It made sense – I got little sleep the previous night because Ryan was clinging so tightly to me throughout the night. This might be the way it would be for awhile, as he needed security and comfort, and I somehow provided that to him. He was just like a scared little boy, and I felt for him.

I woke up with a start. The alarm clock was going off. At first I had that unfamiliar, scary feeling of not knowing where I was, and being disoriented, then I remembered that I set the alarm because I was concerned that I wouldn't wake from my nap on time to see Ryan at the hospital.

"Shit." It was 4:50 PM. Visiting hours were at 5.

I'll just have to be a little late.

I actually got there at 5:45, which wasn't so bad, considering it was a bit of a drive in LA rush-hour traffic. Ryan was waiting for me again.

"I'm so sorry I'm late. I dozed off and, for some odd reason, set the alarm for really late."

"That's fine, beautiful. I have to stay here tonight, so maybe we can eat in the cafeteria and watch some television in my room?"

Which was what we did. I got fried chicken, mashed potatoes and a salad – I was apparently craving comfort food – and Ryan got a Chef's Salad. "Eating light, huh? Well, that's a good thing, because you're getting fat," I teased.

He nodded. "I don't have much of an appetite to tell you the truth." It was then that I noticed how tired and pale he looked. His beautiful eyes were still as aqua green as usual, with the little flecks of blue and gold that danced around, but he still looked tired.

"Rough day?"

He nodded. "Every day I have to force myself to remember my days with Rochelle and with my father. I'm starting to remember names and faces of some of the people at the parties. And some of the people who were at the parties were people that even you'd know. I mean, they're somewhat household names. Wall Street types, and even a few actors and models."

The rich and famous behaving badly. Who knew?

He continued. "I know that what happened isn't my fault, it was my father's fault and Rochelle's fault later. But I can't help feeling ashamed of it all."

I felt for him. Right now, at this moment, he seemed so vulnerable and hurt. He continued. "I don't know why I allowed it all to happen. My father was forcing me, of course, but why couldn't I tell my mother what was going on? She would've protected me."

"Well, don't forget that your mother was being threatened by your father, so you and she had lost contact."

"Yeah, that's true. I just wish I could've done something, tried harder to leave with my mother when I had the chance. I mean, I know why my father kept me around, and got rid of my mother and sister. I was more useful to him because of the way I look, I guess." He looked embarrassed to acknowledge the obvious – that he was physically beautiful, so he was a wonderful asset to his pervert father and his pervert father's pervert friends.

"Your sister, is she attractive as well?"

"Yes, very much so. So, I don't know why Sarah didn't get to stay as well. That's a mystery to me, actually. I wish she could've stayed, because then I would've had at least one ally." He looked down at his food. "That's so shitty of me to wish for that, though. I should just be happy she got out when she could, instead of wishing she had to stay and suffer like I did."

I nodded. "That's normal, I'd imagine. Even though Sarah would've suffered if she were forced to stay, she could've protected you, so it's normal for you to wish she stayed there with you. And that's probably why your father sent her away – he didn't want anybody protecting you."

He looked at me tenderly. Once again, I noticed his color was coming back into his cheeks and his eyes got a little brighter, the longer I was there with him. I did seem to be having a salutary effect on him, and this was heartening to see. "You really have been a godsend to me while I am here. I hate to say it, but I was feeling really lonely before you arrived. I made some friends in here, of course, but I just really needed somebody here who has my best interests at heart and who can listen to me and understand what I'm going through."

I did know what he was going through, more than he could know. He seemed to sense this, but he had no idea how much I truly understood, because of my own experiences.

Then he made another revelation. "You've always wondered why I fell for you so quickly. I've been asking myself that question. And I think it's because I see that you're also vulnerable. You put on a brave face, but I know you've faced tough times."

Yes, I have. I certainly have.

He dug into his chef's salad, and continued. "I've felt

from the start that you would be somebody who could empathize with me, instead of merely sympathizing with me, and that you could get where I'm coming from. I felt that instantly from you." He smiled broadly. "Also, I find you very beautiful. You don't see that in yourself, I know. All you can see are your own flaws. But you're beautiful without trying. You don't need a ton of makeup, the latest designer clothes, or any of that. You're just beautiful when you wake up."

I blushed. Here was this Ralph Lauren model with an MBA from Oxford telling me I was beautiful? I guessed it was true that beauty really was in the eye of the beholder. Just like in that *Twilight Zone* episode with the pig faces looking at Donna Douglas, pre-Ellie Mae Clampett days.

"And you're not pretentious. That's so attractive to me. You have to understand, I'm used to pretense. I've lived with the fakest people imaginable. The kids at school, most of them would stab you in the back right where you stood. Social climbers, spoiled rich kids. You're not any of that, and that's so refreshing to me. And, because I'm kind of an underdog because of what was going on at home, I identify more with you than I do with any of them."

He was implying I was an underdog.

Which I was, of course.

At last, I was starting to feel comfortable in how he felt about me. It was always a mystery, and the mystery was becoming resolved. It turned out the very traits that I thought were my weaknesses – my lack of manners, social standing and money – were what turned him towards me. Where I saw in myself a lack of focus and sloppiness, he simply saw as a lack of artifice and pretense. Now that I knew why he loved me, perhaps, just perhaps, I could bring down my walls enough to truly love him back.

He was giving me the lusty look. As usual, my heart stopped when he looked at me like that. There was so much desire in his beautiful eyes. But, I also knew that he was raw right now. Making love would not be in his best interest, and I was going to take Dr. Silver's advice and only look out for his best interest, at least while I was there in LA with him.

"What time is it? Perhaps I need to leave?" I asked.

He looked sad again. "Yes, it's getting about that time. Visiting hours will soon be over. Let me walk you to your car."

He walked me to my rented Volvo. Giving me a long hug, and a kiss on the forehead, Ryan said "I can't wait for things to get back to normal between us. I miss making love to you more than you can ever imagine." When he said that, my breath caught. Just imagining us making love again was enough to make me weak in the knees. Then he said "I'm going get a pass to leave this weekend. Only for the weekend. Maybe I can stay with you?"

I was instantly excited. Then a little crestfallen. That beautiful, romantic hotel room with the sunken tub, and we were going to be expected to behave? This was going to be a challenge, and I found myself wondering if making love wouldn't be so bad right now.

But, no, he was going through intensive therapy that was centered around some very bad sexual abuse. Sexual contact wouldn't be in his best interest right now.

Still, I found myself saying "Of course you can stay with me, silly."

He looked relieved. "I was hoping you would say that."

Well, of course, silly. After all, you're paying for my gorgeous room.

The weekend couldn't get there quickly enough.

Chapter Twenty-Three

The weekend was finally here, and Ryan and I were going to spend it together, away from the Beverly Hills facility. There were any number of things I wanted to do with Ryan, now that we had a lot of time to spend with one another, and one of these things was to go to the beach. I made sure that I packed plenty of sunscreen and a floppy hat, and I picked Ryan up at 10 AM Saturday morning for our rendezvous.

I was a little bit nervous, because I didn't like the way I looked in my swimming suit, and Ryan, of course, would look amazing in his.

When I got there, Ryan said "You do know, love, that you won't be able to get into the water? I mean, the Pacific Ocean is freezing even in the summer time."

I was a bit crestfallen to hear this. But then I remembered the trip to San Francisco in the middle of August. It was cool that week, even in August, so much so that I ended up buying a coat when I landed at the airport, because I didn't think to pack one. However, going to the beach was another matter entirely. The coastal weather was typically 10 degrees cooler than inland, as I found out, and I couldn't get into the water at all.

Still, I wanted to go to the beach more than anything else. It had been years since I had been on a beach, and I had fond memories of beach visits earlier in my life. Granted, these beaches were on the east coast – Florida and South Carolina – and the water there was considerably warmer. But I wanted to at least try to get into the water. I even brought a boogie board.

We got to the beach, and there were a few people in the water. They looked very brave. Ryan looked at me. "You know, maybe you should have a wet suit. That would enable you to be warmer in the water."

So, we went to a surf shop and found a wet suit. Ryan insisted on buying it for me. It was over $200.

"Now, come on, Ryan, you're spoiling me."

"You deserve to be spoiled a little."

"Yeah, but you spoil me a lot."

"I like to spoil you," he said, as he gave the clerk his black Master Card.

I put on the wetsuit, and, when I emerged, Ryan smiled. "You look cute. You look like a little surfer girl."

I smiled back. "Thanks for the suit."

I played in the water for about a half hour, glad that Ryan was looking after me, again, when he made sure I had a wet suit. The water was absolutely freezing, and I could feel it on my feet and face.

After about an hour, I realized the undertow had taken me far down the beach. Getting out of the water, I had a hard time finding Ryan again. After about 20 minutes of looking, I finally found him. A woman was over where he was, talking to him. The woman was the typical gorgeous woman who always came onto him – long hair, large rack, rocking a bikini. I sighed.

This was another thing I've had to get used to – women glomming onto him like he had some kind of magnet attached. They pretty much didn't care that I was around. They would slip him their phone number, right there in front of me. I guessed they figured they could take me. Ryan never gave them the time of day, of course, and a less secure woman would have been constantly jealous of the female attention. I, however, was philosophical about it all. I knew Ryan was crazy about me and I trusted him implicitly.

He saw me approach, and waved at me easily. I looked at the woman, and she glared back. "Charlotte, this is my girlfriend, Iris."

She smiled fakely. "Hello, it's good to meet you."

I nodded.

She looked back at Ryan. "Call me." And she sauntered off.

I made a face at her as she walked away.

Ryan was smiling. "How was the water?"

"Freezing, just like you said."

"You hungry?"

"Famished, actually." I didn't eat breakfast that morning, because I was so excited about the day that I wasn't hungry. Now it was early afternoon and I was starving.

I was looking over the menu. I looked up and Ryan was studying me. "You know, Iris, I'm so happy that you're here. These past few weeks have been hell for me, but you've made everything so much brighter."

"I'm happy to be here."

We both ordered lunch. I looked at him. *Was he in the mood to talk more about what was going on?*

What he said next surprised me somewhat. "When we get back to Kansas City, I want you to meet Nick."

I sighed. It had to happen, sooner or later. I wanted to put it off as long as possible, but it didn't look like that was going to happen. "Sure, I'm looking forward to it."

Ryan said "Well, you're the most important thing in my life, and I really think you'll be permanent. He's also a permanent part of my life. So, it's important to me that you meet him and hopefully you'll get along."

I smiled tightly. I still wasn't entirely ok with any of it, but, at the same time, I couldn't dictate his life.

I wondered if I was being a little too laid-back about it all, though.

Ryan noticed that I wasn't entirely happy. "Honey, I've the feeling you're nervous about meeting him."

"Well, of course. It's strange meeting my boyfriend's boyfriend."

"That's one way to put it." His face was still friendly and soft, so I knew that he wasn't too upset about my not-so-crazy reaction to the deal. "But it means the world to me that you meet him."

"Well, I had some time to think about it all while I was at my mom's house. I've done research on it, and I realize that it's not entirely abnormal to be sexually attracted to the same sex. So, I guess it'll be ok."

"Not exactly a ringing endorsement."

"It'll take some getting used to. But I really don't object to meeting him."

"That's all I'm asking."

We spent the rest of the day at the zoo and going to Rodeo Drive to shop. We ended up back at my hotel room at 10 PM.

Once in the room, I felt uncomfortable and so did he.

We really didn't know how to be alone with each other and abstain. Yet, abstaining was exactly what was in order.

I had a suggestion. "Why don't we get into our swimming suits and sit in the hot tub?" I was referring to the hot tub bubbling in the middle of the room, as opposed to the two tubs located in the bathrooms.

He sighed. "That's a good idea, but – "

I knew what he wanted. I wanted it as well. Dr. Silver's warning was ringing in my ears – "You need to think of him and his recovery, and not yourself. You need to be a grown up here."

I took a deep breath. "Maybe being here alone is not such a good idea."

He nodded, as he came up to me, putting his hands on my shoulders, kissing the back of my neck. I took a deep breath, trying not to feel the burning sensation in my groin. It had been so long for us, over a month. We wanted each other, that was for sure.

But I needed to be a grownup.

He kissed me passionately, hungrily, urgently. He was leaning into me, his erection evident through his jeans. I wondered what harm it would do to make love.

I soon found out.

Chapter Twenty-Four

We made love with the usual passionate abandon. We acted like we had never been with each other before. It was animalistic and passionate, with his lips all over my body and my lips all over his. *So much for my being a grown up here.*

I was feeling guilty, so the punishment to come that night I felt was justified.

What happened was that, during the third time that we made love, Ryan suddenly started shaking and quivering. I was on top of him, when suddenly he violently threw me off of him.

"Stop! Stop! Stop! Leave me the fuck alone!" His face was contorted with rage. I was stunned. I didn't really know what to do, as Ryan was shaking violently. He was also hyperventilating. He apparently didn't see me. He looked at me, but it was like he was looking right through me. I knew this was what Dr. Silver meant by his having a flashback, but I wondered what triggered it. He was sweating and shaking and still breathing heavily. I sat there, quietly, hoping he'd come back to reality soon.

However, it took the better part of an hour for that to happen. I could tell by the way that he looked at me, without seeing me, that he was in another world, and that he was right back at Rochelle's house, being forced into having sex.

Finally, Ryan stopped shaking and sweating. He looked at me like he knew who I was. This was a good sign.

"God, I'm so sorry, beautiful. I, I...I don't know what just happened."

"I do. Dr. Silver wouldn't be very happy about what I did tonight."

"What did you do? As I recall, there were two of us making love."

"Yes, but I'm supposed to look after you. I was supposed to make sure I'm only interested in your best interests. I failed miserably."

I'd dressed already. Ryan was still naked. He came over to me, putting his arms around me. "You're not failing me. We just have to be more careful. And I hope I can get to a point where I can make love to you like before, without this happening."

I nodded. This was going to be touchy for awhile.

I felt like crying.

He noticed the look on my face. "Hey, come on. Don't feel bad. Now we know that making love right now is not such a good idea. We can still cuddle."

"What triggered this flashback, exactly? After all, we made love twice tonight before this flashback happened. Maybe if we can figure that out, we can prevent this from happening again."

"I'm not sure. All of a sudden, you weren't you. You were her. I don't really know exactly what was the trigger for it though."

I felt discouraged. If there was a certain move I made that precipitated it, I might be able to prevent myself from doing that in the future, and this wouldn't happen again.

It wasn't going to be that easy, alas.

Nothing in life worth having was ever easy.

He got dressed in some boxer shorts and a tank top. He always took my breath away with his beauty, and it was no different now. He made those boxer shorts and tank top look amazing. At the same time, it was going to be strange for us to sleep with pajamas on. Typically we slept in the nude with each other, because we always made love before falling asleep together.

Adjustments, adjustments. There was going to be hell to pay if Dr. Silver got wind of this.

We got into bed. I lay in his arms, him stroking my hair. It felt so familiar, yet so alien at the same time.

He spoke. "I'm sorry for scaring you like that. I feel awful."

"No, please don't. You can't help it if you have these flashbacks."

We slept in the bed that night, him clinging to me tightly again. Although the bed was king-sized, our actual bodies only occupied a very small portion of it.

The next morning, I took a shower while Ryan slept. Ryan was soon awake, and he joined me in the shower. He soaped me up, and tenderly washed my hair. He took a brush and scrubbed my back with it. It felt amazing, the brush exfoliating my skin. I returned the favor, soaping him up, washing his hair and scrubbing his back. I also shaved his face, which was a ritual we enjoyed. I gently lathered his face with shaving cream, then stroked his chin, upper lip and face with a razor. He reared his head back while I was doing this. It was obviously giving him great pleasure.

Usually, after our shower rituals, I would end up playing with him and blowing him in the shower and, if there was time, we would make love. However, this time, there couldn't be any of that.

I felt a keen sense of frustration.

After the shower, it was another full day in LA. We hiked Laurel Canyon and explored the city.

That evening we went to dinner at a Greek restaurant around the corner from the hotel.

Over falafels and gyros, we talked.

"So, what's on the agenda for tomorrow?"

"More of the same. I'm still trying to recover more memories so I can deal with them properly."

I nodded. A part of me, though, wondered if this was the best course of action, making him relive all that stuff. Of course, it was better than it being buried. At least this way he can feel the emotion and handle it as best as he could.

"Have you given anymore thought to how you're going to handle Alexis?"

He looked at me, taking a deep breath. "There's something I haven't told you about Alexis. It's the reason I have to treat her with kid gloves."

I waited, knowing he was finally going to tell me about the blackmail.

He looked pensive. "Alexis can do some damage. She's threatened to in the past. She's told me that she'll go to the press about Benjamin. So cutting Alexis out won't be easy. It might throw her off the deep end, again, and this would put her back into blackmail mode. As I said before, keep your friends close and your enemies closer. Alexis is a special case, however, because she can be considered either a friend or an enemy. It literally depends on the day."

I didn't know her all that well, yet I could see his point. She was rather volatile.

"I agree," I said. "About Alexis, I mean. The last thing you need when you're trying to get better is to deal with her and her volatility."

"I also wanted to apologize to you."

I looked quizzical. "Apologize for what?"

"For sucking you into all of this. You're so normal and it occurred to me that you belong with somebody a little less fucked-up."

I didn't disagree. I just looked at him.

Finally, I spoke. "Well, you do certainly have some drama in your life. Who doesn't?" I tried to sound carefree.

"True, but I think I might be more drama than you can handle."

I shook my head. "Hey, as you said, my life is pretty normal. That means your drama is the only drama in my life. Which means I can devote my energies to you. And my life would be pretty boring without the drama." Again, I was trying to make light of everything.

He looked sheepish. "How much is my life's soap opera going to affect you and your life?"

I smiled. "Let's not talk about that. It's not important. What is important is you getting better."

"Yeah, but I feel I'm going to have to help you get your life back on track. I know this trip derailed you."

"Please don't concern yourself. I can handle myself. I've been doing it all my life."

Again, he looked hurt. "When are you going to let me in?"

I honestly didn't know the answer to that question.

Later on that night, I was unable to sleep because Ryan was wrapped tightly around me like usual. As I lay there, I thought about everything. Specifically, I thought about the "let me in" comment. I was still keeping him at arm's length, and it wasn't for the reason I originally thought. Yes, he was beautiful. Yes, he was rich. Yes, he was generous. Yes, he was stratospheres out of my league. But, somehow, his problems made him more human to me, so all of that "out of my league" business seemed less so. By now, he was simply Ryan, the sweet guy who walked through fire through much of his life and was still dealing with it today. Yet, I *was* still keeping him at arm's length.

I felt sad as I realized my walls might lead to a self-fulfilling prophecy. I didn't want to be hurt, so I shielded myself. Because I shielded myself, I was more distant than I should've been. Because I was distant, he would turn to somebody else. And the cycle would continue with the next guy.

I sighed. The clock read 3 A.M. Ryan was wrapped around me, sleeping soundly, not talking at all. I was awake and obsessing.

Finally, it was 6 AM, time for Ryan to wake up. I gently pushed him and he woke with a start. He looked at me, without seeing me again, for just two seconds, then I saw his more familiar expression. He smiled "Oh, thank God. I was dreaming you couldn't handle everything and you left."

"You should be so lucky." I smiled.

He didn't smile back. "No, I'm lucky for just the opposite reason. I don't know why you stay, but here you are."

We got up and showered in separate bathrooms. Then both of us got dressed in silence. He was lost in thought, probably thinking about the day ahead. I really didn't know what to say, so I just didn't say anything.

On the way to the institution, Ryan stayed quiet. I felt a

little paranoid, thinking he was upset with me because of the way I kept him at arm's length.

However, that wasn't it at all.

"I dread going back," he said. "I've had such a nice weekend. I really don't want to ruin it with more talking about stuff I don't want to talk about."

I nodded. "Well, just remember, I'm here for you."

He looked at me. "I hope to tell you everything sometime."

Everything? There was more? My heart sank.

At that, he got out of the car. "See you at 5?"

I nodded.

And, so it went, for the next two weeks. Me coming to see him for a few hours in the evening, usually having dinner. More and more, Ryan just picked at his food. He was losing a few pounds, although he still had an amazing Adonis body. I would leave around 9 every night, then come back at 5 the very next day.

I was on the hamster wheel.

I did get to spend the night with him one night a week. But he didn't come back with me on the following weekend.

I knew why – he was afraid to be alone with me.

I felt extremely sad about that.

Finally, it came time for his 30 days to be up. Time for an exit interview with the infamous Dr. Silver.

I, of course, had to attend.

Dr. Silver looked just the same as the first time I saw her, except her hair was put up. She had on a silk blouse, a tight black skirt, and Christian Louboutin shoes, a different pair this time. Funny how I was starting to know my designers now that Ryan was in my life.

She looked at me meaningfully. "Okay. Ryan is ready to

leave and get back to Kansas City. And you're going to be staying with him, right?"

I nodded. "Living with him, actually."

"Okay. Do you have any questions?"

I looked embarrassed. "I don't know if I should ask this…"

She looked at me. "You and Ryan can be intimate as soon as he's ready."

"When will I know he's ready?"

Ryan was looking at his hands. Then he looked at me. "I'll be ready, hopefully, now."

I shuddered, remembering the last time.

"Are you sure?" I asked him.

"No, but we have to try," he said.

Dr. Silver, surprisingly, didn't shoot us her withering glance at this admission. She actually smiled. "That's fine. You won't know you're ready until you try."

I looked at her in disbelief, then sighed. That basically meant that what happened before could happen again and I wouldn't be able to prepare for it.

But the interview went better than I thought it would. Maybe she was PMSing the first time she met me.

Ryan came with me to return the car. I touched the car longingly. "Bye, car," I said.

Back to the jalopy. What am I saying? Back to life, back to reality.

I wanted to throw up.

I saw him watching me as I touched the car longingly. I turned around. "Come on, let's go."

We took a shuttle to the part of the airport which had the private planes. I figured it would be like riding on a puddle jumper.

Was I wrong. The plane was the size of a typical puddle jumper, but the interior was all luxury. There was a mini-bar, a large flat-screen television, and a leather sofa. Even the bathroom was nice, with gold fixtures and an actual toilet. I was surprised there wasn't a hot tub in there.

"Buckle up," Ryan said, pouring me a glass of wine, then taking his place beside me on the couch.

I did. The plane took off and it was unlike any sensation that I've ever had. My stomach was in my throat as the plane lurched into the air. I felt a little bit woozy. The wine certainly did help, though, to calm my nerves.

Once in the air, Ryan touched my leg. "I love you," he said, for perhaps the 100th time. I had never told him the same, except that one time when he was asleep.

I smiled and said nothing, taking a sip of the wine. I squeezed his hand a little.

"You scared?" he asked.

"No. Well, a little. I've never been on a private plane."

"So what do you think?" he asked, right as the seatbelt sign went off.

"It certainly is better than the sardine can with crying babies behind my head."

He nodded, but I knew he'd never flown coach in his life.

"Would you like to watch some television?" he asked.

"Sure."

He turned on the TV. There was a selection of movies at our disposal. We both decided on the movie *Taken* with Liam Neeson. I'd seen the movie before and thought it was pretty bad-ass. He thought the same.

He grabbed my hand and rubbed it thoughtfully. I found myself wishing the flight would never end. It was pretty cozy up there, just him and I on the leather couch. I snuggled up to him and he stroked my hair.

"I can't wait for you to move back in," he whispered in my ear.

Well, "move back in" really isn't the phrase for it. The only property I "moved out" were my clothes.

"Me too."

"So, what's going to happen when you get back?"

I didn't want to think about it. "I don't know."

He looked distant. "I was wondering if I could come by tomorrow. To your office. To help you get settled back in."

I looked at him. *What about his job?* "Sure. But what about the bank?"

"I took a leave of absence. They aren't expecting me back right away."

I nodded. *Must be nice.*

We watched the rest of the movie in silence, him stroking my hair. I couldn't concentrate much as I couldn't stop thinking of the disaster that no-doubt awaited me after being gone for three weeks. I could just imagine the volume of e-mails, letters, motions, etc., that awaited me.

This was the Sunday Scaries writ large.

Chapter Twenty-Five

After we got back to KC, it was just like I knew it would be. I arrived at my parent's house and announced I'd be going back to Ryan's. My parents were happy about this, and my sister was a bit sad, because we had some fun bonding together when I was there. But I was relieved, because I knew that, with the forcible eviction and the bad-credit situation, I probably couldn't find another place to rent.

And, of course, I was happy to be moving back in with Ryan. His place was gorgeous, but that wasn't all. I was thrilled to be with him again. Problems and all.

The office was another story. The second I got in, Melinda pounced. "Here are your phone messages. The ones on top are 911." I rolled my eyes. There were no less than 10 messages marked "911." She then produced a stack of mail at least two feet high. "Here's your mail."

"Thanks!" Then I logged into my computer. My day was starting out shitty, might as well go all the way.

As expected, there were about 100 e-mails for me to

look at, all of them professionally related. I was going to have to triage everything.

I felt nauseated.

Most of the mail was bullshit, thankfully. Junk mail, motions I really didn't need to attend to, and some mail that wasn't even addressed to me. However, there was enough important mail that I felt I needed to spend the better part of the day trying to answer it.

One piece of mail was from the State of Missouri. I opened the letter and read. It was a letter informing me I was appointed counsel on a case where the state was trying to severe the parental rights of a neglectful mother.

I groaned inwardly, calculating the untold hours I'd spend on this case, waiting in the crowded juvenile court room. The last time I had a case like this, I literally was waiting for four hours in the waiting room. Then, I was told to come back the next week, because the judge couldn't get to my case. One of these cases would suck up hours and hours of my time and I wouldn't get paid for it. Plus, the hearings for these matters were endless and go on for years.

Juvenile court was the ninth circle of hell.

There was one more piece of mail that made me nauseated. The IRS - they put a lien on my bank account for the back taxes I owed them. The lien was for $60,000, which meant all the money in that account, which pretty much only consisted of the money Ryan wired me, was now gone.

"Crap!" Then I put my head in my hands. So much for the money Ryan wired me. I started to shake. *Now what?*

Presently, Melinda came into my office. "Your gorgeous boyfriend is here," she said, fanning herself and giving me the face like "Oh, my God!"

"Hey," I said, without enthusiasm, after he came into my office.

He smiled. "I'm here to help you."

"What would you like to do?"

"What do you need for me to do?"

I gave him the pile of mail. "Just open these for me and prioritize them, if you could."

He carefully opened every piece of mail with a letter opener. Within a half hour, he had every piece of mail opened and sorted into categories. Letters from opposing counsel was one category. Letters from judges was another category. Motions from opposing counsel for domestic cases was a third category. Motions from opposing counsel for bankruptcy cases was a fourth category. Judgments was a fifth category.

These were the only categories.

I was impressed. He knew what to do with each piece of mail.

"Would you like me to call any of these people?" he asked.

I nodded. I had to smile as he got on the phone with some of the other attorneys who sent me correspondence, asking them questions on my behalf. He knew the right questions to ask, to my surprise.

By the end of the day I had preliminarily tackled everything. With Ryan's help, I got letters out, answered every e-mail I had to answer, and at least left messages to everybody who had called me. He was an enormous help.

Around 6 PM, I was ready to quit. It was a full day of playing catch-up, and I was able to make a dent in my three weeks worth of work in just one day, with Ryan's help.

"Thanks for all your help," I said.

"Please. You helped me more than you know by coming out to see me in California."

"Well, thanks, all the same."

That night, after I moved back in, Ryan prepared a bubble bath for me. Just for me. He had scented candles by the bathtub and had even chosen a book for me to read in the tub. "Relax and enjoy," he said, smiling, as I got undressed and into the tub. I soaked in the tub, and I did end up relaxing and enjoying myself.

So much so that I fell asleep.

Ryan came in the bathroom to check on me, about two hours after I got into the tub. He gently nudged me awake. "Come on, sleepy head, let's go to bed." I staggered out of the tub and into the bed, and he lay down beside me. "Welcome home, beautiful," he whispered before I became unconscious again.

Chapter Twenty-Six

Ryan didn't go back to his own work all that week. Instead, he came to my job to help out. He was wonderful that week, making phone calls when I asked him, filing papers, and helping out Melinda. He even helped me with new client intake, presenting coffee and water to my new people, and chatting with them when I was late seeing them - which was often, because I had to pile up as many people as possible, every day, so that I could make up for my lost time out in California.

Melinda couldn't believe her eyes. "Oh, my sweet Jesus, that man is beautiful!"

I nodded. I was used to hearing that. She continued. "And he's so efficient and kind! Where did you find him?"

"I invented him. Like in *Weird Science*." I almost felt that to be true. I couldn't come up with a more perfect guy if I'd actually invented him.

"Seriously, where did he come from?"

"I met him in a bar," I said, not bothering to mention the fact that I initially had a one-night stand with him.

"I gotta get out more. Hubba hubba!"

I laughed. Melinda had a boyfriend, but they were perpetually having problems. I sympathized with her, remembering my own checkered past before meeting Ryan.

By the end of the week, with Ryan's help, I was not only caught up, but was ahead a little bit.

"Man, you need to come in the office more often!"

"I wish I could. But, alas, I have my own job to get to on Monday." He smiled. "But I sure have enjoyed helping you, for a change."

I sighed. I wished he could come in and help me all the time. But, as he said, he had his own job to go to.

A job he hadn't been to for six weeks, now.

Chapter Twenty-Seven

About a month after I moved back in, around Christmas time, everything changed again. I arrived home early one day to find the lights had gone out. A fuse must have blown. I went to the basement to try to find the fuse box, not wanting to bother Ryan at work to ask him where the fuse box was. It was already dark, even though it was only 4:30 PM, so I had to use a flashlight to navigate my way around the large house.

Seeing nothing in the basement, I proceeded into the attic with my flashlight. When I went up there, I came upon a pile of watercolor paintings, which were exquisitely detailed. Some of the paintings were of an enormous palace on acreages of land, with a lake in front. The palace had two circular towers connected to a rectangular building with a flat façade. This place reminded me of an English country manor I had seen in photographs. I looked at the back of the painting. "Cork, 1994," it read.

Other paintings were of a beautiful, dark-haired lady with sad green eyes. In some of the pictures, she was clutching a beautiful young girl. In others, she was clutching a young girl and a young boy. The young boy looked like Ryan. I looked closer. Come to think of it, the lady resembled Ryan, as well. The paintings were in great detail, and were beautifully drawn, like a professional did them.

Still other paintings were more abstract. There were some that had a surrealist bent, others were cubist. Some of the surrealist influences were evidently Salvador Dali, Max Ernst, and Francis Bacon. The cubist work was evidently influenced by Picasso, Georges Braque, and Juan Gris. There were also works that seemed to transcend genres and others were hybrids.

Flipping through the paintings, my heart stopped. There were several portraits of me! I rubbed my eyes, not quite comprehending what I was seeing. There was a portrait of me made from a photograph. In the portrait, I was wearing a bucket hat and smiling. Another portrait of me was from a photograph of me on skis. A third portrait was of me in the backyard garden, staring at some of the flowers. This was a candid portrait and I didn't recall a picture being taken of me like this. A fourth one was of me sleeping on a couch. I vaguely remembered there was a photograph like this somewhere.

I was dumbfounded, completely forgetting why I was in the attic in the first place.

Just then, I heard a car pull up. *Shit!* I scrambled out of the attic, putting the ladder back and closing the attic opening. I ran into the den and plopped on the couch, the flashlight in hand.

"Hey!" Ryan called. "You wanting to surprise me with a candlelight dinner?"

I called back. "I'm in here. In the den. With a flashlight."

"What's going on?"

"I don't know. The electricity went out. Must've blown a fuse."

"Oh, ok. Did you go to the fusebox?"

"No. I didn't know where it was."

"I showed it to you when you moved in, silly. Give me that flashlight." At that, he snatched the flashlight out of my hand. He walked over to the hallway, where there was a little tiny door, and, inside the door, there was the fusebox. He flipped a few switches, and the lights came on. The refrigerator resumed its familiar hum.

"I guess I'll find it next time."

"You should've found it this time. You don't have a very good memory, do you?"

"I guess not."

He rolled his eyes, making a fist and knocking my head a few times. "Anybody home?"

I shrugged. "I'll remember next time."

"That's all I can ask, I guess." He went to the fridge and opened it.

"Everything needs to cool down in there," he said. "I hope nothing spoiled." He turned to me. "Looks like we'll be going out to eat tonight."

My heart soared. I loved going out to eat, especially when I wasn't expecting it.

We ended up getting Mexican food. Over margaritas, I found a subtle way to ask about his mother.

"You know, you don't talk too much about your mother. What was she like?"

He had a faraway look. "Mom was a wonderful woman. She is a wonderful woman, still. Beautiful singing voice and she always made me laugh. She was very caring, very warm, very funny, very smart." He looked at me. "Why do you ask?"

"Just curious. I know about your father. You haven't talked much about your mother."

He looked a little upset. I wondered why.

Then I asked "What did she look like?"

"Beautiful. Black hair, green eyes. She looked like a movie star."

I thought about the woman in the paintings. Black hair, green eyes. She was as beautiful as a movie star.

Of course, those portraits had to be of her.

He was onto another subject. "So, tell me again why you couldn't find the fuse box?" He was looking at me, expectantly, his right eyebrow raised.

"I don't know, I just forgot where it was."

"Didn't you look?"

"Sure. I looked in the basement."

"Where else did you look?"

"Nowhere," I lied. I wondered how I could bring up the subject of the paintings. He obviously wasn't going to volunteer the information. I would've never known of their existence if I didn't happen upon them like I did.

"Hmmmmm....You aren't a persistent one, are you?" He looked skeptical. However, just at that moment, the waitress approached with our food. I had the chile relleno, he had the shrimp fajitas.

That night, Ryan undressed me, kissing the back of my neck. "I think I'm ready," was all he said. My heart skipped a beat. We hadn't made love since that one night in the hotel room, when he freaked out. I was nervous about trying again. I turned around, and he kissed me passionately, yet slowly. His shirt was off already, and I was in a t-shirt and underwear, no pants. I was ready for bed.

His body was beautiful. He had lost a few pounds in California, as his therapy took away his appetite. However, he had since gained them back, and he looked buffer than ever. I rubbed my hands up and down his arms, as he kissed my neck and my breasts. He picked me up and put me on the sink vanity, pulling down my panties. He then pulled off his pants, revealing his massive erection. I gasped. I hadn't seen it in all its glory for awhile, and looking at it always made me hyperventilate a little, like the first time I felt it through his pants.

He was kissing me hungrily, fingering me, getting me wetter and wetter. The sink was the right height for him, as his erection was level with it. I spread my legs open, and he plunged all ten inches into me, thrusting deep, kissing me the entire time. His hands were in my hair, messing it up and pulling it at the same time. My nails were digging into his beautiful, sculpted back, clawing deep into him. Then my hands were on his butt, as I fingered his sphincter slowly. He groaned, biting my breast hungrily. Then he shuddered, his head now on my shoulders. He was breathing heavily.

"I'm sorry. It's been so long. That was, uh, a little quick."

I didn't care. I had an orgasm, as usual.

Then he grinned. "Let me make it up to you." At that he carried me into the bedroom, and laid a blanket next to the fireplace. We were still naked, and he looked at me longingly, his hands gently stroking my hair. "Such beautiful hair," he said, before kissing me, more slowly than before. He stroked my breasts, and fingered me slowly. He was hard again, but didn't thrust into me right away. "This will last longer, I promise." I could hear him breathing in my ear. His heart was pounding louder than I have ever heard it. "Goddamn, I missed you."

"I've always been here," I said, innocently.

"You know what I mean," he said, as he kissed me passionately again. He kissed my stomach, then my inner thighs, then lightly started tonguing my vagina. I groaned. He was really very good at this part, the oral part, unlike most men I'd known. His tongue was gentle, yet firm, and he took his time, patiently darting his tongue in and out, and up and down. I gasped, and moaned, coming to orgasm again. Then he slowly, slowly thrust his manhood inside of me, filling me up. He gently slid in and out, while kissing me slowly and deeply.

We made like that for the better part of an hour, with me orgasming several times. After it was over, we lay on the floor, wrapped around each other. Ryan looked at me, brushing some of my hair off of my face. He stroked my face lovingly. "Thanks for being patient with me. It looks like things are going to be better now."

That was an understatement. I knew Ryan had continued his therapy with Dr. Halder and he had confided that most of what he was talking about to him was about Rochelle. It was because those memories were new to him. He was slowly getting over what she'd done. I knew he was feeling confident that making love wouldn't trigger him anymore, but I still had my doubts that it wouldn't happen again.

"Sweetheart, I have no trouble having patience with you," I said, as I took a deep breath, and looked into his eyes. "I love you."

His eyes widened, and then I saw that he started to tear up a little. It was my first time telling him this, at least while he was conscious. He smiled broadly. "I love you, too."

At that, we got up off the blanket and got into bed. He wrapped himself around me, and both of us fell asleep.

There was nothing more to say.

Chapter Twenty-Eight

Christmas was only weeks away, and Ryan and I were talking about getting a tree. Actually, two trees.

I explained to him "I grew up with a silver tree. Yes, it was ghetto, but some of my fondest memories surround that tree. And there was a little disk under the tree that made the tree glow different colors. Like a color wheel."

"So, you want a silver tree."

"Yes."

"Ok, but I've always gotten a live tree. I want that this year, too."

I must've looked crestfallen, because he quickly added "but, of course, we'll have a silver tree for you as well. With the color wheel."

I smiled broadly. "Oh, thank you, thank you, thank you!"

He laughed. "Anything for my beautiful girl."

That was how we got two trees. Ryan's tree was magnificent. We chose a fifteen foot spruce, because Ryan's ceilings were a good twenty feet high. I thought about my sad little apartment and how this tree would have been too tall to fit in there.

My tree was bought on Amazon, and it was about six feet tall. We assembled the silver branches on the pole, and it filled out pretty well. I loved my little tree, and I loved the way the color wheel made it glow different colors at night.

Then I got an idea. I knew that the Christmas ornaments were in the attic. I saw them when I was up there the last time. He, however, was not aware that I'd been in the attic. I decided to test him a little.

"Ryan, I'm going into the attic. I assume that's where the Christmas ornaments are?"

"Yeah. Let me get them. You might fall."

"I won't fall."

He gave me a look. "Bitch, please." Then he smiled.

I frowned. He made a good point. I was pretty clumsy.

At that, he brought down the ladder and climbed into the attic. I tried to climb in the attic with him.

"Come on, Iris, I told you to stay out of here."

He called me by my name. That pretty much meant he was serious. I pouted a little. However, his reaction told me he didn't want me in the attic, probably because he didn't want to explain those paintings.

My curiosity about them was killing me.

He brought down a large box, full of ornaments. Then he went back up, and brought back another box, filled with figurines. "This is my little town," he explained.

We spent the evening dressing the trees and assembling the little town beneath Ryan's tree. The town was pretty elaborate – there were multiple buildings, and multiple little people – the women were dressed in bustles and old-fashioned high boots, the men were in top hats and tails. There was a railroad and train that ran on the outside of the town. There were children as well, and little dogs. Also, a horse-drawn sleigh with people inside. There were also multiple churches with little steeples. There was a little newspaper boy, and we put him right in the middle of the town.

"This town is really cute," I said.

"Yeah. I've had it since I was really little. Before my mom left. It was always a tradition for us to put this town up." Then he looked sad. "After she left, the town never went up in Benjamin's house again. But I took it with me when I left home and I started putting the town up again when I stayed with Nick's family. I've been putting it up every year since then."

I stroked his hair. Sometimes he looked like a little boy and now was one of those times. "It's important to keep traditions up."

"Yes. Now, you and I have to make a new tradition to go with the old ones. I have my little town, you have your silver tree. We have to make something together, all our own."

My heart soared. I knew he was serious about me, but I always loved to hear the words which told me he pictured me as a permanent part of his life. If he wanted to create a new tradition, it meant he felt I was here to stay.

We decided our tradition would be to go ice-skating at the Crown Center on December 23rd of each year. Even if it fell in the middle of the week, which it didn't this year. And, on Christmas Day, we decided to make a tradition of going to the casino. Yes, it was unusual, but both of us agreed that Christmas Day was often a let-down, and gambling at the casino was something both of us loved to do. Christmas Eve would always be spent with my family, we decided.

That last decision, however, sparked a disagreement.

"Ryan, I know why you don't want to spend Christmas Eve with your father. But what about your mother?"

He deftly handled it, though. "Listen, you love your family. I love your family. I'll see my mother some other time. I want to spend Christmas with you and your family. I hope they'll officially be my family someday soon."

It was getting peculiar. I had yet to meet Maggie Gallagher, even though Ryan said she lived in town. I wondered if there was a story there as well. I shook my head. How many awful stories can one man have? No, there must be a logical explanation as to why the mother, whom he loved so much, had never met me.

But what?

Chapter Twenty-Nine

On the 23rd, just like we said, we headed down to the Crown Center and joined the throngs of people skating around the rink. The mayor's Christmas Tree, the enormous 100 foot tree with elaborate decorations, glowed in the background.

I was just learning to skate. Ryan, of course, was a pro. There wasn't anything that he couldn't do well, I decided. However, he was very patient with me, showing me how to stroke and glide. At first, I clung to him, when I wasn't clinging onto the wall. However, after a few hours, I was getting my bearings, and we skated, hand in hand, for the rest of the evening until the rink was almost closed. I had to admit, it was one of the most fun evenings I'd ever had. The night air was crisp and cold, and the rink was brightly lit. There were probably hundreds of people on the rink at any given time.

Yet, I felt that there was only he and I there on the rink.

I half expected some other ghost from Christmas past to pop up and say "boo" to Ryan. But, fortunately, that didn't happen. He did, however, see some friends and colleagues. He brought me over to meet one of them.

"This is Nate. He is an old buddy of mine from Harvard." Nate was tall, like Ryan, with black curly hair and blue eyes. He was meltingly handsome.

I took a deep breath, and held out my hand. He hugged me. "Ryan's told me so much about you. I'm so glad to finally meet you."

Ryan was grinning. Looking at me, he said "we e-mail a lot."

"I see." I was at a loss for words. It took me awhile to get comfortable with Ryan, because I felt so inferior to him. Now I was facing another gorgeous Harvard man. I felt that he was sizing me up, and finding me lacking.

However, if he did find me lacking, he didn't show it.

"Ryan tells me that you are an attorney."

"Guilty as charged."

He laughed. "Do you like it?"

"It has its moments." Which was true. Unfortunately, those moments were few and far between. "What do you do?"

"I'm an international man of mystery."

Ryan motioned to him with his thumb, mouthing the words "trust fund baby."

I looked at him. *You should talk.*

Nate said "No, seriously, I'm an investment banker at Goldman Sachs. I'm in town for the holidays. Imagine my surprise to run into this clown."

To which Ryan said "ha, ha."

Just then, a woman skated up to Nate. She had dark hair, hazel eyes, a perfect face and body. Large breasts, long, thin legs. No makeup, and didn't need any.

"Iris, this is my wife, Natalie. Natalie, this is Iris."

She looked at me, her eyes getting wide. "The Iris? Ryan has told us so much about you!"

She seemed sweet. I just stupidly said "Nate and Natalie. That's cute." That was all I managed.

I wanted to get out of there, pronto. I was once again reminded of how I would never, ever fit into his world.

Ryan explained "Natalie went to Harvard with us, too. Nate and Natalie got married right out of college, and they're still like newlyweds."

Natalie grabbed my hand. "Come over here with me, and let's let the boys talk and catch up. They haven't seen each other in years."

Holding her hand, we skated over to the concession stand. "Can I buy you something to drink?" Natalie asked.

"Oh, you don't have to do that. I have my own money."

"Please, I insist. What would you like?"

What was it with these people never letting me pay for anything? I figured that I had the word "broke" stamped on my forehead.

"Uh, I, uh."

She turned to the concession boy. "Two hot cocoas, please."

This was actually a good choice. I love hot cocoa.

"Uh, thanks for the hot cocoa."

"Not a prob."

We sat down at one of the very few free tables, and sipped our cocoa.

"So, uh, what did you hear about me?" I asked her.

"Only good things. You really have that boy whipped like I've never known him."

"I do?"

"Yeah, you do." She sighed. "I always had a mad crush on him, but he was always with Alexis. Well, not always. I mean, they were on and off all the time. But he was always crazy about her, even when they were off."

"Alexis is still around."

"Yeah, but she cheated. That's one thing Ryan will never forgive." She looked at me. "Got that? From what I hear, Ryan is wrapped around your little finger. Don't tell him I told you that, though. But you cheat, even one time…" She took her finger and sliced it across her neck. "Anyhow, I loved Ryan all through college. But I ended up marrying one of his best friends."

"Nate is very handsome."

"Yes, he is. And nice, too. But there was always something about Ryan. I mean, he's jaw-droppingly beautiful, of course. But there is such a, a, um…vulnerability, I guess, is the right word. It's like he has no idea how gorgeous he is, and how much people are drawn to him. He's very humble, you know."

I figured that she didn't know where Ryan's vulnerability stemmed from. I wasn't about to tell her, either.

"Nate isn't vulnerable?"

"Nah, he's a banker with Goldman Sachs. You pretty much have to be a ball-breaker all the time to do that job well."

"And, what do you do?"

She laughed. "I'm also a banker at Goldman Sachs."

I laughed along with her. *So, you're telling me that you are a ball-breaker as well?*

I asked "So, how do you like Kansas City?"

"Love it. We come here every year, because Nate has family in town. It is refreshing to be in a smaller city like this. People are friendlier here, and this town has really come a long way with the new additions to downtown and all." She smiled, her teeth perfect.

I started to realize that I was relaxing around her. Maybe I was getting used to wealthy, beautiful people. Nah, it was just that the particular wealthy, beautiful people that I was coming to know were also very relatable and down-to-earth. Natalie seemed to be a real sweetheart.

"Do you guys have any kids?" I asked.

"Heavens, no. We don't have time to make the kids, if you know what I mean, so we really wouldn't have time to care for them."

I had to smile at that one. I just met this woman, and she was already confiding in me about her non-existent sex life.

"How do you like New York?"

"It's hectic, busy, always on the go. You can get anything at anytime, unlike here. We're lucky, because we can afford a nice apartment on the Upper West Side. When we first moved there, though, we pretty much lived in a sardine can."

"Oh. I guess Ryan was joking about the trust fund baby thing?"

"No, Nate is a trust fund baby. But he wanted to see if he could make it on his own. Ryan is trust fund baby, too, you know."

I figured as much. He did have a very good job, but I didn't imagine that his job would allow him to buy wineries and private planes. I remembered what Alexis had told me, too, about how Ryan's father bought his silence.

I wondered what the price was for that.

As if on cue, Natalie inadvertently answered that question for me, saying "I always wondered why Ryan didn't keep up with his art. He would never be a starving artist. I mean, he has a $100 million trust fund. He could just be an artist his whole life, and never worry about paying the bills. Instead he's a bank president. Go figure."

What? $100 million dollars. What?????

I perked up about something else. "Uh, Ryan is an artist?"

"An amazing artist. I mean, absolutely amazing." She narrowed her eyes. "He never showed you his work?"

I thought about the paintings in the attic. *Well, he has never showed me his work, but I have seen his work.* "No."

"Hmmmm, I wonder why." She shrugged. "Well, maybe he's embarrassed. And, uh, in college he might've been a better artist than he is now. Drugs can make you pretty creative." Then she looked horrified. "Oh, shit, I…" she began, opening her mouth wide, and putting her hand over her mouth. Her eyes got enormous, and she looked genuinely mortified. I saw her visibly shake a little.

"Don't worry, I know about the drugs."

"Oh, thank god. Oops!" She visibly let a breath out, drooping her head.

I nodded my head. "Well, uh, please don't tell Nate or Ryan this. But I came across some of his artwork, I think, in the attic."

Natalie had regained her composure. "Typical. Ryan's very modest. I guess he's hiding this part of himself from you. Don't worry, he'll come clean about it."

"What's Cork?"

"Cork is Ryan's boyhood home. Named after the County of Cork in Ireland. That's where the Gallaghers originated. Guess that Benjamin was crazy about his wife at one time, huh?"

My eyes got wide about that. I remembered seeing the painting of that magnificent palace on the lake. I didn't think that Kansas City had such splendor.

She looked at me. "Why do you ask?"

"Well, I saw some paintings of this palace, and the back of the painting said 'Cork, 1994.'"

"That would be the year that Ryan left that hell hole."

Oh, so she does know something.

I got an idea. "And what about Maggie? Ryan talks about her, but I've never met her."

She made a face. "Oh, uh, I don't know about that." She looked around, nervously. Then, she leaned into me a bit, like she was going to confide in me about something.

At which time, the boys appeared at our table.

Drats, foiled again!

"Hey, you two!" Ryan said. "What's going on?"

"Just a little girl talk, you know." Natalie looked at Ryan, and smiled at me. She got up, and whispered loudly, "charming girl. I can see why you're crazy about her."

I felt a little dumbfounded. First Alexis, now Natalie. How was I charming these beautiful women?

He smiled back at Natalie. "Yes, she is. She certainly is."

He grabbed my hand. "Come on, love. Nate and I would like to treat you and Nat to some well-deserved chow."

We headed over to Ryan's Escalade, and the four of us piled in. The boys were up front, and Natalie and I were in the back. Natalie grabbed my hand and held it the whole way. *She certainly is touchy-feely.*

Not that I minded.

Ryan said "Let's go and see what's happening at the Power and Light, and I can drive you back to your car after dinner."

We ended up at a crowded restaurant in the Power and Light District. This was the District to which Natalie referred when she talked about the improvements in the city over the years. Downtown used to be a desolate, lonely place. That is, until the Power and Light District came into town, along with the downtown arena and the gorgeous performing arts center, just down the way.

The line at this particular restaurant was an hour and a half, so we decided to get some drinks at the bar while we waited to be seated.

Nate brought two scotches, for himself and Ryan, a dirty martini for me, and a Pinã Colada for Natalie.

"Natalie likes the frou frou," Nate teased.

"Yeah, yeah, what of it?" Natalie teased back.

Nate came around and put his arm around me. "So, I finally get a chance to talk to you. How're you doing?"

"Great."

"Yeah. Ryan is doing great, too. You've made him one happy guy."

"He, uh, wasn't happy before?"

"Oh, hell no. He pretty much went off the deep end after Alexis and Paul. And Mia, of course." He looked sad, pensively looking at his scotch. Then he looked up. "But you seemed to have brought him back to life."

I nodded.

"You seem like a solid sort. I think that Ryan made a pretty good choice, from what I hear."

"I hope so."

"You don't sound so sure."

I felt embarrassed. *Would I ever stop being insecure?*

Nate cleared his throat. "Listen, I, uh, think that you feel like maybe you don't deserve a guy like Ryan."

He could tell that just by talking to me for five minutes? I must be completely transparent.

I didn't say anything.

He went on. "Well, whatever you're thinking, stop

thinking it. Personally, don't tell him I told you this, but I wouldn't be surprised if Santa brings you something extra special. Like, you know, an engagement ring."

My eyes popped out. "Why do you say that?"

"Oh, I don't know. I guess it's because I've never in my life seen him this way. Ever. Not even with Alexis."

"Well, you, uh, just saw him this evening. You haven't really been around him recently."

"Sure, but, you know, we e-mail all the time. Ryan tells me everything. I was his second-best friend in college, besides Nick." He looked around. "Again, don't tell him I told you. It's just a hunch, anyhow." He nodded his head meaningfully.

"Oh, I won't say anything, but, uh, Ryan would pop the question without my meeting his mother?"

He made a face and frowned. "Oh, right. His mother. Well, I'm sure that you will meet her soon enough."

I started to think that the mother was like the crazy lady in the attic in *Jane Eyre*. But, I saw Ryan looking at us while he talked to Natalie, so I decided not to press it.

"So, how did you meet Ryan in college?"

"We lived in the same building, so we started running around together, and Nick usually was around as well. Ryan is a great guy, just a really solid guy. You're a lucky girl."

I smiled inwardly, wondering if Nate and Ryan were like Nick and Ryan. *Stop thinking that.*

"I haven't met Nick."

"Well, I'm quite sure that you will, sooner or later. Nick will no doubt be Ryan's best man again." Then he looked at me. "I guess you're ok with their relationship, huh?"

I felt embarrassed. "Yes, yes, of course." I don't know why, but I assumed that Nate didn't know about that. Then again, maybe it was always an open secret.

"That's good. None of his friends ever really cared about that. Yeah, so they're two dudes who are into each other. Big whoop." Then he smiled. "But let me tell ya, the ladies all wanted to get involved when they found out about them. Two hot guys like that – I'd imagine that would be a fulfillment of every girl's fantasy."

"Did they fulfill many fantasies?"

"No, just Alexis's."

I changed the subject. "Why do you think he wants to be married to me? We haven't known each other that long, Ryan and me. I don't think that he's ready to get married just yet."

Nate took a swig of his scotch. "You're living with him?"

"Yes."

"And how long did it take for him to ask you to live with him?"

"Well, a few months, but-"

"But, nothing. That boy wanted you to move in the first weekend you guys met. He saw an opening when you got booted from your apartment and pounced on it."

I was still having a hard time coming to grips with all of this. "But why?"

"Love at first sight. It happens, you know."

"Like Tony and Maria?"

"Like Oliver and Jenny. At any rate, I see wedding bells in your near future."

I felt excited and nervous at the prospect. I was 33 years old, and have never been close to getting married to anybody. Now, somehow, I was close to marrying this sweet Adonis.

Go figure.

"Yeah, and Ryan tells me that you are still referring to your guys' house as 'his house?'"

"Well, yeah, it is his house."

Nate shook his head. "No, it's both of yours house."

"No, actually, it is his house. I just live there."

He looked at me quizzically. "Now, I wonder why he didn't tell you...."

"Tell me what?" These people were ratting out Ryan right and left.

"That he had your name put on the house deed. Don't worry, he owns it free and clear, so you're not on the hook for any mortgage or anything."

Shit. I was now half owner of a multi-million dollar house? I thought about my student loans, which were astronomical. And the IRS, which already had a lien on my bank account, and probably now has a lien on Ryan's home.

Why didn't he ask me first?

I just looked dumbfounded. Nate continued on. "Well, maybe that was supposed to be part of your Christmas present. So, don't tell him that you know."

I started to open my mouth to tell Nate about the student loans, but Ryan came over and put his arm around Nate. "Whatchyou guys talking about over here?"

"Nothing, bro. Just chit-chatting. What are you and Nat talking about? The usual, about how much she is in love with you?" Nate was only half-teasing. He no doubt knew that he was second choice.

I wondered if that bothered him.

"Nah, Nat is like a sister to me, you know that."

"Some sister. Unless you habitually bang your sisters, I don't think that analogy is quite appropriate."

I made a face. Ryan looked sheepish. "It was when Alexis and I were broken up. One of the many times," he said to me. He turned to Nate. "Why do you have to keep bringing that up?"

"Just busting your chops. Just busting your chops." Nate chuckled. "Ancient history."

Somehow I had the feeling that it wasn't ancient history, at least not in Nate's mind, but I didn't say anything. I suddenly felt that I was being pulled into a vortex of dysfunction, once again.

Natalie came up to me, and put her arm around me. She played with my hair a little. "You're such a cutie," she said. I think she was getting a little buzzed, even though she just had one Pinã Colada. That I knew of.

I smiled. She was the hottest woman in the place by a mile. *Stop feeling inferior and take the goddamned compliment.* "Thanks."

Finally, our buzzer was going off. We all got seated, and opened our menus.

Nate looked at Ryan. "So, when are you going to move to New York, buddy? That's where it's at. I can get you a job at Goldman, no problem."

Ryan looked at me. "Uh, I am staying here, in town. Iris' family is here, so...."

"Oh, right. Okay, then. Well, you can always visit, which you haven't done."

"I know, I know. We'd love to come out sometime. Right, Iris?"

"Sure. I've never been to New York."

"Never been? Ever? How's that possible?" Nate asked.

"Well, I had a chance to, in college. My sister won an all-expense trip to New York by entering a trivia contest. I couldn't go, though, so she took my gay friend Richard." I sighed. "Actually, I should've gone. The only reason why I didn't was because my loser boyfriend at the time didn't want me to go. I just figured that I would always have the chance. I didn't know, of course, that I would never in my lifetime get to see the twin towers. I guess it just goes to show that you take your opportunities when they come up, because they may never come again."

We all were quiet for a bit, and then Nate decided to lighten the mood again. "This is getting depressing. Let's talk about something lighter. Like Ryan's charity. I guess he hasn't told you much about his charitable contributions, has he?"

I looked at Ryan, who looked embarrassed and was shooting Nate a look at the same time. "Well, no. I mean, I know that he is on the board of the Humane Society and the Rose Brooks House."

"Ah, well, Ryan has given $10 million to the Humane Society in the past ten years." Nate looked triumphant to have given away yet another secret.

My heart soared. That was a cause which was so close to my heart, and the American Society for the Prevention of Cruelty to Animals (ASPCA). And my Ryan gave $10 million to them? I squeezed his hand, and he looked at me, red in the face.

He raised his eyebrow at Nate. "This may the first and last dinner we all have together, buddy." He wasn't smiling.

"Hey, lighten up. You have more charity in you than I ever will. And those animals do need protection."

Then Ryan smiled, the tension having passed. He looked at me expectantly, and I beamed back. I couldn't have been prouder to be with him. He smiled back at me, putting his arm around me and playfully tousled my hair. I looked at Natalie, who was staring at us sadly. I smiled at her, because I knew what she was thinking – *I wish that was me.*

"I love that about you, Ryan, that you gave all that money to those animals." Then I looked at Nate. "Animal issues are very important to me, as well. I volunteer my time for a pit bull rescue group, although I'm ashamed to say that I haven't been as active with that group lately as I should be. I really need to get back to it. It's a very rewarding endeavor. There's nothing like saving the life of an animal, and they show nothing but gratitude."

I found myself having fun with these people, even though there was an undercurrent of tension between Nate and Ryan. Understandable, because Ryan apparently had a fling with Nate's now-wife, and the now-wife still carried a torch for Ryan. A torch which was obvious for everybody to see. But Nate seemed to be handling things reasonably well, and it was clear that he still admired Ryan a great deal.

After a little while, the three of them started talking about their Harvard days, and, of course, I couldn't contribute much to the conversation.

Nate would say "Remember that time we went to the Hamptons and-"

Then Ryan would say "the bongo drums!" Then they would giggle like school boys.

Or "remember that time that we kidnapped the other team's mascot horse?"

Or "remember the time that we rearranged the letters in that hallway to make dirty words?"

"What about old man Winthrop's class? God, he was like that guy on *The Paper Chase*."

"Don't insult the guy on *The Paper Chase*."

They were laughing like school kids the whole way.

Nat said, laughing so hard there were tears coming out her eyes "Oh, good times. Good times."

I sat quietly, while the other three got fairly drunk and silly.

Finally, the evening came to an end. Ryan paid the bill,

with Nate draped around him. Nate was talking rather loudly. "Listen, buddy, I want to be at the wedding. Why don't you have it in New York? It can be a destination wedding."

To this, Ryan said "New York would not be a destination wedding. Jamaica would be a destination wedding. Geneva would be a destination wedding. New York? Not so much."

"Splitting hairs," Nate slurred. Then "When are you going to ask her?"

"I don't know yet. Shhhh, she is right over there."

"You only live once, buddy. Only once. And I hope that your Iris will always love only you, and not you and some other guy."

"Shhhh. Man, you're wasted."

I looked over at Nat, who also overheard the boys talking. She looked embarrassed. She looked at me and shrugged. "What can I say? My feelings for Ryan have always been a bone of contention between myself and Nate."

At that, she walked up to Nate, and took his arm. "Come on. Hey, Ryan, are you ok to drive?"

I walked up to the group. "I haven't been drinking. I can drive."

Ryan looked at me gratefully. "Thanks, sweetie. I'm so sorry, I was driving, I should have been more responsible with my drinking."

"Not a problem." I was going to drive the Escalade. I haven't driven it before, but it shouldn't be a problem. It was just that I was used to driving jalopies, with the exception of the beautiful Volvo that I drove around Los Angeles. *Too bad we didn't take the Porsche. That would have been amazing.*

We dropped them off at their hotel, instead of their car.

Nate protested this turn of events, but Ryan assured him that he would be able to get to his car in the morning. Daniel would pick Nate up at 8 AM to take him to his car.

"Thanks, Ryan, you're the best. Would you guys like to come up for a nightcap. A kind of after-party?"

"No, thanks," said Ryan. "We're pretty tired. But let's get together before you leave town, ok?"

"Sure, sure." He kissed me on the cheek, and Natalie came up and gave me a hug and a peck on the cheek as well.

"Take care of him," Nat said. "You have a great guy, there. Don't fuck him over. If you do, I'll haunt you." She wasn't joking.

I smiled. "Don't worry, he's in good hands."

On the way home, Ryan tousled my hair. He was still pretty drunk, and I could smell the scotch on his breath.

"Thanks for being so cordial with my friends. They loved you."

"They're very nice people."

"Nate used to hate me, you know. Because of Nat. I mean, when Nat and I had our thing, she wasn't dating him, but it turned out that he always loved her from afar. I didn't know that, though, otherwise I wouldn't have gone there." He sighed. "Whatta mess that was for awhile. It all got sorted out when Alexis and I got back together, but there was a lot of bad blood between all of us for awhile." He laughed. "As sands through the hourglass...."

I laughed, too, at the reference. My mother always used to watch *Days of Our Lives*. Come to think of it, the whole Nate-Nat-Ryan-Alexis quadrangle could be a story on a soap opera. Or Jerry Springer.

"Did you date a lot of other girls while you were on hiatus from Alexis?"

"Oh, yeah. Of course. For some odd reason, getting women was always like shooting fish in a barrel."

Yeah. For some unknown reason. Wonder what that is?

"But none have been as pretty as you. Honest."

I raised both my eyebrows at that one. I've now seen two of his exes, and either one of them would look right on a billboard in Times Square. I kept quiet, though.

"Why do you ask? I mean, I know that you, uh, have been around," Ryan asked.

"You might say that." I had actually stopped counting the number of men that I had slept with, so I hoped that he didn't ask. However, one thing I can say is that I have never, ever cheated on a boyfriend.

"I hope that you and I have a wonderful Christmas together."

"I hope so, too."

Chapter Thirty

We spent Christmas Eve with my family, just like we planned. I spent the better part of the morning, however, trying to convince him that we needed to see Maggie on Christmas Day, instead of the casino thing.

"But we love the casino. That's always a happy place to be," Ryan said.

"Yes, but your mother probably wants to see you. That's a better tradition to keep, don'tcha think?

His eyes darkened a little. He took a deep breath and let it out.

"It's more complicated." He looked at me. He gestured to a chair. "Sit down." I obediently took a seat. Taking a deep breath, Ryan continued. "Oh, boy. Well, if we're going to get married, I might as well lay out the last skeleton."

Again, he brought up marriage. Of course, I'd heard it all before, so I wasn't getting too excited about it. If he produced a ring and we actually walked down the aisle, I would believe it. Otherwise, he was all talk, as far as I was concerned.

"My mother is a lovely lady. But she isn't well. She was diagnosed with schizophrenia when I was 8 years old. That was part of the reason why she and Benjamin divorced. Well, that and the fact he's a bastard, but that really is besides the point."

He waited for my reaction. I just listened intently, holding his hand and rubbing his arm. He continued. "Anyhow, she takes meds and she's pretty good these days. But she was off her meds about ten years ago. The voices in her head told her that a bartender at a bar she frequented was the Anti-Christ. So she waited in the alley for him after hours and stabbed him."

I tried to conceal my horror. A pervert father and a mother in prison? What more can this poor guy endure?

"The bartender didn't die. In fact, it was kind of a superficial wound. Turns out my mother doesn't have that good of an aim." He smiled wryly. "She plunged the knife into his chest, above his heart, so it tore his pectoral muscle. He ended up in the hospital. She was found not guilty by reason of insanity, so she's been locked up in the state hospital ever since the date of her verdict."

I nodded slowly. He went on. "The good news is, she can get out at any time if she is well. The judge said her minimum time in the hospital would be the same amount of time she'd get if she went to prison. In her case, she was charged with first degree assault, so the judge calculated that she'd have served 10 years in prison for that. Not sure how he came up with that, but that was the sentence he gave her. My mother has been in that place for 10 years and she's better. She's lucid and has stayed on her meds. I have a lawyer working on her case and the lawyer has told me she'll probably be out early next year."

He looked pensive. "But, for now, she's in the hospital.

Now that you know, I'd love to take you to see her. I just didn't think you wanted to spend Christmas in that place."

I felt so overwhelmingly sad for him. Yet, even with all that going on in his life, he wasn't bitter. He was the opposite. I took his hand and stroked it lovingly.

"So, there you have it. You now know everything. All the bad, the worse and the ugly," he said.

"Shhh. There's a lot of good, there, too."

He took a deep breath. "So you're staying with me?"

"Of course. Why would there be any question about that?"

He smiled. Then he said "What time do we have to be at your parent's for Christmas Eve?"

"Not until 4 PM."

"And it's now 11 AM. What would you like to do until then?"

"I wonder."

We made love for the next four hours.

Chapter Thirty-One

When we arrived at my parents, the duplex was tidy, or at least tidy for them. Which meant it was picked up but still smelled like dog pee. My mother was in her little kitchen, bringing out the Christmas ham. My father was in the living room, watching some DVD.

Ryan immediately went into the kitchen to help. I sat down next to my dad to find out what he was watching. It was a James Bond movie. Typical. I wanted a traditional Christmas Eve, with carols and Christmas music, and my father was watching James Bond.

However, I was cheered up when my dad said they would be showing *The Nutcracker,* with Mikhail Baryshnikov, on PBS, and he'd also be turning on the Boston Pops. This felt more traditional to me. I remembered coming home from my aunt's house in Christmases past and watching this very version of *The Nutcracker* with my dad. Baryshnikov was the most amazing dancer I'd ever seen.

"Where's Sue?" I inquired about my sister.

"Up in her room, you know how she is."

"Well, tell her to come down. I want to spend Christmas Eve with her."

At that, my mother called her on the phone. I rolled my eyes. My family certainly did put the "fun" in "dysfunctional."

Ryan smiled at it all.

Dinner was great. Ryan once again had special gifts for everybody, much more elaborate this time. For my sister, he bought her a digital camera with a long-range lens. He remembered her talking about how much she loved photography. For my mother, it was a beautiful necklace in her birthstone, aquamarine. My father got a season pass to the performing arts series and a Rolex watch. I knew my father didn't mind going to see these shows alone, so it wasn't a problem that he was the only one who received the season tickets. I also knew he was thrilled about receiving them. I could tell the watch, however, made him less than thrilled. I wondered why Ryan would buy my dad a Rolex. My father was definitely not a Rolex kind of guy. Still, he feigned enthusiasm at the watch and thanked Ryan politely.

My family was extremely gracious, thanking him over and over, and telling him how much they loved the gifts. However, I immediately felt bad for them. They couldn't afford to get Ryan much, but they did present him with a nice pair of pants, that I helped to pick out, and a dress shirt. I took my mother shopping at Kohl's to buy this stuff. My sister gave him a $50 gift card to Nieman Marcus.

I hoped they weren't too embarrassed.

I sighed. I should've stopped Ryan and told him not to spend that much money on everybody. Then a thought panicked me. I, myself, had merely bought Ryan a grind and brew coffee maker. It was the one thing he didn't have.

It was a nice one, and, at $200, it was really beyond my budget. But that was all I could afford.

After dinner, Ryan joined my father in watching the rest of the James Bond movie, and I talked to my mother.

"He shouldn't have bought all those things," she said. "I'm so embarrassed."

"I know. He's rich. He doesn't think. He figures he has the money so he might as well use it."

"My necklace is beautiful, though. I see he bought it at Tiffany's."

My own gift to her was a new Barbie doll to add to her collection. She started collecting them several years back when I gifted her a Grecian Barbie, and, ever since then, I gave her one every year for her birthday and for Christmas. My gift to my father was a book he had his eye on and some new coffees for his Keurig. My sister's gift was a faux pearl necklace I bought at JC Penneys for 70% off.

Their gift to me was $100, which would go towards a new iPad. That was what I asked for and they all three chipped in on it.

The Boston Pops was coming on and we all sat down to watch it and talk amongst ourselves. Ryan seemed really into it. I wasn't aware that he knew much about classical music, but I heard him talking with my dad about the different composers and pieces he heard, so I guessed I was wrong.

We stayed until midnight, drinking eggnog and eating popcorn from a tin. I wanted to stay the night, because I was tired, but there really wasn't a place to sleep, except in the tiny spare bedroom on the double bed. So we headed home.

I found out later that Ryan also left $1,600 in an envelope with my mother's name on it. He overheard me talking to her one day and I was talking about how getting her teeth fixed would cost $1,600 she didn't have. My mother was grateful but overwhelmed. I had mixed emotions about that, too, but I was glad she could get her teeth fixed and not have to worry about the bill.

On the way home, I privately fretted about the next day. How would Maggie be? Would she like me? How would the facility be – a snake pit? Ryan said it wasn't a snake pit but I had my doubts. At any rate, I was very nervous, thinking about meeting Maggie the next day. And I was very nervous about what I was going to get from Ryan, especially because all I could afford was a grind and brew.

Chapter Thirty-Two

Christmas Day was here and I was nervous. I had wrapped Ryan's grind and brew very carefully, much more carefully than usual. Usually I slap something together, or just buy a gift bag if I was really lazy, but I figured that wrapping this present with care would be the least I could do.

"Good morning, beautiful. Merry Christmas!" Ryan called to me, as I came down the stairs on Christmas morning.

Ryan had two glasses of champagne at the ready. We clinked the glasses and sat next to the tree.

Ryan began. "I have several things for you. Some small, some not so small, some big. Which would you like first?"

I held my breath. "Small."

At that, he presented a small, perfectly gift-wrapped box. I opened it up, feeling apprehensive. I figured it wasn't an engagement ring, and I was right. It was a platinum and diamond necklace from Tiffany's, with matching platinum and diamond earrings.

They were the most beautiful things I'd ever seen.

I teared up. I'd never seen something like this, let alone think I'd own something like it. Shaking, I asked him to put the necklace on me, as I put on the earrings.

"There. You look beautiful."

"Thank you. I don't know how…"

"I'm not done yet. What would you like next?"

"The next up."

At that, he presented me with a large, gift-wrapped box. I opened it, and there, inside, were the paintings of me! I was astonished and genuinely surprised. I figured he was hiding them away because he didn't want to admit he was an exquisite artist. Now I knew he was just saving them for a gift for me.

"Where did you get these done?"

"I did them."

My eyes were huge. "Oh my God! These are beautiful!" And they were, even more now that they were a gift to me. "I didn't know you could paint like that!"

"I dabble some."

"Dabble! These are gorgeous!"

"I'm glad you like them."

"Like them? I love them!" I grabbed his neck, burying my face in his shoulder. I was sobbing, honestly sobbing.

"Hey, hey, hey. What's wrong?"

"Nothing. It's just that these paintings of me are so gorgeous and so intimate and personal. So artistic. So made with love."

"Well, of course. I love you. I made these paintings when I was away from you, after our fight, but before I went to Beverly Hills. I couldn't stop thinking about you, so I painted you to help me feel better. It didn't really work to help me feel better but it got me back into my art. Before painting these, I hadn't painted in a long, long time. So it really should be me thanking you. You're my muse."

I cocked my head and smiled. I silently hoped there would be no more gifts, but I knew there were.

"Why don't you paint more often?"

"I have to be inspired. But you make a good point. I used to love to paint and draw with charcoal. I was pretty prolific in college during my drug days. That work was pretty dark, though. I even had a showing at an art gallery and everything sold." He looked pensive. "I was never more proud of myself."

"Why don't you do it full time?"

"I can't just turn it on and off. I wish I could. I was driven to art when I was in college because I had to have a way to exorcise my demons. So I did a lot of drugs and I painted. Two ways to escape. But I haven't been inspired to art since then, really. Until you."

I thought of something. I ran up to the guest bedroom where I spent the night the first night I was here. I motioned him to follow me, which he did.

I pointed to the magnificent painting above the bed. "This is you, right?"

He blushed. "Yeah, that's me. It's one of my better ones from my early days."

I studied it more carefully than before. It was gorgeous - it was a portrait of a beautiful woman's face that was halfway there. The face was painted in blue, with bright red lipstick. On the other side of the face, the part that wasn't there, there were words displayed. Random words. The background was a bleeding background of bright purple and orange. I was very drawn to the painting, anyhow, now much more since I knew who did it.

I looked at him. He was standing in the doorway, his

hands shoved in his pockets. He was looking at the floor. I took his chin in my hand, and raised his face towards mine. "You are an amazing artist." Then I kissed him passionately.

His face was bright scarlet. "I dabble. I'm not as good as-"

"Shhhh. You're the best artist I've ever known." The irony – there was something he was insecure about. We had more in common than I thought.

We went back downstairs and I held my breath. There was more to come, I knew it. "Ok, now for the next present," Ryan said. "Here, put on this blindfold." He wrapped a handkerchief around my eyes. Then he led me by the hand, opening the door that leads to the garage. My heart was pounding, and I was shaking. *Please don't be what I think it is.* He took off the blindfold, and there was a brand new Volvo, just like the one I drove in Los Angeles. Only this one, somehow, had a six-speed manual transmission. As I gaped at the car in shock, Ryan was explaining "I remembered you always said how much you liked the stick, so I had this car custom-made for the six-speed. I hope you like it. I know you liked the car in Los Angeles."

I couldn't speak. I wondered what had befallen my jalopy Priscilla, the purple RAV-4 with her side door still dented in. My breath caught. I was rooted to the ground, unable to lift my feet even one inch. I felt some kind of trance envelop me. Inside I was screaming "This is too much! You got him a fucking grind and brew!" Then I realized I was crying again, sobbing uncontrollably, with Ryan's arm around me.

"Shhhh, beautiful, this wasn't the reaction I thought I would get."

By now, I was on the floor of the garage, crying and

hyperventilating. There was no way that I could have been prepared for this. Ryan was on the floor next to me, stroking my hair, holding my head tightly to his chest. I was shaking. It was as if all the emotion for the entire seven months that I'd known him was coming out of me. Like maybe I was hanging in with everything previously because I'd been in shock that a guy like Ryan would love me, the bullied, unpopular girl, and I never thought it was real. Like he was a fantasy I'd cooked up in my mind. He couldn't possibly be real. Now, he was real after all, the car was real, everything was real, and I just couldn't handle it.

We sat like this on the garage floor for a good half hour. By then I had calmed down.

"What just happened?"

"I don't know. I was overwhelmed, I guess."

He looked concerned. "Well, then, maybe I should tell you about the rest of the gifts later."

I made a face. "No, no, I'm ok. I love the car. I mean, I really, really love the car."

"Ok, then. Here." He handed me an envelope. I opened it and saw it was a copy of the deed to the house, with my name on it.

I looked at him in absolute shock. "Ryan, this is so wonderful. I mean, I know that you want this to be our house. But I have student loans up the wazoo and the IRS has a lien on all of my property. They both will come after this house."

He smiled nervously. "I know about the student loans, love. And the IRS. And I took care of them."

I narrowed my eyes. *How did he know about the loans, and the IRS, and what did he mean "I took care of them?"*

He went on. "Well, I had your background looked into

before I put your name on this house. I paid off your loans, and the IRS, as gifts to you."

"Oh, hell no. Hell, no. Hell to the fucking no. You didn't incur those debts, so you're not going to pay them." I had to draw a line somewhere.

"Calm down. Listen, I have a lot of money. I had a trust fund after I left Benjamin, and I invested in tech stocks and sold them before the bubble burst. The fund increased fourfold because of this. I want to do this for you, for us. We don't need that stuff hanging over our heads as we start our lives together." He was talking fast. I could tell he was nervous.

I felt defeated. He made sense. If we were going to get married, I'd have my name on the house and the student loans would be lurking in the background, accruing interest at the rate of 8%, which wouldn't help anybody out. Neither would it be beneficial for the IRS to attach a lien. It was better just to pay the fuckers off, instead of letting them get astronomical, to the point that the house would be in jeopardy because of them.

Still, it was a blow to my pride. I wished I could take care of my responsibilities on my own, instead of having the white knight come in and do it for me.

Finally, I just smiled. "Thank you," I whispered. What more could I say?

He smiled back. "You're welcome. Truly. It was my pleasure to do this for you."

"Now, slow down. Tell me about the trust fund."

"Okay. Well, as you know, I left the house when I was fourteen."

"Yes, yes. Go on."

"Benjamin, I guess he felt guilty about what he'd done. He made sure I was taken care of when I went to live with

Nick. So, I was made the beneficiary of a $100 million trust fund."

He took a deep breath. "Anyhow, it was the mid 1990s. Tech stocks were just about to take off, but they hadn't yet. Somehow, Nick's father knew these stocks were going to be hot, so he recommended that I invest as much as I could in them. So, I did. I invested all of it in some high-risk, high-reward tech stocks. And I got lucky."

"Lucky, how?" I was genuinely interested in this.

"Well, I got out right when the bubble was about to burst. At the very height of the market, I sold the stocks. They'd quadrupled in price by then, and they were about to be worth a fraction of that. I don't know, it was dumb luck, I guess."

"So, the bottom line is…"

"Well, my trust fund is now up to around a half-billion."

I nodded my head. I knew Ryan had a very good job, but not a job that would allow him to buy a private plane and a winery. The Cezanne was given to him by Benjamin, and the de Kooning probably was also a gift, so these were explained. It occurred to me that the Cezanne and the de Kooning together were also worth about another hundred million.

"So, you see, I have more money than I know what to do with," Ryan said. "Plus, I feel that it's tainted, blood money. Or at least some of it is. Some of it I consider untainted, because it increased by my own initiative."

He gazed at me, and grabbed my hand. "I want to do things for you, Iris. Things you might not be able to do for yourself just yet. I know you've struggled financially. I don't want you to ever feel that I am condescending to you, or patronizing, or that I pity you, or any of that. That couldn't be further from the truth. But I don't want you to struggle, either. It's a tricky thing, helping you out so that you can get out of your hole, yet knowing you need independence. I'm trying to find that line."

I could feel the tears again. He was saying all the right things. I didn't deserve this. I made my mess, I should straighten it out myself.

Yet, what he was saying made sense as well.

I smiled weakly, shamefully handing him my meager gift. "Here. Merry Christmas." I faked a smile. But I couldn't look him in the eye, I was so ashamed of what I was giving him.

He opened the carefully wrapped gift. "Great wrapping job, by the way," he said, smiling. He looked at the grind and brew. He genuinely looked thrilled about it. "This is such a thoughtful gift! Usually I have to grind my coffee beans at the store, and it doesn't taste as good that way. Now, I can grind them while I brew them." He kissed me, long, slow and deep. Looking into my eyes he said "Thank you for this. I'll get a lot of use from this."

I couldn't tell if he was genuinely thrilled or just trying to make me feel better about the paucity of my gift to him compared to his gifts to me. I hoped the former, feared the latter.

"I bought this at Williams Sonoma. It was one of the higher-end models." I felt that I had to make it known that the grind and brew did not come from Wal-Mart.

"I've been eying this very model at Williams Sonoma for months. It's a perfect gift."

I had a little something else. "Here," I said, presenting him with a pound of his favorite coffee, which was dark chocolate flavored.

"I love this coffee. You've really paid attention." He kissed me again. "I love you Iris. And I love your gifts."

I felt a little relieved, but I still felt I was having an out-of-body experience. I was now the proud owner of a brand new Volvo, half of a multi-million dollar house, gorgeous diamond and platinum jewelry, and, most importantly, portraits of myself. Actually, come to think of it, I owned 100% of the house, as did Ryan, because we were joint tenants with the right of survivorship. That meant the house wasn't severable, and each of us owned the house equally, and each of us owned 100% of the house. It was a popular legal fiction, but it worked.

All at once, I had a lot of property and no debt. All at once, I was wealthy myself. To say it felt weird is an understatement.

And the day was only beginning.

Chapter Thirty-Three

We drove in silence to the state mental institution on our way to see Maggie. I was nervous, not really knowing what to expect. Ryan held my hand tightly.

"Iris, I just want you to be prepared. This place is not going to be like the place in Beverly Hills."

"Of course. It's a state hospital. I don't think the state can afford to run a place like that place."

"Right. Anyhow, it's not quite a snake pit, but it isn't a resort, either. It's somewhere in between."

I kind of knew. I had a client once who had a breakdown. Nice guy, but his ex-wife drove him so out of his mind that he threatened to kill her. He ended up in a 48-hour lockup in a place that was not so great. It wasn't like the mental institutions of the past, where people howled, screamed and convulsed through shock treatment. But people did talk to unseen figures, and, occasionally, there were threats.

Then again, I'd been a public defender for a little while and once had a guy confess to me that he'd killed his drug partner with a phone, explaining that he had to do it because she was turning him into the FBI.

I was prepared for anything.

We arrived at the state institution. We saw the receptionist, who recognized Ryan immediately. Then she looked at me. I hoped I looked suitably somber in my Chanel jacket and black dress underneath. The actual jacket was purple and green checked, with fringes and large buttons. It was an earlier gift from Ryan, "just because" – just because my wardrobe sucked. I used to be like a "before" on an old *What Not To Wear* episode, a popular show on TLC years and years ago where some poor schlub was chosen for a wardrobe makeover because they definitely needed one. Now I was a definite "after."

For his part, Ryan was dressed in a dark blue pinstriped shirt and typical Italian mega-dollar suit with his Ferragamo shoes. As usual, he looked like he walked off the pages of GQ.

The receptionist smiled. We no doubt were the best dressed people that ever walked these halls. "Hi, Ryan. And you must be Iris."

I was somewhat taken aback. *Does everybody in Ryan's life know about me?*

"Yes, I'm Iris."

Ryan said "How is she today?"

"Great, actually. She's still lucid."

"Wonderful. I hope there isn't a relapse."

"She hasn't relapsed in awhile. It seems the drugs she's on are really working wonders."

Ryan nodded. Then he turned to me. "Make sure there are no metals in your pocket or anything. Take off your watch."

I took off my earrings and watch and threw my keys

into a container. Then we walked through a metal detector. The detector went off when I walked through, so I took off my shoes. Sometimes shoes had metal in them. This time, the metal detector didn't go off.

Grabbing my belongings and putting my shoes back on, I joined Ryan in the elevator. We took the elevator up to the 8th floor, and, clutching my hand, Ryan led me to a shared room that had a divider in between. An ancient television was positioned above the two beds. A fortyish woman lay on the bed, her wrists bound with leather straps. I prayed this wasn't Maggie, although I was pretty sure it wasn't, as this woman looked nothing like the woman in Ryan's paintings.

"Hello, Rosey. Where's Mom?" Ryan asked the woman.

She looked through us, not seeing us, yet looked right at us. She didn't speak.

Ryan frowned. "Rosey must not be having a great day. Let's go to the TV room and see what's happening there."

We headed down to the TV room. There was a skinny, red-headed guy with wild hair, shouting at nobody in particular. "Leave me alone!" he shouted, his head shaking wildly. "Mother fucker!" he shrieked, punching the air behind him. Another lady came right up to me. "Roxanne, is that you?" she asked, her hand touching my face. She grabbed my hand. "I'm so happy to see you. I knew you wouldn't forget my birthday." She led me to a chair, and, next to the chair, a fifty-ish, heavy-set man sat in another chair, just staring. "Oh, don't mind Robert," said the Roxanne woman. "He doesn't talk. He hasn't talked in 20 years." At that, Robert looked at us, mutely. Then, his eyes got large and he said "Boo!" Then doubled over laughing.

I took a deep breath. I could feel myself shaking just a little bit. Then I noticed Ryan was no longer by my side. I looked around, and saw him across the room, with a small, dark-haired woman who looked just like a movie star. I could see where he got his green eyes. She looked over at me and smiled a perfect smile. She gestured for me to come over.

But the Roxanne lady, whose name I later learned was Peggy, had a firm grip on my hand. "You can't leave yet, Roxanne. You just got here. It's been so long."

I looked over at the dark-haired lady, obviously Maggie, helplessly. She came over. "Peggy, this isn't Roxanne. Roxanne is no longer with us. Remember?"

At that, Peggy looked at me, then got a very faraway look. "Oh, right, right. I'm sorry." Then she turned away and faced the window, while Robert continued to shriek and laugh and the red-haired man continued to shout "Goddamn, it, I told you to leave me the fuck alone!"

At that, Maggie took my hand and led me back over to where she and Ryan sat. I looked at her close up. She was around 55, couldn't be much older than that. Or at least she didn't look it. In fact, she looked ten years younger than that. Her hair was dark with just a bit of grey. Her face was remarkably smooth, even though she couldn't weigh 110 lbs. I always heard that, when you get older, you have to choose between your ass and your face – either you are thin and wrinkly, or you are plump and get to keep your youthful face. Maggie had a small ass and a smooth face. Genetics were kind to this family. Her teeth were perfect, like Ryan's, and her eyes were the same color of mesmerizing green. She was really a lovely woman.

"I'm so sorry about Peggy," she said. "She lost her daughter about 20 years ago and has been here ever since. The poor woman thinks every red-headed girl who comes in here is Roxanne."

Ryan nodded. "Peggy is a good woman but she's not always med compliant."

"I'm so glad to finally meet you," Maggie said. "Ryan has been here every week and he talks about you all the time."

What could I say? Ryan talked about her, some, mostly in generalities. I didn't think he was exactly ashamed of her, but I didn't know too much about her, either.

"He talks about you too."

She smiled slyly. "Oh, I doubt that. Ryan never knows what to tell people about me."

"I hear you're a great singer."

"Well, yes, I'd hope so. I used to fill houses in Ireland when I was younger. When Ryan was very young."

At that, she started singing. Humming, really. Bach's *Air on a G String*. I loved this piece, and her voice was hypnotic. Ryan smiled and I could see his face relax.

After that song was over, she looked at me and asked me if I had any requests. Before I could answer, however, she launched into a pitch-perfect *Fur Elize* on the piano. A gorgeous Beethoven piece, it was breathtaking to hear such a perfect rendition. This was something, considering the piano was old and, no-doubt, second-hand. Yet Maggie played it like it was a baby-grand. Then she started playing Rachmaninoff's *Theme of Paganini*. Then some Tchaikovsky music from *The Nutcracker*, but also his Second Symphony. Then, out of nowhere, came the Gary Jules version of *Mad World*, with Maggie and Ryan both singing harmony on this. Then *Christmastime is Here* from the Charlie Brown Christmas special. Then *Wrapped Around Your Finger* by the Police. Ryan had a huge smile on his face the entire time.

He moved over to me. "Maggie is in her element." I smiled, but I noticed that nobody was paying us much attention. The woman was giving a concerto, and nobody really cared. I was guessing that everybody was, literally, in their own worlds.

"Oh, I'm so sorry. I've been indulgent. I guess I wanted to show off for Ryan's special lady." She smiled knowingly. Ryan was blushing. "Now, you were saying – what would you like to hear?"

"Well, it's Christmas. My favorite Christmas standard is *O Holy Night.*"

At that, Maggie launched into an elaborate version of this familiar tune. Ryan and I joined her in singing. After that, we sang one Christmas song after another – including John Lennon's *War is Over.*

I was treated to this special performance for a few hours and I was in heaven. I loved every tune she played. However, at some point, she had to stop. She looked at me and said "Oh, heavens, I have been playing and singing for hours. I really should stop so I can get to know you, Iris."

But first, she launched into one more song – Michael Martin Murphy's *Wildfire.* One of my favorite songs. By the time she ended the song, I was crying. She finished the song, then smiled angelically at me. Ryan was silently watching the interaction between us, his arm around her. I noticed him playing with her hair, which was always his loving gesture.

Maggie got up from the piano, and took a seat on the other side of the room. She gestured to Ryan and me to join her.

"So, Iris. How was your Christmas?"

"Oh, it was fabulous. The best ever." I meant that and it had zero to do with the elaborate gifts.

She smiled. "Mine, too. I have a wonderful son."

I wondered about Sarah, where she was. Maggie went

on. "And a wonderful daughter, as well. Alas, she's out of the country this Christmas with her husband. I wish you could meet her, but, I guess, some other time."

She continued. "So, I guess you have family in town?"

I nodded.

"You saw them last night?"

"Yes, we went over there to visit last night."

"You're very lucky. From what Ryan tells me, you have a great family."

I realized she was right. My family was financially broke, but they were intact, and we all loved one another very much. Ryan might have love with his mother, but his father....not so much.

"And you have a career," she said.

"Such as it is."

"Don't give that up. Women always need to have skills and support themselves. You just never know when your support might be cut off." I knew she referred to her own situation, but I didn't think she was cut off financially. But maybe she was.

But she didn't seem bitter. She still smiled angelically. And I realized that, even though she fought mental illness, her overall demeanor was very similar to Ryan's. Laid-back, happy, seemingly optimistic. I couldn't imagine this woman violent, even though I knew what she'd done.

She turned to Ryan. "And what is your news for me?"

"Sheldon says you can probably get out early next year. I'm arranging a group home for you to live in for when you get out."

She sighed, and looked a little sad. "I was hoping I could live on my own."

"I hope so, too, eventually. But you have to transition."

"Yes, yes, of course, of course. It's just that those group homes are so depressing."

"Well, let's see how you do and how you stay on your meds. Maybe you can live on your own after a year or so."

She nodded. "Hey, maybe I can meet a guy like John Nash in there and live happily ever after. As long as both of us stay on our meds." Then she laughed gaily. "Oh, could you imagine? Me and a mathematics genius?"

"Well, of course. I'm confident you could keep up with anybody," Ryan said. "You always kept up very well with my Harvard buddies."

"Oh, yes. How is Nick these days?"

I felt a bit funny. *I wonder if she knows.* I shook my head. *Of course not. Why would she?*

"He's great, great. Spending Christmas with his family in Switzerland."

"Oh, they're back in Switzerland? Wonder why they want to live there?"

"I think they go there every year to ski. Nick, his mother and father, and Nick's wife and kids."

"Oh, ok, they aren't living there. Well, I know why they would want to visit. That's a gorgeous place."

"Yeah. Nothing like skiing the Alps." At that, I groaned inwardly. My own skiing was not progressing apace, and I despaired of ever getting off the Snow Creek slopes. Let alone ski in the Alps. *Ryan will have to take his ski trips without me, if he wants to go in the future.*

"Right," Maggie said. "Ah, remember skiing when you were little? We stayed at that little Italian ski chateau?"

"Of course."

"You were on the Black course by the time you were ten. You were really a natural."

Ryan blushed.

Maggie went on "Well, maybe we can go skiing together when I get out of here and I'm well. I'd love to try the double black diamonds with you again."

"That would be great, mom. I can't wait for that." He gestured to me. "Iris is learning to ski. Maybe she can join us?"

"Of course! That goes without saying!"

I kept quiet, not telling her I had never actually been skiing, except on the baby slopes of Snow Creek, which was the skiing park just north of Kansas City. Even those little slopes scared the living crap out of me. *Oh, well, they can ski their double black diamonds. I'll stay behind at the lodge and get drunk.*

The day went along like this, as I chatted with Maggie and Ryan. She was an exceedingly sweet woman, talented, beautiful and smart. Just like he described her.

We had dinner there with her, as well. The food there was not as good as the food where Ryan stayed. However, because it was Christmas, they tried to provide something special. It was mashed potatoes that tasted like they came from a box, cranberries from a can, and turkey gravy. The yams also came from a can, and they had little marshmallows on them, which were not completely melted. Their rolls, however, were divine. Absolutely divine. They reminded me of the rolls I used to get in grade school and high school. My schools served the worst food ever – orange meat, wilted greens, tough ham, mystery food. However, when it came to rolls and breads, nobody did it better. Nobody. The rolls here reminded me of that. I found myself wishing I could make a meal consisting just of bread.

I thought about my father, who was in the hospital with heart surgery all those Thanksgivings ago. On Thanksgiving Day, they served him chili mac that looked like it had been sitting around for more than a week. So, I figured the spread we were getting here was pretty good, considering.

Ryan looked more than pleased to be in Maggie's presence. And mine, too. I caught him looking at me many times during the meal, and I could tell that he was happy. I must've been doing ok.

And Ryan dug into his food like he hadn't eaten all week. Ryan, in general, was kind of a health food guy – he pretty much ate organic fruits and vegetables, very little processed food, and free range chicken. He, like myself, was well-versed on how crappy the food of today was, how many chemicals and preservatives were added into everything, how many pesticides were on our fruits and veggies, and how many antibiotics and hormones were given to our meat producers. I was pleased to know that about him, because I always wanted to go organic, but never could afford to. He could afford to, and he truly believed, so it was the best of both worlds.

Yet, here he was, digging into the processed crap like it was the best thing ever. I supposed to him, it was. Because he was spending Christmas with his mother. And with me. He was like – well, he was a like a kid on Christmas morning.

Around 10 o'clock, we had to leave. I was feeling that I had truly a magnificent time. Maggie was a fascinating woman – besides the fact that she could play piano like Rachmaninoff, and sing like Maria Callas, she truly had a great personality. She was witty, intelligent, well-rounded, and warm. For her Christmas, Ryan had brought her a slew of non-fiction and fiction books on her list.

Upon receiving these books, which filled a shopping bag, Maggie exclaimed "Oh, Ryan, exactly what I asked for! These will keep me busy, at any rate." Maggie didn't have a gift for Ryan, as she wasn't able to get out to get him a gift, but, of course, he understood that.

I found it peculiar that Ryan gave his own mother such modest gifts, and myself and my family such elaborate ones. I figured that he was just trying to impress us, and she was his mother, so he didn't need to impress her.

As we were getting ready to leave, Maggie gave me a long hug. "I'm so happy to finally meet you. Ryan has talked about little else but you for these past few months. You're just as lovely as he describes."

"I'm happy to meet you, too, Maggie," I said, hugging her back. I felt so badly for her, going through all that she had went through – with Benjamin, and her mental illness, and everything else that happened to her. Yet, here she was, resilient, courageous and beautiful. I knew then exactly whose genetics favored Ryan.

He was just like her.

He held my hand and skipped a little as we left. We got outside, into the cold, crisp air. He was practically dancing. "She loved you!" he exclaimed. "As I knew she would!"

I was laughing. "Well, of course. I'm so loveable, you know!"

"You don't understand. She couldn't stand Alexis. I think she knew that Alexis was bad news. So, it's nice to bring somebody to her that she loves."

"What about your other girlfriends?"

"Well, for serious girlfriends, Alexis was the only one. So, pretty much, you're only the second woman to meet her."

I was puzzled by this. I knew he and Alexis were on and off for years, and I figured there was somebody else in there he cared about. But I guessed I was wrong about this.

That night, we made love with wild, passionate abandonment. Since neither of us had to be anywhere the next day – we both took the day off from work – our lovemaking had one of the all night qualities that it had at the first, and periodically since then. I was feeling I couldn't get enough of him, and he obviously felt the same way.

As we lay there, both of us spent after making love for a long time, Ryan took my left hand, and looked at the ring finger dazedly. "That finger looks so naked. We must do something about that soon." Then he kissed me, and we made love again.

Chapter Thirty-Four

It was January now, and we had been home, together, uninterrupted by any serious event, for well over a month. And there had been, as of yet, no mention of me meeting Nick. I didn't bring it up, either. I was too nervous.

However, one Friday night, over a simple dinner of pasta and oil, Ryan casually brought it up. "What do you think about next Saturday night?"

"As in?"

"As in you and me and Nick getting together for dinner."

I took a deep breath. I had hoped to avoid it, but here it was. "Sure."

He smiled. "Good. You've met my mother. Now it's time for you to meet the third-most important person in my life."

I looked at him quizzically.

He kissed me. "You, of course, are tied for number one. With my mother. And Nick is third. And, when you're Mrs. Gallagher, you'll be number one in my life, bar none."

I smiled. *Promises, promises.*

"Ok, then. Let's do it!" I had a tight smile on my face, and Ryan, unfortunately, was learning all my tells.

"Oh, Iris, I know you aren't entirely happy. Just keep an open mind." At that, he went into the other room and I heard him talking. "Yeah, buddy." Pause. "Yeah, Friday night, Piropos." Pause. "8 o'clock." Pause. "See you then."

"8 o'clock Friday it is!"

"Piropos is incentive enough." I loved that place. I could never afford it before meeting Ryan, now it was a place we went to at least once a month.

Little did I know I would never make it to this particular rendezvous. Neither did Ryan.

Chapter Thirty-Five

It was Friday, the day of meeting Nick. I was at work, and feeling queasier by the second about what the night held in store for me. I didn't know what to expect - would they be stealing glances with each other and talking about me when I went to the bathroom? Would they be discussing the possibility of a three-way between all of us? I knew that Nick was basically straight, although was definitely more bisexual than Ryan. At least that was what Ryan told me about him – that Nick loved women, and women loved him, and he had dudes on the side. But that Nick also did like his "dudes on the side," and Ryan did not like "dudes on the side." So, Ryan was pretty much a one guy guy, whereas I guess Nick was a multi-guy guy.

I sighed. I was reading more and more books about this, and I was understanding there were lots of men like Nick – happily married and prowling for men. *Mother never told me about this when I was growing up.* Hell, when I was growing up, Nick would be labeled a closet homosexual. Period. Suddenly, however, it was becoming more known that men liked men and this didn't mean they were gay. Or on the way to gaytown. I thought of Cary Grant, Marlon Brando and James Dean, all rumored bisexuals, and felt comforted.

Anyhow, I had to concentrate at work. Which wasn't easy on the best of days. I dazedly sat through new client intakes, explaining the rules of bankruptcy to one client, and how I could help get custody of their kid to another. To another guy I was explaining how I would get him off his latest DUI charge. Then, in the afternoon, I sat through the endless line at the traffic prosecutor's office, in an effort to reduce a ticket. It was all in a day's work, really, except that I knew that the evening would be anything but routine.

But I could never, in my wildest dreams, imagine just how non-routine it would be.

At the end of the day, I walked to my car. Suddenly, out of nowhere, a slight figure jumped out at me and put a rag over my face. I struggled a bit, then everything went black.

Chapter Thirty-Six

I came to sometime later. I had no idea how much time had passed or where I was. I had on a blindfold, my wrists were handcuffed to the arms of a chair, and my ankles were handcuffed to the legs of the chair. I felt completely nauseated. Then I realized there must have been a bucket of vomit on the floor next to me. I could smell its pungent odor.

I tried to orient myself. *Was I dreaming?* I often got disoriented when I first wake up, not knowing where I was. I waited for the familiar feeling to kick in, the feeling I got when I figured out exactly where I was, and I was able to fall back to sleep.

I had a vague feeling that my upper arm was tied off with something. A tourniquet, maybe. And there was a needle in the crook of my elbow.

What the hell is going on here? I wasn't exactly panicking. I felt too out of it to panic, yet I had some degree of lucidity, because I knew something wasn't right. But I still couldn't yet figure out if I was dreaming or awake.

I prayed I was dreaming.
Then I heard a voice.
"Hello, Iris."
"Hi?" I said, uncertainly.
"I see you're awake."
"Yes, I'm awake," I said, stating the obvious.
"Do you know where you are?"
"No."
"Ryan told you about me, I presume?"

Oh, so this is connected to Ryan somehow. At least it wasn't a random serial killer. If I'm not dreaming, and this is real, at least I have some chance of getting through this. I was amazed at how logically I was thinking it through. My legal brain, I guess. Or maybe it was the Virgo brain.

I nodded. I really didn't know if Ryan had told me about this woman or not. I didn't know who she was. Literally.

"Fucking bastard."

It struck me. *Was this Rochelle?* I knew it wasn't Alexis. I knew Alexis' voice. Besides, Alexis was around a little bit, not as much as before, and she was always nice. Was trying to get her life together. She even had a new boyfriend and we all went out one night. I didn't think she would have a relapse so bad that she would kidnap me.

Again, my mind was thinking excruciatingly logically. I always wondered what kind of mindset I would have if something horrendous happened to me. I was proud of my equanimity.

"Goddamned bastard. I had him followed, you know."
I nodded.
"Fucking asshole went to Tiffany's yesterday. Fucking Tiffany's! He bought you the biggest rock I've ever seen. Platinum setting, five carats. Perfect rock." She was

breathing heavily, almost hyperventilating. "That should be me! He loves me, not you, you little cunt." Then she kicked me hard in my shins. I winced. She brought out a belt and whacked my thighs, which were bare. White-hot pain shot through me. I could feel tears coming to my eyes.

Then she had a knife and she held it to my throat. "I could kill you. He doesn't need to be with you. He's not supposed to be with you. He was always supposed to be with me!" The knife was cold and sharp, the point of it digging into my skin, dangerously close to my jugular vein. At least I imagined it was my jugular vein beneath the point.

I sighed. My thoughts immediately went to my mother. She would be so devastated when I just never showed up anywhere, ever again. She'd never know what happened to me. I'd be like one of those missing women who were just never heard from again. My family would search for me for years and they would never get closure on what happened to me. Somehow, these thoughts dominated me. My mother. Of course, everybody else would be devastated as well, but none like my mother.

This would kill her.

Because I had no doubt Rochelle would know how to get rid of my body.

"What do you want from me?" I decided it was time to bargain, to see if there was anything to say or do that would save me.

"Little cunt. I don't want a thing from you." Then, WAP, she sliced the belt on my thighs again, twice more. I screamed in pain. The woman took the knife and sliced my forearm. Again, I screamed out in white-hot pain. I could feel her run her fingers in my blood, then I heard her lick her fingers.

"Nobody knows you're here. Nobody can hear you scream." At that, she beat me again with the belt. I started crying, the hot tears streaming down my cheeks. The survival instinct was inside of me, I just had to find it, and use it to try to get out of here.

"That mother-fucker wants to marry you. Fucking Tiffany ring! Well, just wait until he finds out you're never coming home" She laughed. "Mother fucker will be devastated. He'll feel just a fraction of the pain I felt when he left me."

Of course this is Rochelle. I knew now that it was definitely her, because she referred to him leaving her.

Then she was calmer. "He was a beautiful boy, you know. Absolutely the most perfect specimen of boy I'd ever seen. Everybody wanted him. And I had him. Me." She laughed. "God, how we could rock those sheets. We couldn't get enough of each other."

Then she said "Fucking every night. I couldn't get enough of him."

My mind searched. *Ok, now that you know this is Rochelle, what can you do?* I desperately thought of what Ryan had told me about her, in an effort to find something I could say or do to get out of there. *Think, Iris, think. Did he tell you anything at all that might trip her up, or soften her up, or bring her back to reality?* I didn't have a clue how I would physically get out of this, so I had to think about how I could mentally get out of it.

She went on. "When he started hanging out with you, I didn't think it would last. I mean, look at you. Not in his league at all." Then she laughed. "Little did I know he'd be more serious about you than anybody else. Go figure. I saw him with some real Victoria's Secret model types all the time. Yet he never liked them much. But you..." Then she wapped me again, hard, with the belt. "You! Of all fucking people, he chooses you! I mean, I could almost handle it if he was with somebody who looks right with him. But you! That's an insult."

"I agree. I don't know why he's with me either." It was honest, but I also thought agreeing with her might be the best course of action at this point.

At that, I heard her light up a cigarette. She took a long puff, then put the lit end on my arm, for a good 30 seconds. I screamed in pain and writhed around.

Then, suddenly, I heard something else. It was Ryan! He was here! I had no idea how he figured out I was here, but he was here to rescue me!

"Rochelle! Oh, shit!" he screamed.

"Ryan. How did you know to come here?"

"Iris didn't show up tonight. I called her assistant and she remembered seeing somebody fitting your description hanging around the office today. It wasn't hard to figure it out."

"Ah, well, of course. I lured you here. I knew you'd figure it out. Now, you'll do whatever I tell you." She grabbed my arm. "See this needle? Black tar. I plunge this into her and she'll not survive." Then she laughed. "Oh, but what a way to go, huh? She'll go to la la land like she'd never experienced before she dies."

"What do you want? What can I do?" Ryan asked. His voice sounded desperate, pleading.

"Tell me about the ring, Ryan."

"What do you want to know about it?"

"Describe it."

He quickly responded "Five carats, perfect diamond, perfect cut, clarity, color. Princess cut. Platinum setting."

"How boring. You really have no imagination, do you?"

"I don't know what you mean?"

"Oh, I don't know. I figured you'd go to the Smithsonian and buy the Hope Diamond itself."

He didn't respond to that.

"What do you need from me? I'll do anything you want, just please let her go."

"Anything?"

"Anything."

"I can think of a lot of things I want from you."

"Ok. If you let her go, I'll give you what you want."

I had mixed emotions about this. I was happy Ryan had come, and was apparently ready to sacrifice himself for me. But I knew what she wanted and I wasn't happy about the sacrifice.

But Rochelle surprised me. "I don't want anything from you. Not like that. You have to want me."

Then she said something that chilled me. "All I want is for you to suffer. And I can think of no better way to make you suffer than to make you helplessly watch your precious cunt die."

I heard him scream "NO!" as I felt the plunger push something into my arm. Then an amazing feeling of euphoria like I'd never felt. I wondered if I was in heaven. It was like the moment in surgery, right before you're unconscious. Like I was floating and nothing could touch me.

Then everything went black again.

Chapter Thirty-Seven

Everything was dark. I was vaguely aware that I was in my body but I couldn't speak or open my eyes. I could hear everything, though.

"I went by your office today," Ryan was saying. "Don't worry, everything's under control there. Melinda had your cases assigned to some guy named David. I even made sure every judge was called, so they know why you're not coming in."

He paused for what seemed like forever.

"I want you to have a successful office to come back to. And you're coming back. Do you hear me? You're coming back."

Then he grabbed my hand. I could feel his head on my stomach. I vaguely heard the steady beeping of a machine, which made me realize I was in a hospital bed. He now had both of his hands on my stomach, along with his head.

Why couldn't I open my eyes? Again, I felt I was dreaming, but I was in one of those dreams where you're halfway conscious and halfway unconscious. You know you're in a dream but you simply can't come out of it.

Then a female voice. "You're still here? You haven't gone home, I see." Alexis.

"No. She's in that bed because of me. If she never would've met me, she'd be living her life somewhere, carefree. I should've never sucked her into my crazy life."

"And still blaming yourself. This is getting boring."

"Well, then, if you're bored, you can leave."

"Hey, hey, now. Don't get defensive. I care about her, too. That's why I'm here."

"I know, I'm sorry." He sighed mightily. He put his head back down on my stomach.

"Well, here. I brought you a change of clothes."

"Thanks."

"I don't know how your job puts up with your constant leaves."

"They probably won't much longer. That's ok, it's run its course."

"So, what're you going to do, become a full-time trust fund baby?"

"I don't know yet. That's the furthest thing from my mind right now. The very furthest. It's like I'm on Tatooine and that concern is on the Alderaan System."

"*Star Wars*? Really? Now I remember why we broke up," she said, but I could tell she was teasing.

Then "Hey, lighten up, I was teasing you." Then she paused. "Ryan?"

I could hear him snoring.

"Now we have two unconscious people on this bed." Then I could feel Ryan's head being pulled off my stomach. "Come on, I'm going to arrange for you to have a cot so you can sleep. Poor guy, you must not have slept much for the past three days."

Then she addressed me. "You better wake up, Iris. This guy needs you." Then I heard her leave the room, but she was talking to a nurse outside the hallway. "Could we get a cot in there?"

"Certainly. We'll bring it up in about five minutes."

Then I heard my mom, dad and sister in the room. My mom said "I still don't understand what happened to her. How could she overdose? She's never done drugs in her life."

My sister talked next. "Maybe she had a secret life. I was addicted to crystal meth for years and you never suspected a thing."

My mother. "But it just isn't like her. She's always been a good girl."

"Sometimes people just lead double lives. It happens," my sister said.

I could hear chairs being pulled up around the bed. Then a male voice I didn't recognize. "Her vitals are stable. There really is not a reason why she can't come out of this." I could feel a blood pressure sleeve tightening over my arm, then loosen. "110 over 70. Pulse 65. Everything's normal."

My mother was crying. My dad was saying "dear, she's going to be fine. She's just going to wake up out of this and ask for a piece of pizza or a bar of chocolate."

"You don't know that!" Now she was really sobbing. Hearing her sobbing made me want to come out of this, to wake up, but somehow I just couldn't. It was so frustrating, hearing everybody around me, and not being able to engage.

At this point, I heard Ryan's voice. "Mrs. Snowe, Iris

isn't an addict. She isn't on drugs. As far as I know she's never done drugs in her life."

"So what happened to her?" asked my mother.

At this Ryan said "I was involved with a woman years ago. She's obsessed with me. She kidnapped Iris and shot her up with black tar heroin. Because Iris isn't used to drugs, at all, let alone a large quantity at once, she overdosed."

He paused. "I'm so sorry. I tried to save her, but I got there just a little bit too late. Rochelle already had her thumb on the plunger by the time I got there to try to save her. There wasn't anything I could do. However, the second that Rochelle plunged the drugs into Iris' arm, I tackled her to the ground and called 911."

"Where's Rochelle now?" asked my dad.

"She's in custody. She was arrested and charged with kidnapping and assault."

My mother was sobbing and my dad was saying "Dear, she's going to be ok, she's going to be fine. Shhhhhh."

Then the doctor's voice "Visiting hours are coming to an end."

I felt a bit of panic. I wanted somebody to stay there. I was scared, now, not being able to communicate or even open my eyes, and I didn't want to be abandoned.

Ryan asked "Can I stay here? I have a cot to sleep on."

"Who are you?"

"Her husband."

"Oh, ok. Yes, sure, you can stay here as long as you like."

"Thanks."

My mother. "You lied about that, but that's ok. I don't want her to be here alone."

To this, Ryan said "me neither. She needs to see a

familiar face when she wakes up." He paused. "Besides, I might be her husband sooner than you think."

My sister. "I hope so. She needs somebody nice to take care of her."

Ryan said "I take care of her, but she takes care of me, too."

My mother. "She's a sweet girl. You take care of her. And don't blame yourself for what happened. You can't help what happened."

I didn't hear Ryan's response, but I figured that he was nodding.

Then the rest were gone, and I heard Ryan's voice. He was reading from my favorite book *The Thornbirds*, from page one. My heart soared. I loved this book and I loved him for reading this to me.

"Beautiful, I'm going to read to you from this book, and other books, too. Hopefully you'll wake up before I end this book, though. It's over 500 pages long."

For the next few hours I heard the story about the Cleary family, their clashes with Mary Carson, and their friendship with Father Ralph De Bricassart. I thought about the first time I knew about this story, and was exposed to it – I saw it on a cable channel when I was little girl, and I couldn't take my eyes off of it. I must've read that book 100 times.

Ryan took a break, just as the action was heating up. Meggie had grown up and she was about the embark on the romance of her life, with Ralph the priest. "We'll pick this back up tomorrow. It's getting pretty good." Then I heard him sigh mightily. "Please come back to me. I need you in my life. Things aren't the same without you."

I tried to open my eyes. I tried mightily, but I just couldn't.

Ryan picked the story back up again sometime later. It must have been morning, but was impossible to tell. Time had no meaning to me anymore.

I found myself involuntarily drifting away from the story, away from the book, away from the hospital, away from Ryan. I was in a city all at once, in the downtown area. I looked up and saw the Twin Towers, intact. Then I realized I was in a large baby carriage being pushed down the street. There were little beads above my head, and I batted them while I restlessly punched the air and moved my hands and feet in the carriage. There were loud sounds all around me. My diaper was wet and I started screaming.

There was a voice telling me this was real and was an actual memory. Then I remembered in my adult mind that when I was very small, my family lived in Rhode Island, and my mother had a cousin in New York City and we visited often. This was one of those visits, and I realized I had actually seen the Twin Towers in my lifetime. I just couldn't remember it, because I was only a few months old. And I somehow felt at peace about this, because one my biggest regrets in life was never getting to see those towers.

Then I was back at the hospital bed. Ryan was still there, and so were my friends, Richard and Debbie. I heard Debbie speak. "Any improvements?"

"None," Ryan said.

"It's been three weeks. Have you left for any period of time?"

"I pretty much stay here in case she wakes up."

Then Richard spoke up. "She'll wake up soon, so it's a good thing you're here all the time."

Three weeks? The last I knew, I was here for a matter of days. Where did I go? I still had my sense of smell, and I could smell

Ryan's scent. He smelled like soap, aftershave and mouthwash.

The three of them were talking some about people in comas, and how they come out of it being no worse for the wear. "I knew this guy with meningitis who was in a coma for a year," Richard was saying. "He said that was the best year of his life, because he literally travelled the world in his head and it was like he actually was at a Stones concert or in London or wherever he was imagining."

To this Debbie said "I wonder where Iris is traveling right now?"

Ryan said "I don't know, but I'm sure that I'll hear all about it. Maybe she's in Amsterdam, sampling all the pot in the red light district."

Ha, I wish!

But I felt myself drifting away again. This time I was on a beach and the water was warm. I was playing in the water, the waves crashing over me time and again. I leaped over the waves and swam under them. I looked on the shore and saw my cousin Terry picking up sea shells. She looked to be about 15 years old. I was extremely skinny, and I realized this was another memory of a time that I went to the beach with Terry and my uncle Justin. We used to go to South Carolina every year.

I started to worry. Was I dying? My life seemed to be flashing before my eyes. It was like God was showing me some of my favorite memories, or at least memories that were previously lost to me, such as the Twin Towers. What if I couldn't come out of the coma?

I was back at the hospital bed again. Ryan and Alexis were arguing.

"Ryan, it's been two months. You have to come back and join the living. Everybody's worried about you."

"What's that supposed to mean? I'm here in the living. In case you haven't noticed, she isn't dead."

"I know, but every day she's like this makes it more unlikely she'll come back. You have to accept this."

"I'll do nothing of the sort. I'm not going to give up on her."

"You may not have the choice."

"Meaning?"

"You might have to say goodbye to her."

"Oh, and wouldn't that be convenient for you? Then you can have another chance, is that what you're thinking?"

"Of course not! Number one, I like her too, if you didn't forget. And number two, things are going pretty good with Todd."

Todd was the guy Alexis had started seeing before I became like this.

"Well, I'm glad things are going well with Todd. Why don't you go and see him and leave me alone?"

"Because I care about you and I know you need a friend."

Just then, I heard another voice in the room, a male voice. Alexis addressed the new guy. "You talk to him. He might listen to you more than he would me."

"Hey Ryan, buddy," the new guy said.

"Nick, if you're here to say anything negative, I swear to God, I'll get in your face."

"Nothing negative, but you need to take a break here. You haven't been at work for the past two months and everybody is concerned."

"I've taken a leave of absence for an indefinite period of time. If they fire me, they fire me. I don't really care about that right now."

"Ok, then, let's at least go down to the cafeteria and get something to eat, ok?"

Oh, so this is the infamous Nick? His voice was very nice, very deep and masculine. He sounded like a jock for some reason and I could imagine he was.

I heard them leave the room. I concentrated on trying to open my eyes or moving some of my muscles.

After what seemed like forever, Ryan and Nick were back. "I do feel a bit better," Ryan was saying. "Thanks for taking me to the Granfalloon. Walking there really did me some good."

The Granfalloon was a bar and grill on the Country Club Plaza, and I knew St. Luke's Hospital was close by this restaurant, so I knew this was the hospital in which I lay in my twilight state. That comforted me, as it it oriented me to time and space and anchored me somewhat.

"Not a problem, buddy, but I'd like it if you'd spend the night with me and Rielle. I know you don't want to go home to your empty house, which is why I'm making this offer now. Hell, you could even move in with us until she wakes up."

"You always come through for me, but no. I need to be here for her when she comes to."

"Suit yourself. You know where to find me." Then he left.

Ryan sighed. "Iris, you have to come out of this. I'm cracking up without you. I can't go home because I see you there, everywhere I look. So I've been staying here, night and day. This hospital is now my home. So, please come back to me. I need you. I need you. I need you."

He was crying softly. My heart went out to him, so I tried, once more, to move something, so he wouldn't give up on me. *A finger, move a finger.* It was a herculean effort, but I could feel my finger moving!

Ryan felt it too!

"Oh my God! Collette, Collette!" He was shouting down the hall. "Where's Collette?"

Then a voice outside the room. "Collette's off duty, can I help you?"

"Get Dr. Maris. Hurry. Iris moved her finger!"

Then he was back. I must've been resuming consciousness, because I opened my eyes and finally saw Ryan. He was smiling bigger than I'd ever seen him smile. His face was close to mine. His hand was clutching mine so tightly that I thought the circulation would be cut off. He was blurry at first, but gradually came into focus.

"You're awake! " He had tears in his eyes. Then he was on his iPhone. He was apparently calling my mother because he addressed the person on the other line - "Hello, Charlene? She's awake!" A pause. "A few minutes ago. Get here now!"

"Your parents are on their way. Hopefully they'll call your friends, too."

I nodded, literally unable to speak. A doctor was soon in the room.

"How are you feeling?" The doctor asked me.

I shook my head and motioned to my neck and mouth.

"Don't worry, your speech will come back. There hasn't been any brain damage, so everything will come back to you in time."

My mouth was in a straight line now, and I was shaking. I wanted to speak so badly, so I attempted that. "Day is this time?" I was vaguely aware this sentence didn't make any sense.

However, Ryan understood me perfectly.

"Today is March 13. You've been away from us for two months."

I nodded. Then I felt my stomach and legs with my hands. I felt different. My belly was concave and my legs were quite a bit smaller. I felt little musculature in either area. I looked at Ryan quizzically.

"You lost about 35 pounds, I'd estimate," he said.

I wanted to lose weight, but not like this.

"Will it be hard for her to walk?" Ryan asked Dr. Maris.

"For a while it will, because she's lost a lot of muscle. She'll have to go to rehab to build that back up."

"That's not a problem at all. I can take her to her rehab every day."

I looked at him. I knew he was at my bedside pretty much 24/7 since I became like this, and I worried about his job. I croaked the best I could "Job you to go." I nodded my head at him eagerly.

He looked at me. "Love, it isn't a problem for me to bring you."

I shook my head violently. "Go job you, mom every day me bring," I said, pointing to him. Once again, I nodded my head eagerly while smiling big.

"We'll talk about that later." He suddenly didn't look happy. He narrowed his eyes at me, and turned to the doctor. "What time will she have to be at rehab?"

"I'll have to arrange that and I'll let you know."

At this point, my parents were in the room along with my sister. My mother saw me sitting up in the bed and broke down crying.

I looked at her. "Cry?"

"I'm just so relieved you're awake," my mom said,

My sister said "We were so afraid that...."

To this Ryan said "I wasn't afraid. I knew you'd make it."

I smiled big, trying to lighten the mood. "Good skinny got I." I nodded my head at everybody. Nobody seemed very pleased about that, though. I figured my sister, at least, would appreciate this.

The doctor was explaining everything to them. My speech would probably come back on its own, but my muscles had atrophied to the point where I would need physical rehabilitation.

Ryan piped up. "I can install a home gym, that's not a problem. You'll give me some exercises she'll need to do, right?" I actually had always wondered why Ryan didn't already have a home gym, for he always worked out at the local gym. I always guessed that was his personal time away from me, which was fine. Now he would apparently put in a home gym, and if I knew Ryan, he'd get the very top of the line of everything.

"Sure, at her first rehab session they'll go over all of that with you."

He looked at me anxiously. "Can I talk to you outside?" he asked the doctor.

I shook my head violently. "No. Doctor here you talk."

He gave me a look, but talked to the doctor in front of me. "Are you sure her speech will come back?"

"Yes, it's very common for coma patients to have some degree of aphasia for a little while after they wake up. It usually comes back on its own with time."

He looked relieved, but I could still read anxiety on his face. Inwardly, I wondered if Ryan would still love me if I couldn't speak properly. In spite of myself, I started to cry.

Ryan was concerned. "What's wrong my love?"

"Love you."

"I love you too." He still looked concerned. "But what's wrong?"

"Speak me love me not?"

"Of course, of course, beautiful. You'll speak fine, but even if you don't, I'll always love you."

I tried to feel relieved, but couldn't.

My mother was still crying, my father and sister were looking worried, and Ryan was just staring at me. I felt self-conscious.

"Sleep need I." I wasn't really all that tired, but I couldn't stand everybody looking scared and worried around me. I was feeling pretty scared myself, so I wanted everybody to seem encouraging to me. I also thought that maybe my speech would come back later and everything would return to normal, so I wouldn't be so self-conscious around them.

My mom said "Ok, dear, we'll be back in the morning."

I nodded my head. "Home I go can?"

The doctor said "Not yet, we need to keep you for a few days for observation."

Ryan looked at me. "Do you mind if I stay?"

I nodded. "Stay."

He smiled. Everybody left and Ryan climbed into the bed next to me. "Thank God you're awake. Thank God," he said, stroking my hair, while my head was on his chest.

I nuzzled him, my hair on his chest. I didn't know if coma patients were bathed, but I guessed I was, because I felt clean. Still, I wanted to bathe, and Ryan seemingly read my mind.

"Beautiful, would you like me to give you a sponge bath?"

I nodded eagerly. He picked me up and carried me into the bathroom. I found myself grateful for Ryan's money, because this was a private room that had a bathtub, as opposed to just a shower. He gently put me in the tub and turned on the water. Just then, he got on the phone. "Charlene? This is Ryan." He paused. "Could you do me a favor?" Pause. "Could you go to the store and bring some bubble bath up?" Pause. "Right now if you could." Pause. "Thanks."

He turned to me. "I apologize for not thinking about that. I know how much you love your bubble baths." At that, he carried me back into the bed to await my mother. He was extremely gentle with me, like he was carrying a priceless Fabergé egg.

I nodded eagerly.

My mother arrived about fifteen minutes later. Ryan got up when she walked in the door. "Thanks, Charlene, here's some money."

My mother protested, but Ryan insisted. My mother called into the bathroom - "We'll see you tomorrow!"

Ryan ran the water, putting the bubble bath into the water. Before long, there were enormous bubbles. Then, he gently picked me back up, and placed me into the warm bath. I had never felt anything so amazing.

He gently got a sponge and soaped me up, scrubbing every inch of my body. Then he gently shampooed my hair. "This is just like old times, huh?"

I nodded. I leaned forward, still not used to seeing my new body. My legs were very thin, my stomach was flat, but my breasts seemed deflated too. They definitely didn't seem as perky.

"Don't you worry, you'll be back to normal in no time. I'll make sure you do all your exercises for your rehab and your speech will come back perfectly. Just wait."

I nodded.

We finished the bath, and Ryan put some toothpaste on my toothbrush, then gently opened my mouth and brushed my teeth. Then he produced some mouthwash, put some in the little cap, and I swished it around and spit it out. Then, Ryan picked me up and carried me to the bed. He produced a bag that had some pajamas in it and some other clothes. "I brought this for when you woke up. I knew you'd need fresh clothes."

I looked at him gratefully. "You thank."

He dressed me in some warm pajamas. Then he frowned. He pushed the call button. A nurse came up. "Hey, do you mind changing these sheets?" The nurse nodded her head, and came back up with some new bedding, and changed the sheets, the pillow case and blanket. "Thank you so much," Ryan said.

I was now freshly washed, and so was my bedding. Ryan and I snuggled in the bed, him stroking my hair, just like old times. "I was so looking forward to this day," he said.

I just lay there silently, hearing his heartbeat. Surprisingly, considering that I just woke up after two months, I was exhausted and I was soon asleep.

Chapter Thirty-Eight

The doctor came in the next day and announced I'd start my rehab that morning. Ryan carried me to a wheelchair and pushed me to the rehab facilities.

I went through some exercises designed to strengthen my leg and arm muscles. The rehab guy said that muscle atrophy was my only problem, and that I'd be able to walk fine when I built up my muscles.

The session was painful and frustrating. I used to be so strong. Now, I could hardly walk. That said, I could walk a little with the help of the parallel bars. I also did a variety of exercises that strengthened all the muscles in my legs, using the very lowest weights possible. Even at the lowest weights, they seemed impossible to lift. Ryan was right there encouraging me, though. I guessed if anybody could help me get back into shape, it'd be him.

I stayed at the hospital all that week, because I had to go through rehab every day, and the doctor ran tests, such as CAT Scans and other tests to make sure there wasn't major brain damage. My speech was gradually coming back, which was encouraging.

Ryan never left my side, giving me sponge baths, dressing me, and hanging out with me. He also slept with me and ate with me, wheeling me down to the cafeteria during the first few days. He made me walk up and down the halls, walking along with me slowly. As usual, he showed an incredible amount of patience with my slow progress.

During the week, my parents and sister came by every day, and Debbie and Richard stopped by several times as well. I also had a steady stream of people coming in – aunts, uncles, cousins, and other friends, such as Patty and Robert. Even Alexis stopped by, her new boyfriend, Todd, in tow. Everybody was considerate, though, only staying for a short time, because I found that I tired very easily.

Everything was a chore – speaking, walking, eating, getting dressed, bathing. I found that I just wanted to lie in the bed, because everything else was just too much effort, but Ryan made sure I was as active as possible. He wouldn't let me just lay in bed. He forced me to walk, to dress for meals, and to go to rehab. He gave me sponge bubble baths every night. He also was sensitive to when I was really tired out, and let me quit when I absolutely had to.

Finally, it was time to go home. I walked slowly out the door after getting my discharge papers. I had to admit that I was intimidated to go home, though. It had been a long time since I was home, even though it really didn't seem that long for me.

First, though, we had to pick up Maximus and Brutus, who had been staying with Daniel while I was in the hospital, because Ryan was in the hospital as much as I was.

Daniel greeted us. He was always pretty taciturn with me, but on this day, he seemed much friendlier than usual.

"It's good to see you, Iris. You're looking well."

"Thanks, Daniel," I said.

"If you need anything, don't hesitate to ask."

I nodded as Ryan went into the house to get the dogs. Daniel stood outside, standing awkwardly. Ryan came back out with the dogs, who were hyper as usual. "Thanks, bro," Ryan said, the dogs pulling him towards the car. They stopped to greet me, almost knocking me over. "Whoa," Ryan said, pulling the dogs away from me.

I started in singing one of my songs for the dogs, happy that I had my voice back. I created songs for the dogs every day, usually putting my own words into a familiar tune. Ryan smiled, obviously happy that I was getting back to normal.

Finally, we arrived back home. Ryan had already had the gym set up in the rec room downstairs. As I knew he would, he got the top of the line equipment – treadmills, Peloton bikes, elliptical trainers, and a full circuit of weight machines that one would find in a gym. I had my exercises that I needed to do every day, and I was getting stronger and stronger.

Everything was returning back to normal, but there was still a problem - I was having nightmares every night and I was anxious and depressed. Ryan was very sensitive to my moods anyhow, because we were starting to know each other so well, and he was also on the lookout for signs of PTSD. Plus, I refused to eat many of my meals, because I was afraid of getting heavy again, so I continued to lose weight.

This worried Ryan.

We were at the dinner table, and Ryan had cooked up one his fabulous meals, but I pushed the food around the plate.

"Don't you like my cooking anymore, love?"

"Of course. I'm just not real hungry."

"You have to eat. You're wasting away."

I shook my head. I finally felt I looked ok and I didn't want to gain the weight back.

"Iris, you really need to eat more. You need to keep up your strength while you're getting better and stronger." Whenever he used my name he meant business, and this time was no different.

I said nothing, just continued to pick at my food, not meeting his eyes. I could see imagine his stare boring into me, and I could see it in my peripheral vision. Sure enough, when I got the guts to actually look at him, he was staring at me, narrowing his eyes when my gaze met his. He looked pissed, confused and concerned, all at once. I quickly looked away, pushed away my plate, and left the table without a word.

That night, which was happening more and more frequently, I had vivid nightmares of being tortured. I was being burned with cigarettes, slashed with knives, beaten with a belt. It was always an unknown assailant. I always thought I was going to die. I would wake up in a cold sweat, and Ryan would get up with me to reassure me that I was safe.

I didn't feel safe, though.

As for going to the office, I just couldn't. Ryan had already arranged for my cases to be taken over by various attorneys, working with Melinda to make sure everything got reassigned while I was in the hospital. So I no longer had an active practice, which was fine with me. I couldn't go to the office after what had happened to me there. Ryan didn't try to force me, either.

And Ryan still hadn't gone back to work. Caring for me was still his full-time job.

However, after a week of nightmares, days when I couldn't get out of bed, and not eating, Ryan decided it was time to drag me to see Dr. Halder.

I shook my head. "Please don't make me go. I'll be good. I can handle this."

"You need help. The woman I love is disappearing before my eyes. I can't bear to see you so tormented."

I didn't want to see the shrink. I didn't want to be forced to relive what had happened.

But, of course I ended up going. Ryan went with me for support, but he said I should talk to him on my own. He waited in the waiting room, flipping through magazines, while I went inside.

"Hello, again, Iris," Dr. Halder greeted me.

"Hello."

He waited a few seconds, then asked me how I was.

"Not so good."

He nodded. "Tell me about what brings you here."

Surely he knows the story. "Well, I was, uh...uh..." I looked at the doctor helplessly. "Could you please ask Ryan to come in here?"

Ryan came in and joined us. I turned to him. "Could you please explain to Dr. Halder what happened to me?

"Honey, he knows what happened to you. He just needs you to talk about it."

"Oh." But I said nothing more.

The three of us sat in silence for a few minutes. I was shaking, and I was suffering a blinding headache that suddenly came on. "I don't feel well," I said. "Do you mind if I leave?"

"Of course, you can leave at any time."

"Thanks." I made an appointment for the next day. I wanted to make the appointment for the following week, but Ryan insisted that I try to come back the next day.

Over dinner that night, with me still pushing around my food and eating small bites, I asked Ryan what happened to Rochelle.

"She's in prison, honey. She can't hurt you anymore."

I shook my head. I didn't believe that. My mind didn't allow me to believe it. I felt Rochelle was still on the loose and was still waiting for me to come out of the house so she could nab me again. This time, however, she wouldn't let me live. I knew that for a fact.

"Prison? Don't you mean jail?" I asked. People were always referring to jail as prison, and prison as jail. As I was a former public defender, I was a stickler for the proper terminology.

"Yes, jail, sorry. She's awaiting trial."

"How come she isn't out on bail?"

"She's a flight risk. She owns her own private plane and has a house in Monaco. The judge decided nothing would stop her from taking her plane to Monaco and never being seen or heard from again. So he denied her bail."

I shuddered. "I'm tired. I really need to go to bed." It was 7:30 PM.

Ryan nodded. "I'll come to bed with you."

Ryan climbed into bed next to me. I lay down and tried to sleep. Ryan, for his part, wasn't tired, so he watched television in the bed next to me, using his blue-tooth headphones so the noise didn't bother me.

I was out within five minutes and didn't wake up the next day until noon. Ryan had long since gone to work. It was his first day back at work, and he'd asked me if I was okay with that. I assured him that I was. Going into the bathroom, I found a note from him, pinned to the mirror. "I love you honey. I'm at work, but I'm thinking about you constantly." That was all the note said.

The new appointment with Dr. Halder was that evening, after Ryan got off of work. I knew, however, that I wasn't going to make it. So, I called Dr. Halder and cancelled. The receptionist asked me if I wanted to reschedule. I told her I didn't know when I could come back, but would let them know.

After getting off the phone, I started to panic. This was really the first time that I was alone since the incident. I called Daniel.

"Hello," Daniel said.

"Hi, this is Iris."

"What's up?"

"Could you drive me somewhere?"

"Sure, where?"

"Ryan's bank." I really had no idea what I would do when I arrived there. I only knew that I was feeling abandoned and alone and was scared to death.

"Iris, it's his first day back after being away for months."

I understood. "Ok, then, could you please drive me to my mother's?"

"Sure."

Daniel pulled up in five minutes, driving a new Jaguar. I hadn't seen that particular car yet.

"Is this a new car?" I asked.

"Yeah. Ryan bought it a couple of weeks ago."

I nodded. I couldn't get excited about the new car, even though I'd always loved Jaguars.

I stared out the window while Daniel drove me to my parent's house. My head was splitting open again. About five minutes into the drive, I started sobbing uncontrollably.

Daniel didn't know what to do, so he stared straight ahead, watching the road, not looking at me.

"I'm so sorry," I croaked between sobs.

"Not a problem." He was obviously uncomfortable.

I cried all the way to my mom's house.

Daniel pulled up in front of the townhouse, obviously happy to be rid of me. He really didn't say anything at all to me. I guessed he didn't really know what to say.

I felt badly for him.

I dragged myself into my mother's house. She was surprised to see me. "What brings you here?" she asked.

"I have a headache. I need to lie down." At that I dragged myself up to the spare bedroom, lay down on the bed and immediately fell asleep.

I awoke to darkness. I gradually became aware there was a figure next to the bed. I looked at the clock. It was 8 PM. I had been sleeping for about 12 hours at my parent's house. My eyes adjusted to the darkness, and I realized the figure was Ryan, sitting in a chair next to the bed.

"Hello, beautiful," he said.

"Hi."

"Can I turn on the light?"

"Sure."

He turned on the light. He took my hand. "I'm so sorry I returned to work today. I had a feeling you were going to have a tough time with my being gone. Daniel told me what happened."

I nodded. "Maybe I can stay here for awhile? At least until I start to feel better."

He shook his head. "I've a better idea. I'm extending my leave of absence until you start feeling better. You're too fragile to be left alone." He smiled, and gently stroked my hair, while looking at me with a dreamy-eyed expression. "I need to protect you," he said softly. "I wish I could've protected you before. But I need to protect you now."

All I could do was nod. Barely. "That's sweet," I said without enthusiasm. "I'm just so tired." At that, I lay back down and fell back to sleep.

I woke up the next day at 10. Ryan was lying next to me. He was reading a book.

He smiled. "You're awake."

I nodded. "I don't feel well."

"Can I take you home?"

I shook my head. "I'm literally too exhausted to get out of this bed."

"Well, I'm not leaving until you come with me."

"Ok. Could you carry me?"

At that, he picked me up and carried me down the stairs. I clung to his neck, my head buried in his shoulder. He called to my mother "I'm taking her home, Charlene."

At that my mother came up to us and kissed my cheek. She addressed Ryan "Take care of her." At that, Ryan nodded and said nothing.

"Beautiful, you need to start eating. You're way too light." Ryan used to pick me up when we would horse around before everything happened. Now, I guess I weighed quite a bit less than that. "You must've lost 50 pounds."

I merely grunted. He gently put me in the car, fastening my seat belt. I immediately fell asleep in the car.

I woke up in our bed. Ryan must've carried me into the house while I was still unconscious. I had no idea what time it was, but Ryan was lying next to me, so it couldn't be too late in morning. But it was light out, so it must have been at least 7 AM. Ryan had his laptop and he was typing. When I woke up, he shut the laptop. He looked at me. "Good morning, beautiful."

I managed a small smile.

"Would you like to get back into your rehabilitation exercises?"

I shook my head. All I wanted to do was lay in bed.

He nodded. I had to admit that he seemed a stranger to me now. I would imagine it was the same for him.

Later on, I was in bed with my laptop on the Internet. Ryan was downstairs somewhere.

I suddenly realized that I was conferenced in on a chat with Ryan and Nick. He must not have known that he conferenced me. I read the chat between them.

Ry1989: I don't know what to do. I'm losing her.

St.Nick90: Give her time. She went through a lot. Being kidnapped, tortured and almost dying can do that to a person, you know.

Ry1989: I know, but how do I help her?

St.Nick90: Have you tried counseling?

Ry1989: Of course. She won't go. She went one time, but had a headache and went home before the counselor could get anywhere. She won't eat and she sleeps all the time now.

St.Nick90: Where is she now?

Ry1989: Upstairs, asleep.

St.Nick90: Just keep trying and be patient.

Ry1989: I feel so impotent. I'm also afraid she blames me. If she never knew me, this wouldn't have happened to her.

St.Nick90: If she does blame you, she isn't being rational.

Ry1989: I've held back asking her to marry me until she gets better. I hope I finally get the chance.

St.Nick90: You will.

Ry1989: I love her so much. My heart is breaking.

St.Nick90: Buddy, you need a break from all of this. Why don't you come on vacation with Rielle and the girls and me? We are heading out to the Lake Como house in a week.

Ry1989: Thanks, but there's no way I can leave her. I have to protect her.

St.Nick90: Maybe she can come too.

Ry1989: Maybe. I think she's afraid to meet you, though.

St.Nick90: I don't bite. Well, except for that one time. LOL.

Ry1989: Ha ha.

St.Nick90: Sorry, just trying to take your mind off of her.

Ry1989: Impossible. She's all I think about anymore.

St.Nick90: Keep trying to get her into counseling.

Ry1989: How do I do that? She won't go.

St.Nick90: Be persistent. That's all you can do.

I stopped reading after this. I was losing him, and, worse yet, I was losing myself. I was a shell of myself. No spirit, afraid to leave the house, not eating, sleeping all the time. I realized how depressed I was.

And I knew what I had to do.

Chapter Thirty-Nine

The next day, as we were having breakfast, I casually asked Ryan what Rochelle's last name was. I was making a show of eating the eggs and turkey bacon in front of me, although, inside, I felt nauseated by it. Ryan looked pleased to see me eating, though, so I felt I had to finish the plate.

Afterwards, however, I discreetly excused myself to use the restroom and threw up. His cooking was great, as usual, but I couldn't keep anything down.

Not with the knowledge of what I would be doing that day.

Back to Rochelle, though. "Anderson," he said. "Why do you ask?"

"No reason." I looked at him, trying to hide the panic in my eyes. As casually as possible, I announced that I would be going shopping with Debbie, my best girlfriend.

Ryan looked thrilled. "That's wonderful, honey. Do you need some money?" He was obviously happy I was getting out of the house. It occurred to me that I really hadn't left the house on my own since I'd been home.

I shook my head. "No, I just want to browse. Get out of the house, get some fresh air, get caught up with her life. That sort of thing."

"Ok, then. What time are you going shopping?"

"In about an hour."

After I showered, I kissed Ryan goodbye and I got into the new Volvo and took off. I was shaking and nauseated and it occurred to me that I should've asked Daniel to drive me. But I didn't want to raise any suspicion on what I was doing. If I asked Daniel to drive me, it would've been a tipoff that I wasn't feeling well enough to drive myself, and Ryan might have insisted on coming along.

But this was something I knew I had to do by myself.

I arrived downtown, and found a place to park.

And headed for the county jail.

Chapter Forty

The county jail was a red building downtown that didn't really look like a county jail from the outside, as it was modern. Inside, however, the cells were just as one would picture. At least the waiting rooms, where attorneys meet clients, were just as one would picture. I would know, having spent two years going in and out of this jail in my role as a public defender.

I never dreamed I would be coming to this jail not as an attorney, but as a victim. But here I was.

I walked into the jail, and asked the guard for the cell number for Rochelle Anderson. The guard looked at his roster. "You here as a professional or as a visitor?"

"A professional." I knew that if I was a visitor, I either couldn't see her if it was not visiting hours, or I'd be relegated to talking to her on a phone from behind a plated glass. I wanted neither option.

"You got some ID?"

I handed the guard my Missouri Bar Identification.

"Please step through the metal detector."

I obliged.

I took the elevator to the fifth floor, which was where she was housed. I went down the corridor to the attorney room, which was where attorneys meet with their clients, and the door opened automatically. I could see the guard in her booth, and I walked into the vestibule right behind another automatic door. I looked at the guard expectantly, and she pressed a button so that the other door opened, and I walked through.

I sat down at a little table with a file in my hand and waited. I brought an empty file to make it look like I was there as an attorney.

I waited for about fifteen minutes, before addressing the guard at the station. "I'm here to see Rochelle Anderson."

The guard looked puzzled. "Did they call this in from downstairs?"

"I thought so."

"Is she expecting you?"

"Yes," I lied.

"Ok, then." I saw her get on the phone and call. I held my breath, hoping against hope there wasn't a problem of some sort. If they told me to come back, I really didn't think I would. It was literally now or never.

I could hear my heart pounding in my chest as I waited. This was more torture than what Rochelle put me through. I was shaking like a leaf.

What was taking so long?

The guard motioned me to the window. I wasn't breathing, but let out a sigh of relief when she said Rochelle was being brought out.

Then I started shaking and trembling anew. A part of me regretted not bringing Ryan there with me, but this was something I knew I had to do on my own.

About fifteen minutes later, with every minute ticking by like an hour, a woman came through the glass door, wearing an orange jumpsuit. She was a slight woman, dark hair, and was not necessarily beautiful but more...handsome. Square jaw, looked to be in her early fifties. I imagined she was quite a beauty about twenty or so years ago, but she looked ravaged now. Rode hard and put away wet. She appeared to be heavily into drugs.

I stood up, and she looked at me. "You," was all she said as the door clanged behind her.

I took a deep breath, willing myself not to back down, and not to beg the guard to take her away. I had to do this for my own mental sanity.

"Yeah, me," I said.

I watched the guard behind the glass window, who was reading a magazine. Rochelle could literally strangle me and they would be very slow to react. I wished she had on handcuffs and leg irons, but I knew that wasn't the protocol for professional visits.

She sat down. "May I help you?" Very cold. If I was expecting her to break down crying with regrets upon seeing me, I'd be sorely disappointed.

"I wanted to meet you, face to face," I said, mustering as much strength as I could. I wished at this point that I'd invested in acting classes, so that I could act like I didn't care I was facing her.

"Why?"

"Because I need to confront you and tell you how you made me feel. I know you don't care, but I need to say my piece so I can move on."

To my surprise, her expression changed. She didn't look as hostile as when she first sat down.

I took another deep breath and began. "I don't know

what I did to you to make you want to hurt me. I don't even know you. Why would you do that to me?"

"Listen, Chica, don't take it personally. I didn't want to hurt you. I wanted to hurt him."

"Why hurt him?"

"Didn't I make that clear? He hurt me. He devastated me, in fact." Her face contorted. "I haven't been able to look at another man since he left. That was twenty-fucking years ago."

I knew that what I wanted from this encounter was to see the humanity in this woman. That would make her less scary. It might also help me forgive. So far, it seemed like I was on a good track.

"Go on."

"What is there to tell? We were in love." She shook her head. "Nah, that sounds pretty silly right now. He was only 14 at the time. But he told me he loved me. I guess I believed it."

"Why would you do that to a 14-year-old boy?"

"I was mixed up. My husband was beating me before I left him. My fucking kid went to live with him, willingly. Willingly!" She looked disgusted. "Fucking ungrateful bastard still won't talk to me. Huh. Talk about giving someone life and in return they give you hell." Then she smiled. She had a few missing teeth. "I broke my dental bridge in this hellhole in a girl fight," she explained. I figured she lost her teeth to meth, which was common.

Then she looked at me. "Ryan had all the qualities my dickwad husband and bastard son didn't. He was kind and loving. Not a mean bone in that boy. And I fell hard for him."

She paused. She looked like she could use a cigarette. "So, well, as I told you before, I've followed him for years.

Surreptitiously, of course. I pretty much hired people to tail him. I knew he and Alexis wouldn't stay together. My people tailed her, too. That woman got more ass than Dennis Rodman." She laughed. "Anyhow, Ryan broke up with her, like I knew he would, after Alexis and Paul were caught together." She looked at me. "Paul was one of many, by the way. Ryan was being cuckolded right and left and had no fucking idea."

She shook her head. "That's why I'm in love with him. He's still so pure, even after all these years. That was why he had no suspicions about his slut wife. He just couldn't imagine that she would do that to him." Then she smiled slyly. "Of course, he always had his boy on the side. But Alexis knew about that the whole time. What fun is that?"

She continued. "Anyhow, after Ryan and Alexis broke up, Ryan started dating these women. These beautiful women. He would go out with a different one every night, I swear. So I felt safe."

"Safe?"

"Yeah, safe. Safe that he wasn't settling down and maybe I still had a chance with him. I was waiting for the right time to make my move."

Next stop, Crazytown. But I let her go on. This was very therapeutic for me.

"Then you came along." She snorted. "Somehow I knew when he met you that he'd found The One. It was just like Ryan to want to settle down with somebody who is, shall we say....I mean, no offense, but you're not exactly a runway model."

"No offense taken. Go on."

"My hunch was right. My people didn't see him juggling one supermodel type after another anymore, he stopped messing around with Nick, and he pretty much settled down with you." She snorted again. "Not 'pretty much' settled down. He did settle down. All the Giselles and Heidis were gone after you came on the scene."

"Were there Heidis and Giselles at the time he met me?" Now I was curious.

"God, yes. He had a regular rotation going with about five of them. He met you and they were all gone. Like they were in the witness protection program." She laughed at her own joke.

"Anyhow, I knew he was serious about you," she continued. "But I still felt that maybe there was a chance you'd go the way of all the others and I could still get in there under the wire."

She shook her head. "But no. He bought you this incredible rock, and I was out of my mind when I found that out."

She looked me right in the eye. "So I kidnapped and tortured you. I'm not proud of it, but I figured that was the best way to kill him slowly."

I raised my eyebrows. She didn't exactly seem filled with remorse. Yet I was seeing the humanity in her, so I could feel myself relaxing.

After a pause, she asked "Did I answer all your questions?"

I nodded. "But I said I wanted to say my piece, so I'm going to say my piece. And you're going to listen to it, because where you gonna go?" I looked up at the camera, knowing that what I was saying was being picked up by the guard's station. If Rochelle wanted to leave, she could leave. All she had to do was ask.

But she didn't. She stayed rooted to her seat.

I took a deep breath. "You've ruined my life. But I'm not going to let you keep ruining my life. I'm not going to give you any more satisfaction in telling you how much you hurt me. But know this. Ryan and I are doing great. And, after today, we'll be doing even better. Because now I have closure on what you did to me. I needed to confront you, and that's exactly what I did. Confront you. Now I can put this behind me."

It was my turn to look her in the eye. "You may have thought that you were getting what you wanted when you did all that you did to me. But it backfired. Ryan and I are closer than ever because of this. Your actions have made us stronger." I paused. "I guess Nietzsche was right after all. What doesn't kill you makes you stronger."

Some of that was a lie – Ryan and I weren't stronger together. We were falling apart.

I felt that would change after today.

She looked at me, her face defeated. "What the hell, I wish you luck."

I looked at her quizzically.

"Sure, sure, I wish you luck. I mean, it's not like I'm going to get him back now. Shit, I'll be lucky if I ever get out of the joint."

My face was impassive. I went up the guard's station. "I need to leave."

At that, another guard came out and took Rochelle back to her cell. The guard behind the window pushed a button to let me out.

I felt like a 1,000 lb. weight had been lifted off of me.

As I walked out, I saw Ryan leaning against a lightpost. I was surprised to see him, yet not surprised at the same time.

At any rate, I was extremely glad to see him.

"Hey," I said.

"Hey." He looked sheepish. "Um, I hope you don't think I've suddenly become a stalker."

"Of course not," I said with a smile. "But I'm curious as to how you knew that I was coming here."

"I had a tracer put on your phone."

"A tracer? Why? You don't think I'm fooling around?"

He shook his head violently. "No, no, no, no, no. Nothing like that." He paused. "After what happened to you at Rochelle's, I vowed that would never happen again. All I could think was that I should've gotten there sooner. I almost lost you. You went through torture. All because I didn't know you were missing for a few hours, then I had to figure out where you were the old-fashioned way." He visibly shuddered. "So, I put a tracking device on your phone."

"So I'm microchipped, like a dog?" I was smiling to make sure he knew I wasn't angry about this.

"I hope you aren't angry?"

"No, of course not. But I'm curious as to why you didn't tell me about this earlier?"

He took a deep breath. "I didn't know how to tell you that I've suddenly become paranoid and overprotective."

I punched him lightly on the arm. "I kinda like paranoid and overprotective these days."

"Anyhow, I found out you were here and I freaked out a little."

"That's why I didn't tell you I was coming here. I figured you'd try to talk me out of it, or insist on coming with me." I saw his hurt face. "No offense, but this was something I really needed to do alone."

"I understand." He wrapped his arms around me. "Are you okay?"

I nodded. "Better than okay. I feel free." It felt so good

to be in his arms. I buried my head in his chest. His heart was pounding like I had never heard it before. It sounded like the drum solo at the beginning of the big band classic *Sing Sing Sing*.

"I'm sorry for scaring you," I said.

"It's ok. Just please don't do it again."

I said nothing, just nodded my head into his chest.

We walked across the street to a little bar and grill for lunch.

"So, tell me about the visit," he said over a grilled chicken sandwich and salad.

"I wanted to see her, put a face to my misery. I wanted to see she was a human being and not a scary monster."

"And?"

"Mission accomplished. She was surprisingly not scary. I mean, she's missing several teeth. Did you know that?"

He laughed. "I had no idea."

"True story. She apparently had some kind of a dental bridge, but she broke it during a girlfight in jail."

We both laughed at this for awhile.

I continued "It's hard to be fearful of somebody who looks like a backwoods hillbilly." More laughter.

After a little bit, I continued. "Anyhow, I found out some stuff that makes me feel her humanity. When I was a public defender, I always saw the humanity in my clients. That was how I was able to defend them, no matter what they did. I figured that if I found her humanity it would help me to forgive."

He had that look on his face, the look that always makes me melt. The look of sheer, unadulterated love.

I drew a breath and went on. "She told me about her abusive husband and her son who won't talk to her. Not that I blame the son. She's pretty wackadoodle." I looked pensively out the window. "She isn't remorseful for what she did. I think she justifies it in her crazy little head."

I looked at him. "But I don't hate her. And she now knows that she didn't break me. I made sure she knew that I was stronger because of what happened. That *we* are stronger because of what happened."

He grabbed my hand, looking me in the eye. "I love you. I love you more than I ever thought I could love anyone. And I've never loved you more than I love you right now."

I smiled. "I love you, too." It was easier to say those words now, getting easier every day.

After we finished our lunch, I told Ryan that I had one more thing to do while I was downtown.

Go to the prosecutor's office.

"Can I come with?"

"Sure, you can wait outside the office while I talk to Cindy. But I really need to do that alone as well."

Cindy was Cindy Johnson, the lead prosecutor on Rochelle's case. I needed to have a few words with her.

We made our way to the prosecutor's office. As I entered the main suite, the receptionist greeted me. "Iris, hello!" She came around and gave me a big hug. "We missed you around here. What a pleasant surprise!"

"Hey, Katherine. Is Cindy around?"

"Sure, go on back." She turned to Ryan, her eyes lighting up. "You must be Ryan. Can I get you anything while you wait?"

"A water would be great!" Ryan said. I turned around and saw Ryan take a seat and start flipping through magazines. He looked at me and gave me a wink.

I knocked on Cindy's door. She was busy at her computer, files piled up on her desk. I started feeling anxiety, not because of what I had to say to her, but mainly because seeing files piled up made me remember my own law days, not so long ago.

She looked at me, her blue eyes big. "Iris!" She, too, gave me a big hug. "Come in, come in. Have a seat!"

"I hope I'm not interrupting?"

"Not at all. I mean, I got a PV docket in a couple of hours." She motioned to her files on the desk. "So I can talk for a little bit."

PV dockets were probation violation dockets. There were typically about 50 cases on these dockets, but they generally went pretty quickly.

"So what can I do for you?" she asked, after I sat down.

"I understand you have the Rochelle Anderson case?"

She gasped. "Oh, of course! Stupid me, of course that's why you're here." She looked sheepish. "I know what happened. How are you holding up?"

"Fine, fine. I wasn't ok but I'm better now."

She nodded. "What would you like to talk about?"

"Well, I know she's charged with various counts of assault one and kidnapping one."

Cindy nodded. "That she is."

"I wanted to let you know how I feel. I know it's your job to cut deals, but I also know that assault one and kidnapping one are both 85 percenters." This means that anybody convicted of assault one or kidnapping one are required to serve 85% of their sentence.

I continued. "I don't want you to cut a deal where she pleads down to an offense that is not an 85 percenter. I don't want her being sentenced to 20 years, getting out in three." This was important, because lesser offenses typically result in the defendant only serving 15% of their sentence.

Cindy spoke. "That's not what I want to do, either. And

there isn't a reason to cut a deal like that. I mean, we have her dead to right."

I nodded. "Who is on the other side?"

"John O'Donnell."

I groaned. I knew O'Donnell's reputation. He was one of the highest-priced attorneys in the area and definitely one of the best. His courtroom flourishes and dirty tricks were legendary.

"John O'Donnell. Johnnie Cochran's dead, otherwise I'm sure she would've hired him."

Cindy smiled. "I know, I hate going up against him. He could've gotten Ted Bundy off on a technicality."

"Well, don't succumb to pressure. I need that woman locked up for a long, long time."

She nodded. "It's good you're here. I was going to call you when the time was right. I need to prepare you if this thing goes to trial, which, hopefully, it won't."

"That'll suck, having to tell this story to a jury. But, if it has to happen, it has to happen."

Cindy hesitated. "So, how are you, really?"

"Fine. Getting stronger every day."

"I heard you closed your practice."

"Yeah, well, that had to happen. I wasn't exactly equipped to deal with my clients for a few months."

She nodded.

"And, besides, I can't go back there. That was where I was attacked."

"Are you going to come back? I mean, I understand that you don't want to go back to that particular office, but are you going to get back into law?"

"Not sure. I'm taking a break right now, trying to plot my next move."

"Yeah. I hear you got a nice boyfriend to help you out, too."

I nodded. "What do you know about that?"

"Well, the word is you are dating Benjamin Whitney's gorgeous son."

"The word is correct. How do you know about his being gorgeous?"

"He was in the society pages a lot. I guess you don't pay much attention to that."

"No, never have paid attention to that."

"He was like our very own JFK Jr. Before the crash, of course."

"What do you mean?"

"Before he got married, he was considered the most eligible bachelor in the area."

"Where have I been? I've never even heard of the guy before I met him."

"Living under a rock, I guess." She paused. "Anyhow, I guess you got set up pretty well, there."

I wondered if that was a subtle dig. "Yes, well, I'm not going to be a kept woman. I'm just taking a break right now. I need to recover mentally and physically before I decide what my next move is."

"Of course. That's perfectly understandable." She smiled. "Well, I have to get ready for my docket. Is there anything else?"

"No. I just want you to keep me in the loop on this case. Please don't cut a deal without notifying me."

"I promise."

"Thanks."

I walked out into the waiting area. Ryan and Katherine were chatting.

Ryan saw me and stood up. "How did it go?"

"Ok, I guess. Rochelle got a lawyer who would rival Johnnie Cochran himself."

"I figured as much."

"I apologize, Ryan. But I now need to make one more visit while I'm on a roll right now."

"Sure. Who you going to see?"

"John O'Donnell."

"You want me to drive you there?"

"Could you?" I had to admit that I was silly not wanting him along. His presence comforted me, calmed me down. Once I broke down my walls, and admitted that I was in love with him, I found that his presence brought me peace.

And peace was exactly what I needed right now.

We made our way to his Porsche, which was parked in a garage. Ryan asked "Now, what is this guy's name?"

"John O'Donnell."

He programmed his GPS.

"Looks like he's in Parkville."

It figured. Parkville was an up and coming area that had some amazing nouveau riche mansions. I figured a high-priced guy like O'Donnell would be located in one of the enormous office suites downtown, but Parkville made sense as well.

"Hold on a sec." He looked at his GPS display. "Looks like he also has an office downtown." At that, he called the downtown office.

"Hello?" The receptionist answered the phone.

"Mr. O'Donnell, please," Ryan said.

"One moment, please."

After a few minutes, there was another voice on the phone.

"Mr. O'Donnell is busy right now. Can I help you?"

Ryan looked at me.

I talked into the display. "This is Iris Snowe. Could I make an appointment to see him?"

"Could you hold please?"

After a few minutes, the woman came back. "When can you be here?"

"In a half hour?"

"We'll see you then."

I was more than surprised. I knew how busy this guy was, and he was going to fit me in within a half-hour?

We headed to his downtown office, which was, just as I expected, one of the high-rise jobs. The office was on the 55th Floor. Holding Ryan's hand so tight that I feared cutting off his circulation, we made our way up to O'Donnell's office.

A busty blonde lady in a low-cut silk blouse and fuck-me pumps, wearing more makeup than Tammy Faye Baker in her prime, greeted us. "Hello. You must be Iris." She eyed Ryan, making no secret that she was mentally undressing him. I inwardly groaned. "And you are?" she asked Ryan.

"Ryan. Iris' boyfriend."

She raised one eyebrow at me. *Lucky girl* her eyes said.

She went back behind the receptionist desk, picked up the phone and called O'Donnell. She looked at me. "He's ready to see you. Let me lead the way."

"Thanks." I looked at Ryan. "I won't be long." He looked a bit hurt. I guess he wanted to be in on this meeting.

"Good luck, beautiful," he said with a smile.

I was led to an exquisite suite with enormous windows that looked out on an expansive view of the city. A 50ish handsome man with greying temples, but a full head of hair, stood up at his desk as I walked in. I'd never actually met this guy before, just knew his reputation. His cases were always out of my league, so we never crossed paths.

"Iris. Come in, come in."

I sat down.

"What can I do for you?" he asked me.

I took a deep breath. This was my most audacious request, and I knew I would be turned down. But I had to try.

"You have the Rochelle Anderson case."

"Yes, about that." He looked at me sternly. "The reason why I was willing to see you is that I was going to call you anyhow. Then you called me and asked to see me, so it saved me the effort."

I had a feeling I knew what was coming.

"I understand you went to see her," he said.

"Yes, I-"

"And you represented yourself as her attorney."

"Well, no, I-"

"No? Then how did you get a professional visit with her?"

"Well, I did represent myself as *an* attorney, not *her* attorney."

He shook his head. "Don't do that anymore. I don't want to file a bar complaint against you, after what you went through, but, I swear to God, I'll do that if you come within a mile of my client again."

I nodded. I didn't think it through when I went down there. But he was absolutely right. I was ethically wrong to do what I did, although I wasn't quite sure exactly how many rules I broke. Probably several.

"I apologize."

His face softened. "It's ok. I really don't blame you for doing what you did." He paused. "But that doesn't mean I won't burn your ass to the ground if you do it again. Now, that out of the way, what can I do for you?"

"I wanted to make a request."

"A request."

"Yes. I'd like you to withdraw from this case."

He gave me a look like *right. Ok. Withdraw from the case because?*

"Not going to happen. Anything else?"

I wasn't going to back down. "Listen, I know your reputation." He looked offended. "Hey, it's a compliment. I know the high profile cases that you've handled. I know about your high profile acquittals." I drew a deep breath. "You just can't get this woman acquitted."

"Oh? If I'm not mistaken, you were once a public defender."

"Yes."

"And you gave all your clients a vigorous defense, even if they were guilty as hell."

"Well, that was different."

"Different how?"

"I wasn't a mercenary, going to the highest bidder."

"Oh, I see. Because you weren't charging $1,500 per hour for your services, somehow you were more noble than me?"

"Well, yes."

"Yet you still gave a vigorous defense, looking for every loophole, gunning for every acquittal, knowing your efforts would put a scumbag back on the street."

I opened my mouth, but no words came out. I didn't know what to say.

"Did you think about the victims in your cases?"

I admitted I didn't.

"Of course not. It was all a game, right?"

To my surprise, I was hanging my head now and crying. I looked up, and his face was impassive. His arms were crossed. He had a box of Kleenex on his desk, but he didn't offer me a tissue.

He raised an eyebrow. "Right?"

Inwardly, I knew he was right. But there was a difference – I really wasn't that good. Not in his league, anyhow. I was an underpaid public employee. Yet that wasn't the point. He was absolutely right. Defense attorneys didn't consider present or future victims. It really was a game. Only a job. But now it was real.

"Please, Mr. O'Donnell. My life will be over if you get that woman acquitted on a technicality."

"You are really the biggest hypocrite, aren't you? It's fine for you to get criminals acquitted on a technicality, but it all changes when you're the victim."

I wasn't going to get anywhere with this guy. "I'm sorry to have bothered you."

He nodded, and pressed the button on his phone. "Alice, could you please show Ms. Snowe out?"

At that, blondie appeared, out of nowhere. She opened the door and motioned for me to leave. I obediently obliged.

I followed her back to the lobby of the office. Ryan stood up, saw my face, and immediately looked concerned. He protectively put his arm around me. I shook my head. "I'll tell you later."

He nodded.

I got out on the street, and burst into tears.

"Love, what's wrong?"

I just shook my head, over and over again. "She's going to be acquitted. I just know it." I was shaking violently. "She'll come after me again. And she'll finish the job."

Ryan was looking at the building that we just came out of. "That guy is that good, huh?"

"You don't understand. You don't know the cases he's won. Impossible cases. If you thought OJ's Dream Team was amazing, you don't know this guy."

"Hold on. Stay right here." At that, he went back into the building.

I stood there, astounded. I was shaking and crying, and he leaves me? This made me sob even more. I sat down on the curb, my head in my hands. I felt abandoned on top of everything else. A car drove by, too close, and splashed dirty water on my pants. This made me sob even harder. My entire body felt like it was spasming, and I felt nauseated. I dry heaved, having no food in my stomach, as I couldn't eat that day, and it seemed like days since I last had a meal. Still, a little bit of acid came up through my throat, and this made me gag and cry even more.

Where was Ryan? How could he leave me like this?

After about a half hour, Ryan appeared. I felt instantly calmed upon seeing him. He had a document in his hand. He handed it to me.

It was a notice of withdrawal. I looked at him, perplexed. "How did you-"

"I found his price."

I nodded, understanding. "How much?"

He shrugged. "Three quarters of a million dollars."

My heart stopped. "Ryan, you can't-"

"Shhhh. Your mental health is priceless to me. This is a small price to pay."

I sighed. I'd never get used to this. This casual throwing around enormous sums of money. He acted like he paid him fifty bucks.

Ryan grabbed my hand. "Now, come on. We need to file this document for him."

It occurred to me that this entire scenario might be enough to get me disbarred. Well, this incident, combined with my earlier visit, under false pretenses, to Rochelle at the jail. At this point, though, I didn't care. All I wanted was for this guy to not represent Rochelle.

Anybody but him.

It also dawned on me there was no way John O'Donnell would turn me in. He would have to admit to taking a bribe. We would take each other down. Of course, Rochelle would be furious and would want to know why he withdrew from her case. With any luck, he had a story at the ready about why he was taking this action.

At any rate, I couldn't worry about it. I wasn't practicing law at the moment, anyhow, and didn't know if I ever would again. So, what did I care? I really had nothing to lose. He, however, had a lot to lose. I figured I was safe.

Ryan and I went to the courthouse, and filed the notice of withdrawal. Then, Ryan drove me to my car. "See you at home?"

"Of course."

He smiled. "I'm getting my Iris back." Then, with a little skip in his step, he got back into his car, and I followed him out.

I was going home.

Chapter Forty-One

That night, we made love for the first time since Rochelle ambushed me. Ryan was tender, gentle, like he was afraid that he would break me. I had to admit that I did feel pretty fragile, both physically and mentally.

Afterwards, we lay in bed together. He stroked my body longingly. He kissed me, and I could feel his hardness again. He immediately stopped kissing me.

"We better get some sleep."

I nodded, but wondered why.

He looked sheepish. "I don't want to rush things too much. I'm afraid of wearing you out."

I smiled and pushed him down on the mattress and straddled him. He was inside me again. He started to protest, but it was my turn to shush him. "I'm fine. More than fine. You aren't going to break me. Now shut up and fuck me."

He smiled and obliged.

We didn't make love again that night after that. But things started to feel somewhat normal. He was stroking my hair from behind, his naked body pressed up against mine.

He spoke. "I have to admit this is different. You've lost so much weight, I feel I'm with a different woman."

I looked at him quizzically.

"Don't worry, I'll get used to it. But I liked you before. You really need to eat."

"You liked me before?"

"Sure. I mean, I like you now, too. But it just seems weird."

I snorted.

"What?" he asked.

"Rochelle told me you had a veritable rotation of women going before you met me. And, from the sounds of it, they were all pretty slim."

"Well, yes. I dated a lot. What's so wrong with that?"

"Nothing. I just figured you liked skinny women."

"I like you. No matter what size you are. I'm just concerned, that's all."

He saw my look and continued. "I'm concerned that you're not eating because you're afraid of gaining weight. And I'm telling you that I'm fine with you gaining weight. I fell in love with you when you were heavier, you seem to forget."

I just lay there and said nothing.

"You really need to eat," he continued. "The last thing you need is to go to rehab for anorexia. And don't think I won't get you into rehab if you get below 100 lbs." He rubbed his hands on my now-bony arms. "I need you healthy. We have a full life together, so you need to keep up your strength."

I nodded, but again said nothing. I was enjoying my new body and was still terrified of gaining the weight back.

Maybe seeing a shrink wasn't a bad idea after all.

Chapter Forty-Two

It was Friday, two days after my whirlwind visits to Rochelle and everybody. I was in Dr. Halder's office. I was going to stay there this time and complete my session. But I wanted Ryan go be in the office with me. He agreed to this.

"So, Iris. You're back."

"Very observant."

"How are you?"

"Better. I don't have a blinding headache today. And my sleeping has gotten back to normal."

"Good. Now what brings you here today?"

"Ryan thinks I need to talk about what happened." I looked at Ryan, who was on the loveseat next to me, holding my hand.

"Ok, then. Go on."

"Well, I'm getting stronger. I faced my attacker. I talked to the prosecutor. And I talked her attorney into withdrawing from her case." That wasn't exactly true, but I didn't want to admit there was bribery involved. I still was worried that this would come back to bite me. Of course, it wasn't like Dr. Halder could turn me in. Doctor-patient confidentiality and all that. But I still felt just a wee bit paranoid because Ryan was also in the room with me. With attorney-client confidentiality, the presence of a third party in the room severs the confidentiality, and I wondered if it was the same with a psychologist. Not that he would turn me in, but I didn't really want to take that chance.

He continued to look at me, silently. I went on.

"I guess there are some residual effects. I've stopped eating and I can't bring myself to start eating again."

"And why is this?"

"Well, I was a bit overweight before." I looked at Ryan, who was looking at his lap and shaking his head. Dr. Halder noticed Ryan shaking his head.

"Ryan, you're shaking your head."

"Yes. Iris is beautiful now and she was beautiful then. I don't know why she can't see that."

Dr. Halder then looked to me. "You hear what Ryan is saying. But you don't seem to believe that."

"No. I know the women he's dated before me. And was married to. I need to look my best for him. He deserves that."

Ryan seemed angry now. "I deserve a healthy wife. That's all I want. And if you don't start eating, you won't be healthy."

Somehow I was back to my insecure self. Some things never changed, I guessed.

I shook my head. "I'm not good enough for him."

Now he was angry. "Jesus, Iris, how can you still be spouting this bullshit? I'm completely devoted to you. I can't believe you can't see that by now." He lifted his hand from my hand and crossed his arms.

I looked at Dr. Halder. "So, you can see, I'm pretty messed up."

Ryan pouted for the rest of the time he was at the session.

He ended up leaving the session about a half-hour early, without a word. When I walked out, after talking to Dr. Halder, I saw Daniel there waiting for me. I groaned inwardly.

He looked sheepish. "Ryan left and told me to come and pick you up."

I nodded. I figured I deserved this treatment.

I decided to engage Daniel in conversation. For a first.

"So, Daniel, tell me about yourself."

"What would you like to know?"

"How long have you known Ryan?"

"About 10 years."

"How long have you been his driver?"

"He hired me after Paul. You know." He looked at me knowingly.

"Yeah. And when was that?"

"About three years ago."

"You drive his other women around?"

"What other women?"

"You know."

He rolled his eyes. "Well, before you there were."

I nodded knowingly. "Go on."

"You get nothing from me." He looked ahead at the road.

I sighed.

I arrived at home. The lights were turned out. Ryan's car wasn't in the driveway. I felt the familiar constriction in my lungs, the feeling of fear. I didn't want to be alone. I found my phone and called him.

"Hello?"

"Hi," he answered.

"Where are you?"

"I'm at the Granfalloon." This was the bar and grill on the Plaza where he and Nick went that one day. I could hear noises in the background.

"Can I-"

"No. I'm alright."

I started to feel slightly panicky. What if he really does want to leave me? What if there was a self-fulfilling prophecy - I was so paranoid about him leaving me that I behaved in a manner that caused him to really leave?

"Ok. I'll see you when you get home?"

"Yeah. See you then."

I dragged myself up to our room. I was feeling exhausted again. And depressed. I fell asleep from the time my head hit the pillow.

I woke up to an empty bed. I crept into one of the guest bedrooms. He wasn't there. I searched the other four bedrooms and the office. Not there. I made my way into the loft, and found him on the couch, asleep, the television still playing. I shut off the TV, found a blanket and put it over him. He was fast asleep. I crawled onto the other sofa, found a pillow and blanket, and went back to sleep.

I woke up again, and Ryan was gone. I made my way downstairs, and found him in his boxer shorts and t-shirt, making breakfast. He smiled at me. "Good morning, Sunshine."

I relaxed. He seemed friendlier.

"Do you want to talk?" I asked him.

"Sure. Here. I made you a screwdriver."

I sat down while Ryan finished off the breakfast, and brought it out to the dining room.

"So," I began. "I guess you're mad at me?"

"No, not mad. Just really confused."

I nodded.

He continued. "I'm just confused on how I can show you that you not only mean the world to me, but you're good enough for me."

"I have my issues," I admitted.

"And how." He shook his head. "I just don't know how you still have these issues."

"They don't just magically disappear overnight."

"Granted. But come on, we've been together now for almost a year."

I looked down at my hands and said nothing.

"Anyhow," he said, and kneeled in front of me. I could feel my pulse quickening, and my breath caught. Like when we first met.

He took my hand. "Maybe I can convince you about how much I love you. Iris, you've made me a better man. Before I met you, I was lost and broken. You've fixed me. You've helped me find my way. I, quite frankly, can never imagine my life without you now. Nor do I want to. So now, I have to ask you the question I've wanted to ask you from the moment I saw you in that bar." He produced a small jewelry box and opened it.

Inside was the most magnificent ring I'd ever seen. But it wasn't the ring described to Rochelle. This ring had a princess-cut red diamond in a platinum setting. The red diamond was several carats and was offset by tiny white diamonds. I'd never seen anything like it, and I knew how rare red diamonds were.

I didn't want to know how much he paid for this ring.

"Will you make me the happiest man ever and do me the honor of being my wife?"

I was shaking uncontrollably. I nodded my head, unable to say anything at all. Once again, I had no voice.

He slipped the ring on my finger. I stared at it. It was beautiful, the most beautiful thing I'd seen in my life. I suddenly realized that I was crying uncontrollably. I wrapped my arms around his neck and sobbed into his shoulder.

Ryan was laughing. "I'm starting to get used to your odd reactions to happy events."

I couldn't say anything at all, but I was nodding my head violently. He held me for what seemed like an hour, while I strangled him, not wanting to let go.

I finally finished crying, then looked down at my rock. My hand was still shaking violently.

I finally spoke. "What is this stone?" I somehow knew it was a diamond without him telling me. It was definitely not a ruby.

"It's a diamond."

"I've never seen a red diamond."

"That's because they're very rare, love." He paused, looking me in the eye. "Like you."

"I thought – "

"That I got you a five carat diamond ring at Tiffany's?"

I nodded.

"I did. But the more I looked at it, the more ordinary it seemed to me. It just didn't suit you at all. You're one of a kind, and the ring should reflect that."

I looked into his eyes. "I love you," I said.

He kissed me long and slow. "I love you too."

At that, he picked me up and carried me into our bedroom.

We made love the rest of the day.

Chapter Forty-Three

Two days later, Ryan and I made our way to the state hospital to visit Maggie. I'd already told my parents, but, of course, they already knew. Ryan, ever the old-fashioned gentleman, had asked my father for my hand. My father, confused about why Ryan would bother asking him, said yes, of course.

I smiled. Of course, my father didn't know about that old tradition. I doubted he did the same when he asked my mother to marry him. In fact, I know he didn't – my maternal grandfather was a drunk who left the family when my mom was only 15.

Now it was time to tell sweet Maggie. And give her a double dose of good news – she was finally going to be released. Sheldon had secured this, and Ryan had found her a room in a group transition home.

It was going to be a good day.

We went through the usual routine – taking off our watches, taking off our shoes. I set off the metal detector because of my ring. I begged the security guard not to make me take it off. He saw my pleading face and let it go.

I was relieved. I never wanted to take off the ring, however unrealistic that would be in the future. If I got back into law there would be many more metal detectors. But, for now, I was secure in not having to take it off.

We made our way up to Maggie's room. She was playing cards with Rosey, the lady who was bound in leather straps the last time. Now Rosey looked normal. Maggie lit up upon seeing us.

She came up to us and gave us both a big hug. Rosey did the same with Ryan, then turned to me with a smile. "Hello. You must be Iris." At that, Rosey hugged me, too.

Ryan and I took a seat in the room. "You wanna play some gin?" Rosey asked us both.

I looked at Ryan. Ryan said "Maybe later, Rose. I need to talk to Mom right now."

Rosey nodded. "I'll go visit Michelle down the hall."

"Don't go far," Ryan called to her. She nodded as she walked down the hall.

Ryan took a deep breath. Maggie looked at us, looking at one, then the other. "What's going on?" she asked.

"Do you want the good news or the better news first?"

"The good news."

"Sheldon has secured your release. You'll be getting out of here next Monday."

"Oh, that's wonderful. Where will I live?"

"I found a really nice transition group home for you. If things go well, you can move out of there in a year and live on your own."

Maggie looked a little sad. "I'll miss the people here. Especially Rosey." Then she smiled. "But I'll be able to see you more. And Sarah."

Sarah. I'd have to meet her, too, now that Sarah was going to be family.

Maggie looked at us again. "And the better news?"

Ryan lifted up my left hand. Maggie let out a little shriek of joy, then hugged us both. "Welcome to the family!" she said to me in my ear. Then she looked closer at the ring. "A perfect red diamond. I've never seen anything like this!" She kissed me on the cheek. "I think you'll make a wonderful daughter-in-law."

I nodded, smiling.

We stayed the rest of the day. Rosey came back in after about a half hour, congratulated us, then we all played cards. I didn't know too many card games, but everybody was patient in teaching me. I did know how to play poker, so we did that, too, with Maggie bringing out her poker set with chips. None of the chips were worth anything, but that wasn't the point. Hanging out was the point, and we all had a great time.

Finally, we left.

On the way home, Ryan said "Well, now, Iris. Uh, Nick is…Nick will be my best man. So – "

I smiled. "Let's meet."

I was, at long last, going to meet the infamous Nick.

Next in the Illusions Series

vinci-books.com/deeper-illusions

From dream wedding to living nightmare. Will their love survive the ultimate test?

Iris and her Prince Charming, Ryan, are married—but their fairytale is unraveling. New tragedies strike, threatening everything they've built. Their past haunts them, but their present may be devastating enough to end their love story forever.

Turn the page for a free preview…

Deeper Illusions: Chapter One

IRIS

It was the Friday after Ryan had asked me to marry him over breakfast, and Ryan and I made plans for Nick and his wife, Rielle, to join us for dinner at our house. Now that I had a ring on my finger, I finally accepted that the house was "ours." Funny, Ryan deeding the house to me as a joint owner didn't make me feel the house was "ours."

The ring made all the difference.

I was nervous, so I drank some wine before they arrived. Ryan noticed me looking nervous and put his arm around me protectively.

I smiled. "Don't worry, I'm fine. This is a first, though, I must admit."

He nodded. "Nick is a great guy. I promise you, you'll love him. And he, you."

"Does Nick, uh. Does he, uh." I blushed scarlet.

"Use your words," Ryan teased.

"Does he love you?"

"As a friend, of course. But I've a feeling that's not what you're asking."

I nodded.

"We've talked about that. We do have feelings for each other, I'm not going to lie. But it's different than how I feel about you and how he feels about Rielle. I hope that makes sense."

I nodded again, bringing the wine up to my lips once more.

"Does Rielle know?"

"Nah. She wouldn't understand." He looked at me longingly. "Most people wouldn't understand this. I admit, it's unconventional, but it's more common than you might think."

Finally, the hour was upon us. I heard the doorbell ring, and, taking another sip of wine, I answered the door.

Nick was just how I pictured him. Sandy blonde hair, blue eyes, a very muscular frame. Extremely handsome, like a young Robert Redford. He was the same height as Ryan. He smiled at me, giving me a hug. I noticed his dimples right away. I was always a sucker for a guy with dimples. "Iris, so good to meet you! And congratulations!"

His wife, Rielle, was a little cooler. She wasn't as friendly as Alexis, who was around less and less now that she and Todd were becoming more serious. Rielle was a rail-thin brunette with enormous brown eyes and alabaster skin. She wore little makeup, but didn't really need to. She reminded me somewhat of my former roommate in college who looked better without makeup than with it. At any rate, like everybody who I have met through Ryan, she was gorgeous and well-dressed.

She held out her hand and smiled. "I'm Rielle. I've heard a lot about you."

"Well, don't believe everything you hear," I joked. Rielle nodded and didn't pretend to laugh.

I had a feeling I would get along fine with Nick. Rielle, not so much.

Nick had a bottle of vintage Scotch in his hand. I saw him in the kitchen, putting his arm around Ryan as they poured out two glasses.

"What are you drinking?" Ryan addressed myself and Rielle. We were standing in the living room together, not saying a word. It was very uncomfortable.

"I'd like a mojito," Rielle called.

"That sounds good, I'd like the same." Beer than liquor, never sicker? I wondered if it was the same with wine. I guessed I would find out.

At that, Ryan went out the back door to pick some mint leaves. Nick motioned me to join him in the kitchen.

"So, you and Ryan."

"Yeah. Crazy, huh?"

"Sure. Let me see that ring." He looked at the ring, then gave a low whistle. "Leave it to Ryan to show the rest of us schlubs up. This baby is custom designed. Must've cost a pretty penny. A VERY pretty penny." He had a look on his face that I couldn't quite discern. Jealousy?

At that, Ryan was back with a bunch of mint leaves in his hand. He pummeled them with some sugar, poured the rum into a glass with the mint and sugar, with some ice, and added some club soda and lime.

The mojito was delicious, of course.

As was the dinner. Ryan prepared some filet mignons and I made the garlic mashed potatoes. The filets were grass-fed, as that was the only type of steaks that we ate, for ethical reasons. I had also steamed some green beans.

After dinner, we had some dessert and a few more drinks. I noticed the two guys sitting across the table, Nick's arm draped around Ryan's shoulders. I wished I didn't know what I knew about these two. They just looked like two best friends. I found myself silently cursing Alexis. *What I don't know won't hurt me.* But I *did* know, and I couldn't stop picturing them together.

"So, buddy. How about having it at my Lake Como home?"

I shook my head at Ryan. No way could my family afford tickets to Italy. *Oh, what am I saying? We can all just fly in the private jet.*

"Well, we can visit sometime. But I think Iris wants to have it right here."

"You can honeymoon at the house, then. And visit your winery. You haven't been there for awhile, you know."

Ryan looked at me. "Nick's Lake Como home is pretty magnificent. It has an amazing view of the Lake."

Nick addressed me. "You ever been to Italy?"

"No. I, uh, have never been out of the country." I felt like such a rube, again.

Nick raised one eyebrow. Ryan immediately changed the subject. "So, we were thinking about something pretty intimate. Nothing churchy, of course."

"What about the country club?" Nick asked.

"Nah. Too formal," Ryan said.

Ryan and I had actually discussed this beforehand. I didn't want the country club wedding, or the destination wedding. I just wanted something simple, in keeping with my nature.

Ryan was perfectly willing to go along with whatever I wanted.

"So, what were you thinking?" Nick asked.

"We thought about just having it here. In the backyard," Ryan said.

I nodded. Nick looked perplexed at this.

"Well, I agree your backyard is pretty bad-ass. But you have the choice of having it at the Lake Como house and you choose just to have it here?"

I was starting to feel more and more intimidated by Nick. I could feel a tension there, a dominance issue with him. It could have been just my imagination, but there seemed to be a subtle undermining of my relationship with Ryan.

I wondered if Nick really just wanted to be with Ryan and he was going to sabotage.

I shook that thought off. There was no indication this was the case.

I was just being silly.

Ryan was addressing the issue of the wedding again. "We appreciate the offer, Nick, but Iris has a lot of family here in town, and I can't put all of them on the private plane."

"Why not? Doesn't it seat like 30?"

"Yes, but not everybody can take off work, you know. And between the friends and family, there probably will be close to 100 people. How are we going to get all those people out to Italy?"

"You buy them first class tickets." Nick looked smug.

"Problem solved," Ryan said, rolling his eyes.

"Whatever. It's your wedding. I'm just along for the ride."

Ryan put his arm around me. "I admit, I'd like to stay at the Lake Como house for our honeymoon." Addressing me, Ryan said "I have a yacht out there, too, that I keep on the Mediterranean."

I smiled. *Yacht, schmact.* I really didn't care. I just wanted to be with him, even if it was in a shoebox.

Later on that night, I found out my hunch was true.

Ryan and Nick were in the living room, talking and drinking Scotch. Rielle had gone to bed early with a headache, and I, too, went to bed around midnight, after staying up with the guys. Nick played 20 questions with me. It wasn't entirely unpleasant, but he did seem to pry.

I was leaving my room to get a drink of water, and I decided to eavesdrop on the guys down below. They didn't notice me up above. They'd been drinking most of the night, so that probably had something to do with it.

Nick said "You mean to tell me she's never been out of the country? Ever?"

"Yes. So what, a lot of people have never been overseas."

"Nobody I know. Or you, for that matter."

"This just in - there are people out in the world who aren't rich."

"Buddy. Bro. I love you. You know that."

Ryan nodded.

"Well, then, I'll tell it to you straight. You can't marry that girl. She strikes me as a philistine."

"She's not a philistine. She's highly educated, very intelligent, and the nicest woman I have ever known."

"Educated at state schools."

"Jesus Christ, when did you get to be such a snob?"

"Ryan, you're slumming here. Whatever happened to Brigitte, the Dutch supermodel? She spoke five languages and could play the cello like Yo Yo Ma. Why didn't you like her?"

"Nick, you obviously don't understand."

"Try me. Iris doesn't even ski, for the love of all that is holy! How is she going to be on our vacations in the Alps?"

I sat, up above, wondering why Ryan was not offering a spirited defense of me. My heart started to sink, but I looked at my beautiful red diamond and felt comforted again.

Nick was continuing. "This isn't an Erich Segal novel here. You can have literally any woman you want." He shook his head. "I'm not seeing it here, buddy."

"Well, then, maybe you don't need to be my best man. Maybe you don't even need to be in the wedding at all."

"Easy, buddy. Sorry about the brutal honesty, but you know that's what I always give you."

"You've always been honest, I admit. But I didn't know you were so judgmental. Is that a new trait, or did you suddenly become an asshole while I wasn't looking?"

You go, Ryan! You tell him!

Nick audibly sighed. "You're right. She does seem nice, and she's kinda cute in her way. And, as long as you're happy, that's all that matters, right?"

To this, Ryan said, "There's something on your mind. I can tell."

Nick nodded. "Rielle and me, we aren't doing so good."

"What does that mean?"

"We're hanging by a thread, buddy. So, yeah, maybe I'm jealous that you found the one, right when my one is slipping away."

Ryan put his arm around him. "Sorry to hear that."

Then I saw them kissing. My heart started pounding. I mean, this was all good in theory, but seeing it in front of my eyes was something else entirely. I immediately went back into the room, and shut the door.

Oh, I didn't need to see that. I didn't need to hear that. Why can't I leave well enough alone?

I wondered what else was going on downstairs.

I could just imagine.

But I didn't want to.

I lay there, trying to get the spectacle out of my head. But, to my surprise, I also felt strangely titillated. After all, Nick was a very good looking guy. Seeing two hot guys together wasn't as bad as I thought it would be. I felt very conflicted about it all. On the one hand, Ryan was, technically, cheating on me. But, not really, because I had indicated I was ok with it. So, was he cheating, really? He wasn't with a woman downstairs, and we had discussed it beforehand.

I was very confused.

I opened the door again to spy some more. They were sitting on the couch now, side by side, Nick's hand once again draped over Ryan's shoulders. Nick was talking.

"Come on, Ryan, it's been way too long. Ever since you met her, you don't want to do it anymore."

"It just feels funny, that's all."

"It never did before."

"Well, for one thing, both of our girls are upstairs, asleep. That may change. Would you really want to be caught?"

"I don't really care anymore. I'm heading for a divorce as it is."

"You don't care? Don't you think Rielle might just use this against you, when it comes to custody issues?"

"Touché, buddy." He paused. "I just miss you, that's all. I miss us."

"I know. But it's different for me now. I've never felt like this about anybody else. I really need to minimize this," he said, motioning his hands from himself to Nick.

I saw Nick take another swig, then drunkenly place his hand in Ryan's hair, patting it. "Well, then, buddy, I guess I need my rest. I hope you don't mind if we just crash here. I really don't want to rouse sleeping beauty up there."

"Of course. I wouldn't want you to drive, anyhow."

"You mean, you aren't going to get Daniel out of bed to come and drive us?"

"Ha, ha. That would be totally rude, don't you think?"

"Joking, buddy. I'll see you in the morning."

At that, I leapt back into bed, realizing Ryan would soon be joining me. In a few minutes, Ryan actually was in the bed, crawling in next to me, fully clothed. I felt him stroking my hair. He whispered "You awake, beautiful?"

I lay there, pretending to sleep. I felt like it was the early days of our relationship, with me pretending to sleep, so that Ryan doesn't suspect that I saw and heard too much.

Ryan continued on, evidently soused. "I can't wait for you to be Mrs. Gallagher. You mean the world to me. I don't think I could love anybody as much as I love you."

He continued to stroke my hair. I lay perfectly still, and, after a few minutes, I could hear him snoring.

He was still fully clothed.

Deeper Illusions: Chapter Two

The night before the wedding it was time to finally meet Sarah. She drove in from her home on Martha's Vineyard, where she lived with her husband and two children. The husband and the children stayed on the Vineyard, however. This was not explained.

She arrived in a brand-new Mercedes, a platinum blonde in a pair of big Louis Vuitton sunglasses and scarf around her head. Wearing a cashmere sweater set, a string of saltwater pearls, slim black pants and Tory Burch shoes, she looked like a cross between a wealthy housewife and Grace Kelley. She had a huge Mastiff in tow, who sat in the front seat.

When she pulled into the driveway, Ryan immediately went to the car and helped Sarah harness and leash the monstrous dog. She looked at me and held out a perfectly manicured hand. I shook it.

"I'm Sarah. I drove across the country for this affair, so you better be worth it." Then she smiled. I wasn't sure if she were joking or serious. I laughed anyhow. "Let me see the ring," she said, taking my hand and bringing it closer to her face. She raised an eyebrow and looked at Ryan. "He does really love you. Ryan, where'd you find that diamond?"

"It wasn't easy, believe me," Ryan said, while trying to control the 175 lb. dog. "I found a connection to a South African jeweler who specializes in different colors of diamonds."

I didn't know that. I knew the red diamond was rare, the very rarest. But I didn't know he had to order it from South Africa.

"Really?" Sarah was interested. "Did you fly to South Africa to get it?"

"I did."

Huh? When did he do that?

He explained, addressing me. "While you were in the coma, I took a weekend off to get it. I prayed the whole time that I wouldn't miss you waking up. That was really the only time I left your side."

I nodded. "I had no idea you went to that kind of effort."

Sarah said "What, do you think you can just buy a diamond like this on the Internet? I mean, you *can* buy red diamonds on the Internet, but they're not perfect like this one."

Sarah was making me feel the way that Nick made me feel – like a total rube.

Ryan took the dog, Coriolanus – Cori for short – into the house, where he romped with Maximus and Brutus. They all apparently knew one another.

Ryan explained that Sarah always drove to his house, not flew, because she never wanted to be without Cori. And the dog didn't do well with flying, so she drove.

Ryan got out Sarah's Chanel luggage and the three of us went into our house.

Sarah looked around. "The place looks the same," she said, looking at me. "Where are you in this house, Iris?"

"I didn't really have much to bring over."

"Ryan, what's up with that? Don't you think this place should have some of Iris' influence here? After all, this house belongs to both of you."

"Really, Sarah, it's ok. I love Ryan's taste," I said.

"Sarah makes a good point," Ryan said. "We should really redecorate now that this will officially be our house."

Sarah smiled. I got the impression she had sway over Ryan.

We had dinner at the house, and, after dinner, Sarah politely asked Ryan if she could talk to me alone.

I dreaded this for some reason.

We got some brandy and took it into the den and sat down.

"So," Sarah said, patting her legs. "I'm not gonna beat around the bush, here. Have you signed a prenup?"

I somehow knew this subject would come up with somebody. I was surprised it never came up before. "No," I said.

Sarah smiled tightly. "Don't you think you better?"

"Ryan hasn't asked me to."

"He will. I'll make sure of it."

"Not a problem," I said, honestly.

"Good. Because you will not have the chance to do what that other witch did to him," she said, emphasizing the words "will not."

"Alexis isn't a witch. I really like her."

She snorted, which seemed odd coming from such a classy woman. "Has she got you fooled." She shook her head, and took another sip of her brandy. "You weren't there."

"I know, she's a piece of work sometimes. But she's very nice underneath."

"Nice? Bitch got him into drugs. She went to rehab so many times that her parents finally cut her off. She didn't have the money for her drugs, so she started running for a Mexican cartel." She shook her head. "That didn't last long. Ryan was in love with her. He didn't want her risking her life, so he supported her. Paid her tuition at Yale, paid her living expenses and thensome, and paid for her drugs. And his, of course." She took another sip of her brandy and stared at the fire. "Alexis was just one of a long line of people to take advantage of Ryan. He always lets them do it, though, because Ryan has one main motivation in life – to be loved."

I nodded. I got that from him.

"So now, here you are. Don't get me wrong. I'm happy he found someone decent. You'd think that someone like him wouldn't have a problem finding somebody real to love. But the ironic thing is, his looks and his wealth have always made it harder for him to find someone good." She shook her head, and looked at her hands. "You seem normal, though. Mom loves you, so that's something."

"Well, thanks for the support," I said, not sure if she really was giving her support.

"Listen, Iris, I don't want to be harsh here. But he's my baby brother and I was never able to protect him when we were younger. I look out for him now. He thinks you hang the moon." She smoothed her platinum blonde hair. "He would be devastated if you ever left him. But if you don't sign a prenup, there would be insult added to injury."

"It's not a big deal. I don't care about money and never have."

"Yeah, but you know the good life now. Private planes, red diamonds," she said. "Do you really think you can just go back to the way you were before? In a tiny apartment, working a job you hate?"

I was somewhat stunned that she knew so much about me. I guessed that she and Ryan were closer than I thought.

"I don't see why not. I got along fine for 33 years."

"You're so naïve." She called for Cori, who came bounding into the den. "Take Cori, here. He's a rescue dog. Lived on the end of a chain for the first two years of his life. It was the only life he was used to, so I guess he was ok. Now he lives with me. I baby him, take him everywhere with me, let him sleep in our bed." I made a face at that one – that huge thing sharing their bed? "It's a king-sized bed," she continued. "Hate to say it, but I like this dog more than my husband most of the time," she said with a chuckle. "And my kids for that matter." She threw her arms around Cori's neck, and he licked her face. "Anyhow, imagine if poor Cori had to go back to living on a chain. I'd think he'd be devastated."

"So, you think I'm like your dog."

"In a sense. Not literally, of course. I'm just saying that you have a taste of the good life. I would think that living in a tiny apartment, just getting by, would be tragic to you now."

"I'm not going to worry about that. Ryan and I are very much in love. There'll be no divorce."

"Yes, of course. That's what they all say. 'We're in love, nothing will happen.' Trust me, shit happens. If it didn't, we wouldn't have so many high-priced divorce lawyers." Taking another sip of her brandy, she continued. "Don't get me wrong, I don't want you left with nothing if you and Ryan break up. I just don't want you taking advantage of him."

"Give me the papers. I'll sign them."

"Don't be silly. There are no papers yet. But make no mistake, I'm going to exert my will on him to make sure there're papers drawn and you're forced to sign them. It's bad enough that you own half this house." She shook her head. "My idiot brother. I can never understand why he does what he does." She shrugged. "Then again, he doesn't get me, either, all the time."

"Not a problem. I'll sign whatever."

"Nothing personal, of course."

"Of course."

Later on, I was alone in the den. Well, not entirely alone. Cori, Maximus and Brutus were all snoring loudly beside me. I was sitting on the floor with them, my back against the sofa. I wanted January Jones, I mean Sarah, and Ryan to bond some. So I got out of their way.

I heard loud shouting, though, coming from the living room.

"Goddamn it, Sarah, I'm not going to do it! Now leave me the hell alone!"

"Fine. You want that girl to take everything you got, then go right ahead. Be a dumbshit."

"She wouldn't do that. She's not like that."

"God, you've always been so stupid when it comes to women. Wake up. She's not a saint. She had nothing before she met you, and, trust me, she won't want to go back to that. She'll take you to the cleaners, just like Alexis tried to."

"I had a prenup with Alexis." Ryan wasn't shouting anymore, but was talking loudly.

"Good. You see - if you didn't have a prenup with her, she would've taken you even more to the cleaners."

"Iris isn't Alexis."

"They all turn into Alexis when enough money is involved."

I peeked out the den door. They were now in the kitchen. They weren't shouting anymore. Sarah was getting a jug of milk out, and was pouring a glass for her and Ryan.

"So, tell me what the problem is. Why'd you give a prenup to Alexis, but won't with this girl?" Sarah asked, taking a sip of her milk.

"This is going to sound silly and romantic."

"You've always been silly and romantic. Go on."

"Iris is my soul mate. Alexis wasn't and I never felt that she was. That's all."

Sarah started laughing hysterically.

"What?" Ryan asked.

"Your soul mate. Oh, Lord. Mama raised a fool."

"Ha, ha. Mama didn't raise me, remember?"

"Then Nick's mama raised a fool. I got something for ya. There's no such thing as a soul mate. Now, don't be ridiculous and get to a lawyer's office pronto."

"No. The answer is no, and that's that. My foot's going down."

"Suit yourself. But when you guys break up a few years from now, and Iris is suddenly this greedy harridan who wants everything, don't come crying to me."

"Won't happen. We're in this for the long haul."

"Right. That's what every person in love says. They're in it for the long haul, until they're not. Be an idiot. What do I care? It's just that I helped you pick up the pieces every time that other witch pulled her crazy stunts. Every.time. I won't be there for you this time. You can handle your shit on your own."

"Thanks, Sarah. What a great, supportive sister you are."

"You don't take my sound advice, then you're on your own, buddy."

"You really are manipulative, aren't you?"

"What," she said with a shrug.

"I don't follow your advice so you're threatening to cut me off."

"Not cut you off. I just don't want to hear about her when she inevitably screws you over. We'll talk about any topic but her."

"Deal. I'm not scared of making this deal, because I know Iris and I will be 90-year-olds in a rocking chair together." He pantomimed having no teeth, then grabbed her around the waist and pantomimed biting her on the neck with no teeth.

She giggled. "Stop that, Peanut." Ryan had explained that "Peanut" was Sarah's pet name for him. When she was four, Maggie showed her a sonogram of her baby brother, and Sarah said he looked like a peanut. That had been Sarah's nickname for him ever since.

She ran off, with Ryan chasing her around, acting like he had no teeth. They ended up wrestling on the floor. Her perfect hair was getting messy and they were both laughing hysterically. Then Ryan started tickling and Sarah started shrieking. The dogs immediately woke up and ran into the living room, barking and growling at the two.

Sarah finally extricated herself from Ryan and the dogs. Her hair was pointing in every direction. She brushed herself off and sat down on the couch. Ryan got up off the floor and joined her.

Ryan said "I know you're just looking out for me and I appreciate that. But, trust me, Iris and I are in it for forever.

And, God forbid, if something happens, and we do break up, I always want her taken care of. You don't know how much that girl means to me."

"Wow. I've never seen you like this."

"Nobody has."

"Soul mate, huh? I gotta find me one of those."

They clinked glasses.

Later on, Ryan joined me in the den. "I suppose you heard that."

"Yeah."

"I will never make you sign a piece of paper. Not ever."

"I know. But I would be willing-"

"Of course you would be. But you're not going to."

And that was that.

Grab your copy...
vinci-books.com/deeper-illusions

www.ingramcontent.com/pod-product-compliance
Ingram Content Group UK Ltd.
Pitfield, Milton Keynes, MK11 3LW, UK
UKHW040627161125
465103UK00004B/137

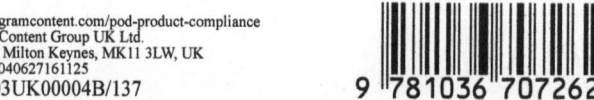